BLUE LIKE ELVIS

The Moody Blue Trilogy
Book Two

Diane Moody

ISBN-13:978-0615625621

Published by

OBT·bookz

Cover design by OBT Graphix

Pink Cadillac image | © Len Green | Dreamstime.com
Guitar Parchment image | © Andrei Krauchuk | iStockphoto.com
Baptist Memorial Hospital image | Public Domain

To Memphis

my hospital,
my co-workers,
my church,
my friends . . .
Thanks for the memories

AN IMPORTANT MESSAGE FROM THE AUTHOR

Writing *Blue Like Elvis* has been such a ride down memory lane for me. The story evolved out of my own experience serving as a Hostess/Patient Representative at Baptist Memorial Hospital in Memphis in the late '70s. The grand building that once filled a block between Madison and Union Avenues no longer stands. The hospital moved out to the east part of Memphis many years ago, but my memories in that butterfly-shaped building will never be forgotten.

This was my first "real" job. I was thrilled when I was hired and proud to wear those classy uniforms as I served our patients at that great hospital. While our jobs were part of the BMH chaplain department, we primarily served in a public relations capacity, attending to the non-medical needs of patients and their families. You will learn more about some of those responsibilities throughout the chapters you're about to read.

The majority of the characters in my book are fictional. Some are based loosely on those I worked with during my tenure there. But I could not write the story without keeping a handful of real people playing their own roles in the spring and summer of 1977. And as with Elvis, the words I put in their mouths are solely mine and completely fictional.

And for those who are die-hard Elvis fans, I ask a special favor. I have taken many creative liberties while writing my story. Some of the dates and events are accurate, but some I have chosen to change in order to flow more smoothly with my story line. I simply ask that you allow me those small "adjustments" here and there and accept them as nothing more than fictional license.

As I researched the last couple years of Elvis's life, I must admit I became more of a fan than I'd ever been before. Elvis ignited a massive shift in the music culture of our world, one that is still recognized today. Whether watching concert footage on youtube, or listening to long play lists of his famous songs, or simply studying books written about his life and the events surrounding his death—all of these efforts helped me to better understand the exquisitely high price of fame.

I hope you enjoy reading *Blue Like Elvis* as much as I have enjoyed writing it.

~ Diane

PROLOGUE

August 16, 1977

Memphis, Tennessee

Ask anyone who was there that day and they'll tell you. The air literally crackled with electricity. As if a nearby transformer had blown and all of us could feel the hairs lift off our arms, our necks. The Union Avenue lobby of the hospital quickly filled as employees rushed to see for themselves. Their questions, hushed but urgent.

Is it true? Please tell me it's not true!

Surely it's just a rumor?

Elvis Presley . . . our Elvis . . . dead?!

Word had spread like a Tennessee wildfire throughout the hospital . . . an ambulance carrying the King of Rock 'n Roll was racing through the streets of Memphis from Graceland to "his" hospital, flanked by police cars and motorcycle cops.

Elvis? Dead? How can that be?

I spotted Sandra immediately and rushed to her side. She grabbed my hand in a death-lock grip. We held our ground there by that expansive wall of windows overlooking the Emergency Room bay. I couldn't breathe, and except for an occasional whisper or whimper, no one else seemed to be breathing either. Doctors, nurses, bookkeepers, administrators. Gift shop clerks, cafeteria workers, visitors. Even a patient or two—some in wheelchairs pushed by family members. And most of my own coworkers . . .

We all stood there. Waiting, hoping, praying.

We were Baptist Memorial Hospital. Elvis's hospital. No, he didn't own our wonderful institution, though he probably could have. But we were so used to his visits, with his entourage taking over part of Sixteen on the Union wing. We always loved when he came to stay, sometimes for a week or two or three at a time. No one had to announce his arrival. Then, like now, the electricity surged through every corridor on every floor.

Elvis is here! The King is in the house!

Only this time, as we waited for him to arrive, we were shrouded in silent grief, fearing the worst.

Don't ask me why, but just then I looked up at the clock on the wall—2:56. Then flashing lights suddenly rounded the corner as a long line of emergency vehicles made the final stretch to the ER entry. As the ambulance rolled into sight, I felt a tear slip down my cheek, then another. I felt Sandra's arm slip around my waist, pulling me closer. I felt someone else's arm drape over my shoulder. In moments, the girls were all around us, drawing closer as the crowd behind us pushed for a better view. I could hear Sandra's whispered prayers in her native tongue. And then I caught a whiff of Mrs. Baker's familiar cologne and heard her utter, "Oh, dear Lord . . ."

I knew it wasn't possible, but at that precise moment, the whole scene seemed to slip into slow motion. The incessant flash of cameras created a surreal landscape of strange strobe-like movements as people rushed across the *lawn* below us toward the ER. The barrage of flashing red lights bounced off the medical building walls as the wailing sirens echoed in that valley of concrete and glass.

And then the sirens went silent . . . all of them, leaving an eerie, foreboding hush in their wake.

Oh God, please don't let Elvis die . . .

Present Day

"Whoa. That must have been bizarre," the young man said, his eyes glazed as if he too was lost in the same memory.

I blinked out of that long ago scene, surprised by the sound of his voice. I cleared my throat, reaching for my cup of hot tea. "Yes, well, it was a moment I'll never forget."

He reached for his bottled water. "I can't even imagine."

I crossed my legs, settling back against the throw pillow on my chintz-covered sofa. The early morning sun filtered through the plantation shutters, drawing a series of lines across the hardwood floor in my sun room. He'd arrived shortly after 7:30 coming straight from the airport, but I'd been up for hours. "Now, Mr. Carouthers–"

"Please, call me Chip. I insist."

"Chip, then. Tell me again, why is it you need to know all this? Why would the memories of an almost sixty-year-old woman be of interest to you?"

"As I mentioned on the phone, I've recently been hired by South Palms Hospital in Pasadena, California as a public relations consultant for the hospital. I've been asked to find some new and innovative programs for our hospital. As I told you, I have family ties here in Memphis, and I remembered hearing about this patient representative program—your *hostess* program—when one of my uncles worked at Baptist. He was an obstetrician back in the day, and always talked so highly of this program. I know it's no longer a part of the hospital, but I wanted to learn more about it with the intent of putting together a similar program for South Palms."

"Did you know the original hospital structure is no longer standing?"

"Yes, ma'am. They razed it several years ago, according to my research."

"I cried that day. We all did. It was like losing an old friend, watching that magnificent building go down into a heap of dust."

"I watched the video of the demolition online."

"Did you now," I mused, imagining such a thing like watching a reel of special effects in a Spielberg movie. He had no idea what I'd experienced that day. Hearing the roar of the blast, the great cloud of dust filling the air, and then the quiet, somber silence when it was over. I looked up at him, a nice young man. Thirty, or so. Well groomed. Polite. Attentive. And hanging on my every word. "And how did you get my name?"

"My uncle is no longer living but my aunt remembered you from her church. Dorothy Carouthers. Do you remember her?"

"Oh, of course. She used to sing in the choir. Soprano, as I recall. Beautiful voice. We worked in the nursery together on occasion. Is she still living?"

"Yes, though she's in a retirement facility in Germantown now. She isn't able to get to church anymore, but she's sharp as a tack. Which is how she remembered your name after all these years."

"My goodness, it has been a long time. What—thirty, thirty-five years?"

"A long time," he echoed.

A long time indeed. More than likely, he hadn't even been born yet. "All right, so what exactly do you need to know?"

"I'm interested in the program. What you did, your responsibilities as a hostess/patient representative. Even the minutest detail. Everything. But I must say, after hearing what you just shared with me about the day Elvis died, I'd love to hear *all* your memories. Even those that might not specifically relate to your job. In other words, tell me everything. Tell me what it was like to be a part of that great hospital."

I set my teacup and saucer back on the coffee table then took a deep breath and closed my eyes. "What was it like? Well, I suppose the best place to start is at the very beginning." I paused, resting against the needlepoint pillows again as my mind drifted back to long forgotten memories.

"I can still smell the new upholstery in my brand new Cadillac Seville—a graduation gift from Daddy. Midnight Blue with a tan landau roof, tan leather seats, fully loaded. And Rick Dees on the radio that bright April morning . . ."

1

April 5, 1977

The wild antics of the radio DJ made me smile as I took a left onto Poplar Avenue and started my first official commute downtown. I'd just moved into town over the weekend after landing my new job at Baptist Memorial Hospital. I was born here in Memphis but hadn't lived here since I was ten. Strange how much you *don't* remember about a place you lived that long; then again, I hadn't even hit puberty when we moved. When Dad was offered the Cadillac dealership in Birmingham, off we went. Roll Tide roll.

So even though I'd written "Memphis" as my birthplace on hundreds of documents and forms over my twenty-three years, I really didn't remember much of anything about this sprawling eclectic town on the banks of the Mississippi. Still, I was excited to be back. After all, my name is Shelby—as in Shelby County, Tennessee, home to Memphis.

Okay, wait. You should probably know my name isn't really Shelby. It's just what everyone calls me. My given name is Rayce Catherine Colter. Hence, the need for a nickname. I mean, we lived in the Deep South and my parents named me Rayce? To this day they swear the "race-related" similarity never crossed their minds, what with the unique spelling and all. But after a handful of unexpected encounters with my black kindergarten teacher, parents of my classmates, and even the nurse at our pediatrician's office, Mom started calling me *Shelby* and it stuck. Dad preferred RC, my initials, which led to no end of taunting from my big brother Jimmy. But I'll save those lovely tales for later.

I'd graduated from Samford University back in June of the previous year, but hadn't found my dream job yet. Not that I have anything against Taco Barn or the photo desk at Walgreens, but I had this crazy notion that a college education would open doors for more than fast food or drug store establishments. My sociology degree had sufficiently equipped me with plenty of analytical reasoning for the socio-economic dynamics thriving in 1976, and yet the kind of job I yearned for had eluded me much longer than I'd hoped.

That was, until I made a trip up to Memphis to visit my former roommate from college. Rachel had married the summer before our senior year then moved to Memphis after we all graduated. Her husband Rich had been accepted into the UT Dental School here, and Rachel quickly secured a job at Baptist Hospital in the heart of the medical community near downtown Memphis. She was an accounting whiz, and apparently the world's largest private hospital needed lots of help with all those numbers. Anyway, she loved her job and loved working at this renowned private hospital.

I'm sure you can see where this is going.

But let me back up and tell you the rest of my story. Rachel may have had ulterior motives that weekend she invited me to come up and visit, but the real reason I made the trek to west Tennessee that second week of March had nothing to do with employment.

"Rachel, I *have* to get out of here. I can't handle this right now."

"Is it your mom? Your dad? Who's giving you trouble, Shelby?"

"No, they're fine. They're actually relieved I had a change of heart before the invitations went out. I mean, they dished out a boatload of money for everything, and naturally, we can't get refunds on most of it. But they're being so great about the financial stuff. I mean, they never really liked Will—"

"Oh, sure they did."

"No, Rachel. They *pretended* to like him because they didn't want to disappoint me."

Rachel was silent. Even without seeing her, I knew she was twirling a strand of her long blonde hair, her blue eyes staring off into space as she mulled over the entire doomed relationship in her mind. "Could've fooled me."

"Yeah, well, they didn't fool me. And in my heart of hearts, I knew all their concerns were valid. While I found the whole notion of being a Navy wife extremely romantic, they knew I'd be miserable on my own in San Diego, so far from everyone I know and love."

"Seems like I brought that up a time or two myself . . . that and the fact he had no interest in sharing your faith."

"I know, I know. But no, it's not Mom and Dad. It's me. It's Birmingham. It's driving by the church where we were supposed to get married. It's having to explain a thousand times a day why I'm not getting married."

"I'm so sorry, Shelby. Hey, come see me! Throw your stuff in a bag, get in your car, and come stay with me for a few days. Rich is leaving for a seminar in Knoxville. He'll be gone for a week. It'll be great! I can take a few days off. We can talk, we can shop, we can get manicures—c'mon, say you'll come!"

And so it was I headed to Memphis for a visit with my sweet friend. And we did, in fact, talk and shop and get manicures. We even shopped for some baby clothes, a first for me. Rachel was five months pregnant at that point with Cooper Christopher Bauer. She was the cutest pregnant thing you ever saw. Thankfully, she was past the morning sickness stage and positively glowing.

I had to admit I was ready to begin a new life. I fell in love with Memphis, and Rachel helped me get an interview to work at Baptist where she worked. No, not in the accounting department. I'm horrible with numbers.

Rachel told me about a unique program at Baptist. Turns out the hospital president, Dr. William Grieve, had pioneered the program patterned after that of stewardesses. Apparently, the highly-esteemed Dr. Grieve loved to fly and he especially loved those classy young women who waited on him on board. Now, I mean that in the good sense of the word. He was a true Southern gentleman who loved the Lord. It would never have crossed his mind to view these young women with anything but pure respect. He appreciated their professionalism, their attention to detail, their friendly manners, and their genuine desire to help everyone aboard feel relaxed and comfortable—even if flight conditions deteriorated or became perilous.

I'm told Dr. Grieve returned from a trip to New York City with the idea for a cutting-edge hospital program that would be yet another revolutionary concept in hospital care. He dubbed it the *Hostess Program,* though they would later be called *Patient Representatives.* I suppose that sounded more professional and less like a hospital version of Welcome Wagon. These young women would be carefully selected from good families with good reputations. A college degree was mandatory. They would be part of the chaplain department, and as such, each hostess was required to be a member in good standing at a local Southern Baptist Church. They would be provided uniforms, much like those the stewardesses wore—impeccable suits designed to set them apart from other hospital employees. Each hostess would be assigned a floor of the hospital and be responsible for visiting all of her patients every day, offering a warm smile, an outstretched hand, and an offer to run errands or to simply be a listening ear. If the patient was so inclined, she would gladly pray for them.

It seemed like a dream job, and I couldn't wait for the interview Rachel set up for me. I met with Virginia Baker, the head of the hostess department, and by the end of our meeting, she offered me the job. I'm sure the fact that Rachel and Rich were members of the church where her husband served on staff might have influenced her decision to hire me. But I like to think it was an answer to prayer.

A flutter of butterflies drifted through my stomach as I drove closer to the hospital. I uttered a brief prayer for a sense of calm on this, my first day. Then that funny DJ on the radio caught my attention again.

"Rick Dees in the A.M.!" It was a jingle I'd grown fond of, even in the few short days I'd been in Memphis. Dees was a local disc jockey who possessed a truly bizarre sense of humor. He made me laugh out loud—something I'd forgotten to do the last few months. His silly parodies and wild impersonations always put a smile on my face. Perfect for a morning like this.

"Good morning, it's ten before eight on this beautiful spring day here in the Home of the Blues . . . Wait! What's this I hear? Who's that knocking at the door?"

A door squeaked open. "Hu-hu-hullo?" Dees mimicked in his Elvis-mode.

Rick responded, "Why looky here, it's the Big E himself! Ladies and gentlemen, welcome my good friend, the King, Elvis Presley!" Raucous canned applause filled the radio waves.

"Why, thank you. Thu-thu-thu-thank you very much. I just stopped by for a juh-juh-juh jel-ly donut and a geetar strangggg.

You happen to have those here, Rickuh-Rickuh-Rickuhdees?"

It seems dear "Elvis" felt the need to launch into song with every sentence. I couldn't help laughing.

"No, nossir, Big E. I don't. You and me, Elvis, we're like burgers 'n fries, milk 'n cookies, pork rinds and Cheez Its, know what I mean? We're tight. If I had 'em, they'd be yours. But no can do this morning, Big E. No donuts, no stranggggs."

The sound of a door slamming broke a brief silence. The King had evidently left the building.

"See?" Rick continued. "We're tight. Like brothers. So while Elvis goes'n hunts him some juh-juh-juh jel-ly donuts, let's play us "A Little Less Conversation."

"Sorry, Rick," I said out loud, "but I can't handle any Elvis today." I switched the station, finding some Crosby, Stills, and Nash singing "Just a Song Before I Go." Much better.

You'd think as a native Memphis belle, I'd love Elvis. I don't know why, but he just never did much for me. Granted, his music was a little before my time. I was born in 1953. By the time I was a teenager and started listening to music, he was already thirty years old. *Old.* My mother played his songs day and night, but I was much more interested in the Beatles, the Herman's Hermits, and Paul Revere and the Raiders.

That and the whole Cadillac thing. I mentioned my dad was a Cadillac dealer. Before he got his first dealership in Birmingham, he worked at Brentwood Cadillac in Memphis. I was much too young to know it at the time, but the story goes that a young, relatively unknown Elvis strolled into the showroom one day and wanted to know about one of the convertibles on the floor. The salesman thought he was just a hood, so basically ignored his questions and refused to let him test drive the DeVille. Dad saw what was happening and made sure he picked up the slack of his stupid colleague. He had no idea who the kid with the jet black hair was, but he knew a customer when he saw one. Elvis bought twelve Cadillacs that day, and Dad became his go-to guy for all his Caddies. And oh, how Elvis loved buying Cadillacs. The longer, the flashier, the better.

And even though Dad was known throughout Memphis for being Elvis's Cadillac connection, I still didn't get what all the fuss about Elvis. Maybe I was just too young.

Crosby, Stills and Nash finished their beautiful harmonies just as I pulled into the gated parking lot in the shadow of Baptist Memorial Hospital. The largest private hospital in the world, BMH stood as a proud landmark, its massive stone butterfly shape spanning from Madison Avenue to Union in midtown Memphis. I took one last look in the rearview mirror, making sure I looked okay. I was pleased to see my hair shine in the morning sunlight, always a good thing for a brunette. The emerald blouse I'd chosen to wear seemed to really bring out the green in my hazel eyes today. Even my mascara looked good for a change, always a challenge for me. I dashed another swipe of gloss on my lips, grabbed my purse, and stepped out of my car.

I was proud to make that walk from the parking lot to my new place of employment, and proud to finally put some of my training to work. As I entered the building from Union Avenue, I tried once again to steel my nerves. I loved knowing I was going to be a part of this great institution and one of its nearly five-thousand employees.

My first real grown-up job. Time to do this!

2

I made my way to the hostess office on the first floor of the Madison wing. Mrs. Baker was seated at her desk in the small outer office.

“Welcome, Shelby! How nice to see you again. Are you excited?” She stood up, extending her hand to me.

I shook it firmly as Daddy had always taught me to do. “I sure am. A little nervous, but very excited. Thank you so much for hiring me, Mrs. Baker.”

“My pleasure. Now come on back and let me introduce you to the other girls. You'll be heading to orientation this afternoon, but I want you to get your feet wet this morning.”

Feet wet? Whoa. I thought I'd have more time to learn the ropes.

“Girls, I want to introduce you to our newest hostess. This is Shelby Colter. Shelby's a graduate of Samford University, raised in Birmingham, but she was born right here in Memphis. You girls introduce yourselves and make her welcome. Shelby, after you say hello, you and I will go have coffee and chat for awhile.”

“Sounds good. Thanks, Mrs. Baker.”

"Girls, be nice to her." With that she sashayed back to her desk.

I couldn't believe how small the back room was. How on earth could it accommodate a dozen hostesses? Two vinyl sofas lined the walls with a corner end table between them. The girls were crammed on the sofas, on the arms of the sofas, on the floor, with several of them standing in front of a full length mirror putting final touches on their make-up.

"Hey, Shelby. I'm Sarah Beth McCracken. I've been here the longest so I'll introduce everyone."

Sometimes you can size up a person in the first few seconds you meet them. I had Sarah Beth pegged before the first introduction was made. Type A personality. Self-appointed queen of the hostesses. Brunette, attractive, in a business sort of way. Perfectly groomed, right down to her polished nails and immaculately coiffed hair. Not a hair out of place.

She went around the room, telling me names I knew I'd forget along with their assigned floors.

Debra, who had maybe the bluest eyes I'd ever seen, worked the Urology floor. "Or the waterworks floor, as we like to call it," she said with a friendly wink. "Hi, Shelby."

Debra. Blue, blue eyes. Ash blonde. Friendly, I said to myself, trying to make mental notes.

Mindy worked the obstetrics floor. "That's on Five. I'm also in charge of the newborn pictures, so I have my own office up there in the prayer room." She leaned closer to me. "It's also where we hang out when we need a break from Mrs. B. Come on up anytime." Her eyebrows danced along with her smile.

Mindy. Long blonde hair. Tall and slender. Confident. Obstetrics. How would I ever remember all their names?

"Leila works the pediatric floor," Sarah Beth continued, "but you won't see much of her. They keep her running."

Leila, gave me a quick wave as she rounded the corner. "Nice to meet you. We'll talk later, okay? Gotta run."

Leila. Another short one. Sable brown chin-length hair. Pediatrics. Cute girl.

"Chelsea works on Twelve with our neuro patients. But don't assume that makes her any smarter than the rest of us," Sarah Beth quipped.

Chelsea smiled. "Ah, but I *am.* It's all that extra brain fluid flowing up there. Sticky stuff, but it does tend to make you smart."

"Gross!" one of the girls said. "Did you have to say that? I'm eating my yogurt here."

And on and on it went. Two of the girls weren't in the office, already up on their floors. Another was home sick. Twelve hostesses in all, all beautiful and dressed in gorgeous rust-colored suits. I noticed they all wore hose and heels. It had been a long time since I'd stepped into anything but running shoes, but I'd adjust. Their pin-striped blouses had matching ties attached, which were tied in the latest style to form a classic bow at the neck.

Just then, a door in the corner of the office opened. Out walked a drop dead gorgeous brunette from the small restroom. I wasn't sure how she'd kept a tan like that this early in spring, but I was sure it was from some recent tropical vacation and not a bottle of Coppertone. Her blue eyes sparkled beneath thick black lashes, her smile radiant with the whitest teeth I'd ever seen. "Well, hey! You must be Shelby, my replacement. I'm Pamela Smythe." Suddenly I was engulfed in a hug and dizzy from a cloud of Chanel No. 5.

"Nice to meet you, Pamela."

"Babe? You ready?"

We all turned toward the door which was now filled by a god. Okay, not a god. But maybe the most handsome man I'd ever seen in person. His white lab coat contrasted with a tan that matched Pamela's exactly, a navy silk tie knotted under his heavily starched blue oxford cloth shirt. His full name was embroidered on the left pocket. *Franklin Warrick, M.D.*

"Oh hey, honey. I'm ready. But I want you to meet Shelby. She's taking my place up on Nine. Shelby, this is Franklin, my fiancé."

Thankfully, he didn't try to hug me. Though even a handshake away, I caught a whiff of his Aramis cologne. It made my knees go weak. "Shelby. Nice to meet you," he said, taking my hand.

Pamela peeked at the mirror one more time, touching a manicured pinky to the edge or her lips. Then she turned, placing a hand on my arm. That's when I glimpsed the rock on her finger. A marquis, easily two carats. I tried not to let my jaw drop, but I'm fairly sure it did.

"I'm going to grab a quick bite of breakfast with Franklin, then I'll meet you back here and we'll head up to Nine. Cardiology! You'll love it up there. We call it 'the floor with heart.'"

A round of moans followed her out the door. "That's because she hooked that big delicious heart throb up there," said the short Puerto Rican whose name I recalled was Sandra. They all laughed and made a few playful digs about the striking beauty and her doctor—all in good taste, of course.

"Shelby?" Now it was Mrs. Baker filling the door. "Let's go for coffee, shall we? Girls, get up to your floors. Time's a wasting."

We took our seats in the dining room that overlooked Madison Avenue. Linen tablecloths, fine china, and silver. A far cry from the usual hospital cafeteria.

As if she'd read my mind, Mrs. Baker took a seat and motioned for me to do the same. "This is our more formal dining room. Many of the doctors and administrators eat here, as well as visiting pastors and other guests. There's also a large cafeteria on the Union side where most of the employees dine. I prefer it here. Much more quiet."

She ordered two coffees for us and I studied her as she began telling me all about the hospital. She was actually very pretty, with a head full of thick white hair, obviously teased into the "do" common to women her age. I'd guessed she was somewhere in the neighborhood of sixty or so. Not exactly lean, but not plump either. Friendly gray-blue eyes with a slight hint of mystery, but overtly authoritarian. No question there.

Suddenly I realized she was no longer talking about the hospital but about her latest golfing trip to Florida. "When spring comes, I try to take off early a couple days a week to work on my game. Do you play, Shelby?"

"Me? Oh, no, ma'am. I've never played. My brother's pretty good. He and Dad play a lot, but I never learned to play."

"That's a shame. I've tried to interest some of the other girls in learning, but so far I've had no takers. Such a wonderful game."

I realized her eyes were lit up like a Macy's Christmas tree. She continued telling me about some of her better shots, which of the doctors at the hospital belonged to her country club, and the locations of her favorite courses around the country.

Note to self: sign up for golf lessons.

Half an hour later, she signed the tab and we headed back to the office. So much for my introduction to Baptist Hospital.

As we rounded the final corner to the office, she said, "Be sure to be at orientation by 1:00 sharp. I'll have Pamela take you to the conference room . . . well, speak of the devil."

Tucked in a dark hall corner closest to the office, the good doctor and his stunning fiancée were sharing a rather tender moment just as we passed.

"Dr. Warrick, I'll thank you to part lips with Miss Smythe and let her get back to work. Time's a wasting, you two."

I felt like a pimple-faced school girl in tow behind the principal watching the cool kids make out. I had a feeling it wouldn't be the last time I felt that way.

Pamela caught up to me as I entered the back office. “Ready to rock and roll? Oh! I almost forgot.” She jumped into the back room where half a dozen other hostesses still lingered. “Did you all hear Elvis checked out this morning?”

“About time!” the feisty Puerto Rican chimed in. “He’s been here almost two weeks this time. Think he’s dried out yet?”

“Sandra, bite your lip!” Pamela scolded with a laugh. “You know Elvis doesn’t drink.”

“Who said anything about booze?”

A tiny wisp of a thing, Sandra was no more than 5’2” with a head full of black curls, a perfect olive complexion, and a ready smile. I could tell immediately Sandra held nothing back and liked to have a good time. I had a feeling we’d get along great. Especially if I remembered to pronounce her name correctly—Sandra, as in “Sahndra” not Sandra as in Sandra Dee.

“Sandra, let it go,” Mrs. Baker warned from the outer office. “You represent this hospital, so watch your tongue, young lady.”

Sandra made a face which our boss couldn’t see, but I kind of loved her for it. No offense to Mrs. Baker, but I wasn’t a big Elvis fan, as you know. I chuckled quietly. Sandra smiled as if we were co-conspirators.

“Miss Garcia, why aren’t you on your floor yet?”

“Oh, I’ve already been up there. I ran out of my cards. I was just leaving.” She made another wild expression then headed out the door. “¡Adios, amigas!”

“That reminds me, Shelby,” Mrs. Baker continued from the outer office. “I’ve ordered your cards and your name tag. They should be ready in the next couple of days, and I’ll call Casual Corner this afternoon and order your uniforms.”

“Great,” I answered. I’d noticed the gold name tags pinned to the other girls’ jacket lapels, but hadn’t noticed the small handful of business cards the girls kept tucked onto their clipboards.

"We give these along with our brochures to each of the new patients." Pamela showed me her card with her name and the office extension below the title, *Hostess,* and handed me one of the small brochures. More like a pamphlet actually. It had a picture of the front of the hospital on the cover with the words "At Your Service" across the bottom. "That's how they contact us. They put a call into the office, then Mrs. B. or whoever's here calls it in to paging. You'll get used to hearing your name all the time. 'Miss Colter, Miss Shelby Colter,'" she mimicked, "then you just pick up the nearest phone, call paging, and they give you the message."

"Do you get a lot of pages?"

She laughed out loud. "Oh, girlfriend, you have no idea. You'll start hearing them in your sleep. Well, let's do this. You ready?"

"Sure," I lied, following her out the door.

As we rode the elevator up to the Ninth floor on the Madison wing, Pamela asked, "So have you ever met him?"

"Who him?"

"Elvis! You know, we all go a little crazy when he's here. I've met him several times. Mostly at social events I've attended with Franklin. Franklin and Dr. Nick are good friends."

"Who's Dr. Nick?"

"George Nichopoulos. Elvis's doctor. Would you believe every time I've been around Elvis, he's asked for my number? Of course, I always refuse to give it to him."

Why am I not surprised. Pamela certainly had the looks to attract a king.

"Why didn't you give it to him?" I asked, curious.

"Because I'm engaged, silly!" she scoffed, looking at me like I'd sprouted horns on my head. "Besides, everybody knows Elvis likes lots and lots of girls. That's just not me. Oh, no no no."

"So what's he like?"

"Once you get passed the flirting, he's the nicest guy. He

really is. Not at all like the wild stallion everyone makes him out to be. He's very generous, very kind. The last time I saw him, he didn't look well. But then, that's why he comes here when he's sick or needs to . . . get better. Of course, you can't just go walking up there on his floor. He's got quite an entourage surrounding him every time he comes in. And then there's Marian."

"Marian?"

"Marian Cocke. Elvis's nurse. Let's just say she's extremely 'protective', but then who can blame her? That's quite a responsibility. She's got her hands full when he's here. Plus she just adores him. Like a mother hen, you know? I really respect her for the way she looks out for his best interests while he's here. And he absolutely loves her in return."

The elevator door opened. We threaded our way through a throng of doctors, orderlies, and visitors, finally making our way to the nurses' station on Madison Nine. I noticed a group of nurses, a medical records clerk, several orderlies, and others working around the station.

And then the former beauty queen (yes, I'd already found out she was Miss University of Mississippi just a few short years ago), looking every bit the radiant glamour queen that she was, introduced the plain peasant girl from Birmingham who'd come to take her place.

"Hey kids! Who wants to meet the new kid in town?"

3

I'm pretty sure my head was spinning and would topple off any moment. Pamela was wonderful, showing me around the floor, introducing me to everyone I'd be working with. But it was a lot to take in all at once. Especially after meeting all the girls in the hostess office. Mostly I shadowed Pamela, observing as she visited all the patients on her floor. She showed me the computer printed cards for each new patient admitted in the last 24 hours. The cards gave all kinds of information, more than we probably needed to know—name, age, address, phone number, person to contact, insurance carrier, social security number—that sort of thing.

Loaded with all these cards, Pamela would visit the new patients first, then later start making rounds to all the others. Most of the people were very pleased to hear of our service. A few weren't terribly cordial, but that was to be expected. This was the cardiology floor, after all. Many times they'd be asleep or out of the room having tests run. Pamela would just leave the hostess brochure and her card on the tray table.

"Remember," she told me, "the best visit is in and out. At least on the initial visit. You don't want to take too much of their time. They're usually overwhelmed to be here in the first place, so it's best just to let them know who you are and how to reach you."

And that's what we did. Well, most of the time, anyway. Occasionally we'd encounter a chatty patient or family member who wanted to share their entire life story and that of everyone they've ever known.

"In those cases, unless you're already done with your rounds and you just want to visit, you've got to learn some tricks. Listen and learn."

She tapped lightly on the door of a patient who'd been on the floor for almost a week. "Good morning, Mr. McKinley. How are you this morning?"

The elderly man launched into a tirade about his good-for-nothing son, the blankety-blank nurses, and President Carter's latest gaffe. How the man carried on such long diatribes was a medical wonder, as sick as he was. After a few minutes, Pamela stepped closer to his bed, patted his hand, and said, "I know exactly what you mean. But right now I've got to run some errands for some of the other patients on the floor. How about I check in on you later?"

And before he could answer she was halfway out the door. "You take care, Mr. McKinley, and get some rest now." As the door silently whooshed behind us, she added, "And that, my dear, is how it's done."

How would I ever remember all her tips and suggestions? I'd brought along a steno pad and made as many notes as I could, but I didn't want to appear rude to the patients. I wasn't kidding when I said my head was spinning.

Pamela looked at her watch, a dainty Rolex, its face surrounded by tiny diamonds. *No doubt a gift from Dr. Warrick.* "Hey, are you about ready for some lunch?"

"Yes!"

"I know. It's a lot to take in," she said, herding me down the hall. "But it's really no big deal. You'll get the hang of it. After a day or two, you'll come up with your own words, your own presentation, and they'll be eating out of your hands. I promise." We'd arrived at the elevators and she pushed the down button. "Would you like to have lunch with Franklin and me? We'd be happy for you to join us."

"Oh, well . . ." I couldn't see it. I just couldn't. A third wheel on the Love Boat. "Actually, I was hoping to get to know some of the other girls in the office. Would that be okay?"

"Oh, sure, Shelby. That's probably a better idea anyway. You're gonna love the girls. I do. I'm going to miss them so much!"

The door opened and we joined the busy main hall of the first floor. "So when is the big day? Your wedding," I asked.

"Three weeks from Saturday. I can hardly stand it, I'm so excited! Franklin has accepted a position at a hospital in Hawaii, so we decided to just have the ceremony there."

Thus, the tans. No doubt a house-hunting trip or two.

"Hawaii! Wow, that must be beautiful. I've never been to Hawaii."

She grabbed my arm. I realized it was something she often did to whoever she was talking to. "Oh, Shelby, you just have to go! You and the girls need to come over and visit sometime. It's so gorgeous, you can't even imagine."

She was right. I couldn't. Not even close.

"Anyway, my last day will be—"

"Moonpie?"

I stopped dead in my tracks. I knew the voice. At least I thought I did. There were only two people on the planet that called me by that name: my brother, who was currently overseas; and his ornery childhood friend, Tucker Thompson. A thousand memories flashed through my mind, taking me back to my childhood before we left Memphis. My brother Jimmy and his annoying friend Tucker, forever aggravating the life out of me just for the fun of it. Sneaking up on me and scaring me so bad I'd wet my pants. Prank-calling me, pretending to be my crush from school. Putting worms in my Spaghetti-O's and vinegar in my Kool-Aid.

"Moonpie, is that really you?"

By now, Pamela had turned around and was enjoying a good laugh. I closed my eyes, wishing I could just fall through the floor and avoid this little reunion altogether. I blew out my breath as I turned around to see the little creep—

Only he wasn't.

He was tall and all grown up and . . . oh my goodness, so incredibly handsome.

Tucker Thompson? Handsome?

"Tucker?" I said, having trouble finding my voice.

"I can't believe it! It *is* you! How in the world are you, Moonpie!" He grabbed me into a bear hug, squeezing what little breath I had left. At this rate, I was pretty sure I'd be passed out on the floor soon.

"Hi, Dr. Thompson." Pamela gave a little wave, smiling from ear to ear.

"Hey, Pamela. Nice to see you."

"Okay, somebody tell me," Pamela began. "How on earth did you *ever* come up with the name 'Moonpie'?"

Tucker stood back, holding me at arm's length. "You wanna tell her or do I?" he asked, as if we were about to share the world's best kept secret.

I covered my eyes with my hand. "No, by all means. You go right ahead."

"Well, let's just say Shelby here had a real passion for Moonpies when she was growing up. Mrs. Colter used to buy them by the case for her little Shelby. She was the cutest little thing you ever saw. Those dark raven curls dancing all over her head, her eyes all narrowed just daring us not to bug her. But you would never, and I mean *never* find little Miss RC here without a Moon Pie mustache. Right there on those pouty little lips." He drew an imaginary mustache just inches from my face. If he'd touched me, I might have smacked him.

"Tuck, do we have to—"

"Wait, wait—'RC'?" Pamela asked, clearly enjoying this way too much. "Are those initials or some kind of nickname?"

"Those are my initials," I explained. "My real name is Rayce Catherine—that's Rayce, spelled R-a-y-c-e. Dad preferred 'RC' to avoid some unfortunate misunderstandings, which you might expect back in the early '60s . . ."

"Ah," Pamela said, figuring out the connection. "'RC Cola and a Moonpie. Got it. Every Southern kid's favorite snack."

"Her brother Jimmy was my best friend," Tucker continued, unfortunately.

Then again, it did give me an opportunity to look him over. He still had the same chocolate brown hair, still a shaggy mess. I'd forgotten the unusual color of his eyes—almost a smoky caramel—now warmed with a permanent smile. But my oh my, he was so tall! Had to be 6'3" or more? It felt so strange looking up to him. In more ways than one.

" . . . and Jimmy and I, we were inseparable. I practically lived at their house half the time. And it was our sacred purpose in life to aggravate his kid sister here as much as we could. And let me tell you, we were *bad*."

"The stories I could tell," I moaned, still trying as best I could to avoid eye contact with him.

"Oh, the stories *we* could tell!" He laughed again with the same contagious laughter I remembered all too well. I hated "Chubby Tucker," which I'd called him for years until it dawned on me it didn't bother him a bit. But I could never stay mad because he always made me laugh.

"So, Moonpie, what are you doing here? I thought you still lived in Birmingham?" He stepped back, taking a good long look at me from head to toe. "And I must say, the years have been kind to you. I can't get over it! Jimmy's scrawny little sister, all grown up and beautiful."

"Hey, if you two will excuse me," Pamela said, squeezing my arm, "I'm sure you have lots of catching up to do. See you after lunch, Shelby?"

"Sure thing. Thanks, Pamela."

"Bye, Pamela," Tucker added.

"Bye, Dr. Thompson."

"Pretty girl," he whispered as she walked away.

"Ya think?" I answered, turning back to look at him. I still couldn't believe it. It simply would not compute in my mind that the obnoxious kid I put up with all those years was standing right here in front of me . . . looking like *this*? His hair was still curly, and a handful of freckles still splashed across his nose. The years had been more than kind to Tucker Thompson, if the gentle laugh lines crinkling around his eyes were any indication.

I suddenly realized he was wearing a white lab coat. With his name embroidered on the pocket. "Tuck, are you a *doctor*?"

"Well, thanks for that bold vote of confidence. But yes, I'm a doctor. This is my first year of residency."

"But how did you end up here? Didn't I hear you went to Vanderbilt?"

"Yeah, I did my undergraduate work there, then lucked into my internship there at the Vanderbilt Hospital. But what about you? What are you doing here? Last I heard you were at Samford."

I had to take another deep breath. "Oh, well, I graduated last spring. Actually, today is my first day on the job."

"Really? Here at Baptist?" Same goofy smile. But somehow, it looked downright mesmerizing now.

"Yeah, I'm going to be working in the hostess department. We visit patients and—"

"Oh, I know all about the hostesses. Everybody does. Great program. The patients all love them. Doctors do too," he smirked, doing a bad Groucho imitation with an imaginary cigar.

He just stood there smiling at me. I felt all woozy inside. Which only made me mad, of course. *Woozy? Over Chubby Tucker Thompson?*

"Listen, Moon—"

"Tucker, you've got to stop calling me that. I'm working here, okay?"

"Fine, sure. No problem. So *Shelby,* do you have plans for lunch? Wanna join me in the cafeteria?"

Oh dear. By this point, I was on brain and emotion overload. I could almost hear the fog horn blasting through my mind. *Aoogah! Aoogah!* Wasn't that the warning signal heard on submarines? *Submarines? Where did that come from?* Oh, for the love of Pete. I had to get a hold of myself. *Grow up, Shelby. It isn't Robert Redford. It's Tucker Thompson.*

I scratched my eyebrow. "Lunch? Um, well . . . yeah, I guess."

His smile faded. "Gee, don't sound so excited. I don't want to put you out or anything."

"No!" I reached out and touched his arm. I pulled it back, as if it had done the deed on its own. "No, Tucker, it's not that. I . . . I'd like that. I would. But can you give me just a minute to check by the office first?"

His face relaxed. "Sure. I'll just wait right here. Take your time."

Remember when I said it felt like my head was about to spin off? It did. Right then and there, toppling off down the hall.

Good heavens.

4

Ten minutes later we'd gone through the cafeteria line and found a table near the windows. The smell of the food. The memory jolt. The information overload. It was definitely taking its toll. I'd picked a salad and hoped I could park it where it belonged—in my stomach, not on Tucker's nice white lab coat.

It was strange at first, trying to reconnect when our original encounters were so . . . bizarre. But glory, I could hardly take my eyes off him. It was so weird. Completely surreal. Him sitting there, looking so handsome. Me, sitting here trying to fork my lettuce and get it in my mouth. We caught up on each other's lives, filling in the gap of so many years. We talked about our families and memories of growing up in Memphis.

"So, how's Jimmy doing?"

"He's still overseas. We're hoping he'll be home soon. Mom's been a basket case ever since he deployed for Vietnam four years ago. But when the war ended, he still had a couple of years to serve out his term. So the Army sent him to the Philippines. At least, that's the last I heard. He's not great about keeping in touch."

"I can't imagine," he said, biting into his BLT. "I really hate that we lost track of each other. School has devoured me the last few years, but that's no excuse. You'll have to let me know when he gets back stateside. I'd love to see him again."

"Me, too. So, tell me how you ended up here at Baptist. I never figured you for someone to stay so close to home after all these years."

Tucker wiped his mouth then took a sip of iced tea. "It's all about who you know. Med school was tough. But I survived. Only by the grace of God, I can assure you. When my internship at Vandy was winding down, I started checking out my options. Dad was a fraternity brother of Dr. Grieve when they were both at Vandy."

"Grieve," I interrupted. "Unfortunate name for a hospital administrator, don't you think? I mean, what are the odds?" I pondered.

He laughed. "But then we all do. Eventually."

"Do what?"

"Grieve."

"Well, there you go. I'm sorry, you were saying?" I asked.

Honestly, I've got to stop this. Every time he smiles, I find myself wondering . . .

"Oh, right," he continued. "So Dad was in law school, but he and Dr. Grieve got to be good friends. So when it came time for my residency—"

"Daddy pulled some strings, and voila! Plumb residency at one of the premiere private hospitals in the world."

"Voila, indeed."

"Tucker?" a voice interrupted. "What are you doing?"

We both looked up at the blonde standing beside our table. "Cassie! I thought you had jury duty today." Tucker stood up, wrapping his arm around her waist. "I would have waited if I knew you were coming."

"Am I interrupting . . . ?" She looked back and forth between us. I didn't need to look in a mirror to know I was eight shades of crimson by then.

"No, not at all. Cass, I want you to meet an old friend of mine. This is Moonpie. Remember me telling you about my childhood friend, Jimmy Colter? Well, this is his kid sister, Shelby. Only we knew her affectionately back then as Moonpie."

"Ah, Moonpie. The girl you and Jimmy used to torment. Hi, Shelby. Nice to meet you. I'm Cassie."

"Hi, Cassie." I held my hand out in an awkward attempt at normal.

"Sweetheart, you want to grab some lunch?" Tucker looked at his watch. "I've still got fifteen more minutes."

"No, I'll just eat the other half of your sandwich if that's okay. I only have half an hour before we have to report back." She took a seat and helped herself to the rest of Tucker's BLT. "Shelby, whatever you do, avoid jury duty. It's such a pain. All the waiting. It's just ridiculous."

"I'll try to remember that," I said, standing. "But I've got to run. I have orientation starting in a few minutes." *Thank God.* "But it was nice meeting you, Cassie. And Tucker, what can I say—it's been . . . interesting."

Tucker stood again, good Southern gentleman that he was. "Hey, I'll see you around, okay? And congratulations on your new job."

I said my goodbyes, grateful for the chance to get out of there. In less than half an hour, I'd gone from a blast from the past shock of a lifetime, to a quite sudden and unexpected goo-goo-eyed, adolescent crush . . . to a deflated ego as I watched the perfect couple across from me sharing a lunch.

And so it goes.

I made my way back to the hostess office to freshen up and psyche myself for the long afternoon orientation. Mrs. Baker was apparently at lunch as her desk was vacant. As I rounded the corner into the back office, the cackle of female chatter riddled the air.

"Shelby! Is it true you had lunch with a resident?" a redhead asked. "Goodness, girl! That's fast!"

I couldn't remember her name. I couldn't remember any of their names at the moment. But I knew I had to set the record straight. "No, no, no. He's just an old friend. Well, actually, a friend of my brother's. No big deal, I assure you."

"Oh, don't be so modest!" a blonde chimed in. "Half the fun of working here is window shopping, if you know what I mean." They all talked at once, laughing and cutting up.

"Well, that may be true, but this resident is taken. His girlfriend showed up, so you can put away your bridal gifts."

They all laughed at that one. I had to admit, they were a lot of fun. After my momentary pity party, they'd make me feel good. I think I was going to like working here. In fact I was sure of it.

The rest of the week was a blur as I continued shadowing Pamela and attending orientation sessions in the afternoon. Gradually I began to relax and enjoy my days. I only ran into Tucker a couple of times, though Mrs. Baker told me he'd called once while I was up on Nine. It just seemed better to avoid him at this point. Better all the way around.

I was already loving the girls, and it seemed mutual. We all came from diverse backgrounds, but still had a lot in common. Toward the end of the week, I actually felt a few moments of genuine joy, thankful I'd found such a perfect fit for my first real job. It beat the heck out of Taco Barn.

On Friday, around 3:00, our orientation concluded with our introduction to Dr. Grieve. By this time, I was expecting someone who was part John Wayne, part Marcus Welby. He was neither. Standing only 5'5", the beloved president of Baptist Memorial Hospital joined us in the conference room, making his way to the head of the table. He introduced himself and shared some of his personal background and that of the hospital.

Dr. Grieve, I pondered yet again. *Dr. William Grieve. Did the kids call him Willy when he was young? Willy Grieve? Won't he? Did he go into hospital work because of his name? I once knew a dentist named Dr. Molar and a podiatrist named Dr. Foote. It does make you wonder. Can a name determine your future? And if so, what does that mean for me—Shelby Colter? Well, okay—Rayce Colter. Should I be training for the Olympics? Running marathons? Or was I destined to win a Nobel Peace prize, bridging the gap between the races? Then again, everyone knows me as Shelby. Maybe I was supposed to run for office. Mayor of Shelby County?*

Then again, there was that other *name. Would I eventually be CEO of the company that made Moonpies . . . ?*

"Of course, I'm always delighted to meet our new hostesses. Miss Colter?"

Hearing my name snapped me back from the rabbit trail to the moment at hand. "Yes, sir?" I answered, half standing.

"Welcome, welcome!" he gushed, making his way to me around the long conference table. "Since I first initiated this program in 1953, I've welcomed many a young lady to our ranks, and I'm always proud to do so. Virginia tells me you're a Samford graduate?"

"Yes, sir. I graduated last spring. Class of '76."

"And what do you think of our grand institution so far?" He practically beamed, like the proud papa he was. I had to make this good.

"I couldn't be happier. It's an honor to be here, Dr. Grieve."

"Splendid! Splendid!" He patted me on the back and made his way toward the door. "Welcome, one and all. Now go out there and make us proud!"

And with that, he left the room.

Moments later, I returned to the hostess office, ready to wind down the week. By this time of day, most of the visits had been made and errands run. For the most part, the last hour or so was just a matter of waiting for any late calls. I noticed an empty seat on the sofa. By now I'd learned to grab them when I could. Top real estate in such cramped quarters.

A serenade in Spanish filled the room. Sandra danced all around us, but I had no clue what she was singing about.

"Sandra, give it a rest," Sarah Beth complained.

"What? It's Friday, the weekend is here! What's not to sing about! Time to dance!" She stomped her wedged heels in a flamenco of sorts then parked her tiny self on the arm of the sofa beside me. "So, Shelby. Where do you live?"

"Me? I'm staying with some friends out in Germantown. Why?"

"I'm looking for a roommate. Mine moved out last weekend."

"Ask her why she moved out," Chelsea said. I already loved Chelsea. She was sweet and adorable with a quick tongue.

Sandra fake-grimaced and whined playfully. "Oh now, why do you have to go and—"

"Greta moved out because she found a week-old pot roast in the oven. Maggots and all," Tess added.

"That's not what happened!" Sandra barked, fighting a laugh.

"No, it was that salsa music, night and day, day and night." Chelsea chuckled.

"Oh now, you guys aren't being nice. You're going to scare the girl!" Sandra suddenly grabbed me in a fierce embrace, her head on my shoulder. "You've got to move in! I need help with the rent. It's a beautiful townhouse. Two bedroom, two bath. Cathedral ceiling. Balcony overlooking a lake. You'll love it. Don't listen to these busybodies."

They all laughed, then continued to tease their miniature colleague.

I had to admit it sounded good. And I wouldn't have to go on the hunt in a town I really didn't know anymore. I just hoped I could handle a little Latin spice in my life.

"When can I see it?"

5

Moving day was . . . interesting. Mom and Dad drove up, bringing my furniture and the rest of my belongings. They immediately bonded with Sandra, enjoying her feisty spirit and constant singing in Spanish. Mom was especially impressed with her floor-to-ceiling bookcase in our living room filled with the classics. Who would have thought a twenty-five-year-old Puerto Rican girl would have such an appetite for those old books? Mom kept wandering over to the shelves, running her fingers along the spines of Hemmingway, Jane Austen, Tolstoy, Victor Hugo, and Sir Walter Scott. And I have to admit, I'd already picked out a few titles I wanted to read myself.

But I wasn't sure how I'd adapt to living in an apartment with such a huge birdcage filled with finches and their legion of offspring. They seemed to chatter incessantly and scatter birdseed everywhere, but I still wanted to give it a try. Otherwise, Sandra's townhouse was cozy and well kept. Though I admit to sneaking a quick peek in the oven. Clean as a whistle.

After helping me get settled, we all went out for burgers at a nearby Danver's. Mom and Dad remembered the hamburger chain from years gone by and wanted to reintroduce me. It was much nicer than the usual fast food environment, and the food was amazing. I loved this part of Memphis near the MSU campus. The quaint older homes, the variety of restaurants and shops. Plus the whole university ambience. I was already starting to feel at home again.

Mom and Dad headed back to Birmingham after we ate. Dad never liked to miss Sunday mornings at church. He'd taught the senior high Sunday school for more than a decade. They loved him, which was no great surprise. Everybody loved Jack Colter. And Mom never liked to miss her ladies class, comprised of her dearest friends. We said our goodbyes then I went home and finished unpacking.

I'd promised to meet Rachel and Rich at their church the next morning. First Baptist graced a huge corner where Poplar and East Parkway intersected near midtown. It was a traditional Southern Baptist church and looked every red brick the part. White pillars, steeple, and beautifully manicured grounds. I hadn't gauged my driving time right, so I was late meeting Rachel and Rich in the broad lobby at the back of the sanctuary.

"I'm so sorry. Couldn't find a parking place."

"No problem, Shelby. We're just glad you're here," Rachel said, hugging me. "There are still some seats here at the back, so we're good."

We followed Rich to a pew on the aisle just three rows from the back. The auditorium was filled with glorious music, accompanied by a full orchestra and massive pipe organ. Just like our church back home.

Except for a most unusual interruption. Located so close to the medical community of Memphis, ambulances frequently zoomed by the church. As one wailed by the church just after the service began, the sanctuary's frequency was interrupted by that of the ambulance driver calling in the condition of the patient. It made for a quite colorful break in the service.

"You've got to be kidding," I whispered quietly to Rachel.

"You'll get used to it. Everyone does."

Here's hoping we never hear the gory details of a severed limb or someone's brains spilling out . . .

When the final chorus of *O God Our Help in Ages Past* finished its crescendo, we took our seats. As one of the staff members rattled off a list of announcements, I settled in. I gazed around the enormous auditorium noticing the huge chandeliers high above us, the deep crimson carpet surrounding us which matched perfectly to the pew padding beneath us. I leaned to one side for a better view of the platform to check out the ministers and the large choir seated behind them. At the same time, the people in the row directly in front of me leaned toward each other, catching my eye. It took a moment before I recognized the beautiful head of blonde hair on the young woman and the tousled brown hair of her companion.

Tucker and Cassie.

Great. Just great. I felt my face heating and mentally chided myself when it did. *How ridiculous. Why should it matter who's sitting in front of me?*

When a rather large woman floated out of the choir loft to the soaring introduction of her solo, I concentrated on her every move, every lyric of her song, and every note of her contra-alto solo. Of course, half-way through I caught myself zoned in on Tucker's broad shoulders, the freckles on the back of his neck, and the messy loose curls just grazing the top of his white shirt. So much for good intentions.

When the service was over, I turned around, busying myself with my purse. If I was lucky, I could slip out without being noticed.

"Rich, Rachel—how are you?" I heard Tucker say behind me. "Goodness, woman, take a look at you—are you carrying twins in there?"

"Very funny, Tucker. No, just little Cooper," Rachel said patting her protruding stomach. "Hi, Cassie. Nice to see you. Oh, I'd like you to meet my friend Shelby. She just moved here and—"

Oh no she did not. I closed my eyes before turning around and plastering a smile on my face. "Hi, Tucker, Cassie. How are you?" I said, sickened at the sound of my fake friendliness.

"You know each other?" Rachel asked.

"Oh, Moo—I mean, *Shelby* and I go way back," Tucker said, obviously pleased with himself for almost avoiding the forbidden nickname. "But we just bumped into each other last week at Baptist."

Rachel tapped her forehead. "Well, of course you did. I can't believe I didn't think to introduce you earlier since Shelby's working there now." She turned to me. "We met Cassie and Tucker in our Sunday school class a few months ago. In fact, we're heading there now, so you'll have to join us."

"Great idea. You should come," Tucker added. "You'll enjoy Dr. Krause. He's on faculty at MSU. Best Bible teacher I've ever heard."

I started backing out into the aisle. "Oh, I don't think so. I'd feel out of place in a couples class."

Rachel laughed. "It's not a couples class. It's a singles class. Rich and I just help out. It's mostly college students and young professionals. You'll love it!"

I turned just in time to see Cassie whisper into Tucker's ear. That pretty much sealed the deal. "Well, thanks, but not today. Maybe next time. But thank you for the invitation."

Rachel made a face at me just as Tucker and Cassie said their goodbyes. Rich chatted with someone behind us. "What was that all about?" Rachel asked, following me in the opposite direction.

"What? I can't skip Sunday school this morning? What are

you, my mother?"

Rachel blinked as the smile faded from her face. I felt like a jerk.

"No, Rachel, I'm sorry. That was rude. I'd just like to take a pass this morning, okay? I'd kind of like to just look around, check out the library, maybe get a cup of coffee."

"Oh, okay. That's fine. I didn't mean to nag. So you know Tucker Thompson? What a small world. How do you all know each other?"

"He's a childhood friend of my brother's. Long story. No big deal."

"And Cassie? How did you meet her?"

"Oh, well, I actually just met her with him the other day at the hospital. Who is she, by the way? Tucker introduced us, but we didn't really have a chance to talk."

Rachel pulled me into the ladies restroom. We did that a lot. I guess it goes with the territory when you're pregnant. After she emerged from a stall and washed her hands, we slipped back out in the hall. "Cassie is the daughter of Judge McElroy. She's a blue blood. One hundred percent."

"Debutante? Cotillions? That whole thing?"

"That and then some. Their family has Memphis roots that go way, way back."

"So how did Tucker hook up with someone like her? I mean, she's beautiful—don't get me wrong. It's just that he was always so down to earth and kinda goofy, y'know? At least he used to be. I can't really see him as the socialite type."

We turned a corner, passing the church offices. "Well, don't forget Tucker's daddy is a prominent lawyer here in Memphis. He's known Judge McElroy for years. So when Tucker came back from Vanderbilt a few months ago to begin his residency, his father introduced him to the judge's daughter."

"Rachel, Tucker isn't blue blood. And I know enough about Memphis to know how it works here. You can be the best of friends, but if you don't have that elite blood flowing through your veins, you're never gonna stand at the front of the church while little Miss Debutante enters to the bridal march on her daddy's arm. It's never gonna happen."

We stopped in front of the church library. "That's true. But being a doctor *and* the son of Roy Thompson—well, let's just say Tucker's on the 'approved' list of eligible bachelors for Cassie. And besides, she really is nice. They make a cute couple, don't you think?"

"Oh sure!" I said, hoping she didn't pick up on my insincerity. "Just cute as can be, those two. Well, you head on to Sunday school, okay? I'll meet you afterward."

"Okay, if you're sure you don't want to come? We have *so* much fun, Shelby. You would love this class. We do all kinds of parties and trips together, and we have Bible studies on Tuesday night—"

"I promise. I'll come sometime, I will. Just not today."

"Okay, then we'll meet you right here after class, okay?" She headed down the hall. "Rich wants to take us out for lunch."

"Great. Sounds good."

I wandered into the library and started browsing the shelves. Mostly I just needed some space. Things hadn't gone at all as I'd expected them to. Silly me, thinking I could just go to church, enjoy a service, and leave. *Maybe I can find a good book to read and park myself in some out of the way corner.* I pulled a book from the shelf and mindlessly skimmed the pages. I quickly noticed they started to blur on me.

Oh good grief. Why am I crying? This is ridiculous. It occurred to me it wasn't just because of Tucker that I'd avoided the singles class. I wasn't ready to jump back in that pond just yet. Not even close. I'd never doubted my decision to break off my engagement with Will, but I still felt so raw from the whole experience. It had been so much more painful than I'd ever expected. There were things I still missed about him. His rugged good looks. His wild sense of humor. He was easily the most romantic man I'd ever known, hands down. But he wasn't right for me. And I think deep down, I'd always known it. Even before he broke my heart.

"That's a wonderful book. I've read it myself, many times."

I took a swipe at my tears before looking up. I was surprised to find Dr. Love, the senior pastor who'd just preached the sermon I'd inadvertently tuned out. He was not much taller than I was, barrel-chested, with a thick head of gray hair. Pronounced creases defined his friendly face with a couple of caterpillar brows framing his deep-set eyes. A faint waft of cigar smoke drifted from his direction, catching me completely off guard. It reminded me of those late summer nights when Daddy used to puff on one of his rare stogies out on the back porch.

"Hello," I croaked.

He looked up at me over the top of his glasses. He seemed to study my face before a smile slowly broke free. He held out his hand. "Thomas Love. And you are?"

I cleared my throat, taking one more swipe at my stupid tears. "Shelby Colter. Nice to meet you, Dr. Love."

"Colter? I knew a Jack Colter once. You any relation?"

Hearing my dad's name put me at ease. "Yes, I'm his daughter. How do you know my dad?"

"Why, everybody in Memphis knows ol' Cadillac Jack. Gave me my first Caddy. A '65 DeVille. Oh, that was a sweet, sweet ride. How's he doing? He still down in Birmingham?"

"Yes, he is. Actually he and Mom were in town yesterday helping me move."

His eyes lit up. "So you're new in town?"

"Well, I grew up here until we moved away when I was ten. But I graduated last spring and just started working at Baptist

Hospital this week."

"Did you now! I get over there at least two or three times a week. Visiting the flock, don't you know. What kind of work? Are you a nurse?"

"No, I'm a hostess. It's part of the—"

"You're one of Virginia's girls! I know all about the hostess program. Great concept. Bill Grieve's pride and joy. Well, good for you. You'll do fine, just fine." He glanced down at his watch. "So why aren't you in Sunday school? We've got lots of wonderful classes, you know. Are you married? Single?"

"Oh, single. And thanks, but . . ." I stalled and stammered. I mean, how do you tell a pastor you don't want to go to Sunday school? "But I just wanted to roam a bit this morning. Maybe next week."

"Well, you just make yourself at home. Miss Colter, it's such a pleasure to have you here worshiping with us. Next time, you go check out George Krause's class. Those singles have a good, good time together in there. You'll want to jump right in."

And then, for no particular reason, my eyes filled again. I couldn't believe it. Like I didn't possess one ounce of composure.

He took hold of my hand again and stepped a little closer. "There, now, what's all this? What could possibly bring a pretty young woman like you to tears on a morning like this?"

Through my tears I could see the honest sincerity in his eyes, which only undid me even more. I took a deep breath, blowing out my frustration. "I'm sorry, I don't know what's wrong with me this morning."

He patted my hand. "Is there anything I can help you with?"

"Um . . . I don't know, I just . . ." And that was it. I couldn't seem to find another word and was too embarrassed to try.

He patted my hand again. "I tell you what. You call the church office and set up a time to come see me this week. Let's have us a nice long chat. What do you say?"

I just nodded. Apparently that was all I could handle.

"Good. I'll look forward to it." He gave me a wink and disappeared around the corner.

I dug in my purse for a Kleenex, wiped the snot off my face, and left the library . . . in all my glory.

6

Monday morning, Sandra and I made the drive to town with all the demented Memphis drivers. We planned to take turns driving to work, and I'd insisted we take my car that morning. We tuned in to hear Rick Dees as we drove. The DJ was in rare form, doing a parody conversation as someone called Lester Roadhog Dees, a crusty old country DJ who kept touting something about "Roadhog's used cold cuts and left-over deli treats." Sandra laughed so hard I thought she'd spill her coffee all over my leather seats, but I had to admit he was funny. A nice companion on our morning commutes.

I'd already grown accustomed to wearing a suit to work. It felt good to be dressed like the rest of the girls. And I couldn't believe the difference it made, wearing such professional clothing. I felt proud to be part of the team. More mornings than not, I couldn't wait to get to work.

Half-way there, my Caddy started to sputter.

Sandra turn down the radio. "What's the matter with it?"

"I don't know. It's never done this before."

It coughed and kicked then seemed to rattle a couple times for good measure. "Great. Just what we need on a Monday morning." I tried to pull over to the shoulder but a semi was blocking me. Then, as if we'd just imagined it all, the Seville stopped complaining and drove like a gem.

"That's just weird. I'll have to give Dad a call and see what he thinks. I'm sure he'll want me to take it by the dealership."

"No problem," Sandra said, finishing her make-up in the mirror on the back of the passenger shade. "We can drop by on the way home. It's not far from the hospital."

Thankfully, we made it to work with no more problems. We parked in the garage and began our long walk to the hospital in the bright April sunshine.

I was slowly beginning to understand the more relaxed schedule of our department. Don't misunderstand me. We worked hard, and we were on call the entire time we were on the clock. But Mrs. Baker was often away from her desk or in meetings a lot, so the routine wasn't nearly as rigid as I'd first thought. Most days, we'd arrive by 8:00, check in, then mosey down to the cafeteria for breakfast until around 8:30. I loved the relaxes start. The cafeteria bustled that time of morning as the entire range of employees grabbed a quick bite to go or took more leisurely breaks over eggs and bacon and grits, and tapping the enormous urns of coffee.

After breakfast we'd hustle back to the office, gather our new patient cards and supplies, then head up to our floors. By now, I was getting to know my fellow workers up on Nine fairly well. Pamela was a natural when it came to people. She'd helped me learn their names, told me about their families and backgrounds, and instructed me what roles they served. They all adored Pamela, so I knew I'd have to work hard to fill her designer shoes.

That morning, she had an appointment in one of the administrative offices to begin finalizing her departure, so I was on my own. I stopped in to greet the staff then made my way to the desk roster to verify my patient information against their list. After culling the cards of patients who had already checked out, I began my rounds.

It was all becoming more natural for me, these patient visits. Most of them, surprised and pleased to know the hospital provided a service like ours, were extremely grateful. Some asked a barrage of questions while others simply accepted my card and brochure, said thank you, and sent me on my way. By 10:00, I had already made two inquiries for patients down at the insurance office, picked up some magazines in the gift shop for the fifty-something lady in 905, delivered a sealed envelope of valuables from the man in 941 to the business office for safekeeping, put in a request for a chaplain to stop by and see the gentleman in 936, and bought some Sour Tarts for the guy in 950.

I only had two more new patient visits to make, then I planned to take a break. I tapped gently on the door of 922. “Good morning, Mr. Underwood, I’m Shelby Colter, your hostess, and I just wanted to stop by and say—”

I stopped. The tears on the face of the elderly gentleman staring back at me broke my train of thought. He was sitting up in bed under the soft glow from the light above him. “Mr. Underwood?”

He quickly rubbed his face as if he could hide his tears, then pulled a tissue from the box on the bedside table and blew his nose.

I approached the side of his bed, unsure what I should say or do. “Are you okay?” I asked quietly.

He took a deep breath and let it out. “Oh, well, I . . . who are you again?”

I handed him my card. “Shelby Colter. I’m your hostess. I’m here to run errands for you, make contacts for you—that sort of thing." I smiled at him. "Is there something I can do for you, Mr. Underwood?"

He stared at my card then dropped his head back against his pillow, stifling a sob. "I'm just so worried about my wife . . ."

I pulled up the chair beside his bed and took a seat. "What's wrong with your wife?"

He wiped his nose again. "We're in here . . . in this hospital because of me. I was driving and I . . . apparently I blacked out. They said I had a mild heart attack. I don't know. I don't remember . . . but my wife . . . she wasn't wearing her seat belt and she—" He stopped, breaking down again.

I waited, giving him time to compose himself. This was a first for me. None of the patients I'd visited with Pamela had responded anything like this. But she told me of several experiences she'd had with distraught patients. *Sometimes they just need a listening ear. Don't feel like you have to fill the silences with chatter. Let them talk.*

And so I waited. And prayed for wisdom.

"She's in intensive care. She was thrown from the car . . . they told me she had a ruptured kidney. They had to operate . . . she also had a concussion and broke her arm. She's really banged up."

"I'm so sorry, Mr. Underwood. Have you been able to see her yet?"

"No, not yet. I think my doctor's afraid my heart can't take it." He looked down at the line of red, raised skin stapled together down the center of his chest, disappearing beneath his hospital-issued gown. His eyes welled up again. "It must be really bad if they won't let me see her. Don't you think?"

Careful, Shelby. "I'm sure they just want to make sure you're okay first. You had surgery too. I'm sure your doctor doesn't want you to exert yourself or risk something else happening to you."

"But she must be so scared. We're from Arkansas. We were on a trip to see our children in North Carolina. We don't know anyone here, and now we don't have a car, and—"

"Has anyone notified your kids yet?"

"I talked to my son this morning. He's trying to make arrangements to get here. But it could be a day or two . . . he can't just up and leave. He's got people depending on him at work and . . ." He stopped again, unable to continue.

"Mr. Underwood, would you like me to check in on your wife for you? See what I can find out?" Even as the words came out, I wasn't sure what the protocol for this type of thing might be. Would they even allow me into ICU?

"Would you?" he asked, his bushy eyebrows lifted with hope. "If you could just tell her I'm okay, tell her I love her . . ."

We talked a while longer and I jotted down some notes to find out exactly what he wanted me to say to his wife. By the time I left, his expression was visibly relieved. Now, if I could just deliver on my promise.

I called Mrs. Baker and told her about the situation. She told me to come to the office and in the meantime, she would make a quick call to ICU. By the time I got downstairs, she had the information I needed and told me who to check in with once I got to ICU. A few minutes later, I was at the bedside of Margaret Underwood.

I knew immediately why her husband had not been allowed to see her.

An unbidden thought rushed to mind—*she looks like a corpse.* So frail and tiny in that bed, surrounded by tubes and monitors and the constant beep-beep-beep of the machines. Her face was horribly bruised, her head wrapped in gauze with wisps of white hair sticking out here and there. Her arm was in a cast, held in a sling against her chest. And she was clearly out of it. The attending nurse told me she'd been in and out of consciousness and completely incoherent, though her recovery from surgery had gone well. I tried to decide what to do. Finally, I wrote a note on the back of my card and left it on her bedside table.

What on earth would I tell Mr. Underwood?

"Shelby, it's not your responsibility to share the details of Mrs. Underwood's physical condition with her husband," Mrs. Baker told me when I returned to the office. "Still, it sounds like he could use some reassurance. Here's what I would suggest . . ."

Half an hour later, I was about to leave Mr. Underwood's room. I had told him his wife was sleeping when I'd stopped by and that the doctors and nurses were taking good care of her. He seemed relieved just to know someone had checked on her for him, and he was especially happy to hear I'd left a note conveying his love. We talked briefly, then I told him to call anytime he needed me.

As I gently closed the door behind me, I finally let out a long breath. I still didn't feel totally confident in what I was doing yet, but I had to admit it felt good knowing I was there for someone in their time of need. As I knocked on the door of the new patient in 931, I wondered what kind of ministry opportunity I might find next.

"Hello, my name is Shelby Colter. I'm your hostess—"

"It's about *#%! time you got here," growled the disheveled middle-aged woman in the bed, flashing a couple of dollar bills at me. "The nurse told me you could go get me some cigarettes. I want a pack of Marlboro's."

Reality check. From Florence Nightingale to cigarette girl in mere moments.

7

By 2:00 that afternoon, I'd finished my rounds and was trying to decide if I wanted to go get a Tab. As I stepped off the elevator, I ran into Tucker.

"Moonpie! I was beginning to think you'd fallen off the face of the earth. How's it going?"

We stepped off to the side of the hall, allowing the other passengers to exit the elevator. I knew I'd eventually run into him again, but I had no clue what to say.

"Good. It's good. Just getting acclimated around here. How are you?"

He tugged at my sleeve, pulling me along. "Come have coffee with me. I need to ask you something."

Whoa.

He turned to look at me. "Oh, c'mon. You have time. It'll only take a few minutes. You're allowed a break now and then, you know."

"I know," I answered a little too defensively.

We entered the café at the far west end of the first floor on

Madison. It was more of an oversized snack bar than café, but there were a dozen or so small tables for seating. We got our drinks and found a table in the corner.

I stuck my straw into my fountain drink. "So how many cups of coffee does a resident drink during any given 24-hour period?"

"You don't even want to know. But I'd never make it without it. The hours are brutal."

"Yeah, I've always heard that. How's it going?"

He ran his hand through his hair and shook his head. "It's tough. I keep asking myself why I thought I wanted to go into medicine. Course, then I work with patients, see a few miracles, and it all comes back to me. I just need to handle my off-hours better. Maximize my sleep time. That sort of thing. But enough about me."

I took a sip of my diet drink and waited. Finally I asked, "And? What was it you wanted to ask me?"

"Oh, yeah. I want you to come to Bible study tomorrow night. It's at Dr. Krause's house. Great study. We're going through Genesis right now. Very laid back, but we always have a good time. And it'll be a good chance for you to get to know some of the singles."

Oh, the bliss.

"Tucker, I appreciate it, but I'm just not ready for the whole singles thing right now."

"Right now? What does that mean?"

I toyed with the wrapper from my straw then flattened my hands on the table. "Okay, I might as well just level with you so you won't keep inviting me to these things. I just recently broke off my engagement. It was painful, I'm still not totally over it, and the last thing I want to do is being around a bunch of singles. No offense, but I'm just not ready to be back in a meat market environment."

"Well, I'm glad you told me about your situation. And I'm really sorry to hear about the broken engagement. That had to be tough. But Moon— I mean, *Shelby*—it's just a Bible study. It's not a 'meat market' as you so delicately put it. Seriously, this group isn't like that. I promise you. We all have a blast together. Just come one time and give it a shot. If you don't like it, fine."

"We'll see. I'm having some car problems so I'm not sure if—"

"That's no problem. I can give you a ride."

"Oh, that's okay. I wouldn't want you to go out of your way."

"Please. Will you stop acting like I'm some stranger and just come? Rachel and Rich said you moved out. You're over near MSU, right?"

"Look, Tucker, don't worry about me. Besides, I'm sure Cassie wouldn't appreciate me tagging along."

He drained the rest of his coffee and stood up. "Oh, Cass can't come to Bible study. She has class on Tuesday nights."

Oh?

He tossed his empty cup in the trash and pulled a card out of his pocket. "Give me your phone number and I'll call you tonight to get directions to your place. And I won't take no for an answer, so don't even bother."

I huffed. "You're relentless, you know that?" I grabbed the card out of his hand and put it on my clipboard. I wrote down my home number and handed it back to him. "But so help me, Tucker, if one goofball starts clinging to me, I'll never speak to you again."

"Fair enough. Gotta run. Talk to you later."

I shook my head, wondering why I'd caved so easily. Why couldn't I just stick to my guns?

This has trouble written all over it . . .

Sandra caught a ride home with Chelsea, so I headed to the

dealership. I'd called Dad earlier in the day and he insisted I take my car right over to Brentwood's Cadillac as soon as I got off work. Since he'd worked there for so many years, he called ahead and made arrangements for them to take a look at my baby and see what was wrong as soon as possible. He also reserved a courtesy car for me to drive while it was in the shop.

I had vague memories of Brentwood's from my childhood. We were in and out a lot of the time, stopping by to see Dad at work. Occasionally he'd take me to work with him on Saturday mornings. But I guess I was too young to remember much, and I certainly didn't recognize anyone there. Still, as soon as I walked through the door, the familiar car dealership smell hit me like a wave, making me miss my daddy.

"So you're Jack's girl," a rather portly man said after I'd checked in at the repair shop. "I'm Burt Brentwood, good friend of yo' daddy's. My goodness, how you've grown! Why, last time I saw you, you weren't this high." He held his hand low, as if I'd magically remember. I had no memory of this man, but since he was a Brentwood, I'm sure we must've met before.

"Nice to see you," I said. "Did Dad talk to you this morning?"

"Sure did. And I promised him I'd take good care of you. We'll make sure the boys get your Seville back running like a top. Meanwhile, I had that pretty little coupe out there washed and waxed for you this morning. That'll keep you running while we've got yours in the shop."

He handed me the keys as I looked out to see a shiny red clone of my baby. "Thanks, Burt. I appreciate it."

As he waited for me to sign the form at the desk, he talked about my dad and how much they all missed him. "But no one misses him more than Elvis. Fact is, he was in here just this morning and asked how ol' Cadillac Jack was doing down in Birmingham."

I looked up. "*Elvis* asked about my dad?"

"Oh sure. Always does. Elvis loves yo' daddy. He still buys his cars from us, but he always lets us know he wishes Jack was still here."

"Wow. What do you know," I mused, signing my name and handing the form to the clerk behind the desk.

Burt escorted me to the loaner, its shiny red coat glistening despite the long afternoon shadows. "Yeah, ol' Elvis likes his Caddies. Bought six today."

"Six?!"

"Oh, that's nothing. Sometimes he orders 'em by the dozen." He opened the driver's door for me.

"I guess I shouldn't be that surprised. Dad said he used to come in and buy several at a time. He said sometimes they were for complete strangers. He just enjoyed giving them to folks."

The wind whipped under Burt's sad toupee and he quickly patted it back into place. "It's true. Waitresses, movie theater cashiers, lawn guys—you name it. He just has a ball surprising folks. Though this time, these were what he calls his 'guilt cars' . . . Elvis can't stand knowing somebody's upset with him or disappointed in him. So if he gets sideways with anyone, even over something trivial, he has to make it right. Buys 'em a Cadillac. Can you imagine?"

I slipped into the car. "No, I can't. I wonder if people take advantage of him just to see if he'll give them a Cadillac."

"Oh sure. Happens all the time. He's just too blind to see it. But he's a good guy. Has his faults like everyone else, but a good man. You ever meet him?"

"Dad tells me I did, but I don't remember it."

"That's a real shame. You'd love the guy. We all do."

I bet. I couldn't imagine what the commission on those six Caddies had been, let alone a dozen. Love indeed.

"Thanks, Burt. Let me know when my car is ready."

I drove off with thoughts of Elvis swimming in my head. I remembered the story Dad often told me of the night Elvis called, asking him to give a private showing for some of his "Memphis Mafia"—his entourage of friends and bodyguards. He wanted to let them each pick out their own cars for Christmas and special order all the extras they wanted on them. Dad thought it would be fun for Jimmy and me to meet "the King" so he let us tag along. Mom was home sick and none too happy about our little outing, especially since it was at midnight. But Dad convinced her it was a once-in-a-lifetime opportunity. And since Elvis was a night owl, midnight it would have to be.

I wish I remembered it, but he says I was only four at the time, so my little brain cells apparently weren't yet cranking out the memory field at the time. He said it was like one big party, all these grown men acting like kids in a candy store. Dad was busy, of course, so he said Jimmy and I just kind of hung around and watched. Then later, when Elvis was in Dad's office signing some papers, he said I walked in and backed along the wall never taking my eyes off Elvis. Dad said Elvis immediately took to me.

"Well, who have we here? Jack, is this little angel yours?"

"Elvis, meet Rayce. Rayce, can you say hello to Mr. Presley?"

He tells me I just stood there with eyes wide open, chewing on my pinky.

"C'mon over here and let me take a good look at you, sweetheart," Elvis said.

Dad said I slowly approached him, twisting one foot back and forth and back and forth. When I got close enough, Elvis picked me up and sat me on his knee.

"Well, aren't you just the cutest little thing? How old are you, Rayce?"

Dad says I whispered "four" and never once took my eyes

off the King.

"Four? Well, you're just about all grown up, aren't you? I hope some day I have a pretty little girl like you."

"What would you name her?" I asked.

"Well, now, I don't guess I've thought about that too much, seeing how I'm not married yet. What do you think I should name her?"

"You could call her Rayce."

He threw his head back and laughed. "Well, I just might do that. I like cars that go real fast, so maybe that would be the perfect name for her."

Of course, Dad says I had no clue what my name and fast cars had in common.

"Rayce, maybe some day your daddy will bring you and your mommy out to Graceland to see me sometime. Would you like that?"

"What's a grassland?" I asked.

Dad says Elvis had a good laugh at that one, then went on to explain it was where he lived. Dad said Elvis gave me a big kiss on my cheek before setting me back down.

Imagine that. I was kissed by Elvis.

I shook off the memories. Well, the memories I knew only because Dad had shared them over and over. And I tried to remember why it was that I didn't really care that much about the superstar. I guess I should've, what with having met him and all. It wasn't that I didn't like him. I was just indifferent. Well, who knows, maybe that would all change now that I was back living in Memphis.

Heck, we're practically neighbors.

8

Tucker called later that evening. We only talked a few minutes. Apparently one of his friends had a family emergency come up and Tuck was going to have to cover his shift for him the next night. Which meant he wouldn't be able to make it to Bible study. Which meant I wouldn't be going either.

After I hung up, I uttered a quick prayer of thanks for that resident's family emergency.

Then I uttered a quick prayer for forgiveness for thanking God for that resident's family emergency.

I decided to go downstairs and watch some TV, but as I left my room, I could hear Sandra crying in her bedroom. I tapped on her door. "You okay?"

She was sitting in bed with a book on her lap, her face buried in her hands. She mumbled something in Spanish as I took a seat at the foot of her bed. "Sandra, what's wrong? What's the matter?"

She wiped her face with the edge of her bed sheet, sighing and carrying on and on. I braced myself, trying to figure out what in the world could have happened in the ten minutes I was on the phone with Tucker.

"It's just . . . it's just . . . oh, it's just so sad. I can't bear it."

Someone must have died. A family member back in Puerto Rico? Sandra was the only member of her family who lived in the states. She'd come to America to go to college, graduating from Mississippi College, a Baptist women's school not far from Memphis. I'd had trouble imagining my spunky little roommate at a women-only school. She was so high-spirited and expressive—and oh, how she loved to flirt. She took the art to a whole new level. I couldn't even begin to imagine her towing the line at a small Baptist college with no male students.

"Sandra, did someone die?" I asked quietly.

She shot me the strangest look. "What?"

"I mean, you're obviously upset and crying and—"

Her mouth formed a long, oval "O" just before she broke out laughing. "No!" she said, sucking in air between her guffaws. "No! It's Anna Karenina! She's in this impossible situation, and she's pregnant with the count's son but her husband refuses to give her a divorce and warns her if she leaves him, she'll never see their son Seryozha again. Then the count's horse falls, throwing the count off, and the horse has to be shot and . . . and it's all so terribly tragic, I can hardly bear to read another word." Sandra blubbered through the woeful tale, hardly taking a breath as she rambled on.

I swatted her leg and rolled my eyes. "Don't do that to me! I thought something bad had happened."

"It did! I just told you! Anna is in this impossible situation and—"

"Well, don't let me interrupt." I stood up and headed toward the door. "I wouldn't want to intrude on your heartache."

"Oh, stop," she teased, still cackling. "I can't help it. It's the most beautiful love story. Hey, I'm starving. Want to go to Frankie's for some fried pepper rings?"

Sandra could switch gears faster than anyone I knew. I loved that about her.

"Be still my heart," I quipped, dashing to my room to find my flip flops. "Do they have fried green tomatoes too?"

"To die for!" she yelled. "In fact, we'll get the Fried Sampler Plate and try them all!"

I could feel the fat jumping on my thighs with the mere thought of it, but that didn't slow me down. Less than fifteen minutes later, we were sitting in a booth at the cozy pub. We placed our order and sipped our drinks while we waited.

"I'm pretty sure the waitress was smirking when we ordered these diet drinks with that plate of fried veggies," I noted.

"Yes, but did you see her?" Sandra whispered. "She hardly has room to talk. How many chins did she have? Three? Four? I lost count."

I flicked her wrist. "Stop! That's so mean. We're in no position to make snarky remarks about someone else's weight issues. Well, at least not me. How is it that you eat so much and never gain an ounce?"

She took a sip of her Tab and sat back. "Don't I wish. I've got to start running again now that the weather's so nice. I've gained half a pound since Christmas."

"Half a pound?" I scoffed. "Please. I gain half a pound just *thinking* about food."

"So we should start getting some exercise. Do you play racquetball?"

"Love it. I played all the time in college."

"Great. I'll get us a court time. They have four courts at your church, you know."

"*My* church? I don't have a church here."

"Okay, fine, whatever. First Baptist. Didn't you go there Sunday with your friends?"

"Well, yes, but it's not *my* church."

Sandra pursed her lips. "Well, it's not mine either, but I play racquetball there all the time. I also have dinner there on Wednesday nights. Best deal in town. Only $3 for a full-course dinner including beverage and dessert. Lots of the girls in the office go."

"You're kidding me. Just for the food?"

"No, silly. Several of them attend church there, but there are a few of us who just come for the bennies."

"Bennies?" I asked.

"Benefits. Oh, here we are!" The waitress placed an enormous platter in the center of the table. "Get a load of these babies!"

It was easily the biggest appetizer platter I'd ever seen. But I had a feeling we'd make a serious dent in it. Fried green and red pepper strips, fried green tomatoes, fried mushrooms, fried pickles . . . all surrounding a small bowl of buttermilk dipping sauce. Heaven!

Once we got past the initial moaning over the delectable flavors, we continued our conversation.

"So, Wednesday after work," Sandra began, wiping her mouth with her napkin, "we can just go straight from the hospital to the church. They start serving at 5:00. You'll love it. We fill up a whole table. Well, not just girls from work. Some of the singles too."

Uh oh. I wondered if Tucker and Cassie were Wednesday night regulars.

"Wait, I just remembered," I said. "I have a 4:15 appointment with Dr. Love."

Her brows arched up her face. "Dr. J. Thomas Love? The pastor?"

I felt my face warm. "Well, yeah, I met him on Sunday and . . . it turns out he knows my dad and wanted me to stop by and say hello." I said that last part a little too fast. *Well, it's true. All of it. No reason to tell her more, right?*

"Oh," she said, clearly perplexed. "That's fine. You can just come downstairs and join us when you're done."

I dragged another pepper strip through the dressing, eager to change the subject. "Tell me how you ended up in Memphis, of all places. You were born in San Juan, right?"

"Born and raised. I have two brothers and three sisters, all younger than me. They're all still there with Mama and Papa. My father has a sugar cane farm. He does very well. At least by Puerto Rican standards, anyway. But when I was about to graduate from high school, he told me he wanted me to come to the states to go to college. He had ambitions for his children, particularly his girls."

"How did you know which school to go to?"

"We had some good friends who were missionaries in San Juan. They were originally from Mississippi and spoke so lovingly of it, I knew it's where I wanted to go. In fact, Aileen was an MC grad, so I never really considered going anywhere else."

"Mississippi College. But it's a girls' school. I'm still having trouble visualizing you in a girls' school."

She laughed. "I know! I don't exactly fit the profile, do I? But it was really an easy decision. Papa said I'd either go to a girls' school or not at all. He had ambitions for me, but he's also very, very protective."

I tried to picture this man, wondering what he was like. I'd seen a few photographs in Sandra's room, but hadn't paid close attention. "Is he short like you? Your father?" I asked.

"Who says I'm short?" she barked. "Back home, I'm not short. Papa, he is much taller than I am. At least 5'5". But every inch of it muscle and determination."

"That explains a lot. And your mother?"

Sandra's smiled widened. "Ah, mi madre. As wide as she is tall with a heart to match. Oh my goodness, can she cook. Someday I should take you home with me. Just so you can taste her tamales. She's known for them. Famous. Oh, what I would give to have one of those right now."

I tossed my napkin on my plate. "How can you even think of food right now? I'm so full, I can hardly breathe."

She forked another green tomato. "That would be fun—you coming home with me sometime. We'll have to do that one of these days."

"I'd like that. I really would," I said, trying not to belch.

"Ah, then you'd get to meet Pedro . . ." she teased, her eyes waggling mischievously as she chewed.

"Pedro? Is he one of your brothers?"

She cackled again, high and loud. "No! Pedro is my boy. My man. El amor de mi vida."

"Your boyfriend?"

She shook her head, her dark curls bouncing wildly. "No, no, no. Pedro is not my boyfriend. Pedro is my parrot."

Now it was my turn to laugh. I'd been envisioning some dark, handsome young man, suitable for my little friend here. "Your *parrot*?"

"Oh, he's gorgeous, my Pedro. He's a Yellow Headed Amazon. Smart as a whip. Next time I call home, I'll let you talk to him."

"He *talks*?"

"Good heavens, he talks more than I do. Never shuts up until we cover his cage at night."

"You mean he just carries on conversations, like you or me?"

She took a long sip of her Tab. "Oh, you should hear him. He'll ask about your day, ask you what time it is, tell you how beautiful you are—I taught him that one, of course."

You would have thought she was talking about her firstborn child the way her face beamed with pride. Then again, you'd rarely see her without a smile lighting up her face and those dark lashes accenting eyes that rarely stopped dancing.

"I'll show you pictures when we get back to the townhouse. He's ridiculously handsome, but he knows it too."

"Is it hard teaching a parrot to talk?" I asked, pushing my plate aside.

"Not at all. You just start early, and never let an opportunity pass without talking to him. Tell him what you're doing, what you're feeding him, where you're going, that sort of thing. Eventually he starts mimicking you. It's hilarious. Of course, at first it just sounds like babble. Then gradually it gets more distinct. He's quite brilliant, if I say so myself."

"Has he ever embarrassed you? Said something you weren't expecting in front of someone else?"

She laughed again. "Oh my goodness, yes. But the funniest is when he flirts."

"Gee, I wonder where he learned that?"

"Not from my brother Carlos, that's for sure. Carlos taught him all kinds of dirty stuff. Well, not dirty like obscene, so much. More suggestive, but silly, you know what I mean?"

"Like what?"

"Like, when one of Carlos' girlfriends visits, Pedro will ask her what color undies she's wearing."

I almost fell off my chair. "No!"

"Or he'll pester them saying, 'What yo' number? What yo' number?' Then, 'Dump the loser, call me! Dump the loser, call me!'"

I couldn't stop laughing, as much at her imitation of Pedro as his antics.

"And if he's *really* feeling bold, he'll say, 'One on the lips. One on the lips. Dump the loser, one on the lips!' Sometimes we laugh so hard we need oxygen."

She ordered another Tab and told me more of Pedro's adventures and boisterous vocabulary. I was about ready to ask for a canister of oxygen myself. Finally we left our fried heaven and made our way home, sufficiently covered with grease and aching from so much laughter.

We climbed in my loaner and headed home.

Sandra rubbed her hands together. “Next time I’ll tell you about Pedro’s secret mission. You see, he’s actually my secret weapon . . .”

9

Wednesday, as soon as we got off work, Sandra and I drove the short distance to First Baptist. She was planning to camp out in the library since she was on the hunt for a book she'd been trying to find. I made my way down to the church offices where I told the receptionist I had an appointment with Dr. Love. She introduced herself as Dorothea Foster. I think? I'm pretty sure I counted fourteen syllables in her first name alone. Thickest Southern drawl I'd ever heard.

"He-uhll be raughhht wee-uth you, Shehhhlby," she said.

I pressed my lips together to hide my smile, then thanked her.

"Juhhst hayuv uh sea-uht ovah thayah on the sohhfah," she said with a wink.

I took-my-seat-on-the-sofa, wondering how in the world different dialects came to be. I loved a good Southern accent, but sometimes it felt like you needed waders just to tip-toe through the pronunciation. I often thought many of them were affected and put-on. It was a common practice for some of the girls I'd known growing up in Birmingham. And Samford had more than its share of accents with a side of thick. But I had no doubt that the delightful melody accompanying Dorothea's greeting was one-hundred percent the real deal.

Less than a couple minutes later, Dr. Love welcomed me into his office. The comforting scent of cigar lingered in the well-appointed room. Instead of sitting behind his large desk, he came around to sit across from me in two face-to-face leather wingback chairs.

"Well, I must say, it's a delight to see you again, Miss Colter."

"Please, call me Shelby."

"Oh, I'll try but my dear mother, God rest her soul, always taught me to show a lady respect. And old habits die hard, but we'll see. So tell me, how are you today?"

He was so kind, so genuine. His face, wrinkled in all the right places from a life obviously filled with laughter and smiles. His head still graced with thick white wavy hair. His pale blue eyes, warm and endearing. He seemed relaxed and ready to listen, as if we had all the time in the world.

He asked all the right questions, putting me immediately at ease, not rushing into any sensitive areas. And yet, once we began chatting, I seemed to have no trouble traveling down those paths with him. I told him about Will, about our relationship, and our plans to live abroad as he made a career with the Navy. I told him how hard I'd fallen for Will and how much I had loved him.

"However, you couldn't marry him," he interjected, as if making a statement we both understood.

I looked down at my skirt, running my fingernail along the pleat. "No, I couldn't. I thought I could. I wanted to. Well, at least I thought I did."

"What was it about your romantic young sailor that made you change your mind?" he asked, resting his elbows on his knees, his hands clasped together.

"Dr. Love, I hate to take up too much of your time like this. It's no big deal."

"First of all, you're not taking my time. You made the appointment. This is *your* time. And second, if it's no big deal, then where did those tears I saw Sunday come from? I doubt you were just overly excited about our lovely library."

"No, of course not. But I—"

"Miss Colter, I knew your daddy well. He's a good man. And your mother is as sweet as they come. I know you come from good stock. Solid folk. So maybe I'm going out on a limb here, but could it be your sailor wasn't all you wished for deep in your heart? Is it possible he may have been quite the romantic, but missing some of the things you'd always yearned for?"

My head snapped up as I looked into his eyes. "How could you possibly know that? Why would you ask me something like that?" I suddenly felt uncomfortable, wondering who had talked to him. Had he called Dad? Had Rachel told him something?

"Because I've sat in this chair a hundred times asking the same question to a hundred others not unlike you. Miss Colter—Shelby . . . you haven't once mentioned if your fiancé was a believer. Was he?"

I looked down again. "No, he wasn't."

"And was he comfortable with the fact that your faith is important to you?"

"No, he wasn't. I thought I could handle it. I thought somewhere down the line, he'd want what I had. Then we could raise our kids in a Christian home. It's what I've always dreamed of."

"Yet your heart fell for someone promising you the moon but not willing to share your belief in God."

"Exactly," I answered, though it came out more of a croak. The tears returned. "All my life I wanted someone who would love me, someone who would be excited to share a life with me. I was always that girl who never got the guy she wanted because he always had eyes for someone else. The girl who got stuck with the guys who were nice enough, but never set her heart to pounding. The girl who was serving punch at the prom instead of dancing with the cute guy from her history class. I didn't want to be that girl the rest of my life.

"But when I met Will, I *wasn't* that girl anymore. He fell head over heels in love with me. It was literally love at first sight. For both of us."

"Where did you meet him, if I may ask?"

"The first week of my senior year at Samford. He was a friend of a friend. He was on leave from the Navy and had flown in from San Diego for a couple of weeks. He showed up at this party and . . . oh, you don't need to hear all this."

"No, no. Go on. Please."

"He showed up at this party and the minute my friend introduced us, it was like he was smitten with me. I'd never had that experience before. I mean, he couldn't take his eyes off me. He wanted to know all about me, about my family, my childhood . . ." I caught myself smiling, remembering the night. "We ended up talking all night. We never left my friend's apartment. Sat right there on his sofa and talked all night long.

"I couldn't believe it. Here was this handsome, articulate, intelligent man—interested in *me?*"

"Wait. Why do say that—'interested in me'? Why *shouldn't* he be interested in you? You're a beautiful young lady, you're obviously articulate and intelligent. Yet you say it as though no one in his right mind would be attracted to you. Why is that?"

"No, I didn't mean it that way. It's just that . . . well, like I said. I was always the third wheel. The one who was buddies with all the guys in the Latin club. The guys I had crushes on never even knew I existed. And now here's this fascinating, wonderful man—*smitten* with me? But I didn't care. I didn't try to analyze it. I just let go and fell in love. By the time he flew back to California, we were hopelessly in love. Three months later, he invited me to visit him. By the end of the week, he took me to a breathtaking view overlooking the beach and proposed to me."

"And?"

I glanced at his clock on the wall. Ten minutes to five. "And to make a long story short, one day I woke up and realized I couldn't marry this man."

"Out of nowhere? You just came to that decision?"

It took a few minutes for me to find the words. "No, Dr. Love. Not out of nowhere. I found out this man who had pledged his life to me on that beautiful mountain overlooking the Pacific . . . was also engaged to someone else."

The clocked ticked. He said nothing.

"She wrote me a letter . . . sent pictures . . . they made a lovely couple." I looked up, unable to force a sarcastic smile.

"Oh, my. That must have been awful."

"I couldn't believe it. I thought I *knew* him. I didn't have one trace of doubt about his love for me. But it was all true. She even sent the engagement announcement from their newspaper, including a photo of them together. How could I have been so easily duped?"

He rubbed his hands together as if deep in thought. Or wanting to strangle Will. I wasn't exactly sure.

"The thing is . . . I never told anyone."

"About his double life?"

"Yes. I couldn't. I was too ashamed that I'd been so stupid and so blind."

"But Miss Colter, you couldn't possibly have known."

"I know. At least that's what I kept telling myself. But the fact is . . . well, Mom and Dad were never comfortable with my relationship with Will. They tried so many times to talk to me about being in a relationship with someone who wasn't a believer. The old "unequally yoked" thing. But I just knew . . . I knew God had led Will into my life. I was so sure he'd come around eventually. And to be quite honest, it caused a distancing between my parents and me. I was tired of hearing their concerns. I wanted to marry Will. I resented their constant questions and doubts and . . . and bottom line, I was sure I knew better. I was sure they'd come around and love him no matter what. Especially when he turned his heart to God. I just knew he would.

"But in the end, they were right. No, they didn't know the details, but they were right to be concerned. They loved me and wanted nothing more than to protect me. Instead, in essence, I shoved my hand in their faces and told them to butt out of my life if they couldn't be happy for me."

He let out a long sigh. "Well, as a parent, I assure you they don't hold it against you. Breaks our hearts to see our kids suffer, but I'm guessing they held no hard feelings once you told them it was over."

I pulled out a tissue from the box on the coffee table and wiped my nose. "You're right. They were wonderful. Of course, they think I called it off just because I realized Will and I were 'too different' . . . but they have no idea what really happened."

"And how are *you* in your heart of hearts? Struggling with trust?"

I blew out a scoff. "Yes. Well, that and my general mistrust of all men on the planet." I looked up at him. "Present company and my daddy excluded."

He smiled. "And that's natural. I'd worry if you *weren't* a bit mistrusting after what happened. But that gives us something to work on. And with your permission, I'd like to help you find your way again. Are you up for that?"

I wiped my tears and attempted a weary smile. "Yes, I'd like that. I really would."

"Good!" he said, reaching over to pat my hand. "Let's set up a regular time every week and see what the Lord has in store for us. In the meantime, will you permit me to pray for you?"

The lump surfaced in my throat again so I just nodded.

He took hold of my hands in his and began. "Lord God, You are our Abba Father. Our King of Kings and Lord of Lords. And oh, how You *love* us. Even when our hearts are broken and our minds are confused, still You love us. Father, I ask You to pour out Your Holy Spirit even at this moment. Fill Shelby with Your presence. Help her to feel Your embrace and make her know without so much as a trace of doubt, that You love her and want her to begin anew. Help her learn to trust again by first trusting again in *You*. Lord, You are full of grace and wonder and we are filled with awe at the way You reach down and touch our lives. How You take the most trivial things to nudge us this way or that at any moment in time. The way You led me to the library last Sunday just to dig through the librarian's drawer in search of some breath mints." He chuckled. "And how You helped me find Miss Colter there by the bookshelf, looking for books and instead finding a friend." He laughed quietly again.

"Oh, Lord God, how we love Your sense of humor . . . Your divine purpose in the smallest of things we do at any given time. You are Lord. You are Jehovah-Jireh! You are GOD, and we love You with all our hearts. Amen and amen."

He squeezed my hands and gave me a quick hug. "You okay?"

"Yes," I whispered. "Thank you so much, Dr. Love."

"Stop by and talk with Dorothea to set up a standing appointment. I'll see you next week, okay?" He opened the door for me.

"Will do. Thanks again." I smiled on my way out, inhaling the faint scent of cigar . . . with the hint of minty fresh breath mints.

Of course, I was the last one seated at the big round table. I'd debated about skipping the church dinner altogether, but I'd promised Sandra and knew she still needed a ride home. She'd met me at the door to the fellowship hall, took my purse and pointed me in the direction where she and several others were seated, then showed me where to go through the cafeteria-style line. Since it was my first time, the meal was complimentary. I hadn't realized how hungry I was, and the home-style entrees made my mouth water. And then there was the dessert table. If nothing else, Baptists sure know how to eat.

I took my seat next to Sandra as she introduced me to everyone at the table. My fellow hostesses Chelsea, Debra, and Leila were there along with a handful of guys I'd never met before. Then I noticed Cassie seated next to Chelsea. When Sandra introduced her, she gave me a little wave and got back to work on her salad. With all the seats taken, I assumed Tucker must be working.

It bothered me that I let Cassie get under my skin. It made no sense. She was nice enough. But knowing what I knew about her background and the blue tint of the blood in her veins, I couldn't help noticing a distinct air of superiority. Then again, maybe it was just my imagination. We'd never really talked. I chided myself for being so critical of someone I hardly knew. How tacky.

"How did it go with Dr. Love?" Sandra whispered, leaning toward me.

"Good. What a big sweetheart he is," I added, before taking a bite of fried chicken.

Oh my goodness. The fried chicken was just like Mom's. I tried the mashed potatoes. *Heaven.* I immediately considered making this a weekly habit after all. That, and shopping at a plus-size women's clothing store . . .

"Everything okay?" Sandra pressed harder, still keeping her voice down.

"Sure." She knew I'd stopped by the pastor's office to say hello. A visit from the daughter of Jack Colter and all that. "Why do you keep asking?"

"Because your mascara is smeared and your eyelashes are wet."

Oh no. "Bad enough for a trip to the restroom?" I asked.

"No, you're fine. Here—" she said, handing me her compact. I discreetly opened to use the small mirror, took care of the problem, then handed it back to her.

"Thanks."

"No problem. We'll talk later."

Yeah. I guess we will.

"Sandra tells us you're new to town," one of the single guys asked. I think his name was Trevor? He was kind of cute, actually. Sandy blond curly hair cut fairly short, nice smile. He looked as if he laughed a lot. I liked that.

"I was born here," I answered. "But I've lived in Alabama since I was ten. But yeah, I just moved back a couple weeks ago. I'm working at Baptist. I'm one of the hostesses."

"Really? I never would've guessed."

The girls and I were all dressed alike. "Good one. So you're, what—a brain surgeon or something? Being so smart and all?" I laughed at my quick wit, stabbing a renegade green bean as I enjoyed my snappy comeback.

"Well, actually, yes. I am."

Everyone laughed. Evidently we made quite an entertaining duo, this comedian and I.

"Right, and Sandra here is the Queen of England. Royalty and neurosurgeon, all at the same table. Aren't we blessed?" I laughed again, enjoying the camaraderie.

"Um, Shelby?" Chelsea said with a big grin. "Trevor is a neuro resident at Baptist. I don't know how smart he is, but he really *is* a brain surgeon."

Trevor shook his head as he stood, clearly amused. "Nah, I'm not that smart, Chelsea. I forgot my drink. Anybody need anything while I'm up?" He looked at me. "Some humble pie, Shelby?"

"Funny. Very funny."

And so it went. The easy teasing and lots of good conversation. Everyone seemed to jump right in and take part.

Well, almost everyone.

Cassie stood and draped her designer purse over her shoulder. "I've got to run. I'm meeting Tucker in a little while at Taylor's."

"Ooohhh," Debra swooned. "Ring shopping?"

"Oh, whatever gave you that idea?" Cassie teased demurely, then waved her bare left hand. "Bye bye. See you all Sunday."

I focused on the generous slice of chess pie on my plate, cutting a large bite. *Tucker's engaged? Why didn't he tell me? Then again, what business is it of mine?*

"Ah, the life of the rich and famous," one of the other guys teased. "Anyone care to make a wager on carat size?"

"Put me down for one," Trevor said. "Wait, make that two. Tucker may not cough it up, but Cassie won't settle for anything less."

"Nah," Leila added. "Tucker's too sensible to spend that kind of money on jewelry."

I tilted my head to look at her, wondering how well she knew Tucker. In fact, they all seemed to know Tucker. And certainly better than I did.

I set my fork down beside the pie. For some reason, I'd lost my appetite.

10

Arriving at work the next morning, Sandra and I had just entered the main floor when a team of white coats flew by us, two of them pushing an unusual cart. I noticed everyone seemed to back out of their way.

"What's that all about?" I asked Sandra.

"That's the Harvey team. Whenever you hear them paged, you'll know there's an emergency somewhere in the building. They're all on call to drop everything and run when there's someone in cardiac arrest or some other life-threatening situation. Their job is to resuscitate if at all possible. Which explains why everyone always gets out of their way. Seconds count. Literally."

I'd heard them paged before but never thought to ask. Good to know.

As we entered the office, Mrs. Baker greeted as she always did. "Good morning, girls." Only this morning she sounded terribly congested. As Sandra said hello and rounded her desk heading to the back office, I got my first visual of our boss. Seated behind her desk, filing through the new patient cards for us, there she sat . . .

with a Kleenex looped and protruding from both nostrils. I blinked, sure I was seeing things. Apparently she'd fashioned a nose-stopper of sorts by twisting the tissue into the shape of a short rope, then sticking each end into a nostril. I'd never seen anything quite like it.

"Mrs. Baker, you sound terrible," I said, wondering if she knew the thing was still gracing her face.

"I know," she answered, sounding as plugged up as she looked. "But it's just allergies. Always hits me this time of year when everything's in bloom. Nothing to worry about." She smiled and went back to work.

I made my way to the back office pressing my lips together. As we all put away our belongings, I picked up on a considerable amount of snickering from my co-workers.

"What's with the Kleenex up her nose?" I whispered to Debra.

"It's her own invention. We call it the Schnauzer Stopper. Not to her face, of course."

"She just leaves it there?" I pressed. "Even with the office door wide open and hundreds of people passing by all day?"

"Doesn't seem to faze her," Leila whispered. "It does the job, she can keep working, and all is well with the world."

I wasn't sure I could keep a straight face, so I tried to avoid her on my way out the door.

Pamela told me she'd be upstairs in a few minutes. Today was her last day, and we had a going-away party scheduled for later that afternoon. I really hated to see her go, but then again, if she wasn't leaving, I wouldn't have a job.

My first visit was to the room of a gentleman who'd had emergency bypass surgery the night before. I was fairly sure he'd be lights out, but I stopped by anyway, first tapping quietly on his door. "Mr. Gerard?"

As I stepped into his darkened room, the window blinds

closed tight, the first thing I saw were his feet. They were sticking straight up in the air. Unfortunately, his hospital gown wasn't covering the . . . subject. His hands pawed the air as if he were climbing something. I quickly turned my back, unsure what to do. "Mr. Gerard?"

"Milwaukee Tower, four-five-six-seven-Foxtrot is holding short runway seven, ready for takeoff."

Oh boy.

"Mr. Gerard, can you hear me?" I asked, my back still turned.

"Cleared for takeoff, runway seven-right."

"Good. That's good. Okay, then. I'm just going to leave my card here and if you need anything, you just give me a call, okay?"

"Copy that. Wind twenty-seven at ten."

All righty then. I slipped out the door and caught up with Samantha, one of the nurses. "Has anyone looked in on Mr. Gerard in 903 in a while? He's coasting at about three-thousand feet by now. I think that's a 747 he's flying in there."

She laughed. "Morphine drip. Makes 'em all loopy. But thanks, Shelby. I'll take a look."

I was still trying to banish the visual from my mind as I stopped in to check on Mr. Underwood a little while later. "How are you today, Mr. Underwood?"

"Shelby! I've been waiting for you. I wanted to tell you—I got to see Margaret last night!"

"Really?"

He was seated in one of the chairs by the windows and motioned me over. "Yes! Dr. Montgomery finally relented and allowed me to see her. He had one of the orderlies roll me down there to ICU."

I couldn't imagine his reaction at seeing his wife in that condition. "How was she?"

"Oh, she's fine. Just fine. Just like you said. Mind you, she wasn't awake. They told me the pain medication she's on keeps her asleep most of the time. But she's going to be fine."

Wow. Speedy recovery? "What all did they tell you?" I took a seat in the other chair.

"Oh, not much really. They were very nice, of course. But without Dr. Montgomery there, I suppose they wanted to leave it to him to tell me how she's doing. But she looked good. Beautiful as ever, my Margaret."

How sweet was that? His poor wife, all banged up and bruised and frail, and he still thought she looked beautiful.

"That's wonderful. I'm so glad to hear it."

"Isn't it? I hope to get back down to see her this afternoon sometime. My son should be arriving sometime tonight. I'll feel better when he gets here."

"That's great. And I'm so pleased you got to see your wife."

"But say, did you tell me you could help me make some phone calls?" he asked.

"Of course. What do you need?"

He had a bunch of papers in his lap—a lap thankfully covered by a blanket. "I need you to talk to my insurance people. I've tried twice and can't make heads or tails of what they're saying. I want to make sure they've been notified that my SU-BA-RU was totaled."

SU-BA-RU? I'd never heard it pronounced quite like that.

"Sure, I'd be happy to help."

Or so I thought. An hour later I was still on the phone with his insurance company. It was ridiculous. Of course, it didn't help that Mr. Underwood kept talking to me the entire time the agent was talking in my other ear. After getting the agent's name, I finally hung up and assured my patient they were looking into it.

"That's what they all say," he grumbled. "That's the last time I ever buy a foreign car, I'll tell you that much for sure!"

"Why's that?" I asked, confused.

"Those SU-BA-RU people are no help. A bunch of foreigners,

they are. Haven't got a clue how we do things here in the good ol' U.S.A."

"But those were insurance agents we were talking to. They don't work for Subaru. It's an American company, your insurance people."

"Doesn't matter. They don't know what they're doing."

By now my had begun to throb. I stood up. "Well, I'll check in later and see how you're doing, Mr. Underwood. You should probably get some rest."

I wasn't finished with my rounds but I needed some Tylenol, so I headed to the office. On the elevator, I ran into Leila.

"Hey, Shelby. Where are you headed?"

"The office. How about you?"

She leaned closer. "To Mindy's office on Five. Wanna come?"

I'd never been to the mysterious "office" on Five, so I decided to tag along. Each floor of the hospital had its own prayer room, a small room tucked around the corner from the elevators. Pamela had shown me the one on Nine and told me the prayer rooms were basically all alike. Dim lighting, sofas, chairs, a small desk with a Bible, hospital stationery and pens, and several boxes of tissues. At the opposite end of the room, a fake stained glass window, backlit to look like the real thing.

Leila used her key to open the door. "Since Mindy keeps supplies in here for the baby pictures she sells, her prayer room has a lock."

I stepped in, surprised to find four other hostesses. "Hey y'all," they said. Debra was reading, Tess was doing needlepoint, and Rebecca was curled up, sound asleep.

"Well . . . hey," I said, following Leila to an empty loveseat near the desk.

"Welcome to my happy little home," Mindy teased, seated at the desk. "Come see my babies."

There on the desk and on a rolling cart beside it were a couple dozen packets. Mindy opened one to show me one of the newborn photographs. “Look at this little sweetheart,” she said, holding the 8x10 portrait of a tiny sleeping infant, its light brown face all wrinkled beneath a pale yellow stocking cap.

“So cute,” I said. “Boy or girl?”

She checked the information on the packet’s label. “Girl. LaTeesha Lorraine Jameson. Born yesterday morning at 3:45 a.m. Isn’t she adorable?”

She explained her work, making rounds to visit the new mothers on her floor, offering them our usual services as well as the option to buy the baby pictures taken by a hospital photographer on their child’s first day. Many of the photos weren’t that great, the babies’ faces all scrunched up in a good cry or temporarily misshapen from the recent tour down the birth canal.

“The moms don’t care. They all love the pictures regardless. And I always make a fuss over them, no matter how pitiful the little munchkins look.”

“This must be the happiest floor in the hospital,” I said.

“It is. Have they told you about the Christmas stockings?”

I shook my head.

“During the entire month of December, every newborn goes home in a Christmas stocking. The women’s auxiliary makes them out of soft flannel. They’re adorable. The parents always want pictures of their little Christmas babies in those.”

“What a great idea,” I said. “Can’t wait to see them.”

The girls rambled on a bit, telling me some of the other fun parts of the job. I learned that the hostesses dress in costume on Halloween, making the rounds on the pediatrics floor. Then, come Christmas, I learned that we help deck the halls, including painting a giant Christmas mural on the window of the Madison Avenue lobby.

"You like to paint?"

"I do. I'd love to help."

"Then you'll be *most* popular. I can promise you that," Mindy said.

I sat back and noticed Leila was already engrossed in a Sidney Shelton paperback.

"So explain this to me. You all just hang out here when you've got nothing to do?"

Tess pulled a thread of yarn from a skein. "Yes and no. Sometimes we come in here when we've still got stuff to do, but need a break. Mrs. B doesn't like us hanging around the office til later in the day. So we come here. It's nice and quiet. Out of the way."

"Do you ever get caught?"

Debra looked up from her book, some kind of Bible study. "Ohhhh yeah. Major, major embarrassment. Sometimes a doctor will bring family members in here to discuss their loved one's case. Or sometimes visitors or family members stop by for prayer."

"Thus the name, 'prayer room,'" I teased. "What do you do?"

Mindy snorted. "They scamper outta here like a bunch of rats. I'm the only one who's got a reason to be here, so it's not a problem for me."

Everyone went back to what they were doing. I bummed a couple of aspirin off Rebecca then leaned my head back against the sofa and closed my eyes. Except for Mindy's quiet humming of Carly Simon's "Nobody Does It Better," the room was quiet. I was glad we could still hear the paging system. *Must be a speaker just outside the door.*

For no particular reason, I thought about Tucker and wondered how the ring shopping had gone last night. I still couldn't understand why the thought of it bugged me. Yes, I had to admit, it was nice to get reacquainted with him again after all these years. Especially since he'd grown up and was no longer intent on pestering me to death. But I had no interest in getting involved with anyone, least of all Chubby Tucker, so why did it bother me? Why should I care?

Good question.

I woke up half an hour later as the girls were gathering their things.

"C'mon, sleepyhead. It's time for lunch," Debra said, stashing her book in the closet Mindy kept locked. Tess stowed her needlepoint in there as well. I wasn't sure how I felt about this little subterfuge. It felt a little strange. Dishonest, somehow.

Then again, it was nice to know there was some place to go after dealing with naked patients and insurance agents.

11

We gave Pamela a sweet send off for her going-away party. We held it in one of the conference rooms in the administrative suite. We'd ordered a cake with *"Aloha Pamela"* scripted around little palm trees and a much-too-blue beach. We all brought gifts and she seemed genuinely pleased. Her handsome doctor stopped by toward the end, wrapping his arm around his beauty queen. I could only imagine the babies those two would produce. I somehow doubted there would be pointy heads or scrunched up faces on *those* newborn pictures. Not a chance.

We all said our goodbyes, promising to stay in touch. Only Chelsea would be making the trip to Hawaii for the wedding. As a bridesmaid, she'd be flying over with Pamela on Saturday and staying a full week. Naturally, Mrs. Baker would be making the trip along with her husband, Reverend Baker. I figured that had more to do with the famous golf course at Kapalua than the wedding, but I kept that thought to myself.

After work, Sandra and I stopped by Brentwood's to swap the loaner for my Seville. Gotta love having a dad in the business. The statement was marked *Paid in Full.* I made a mental note to remember to thank him.

When we got home, Sandra cooked one of her favorite Puerto Rican dishes. The house smelled amazing, making my stomach growl as I gathered a load of laundry. I had just started the washing machine when the phone rang.

"Hey, baby sister!"

"Jimmy! Where are you?"

"I'm in Guam!" he yelled over all the static. "But I'm flying out in a couple of hours. I'm coming home, Sis!"

"Oh Jimmy, that's great! When will you be here?"

"What's that?" he yelled.

"WHEN WILL YOU BE HERE?"

"I'm not sure, exactly. I'm catching a hop to Millington and wondered if you could come pick me up."

"Where's Millington?"

"WHAT?" he yelled again. I could hear engines roaring in the background.

"I SAID, WHERE'S MILLINGTON?"

"It's the Naval Air Station just north of Memphis. Easy to find."

"How'd you get a Navy hop? You're Army!"

"WHAT?"

"Never mind. I can't wait!" I squealed. "How long can you stay?"

"I don't know yet. We'll see. Mom and Dad are anxious for me to get down to Birmingham, but I figured with you so close to Millington, that would be my best bet. Hey, I've gotta run. My time's almost up on the call. I'll be in touch, okay?"

"Sounds good, Jimmy. Hurry home!"

Over dinner, I could hardly contain myself as I told Sandra all about my older brother. It felt strange, talking about him as a war veteran, especially for someone who's only twenty-eight. He hadn't talked much about his experience over in Vietnam, but I knew he'd lost a lot of friends during the war. I wondered how he would settle back into civilian life. Would he go to school? Would he live back in Birmingham? I wished he would move here.

"I can't wait to meet him," Sandra said, taking a sip of tea. "He's very handsome. At least as far as I can tell from those pictures you have in your room. How tall is he?"

I looked at her, trying to imagine the two of them together. *No way.* "Um, he's 6'2". Way too tall for you, girlfriend."

She scoffed indignantly. "I beg your pardon? I like my men tall. Besides, it's the least I can do for my country, welcoming home the troops." She laughed at herself.

"Hey, that's not a bad idea," I said.

"That's more like it."

"No, I mean welcoming him home. We should do something really nice for him."

"Oh! That would be great! We could plan a huge welcome home party and have all girls come with us to the base when he flies in! Get a bunch of red, white, and blue balloons and—"

"Whoa, whoa, whoa! Take a breath, Sandra! Jimmy wouldn't like the fuss. Trust me. He wouldn't. I was just thinking we could have a party for him or something. Invite a few friends. Oh . . . I guess I should invite Tucker, shouldn't I?"

She looked at me for a moment then mumbled something in Spanish under her breath. I'd grown used to these running commentaries, though I was never quite sure what they meant.

"Why not pull out all the stops and greet him at the base?" she groaned playfully. "Don't be such a kill joy."

"Sorry. It's just not something he'd like. But I know he'd enjoy meeting some of my friends. Tucker would probably know some guys to invite. Some of his old friends."

She tilted her head staring at me. "Tucker, huh?"

"Well, yeah. They were really good friends when we lived here way back when. I know Jimmy remembers a lot of the guys from here. He was a teenager by the time we moved away, and I know he's kept in touch with some of them."

"Fine. Plan your little party," she smirked, picking up our empty plates and taking them to the sink.

"Enough with the pouting. It'll be fun. You'll see."

She rinsed our dishes and placed them in the dishwasher. "Speaking of Tucker, what's with his girlfriend?"

"What do you mean?"

"She's not his type. What's he see in her?"

"I don't know," I mumbled, clearing the rest of the table.

"What do you mean, you don't know? I thought you knew him?"

"Well, I know him, but not really. We've talked a few times, that's all. He's Jimmy's friend, not mine."

"Oh, I guess I thought you all were close too."

"Me? And Tucker? No. Not at all. To me he'll always be the kid who stole my Halloween M&Ms and stuck them up his nose."

Sandra threw her head back and laughed hard. She had the cutest laugh. "No, no, no—don't tell me stuff like that! Now I'll never look at Dr. Thompson again without imagining those colorful candies in his nose!"

You and me both.

The next day at work, I was making my rounds but my mind was preoccupied with Jimmy's return. I knew I needed to let Tucker know and get him to help round up some of Jimmy's old friends. But I was hesitant. That whole ring thing still bugged me. And it still bugged me that it bugged me.

I tapped on the door of my next patient in 907. "Mr. Wilcox?"

"Come in!" a woman called out.

"Good morning, I'm Shelby Colter, your hostess."

A short, rotund woman stood by the bed, her face expectant. "Well, how nice! Wilbur? Do you see the nice young hostess? She's come to visit."

Mr. Wilcox sat up in bed, his face equally expectant. "Come in, come in! I'm Wilbur, and this is my wife, DeeDee."

"Nice to meet you."

I gave them my usual spiel, detailing our services and handing them my card and brochure. DeeDee took the card, cradling it in her hands as if the White House had sent it. Wilbur browsed the small brochure.

That would be the last moment of silence I would know for more than an hour and a half. I'd seen it before, patients like this and their family members. First timers. Usually they came from small rural communities outside of Memphis. They'd never experienced this kind of environment before, having doctors and nurses "wait" on them, staff taking care of them, bringing them their meals—all by a mere touch of the call button attached to their bed. Whatever malady may have brought them here, they actually enjoyed all the fuss and attention. Strange but true.

Turns out, Wilbur Wilcox was a railroad man. An engineer. And oh, how he loved trains. By the end of our long visit, I was fairly sure he loved *talking* about trains even more. I learned more than I ever wanted to know about the whole industry. DeeDee listened attentively, though I had no doubt she'd heard it all at least a thousand times before.

"So you see, by the end of the Industrial Revolution, the train was much more than just a mode of transportation. We were a pivotal part of the growth of this country, with thousands of miles of track. Then, after the beginning of the next century—"

"Miss Colter, Miss Shelby Colter."

Thank you, thank you! I'm being paged!

"I'm so sorry, Mr. Wilcox, they're paging me. I've got to go. But it was such a pleasure meeting you." I bit my tongue, resisting the usual reminder that he could reach me by calling the number on the card. Somehow I was all too afraid he'd figure it out.

I said another silent prayer and headed to the nursing station to use the phone. By now I'd grown used to hearing my name paged several times a day. Beepers were common among doctors, but the rest of us didn't have that luxury. I called the switchboard and was given a number to call. I didn't recognize it, but that wasn't unusual.

"This is Shelby Colter."

"Shelby, it's Tucker. I'm in the cafeteria. Do you have time for a break?"

I felt a wave of mild panic, not sure I wanted to go. I appreciated him wanting to look out for the new girl, but I really didn't want to make a habit of getting together like this. Then I remembered Jimmy's call.

"Oh, okay. Sure."

"I just had a few minutes and thought I'd check and see how you were doing with the new job."

"Oh, it's fine. But I'm glad you called. I had a call from Jimmy last night, so I wanted to talk to you about something."

"Great! See you shortly."

Self-talk can be good and it can be harmful. I seemed to be doing a lot of it lately. Naturally, I reminded myself this was all about Jimmy. I also reminded myself Tucker was by now officially engaged. I further reflected on the knowledge that the girls in my office never missed a thing. Any one of them could spot me having coffee with Tucker, and I'd spend the rest of the day convincing them all over again that we were just friends. My conversation with myself was still going strong as I walked into the Madison cafe and spotted Tucker at a table near the back.

"You said Jimmy called?" he asked a few minutes later as I sat down with my coffee.

"Yes, and he's coming home! He was leaving Guam last night

when he called."

"I thought you said he was in the Philippines."

"Yeah, I did. I had no idea he was in Guam. But it doesn't matter. I'm just glad he's finally coming home."

Tucker reached over and squeezed my hand. "Shelby, that's great! You must be so relieved!"

"I am. I just can't believe it. And he's catching a flight to the base in Millington. I guess that's not far from here?"

"Not at all—it's just up the road. What a relief to get him back in the states, huh? When will he come in?"

I stirred the cream in my coffee. "I'm not sure. He had no idea. I get the impression they catch a flight here, a flight there, just trying to make it home."

"Well, let me know when he's due in. I'd love to see him."

I tucked my hair behind my ear. "Actually, I was wondering if you could help me. I'm thinking of throwing a welcome home party for him and—"

"Count me in! How can I help?"

"Really? Well, thanks. I'm not sure yet. I'll let you know, but I was wondering if you could get in touch with some of the other guys you all used to hang out with. Are any of them still here in Memphis?"

He yawned then scratched the day's growth on his chin. I figured he must have been on a long shift. "Let's see. I know Pat Sulley is still in town. Blake Fenton's around somewhere. Oh, and Chris Hawley's back, coaching football over at Briarcrest. Andrew Mitchell lives in Jackson, but he'd drive over if he knew Jimmy was coming in. Then there's Lance and—"

"Okay, I'll let you work on that. I don't remember any of those guys."

"You don't?" He actually looked shocked.

"No, none of them. You might find this hard to believe, but I tried to avoid you and Jimmy and your legion of pests."

"Well, yeah, I guess I can't blame you."

"If you can get in touch with those guys, then I'll let you know as soon as I hear when Jimmy will be here."

"Shelby! There you are!"

I looked up just as my roommate approached the table. "Hey, Sandra. I was just taking a break. You know Tucker, right? Tucker Thompson?"

Refined gentleman that he was, he was on his feet, extending his hand to Sandra.

"Sure, I've seen you around," she responded. "Sandra Garcia. Nice to make an official acquaintance." She shot him her biggest smile.

"The pleasure's mine. Will you join us?"

She looked at me, so I waved her to the seat beside me.

"Thanks," she said, still smiling and looking back and forth between us.

"Tucker, Sandra is my new roommate."

"Oh? Well, that's great. So how's that working out? Any regrets?"

"Aside from some rather messy finches, it's fine."

"Hey, those are my babies you're talking about!"

"Her messy, messy babies," I told him, rolling my eyes.

She laughed and chatted like a magpie. It was truly a gift. She was such a natural around men. I should take lessons. Stop the self-talk and learn to relax. Go with the flow. Within five minutes, the two of them were like old friends.

"Oh." Suddenly Tucker was on his feet again, his attention focused somewhere behind us. Sandra and I both looked over our shoulders just in time to see Cassie turn on her heel and go out the door she'd apparently just come in.

He picked up his empty cup and saucer. "Ladies, if you'll excuse me?"

With that, he was gone. We finished our break, and left a few minutes later. We should have waited longer. Just outside the cafeteria, Cassie was giving Tucker a verbal lashing. We couldn't help but overhear as we passed—us and everyone else within a two block area.

"I'm not gonna have it, Tucker. I'm done. First, you refuse to buy me the ring I want, then you avoid me for two days without a single phone call—"

"Cass, I was on a double shift! Give me a break."

"Yet I see you have plenty of time for your hostesses."

"Oh, c'mon. I told you Shelby's an old friend—"

"Stop! Just stop! It doesn't matter. It's over, Tucker. OVER!"

Sandra and I hurried away, hoping they didn't see us. As we hustled down the hall, Sandra started to giggle.

"What's so funny?"

"Are you kidding me? Didn't you hear?"

"What do you mean?"

"Tucker Thompson's back on the market!" She did a little Latin two-step before going into the office.

I paused for a moment. It was true. It sounded like whatever Tucker and Cassie had, it was probably finished. And yet hearing Sandra's giddy reaction . . .

What I felt didn't come close to giddy.

12

The following week was most unusual. With Mrs. Baker away in Hawaii for Pamela's wedding, things were much more relaxed in the office. Apparently the old adage is true: when the cat's away, the mice will indeed play. And some of our mice played a little more than others. I'd noticed a couple of them waltzed in routinely late in the mornings, and others didn't seem quite as motivated to attend to their patients to the normal extent. The extended lunch breaks were often followed by nail painting, magazine reading, and recipe swapping that kept several of them from getting back to their floors on time.

Like the hideout up on Five in Mindy's "office," our relaxed schedule in Mrs. B's absence made me nervous at first. That said, by the end of the week I'd learned to do needlepoint and had a whole file of new recipes.

Of course, not everyone relaxed along with us.

As the hostess with most seniority, Sarah Beth took over Mrs. Baker's responsibilities at the front desk. She made it known that she didn't approve of our laid-back approach. If we made too much noise laughing and cutting up, she would clear her throat—the exact same way Mrs. Baker often did. When the back office started resembling a pig sty, she went on a tirade picking up our things and filling the trash can. If we were slow getting up to our floors in the morning, she would march into the back office and individually hand us our new patient cards, announcing our counts with the precision of a full-fledged accountant.

Most of the girls just rolled their eyes. I found her quite fascinating. She was always immaculately dressed, uniform pressed, blouse starched, nails polished and perfect, her posture straight, her head held high. I'd learned in earlier conversations she was quite the housekeeper. She loved to brag about her long hours ironing at home. Well, good for her.

"Yes, Mrs. Baker, we're fine."

We all piped down hearing Sarah Beth on the phone with the boss.

"No news, I suppose," she continued.

"Oh Lord, help her keep her mouth shut," Sandra whispered, crossing her fingers.

"Well, I think we'll need to have a meeting when you get back. I'll leave it at that."

Busted.

"No, nothing for you to worry about. Just have a nice time, and we'll see you Monday. Bye-bye."

We heard her hang up the phone and clear her throat again.

"Way to go, Sarah Beth," Leila chided. "Was that really necessary?"

She walked into our back office, her head stretched higher than normal. "I have no idea what you're talking about. C'mon, girls. Back to work. Time's a wasting."

Time's a wasting? Oh, please. I think every pair of eyes in the back office rolled simultaneously at that one.

"Careful, Sarah Beth. You'll get a nose bleed up there," Sandra quipped.

"What's that supposed to mean?"

"Nothing. Skip it."

She whipped around, hands on hips. "Well, somebody has to be in charge. You all are a disgrace. And don't think I won't tell Mrs. Baker when she gets back. You act like a bunch of school girls. Dr. Grieve would be absolutely ashamed of each and every one of you. As am I."

With that, she zipped back to the front office. We could hear drawers opening and slamming.

"Lovely," Debra groaned.

"Well, she has a point," Mindy said.

"What's that supposed to mean?" Rebecca asked, tossing her copy of *Southern Living.*

"It means, we're all taking advantage of Mrs. Baker's absence. We're not kids anymore. We should be responsible enough to do our work whether or not she's here."

I didn't like the tone flying around the four walls. I'd heard the girls get snippy from time to time, but nothing like this. I decided to play the peacemaker. "Hey, we can all do better. Let's just try a little harder and try not to get on each others' nerves."

"Oh, so the new girl wants a piece of it," Sarah Beth added from the front office. "Might be a good idea to stay out of this, Shelby, unless you're taking sides."

"Taking sides? I don't want to get into this at all," I said. "But I can't just sit here and listen to you all pick on each other like this." I grabbed my stuff and left the office.

Whoa. I hadn't seen a cat fight like that since grade school. I headed up to Nine for some peace and quiet. As I rounded the corner on the Madison wing, I heard myself paged. I used the phone at the nurses' station and called the switchboard. The operator put me through to an outside call.

"Shelby, it's Jimmy!"

"Jimmy! Where are you?"

"I'm in Hawaii. On a layover. But I should be stateside in a couple of days. I'm hop-scotching. I only get a flight if they've got seats available. Then I'll have a few days of debriefing at Ft. Lewis up in Washington state. I'll call you once that's winding down."

"Sounds good. I can't wait to see you!"

I was thrilled to have a party to think about instead of the mess in the office. I'd have to talk to Sandra and put the wheels in motion for Jimmy's party. But I wasn't about to call Tucker. I hadn't heard from him or seen him since that big scene in the hall. I felt bad for him, but it wasn't my place to offer a shoulder to cry on. Or whatever.

I spent the rest of the day revisiting every one of my patients. And yes, that included Mr. Wilcox. Thankfully, he was out having x-rays when I stopped by, and Mrs. Wilcox was nowhere to be seen.

That evening Sandra and I grumbled about the tension in the hostess office and agreed to try and stay out of it. She said this kind of stuff happened from time to time in the cramped quarters of our office, but she'd never seen it this bad. I'd never worked in an all-female office before. I wondered if there was just too much estrogen in the air. But what did I know?

One thing I did know. I dreaded Mrs. Baker's return on Monday.

13

On Thursday, Rachel called after dinner and tried to talk me into going to the singles bonfire and cookout on Saturday night. I'd used every excuse I could think of. As I hemmed and hawed, Sandra worked on me as well. She was always ready to party. I finally caved, against my better judgment, and agreed to go—for Sandra's sake.

The week finally ended, not a day too soon, and Sandra and I spent most of Saturday doing laundry and cleaning the townhouse. It took her forever to clean out the finches' cage, but oh, what a difference. The place actually smelled nice again.

That evening, we met the other singles just outside of town at the home of a church member who lived in a sprawling ranch-style home on fifteen acres. Rachel and Rich were already there, along with some of the other sponsors and probably forty singles. The bonfire was already stoked and burning, creating a cozy outdoor atmosphere. The crisp cool spring air felt wonderful. I was glad I'd come.

From the moment we stepped out of Sandra's car, she was smothered by a couple of rather unusual guys. I'd not seen them at church before. One was a little heavy with a rat's nest of dark hair on his head and long sideburns. His friend was a string bean, at least 6'4" and not an ounce of fat on him. He was more hair-challenged, working a wicked comb-over for someone his age.

I clung to Rachel's side, glad to avoid their attention. "What's up with those two?" I asked quietly.

She placed a basket of hot dog buns on the large picnic table, glanced over her shoulder at them, then laughed. "Oh, that's Burt and Bobby. Rich calls them 'the Killer Bs.' They drift in and out of our group. My guess is, they church hop, scoping out other singles groups for dates then come back here when they find slim pickins elsewhere. We haven't seen them for months. The thing is, they have no social skills whatsoever, but think they're really suave. We get a kick out of watching them operate . . . but unfortunately, whenever they drift back in, they chase away a lot of our girls. We'll have to rescue Sandra at some point."

"Oh, trust me. She can handle them." I turned to help Rachel. "Hey, how are you? How's little Cooper doing?" I patted her tummy beneath her long maternity top. "Wow! He's kicking! Do you feel that?"

"Do I ever." Rachel placed her hand over mine. "Isn't that funny? He's been an active boy all day. But I just *love* it. I keep thinking he's in there saying 'Hi Mommmy!'"

"You and Rich will make the best parents. I'm so happy for you, Rachel." I hugged her hard, careful not to squish Cooper.

"We're excited!" she said, hugging me back. She grabbed a covered tray of hot dogs. "Hey, Shelby, have you talked to Tucker lately?"

"No, why?"

"Well, I got a call the other night from—"

"Hey, Rachel, let me help you with those!" Sandra rushed between us. "You guys have GOT to help me!" she whispered urgently. "What is up with those guys?"

Sure enough, Burt and Bobby closed in on us. "Hi, Rachel.

Can we help too?"

"Absolutely. Here, you guys can start cooking some hot dogs for us. Here are the sticks. Just line a few up on there and let 'em roast in the fire."

"Oh! Cool!"

"Wait, wait, wait—first go wash your hands. I don't even want to know where those hands have been. There's some water in that jug over there. Pour it over your hands."

Suddenly they were busily mastering the task at hand, giving Sandra some breathing room. "Thank you," she mouthed to Rachel.

"Who's hungry?" Rick yelled, armed with a tray of condiments and several bags of chips tucked under his arm. "Let's eat!"

Sandra and I found a couple of Adirondack chairs at a safe distance from the fire. We'd just settled in to enjoy our hot dogs when Bobby and Burt launched a secondary attack.

"Hey, beautiful ladies," Burt said, taking a seat in a lawn chair to my right. "May we join you?"

"Burt, it's our lucky day," Bobby said, sitting next to Sandra. "The two prettiest babes at the party and they're all ours."

I'd just taken a sip of Tab. I tried really hard not to spray it out my nose at his proclamation. This could be a painfully long evening . . . after which I would kill Rachel. She'd promised me this group didn't have any annoying guys. I guess their recent absence made them slip her mind.

"So what's this about your boyfriend?" Bobby asked, scooting his chair closer to Sandra's.

"Oh, yes," Sandra answered, giving me a look. "My Pedro. The love of my life."

This time the Tab flew. I wiped my face and tried to wipe my nose.

"What's wrong with you?" Burt asked, handing me his napkin.

I ignored him, feigning concentration on my Tab-sprayed jeans.

Bobby pushed harder. "If he's the love of your life, how come he's not here tonight?"

"Because he's back in Puerto Rico," Sandra said. I noticed her accent was stronger than usual. "He owns a vineyard. VERY wealthy. Very busy. Busy, busy, busy. Works day and night."

"But if he's there and you're here, how come you can't date?"

"Oh, I could *never* cheat on Pedro! I wouldn't want to . . . ruffle his feathers, you know."

This time a piece of hot dog wedged in my throat. I coughed and coughed as Burt patted my back to help. It flew out of my mouth and into the fire.

"You're weird, you know that?" he said in total sincerity.

I just nodded, unable to make eye contact for fear I'd lose what was left of my composure.

Sandra's eyes were huge. Yes, this was going to be a very long night.

An hour later as we finished singing some goofy songs and tried to get the stickiness off our fingers after indulging in S'mores, a car pulled up. To be honest, I was ready to call it a night. But Sandra had finally convinced the Killer Bs she wasn't interested, and she was having a blast hanging out with everyone else. Just then, Trevor Knight stepped out of the Jeep Cherokee.

"Am I too late?"

Everyone welcomed him, Rich rustled up a couple of hot dogs for him, and he quickly joined the party.

"Shelby, how's it going?" He took the seat Burt had vacated.

"Good, Trevor. Late shift?"

"Yeah, but I needed some fresh air. I decided to chance it and make the drive. Glad everyone's still here."

"Good. I'm glad you made it."

He chomped on his meal for a minute then washed it down with a Coke. "Have you talked to Tucker lately?"

I realized then that Rachel had never finished what she

started to tell me about Tucker when I first arrived. "Oh, uh, no. Haven't seen him or heard from him. You?"

He looked around, obviously making sure no one else was listening to our conversation. "Well, sure. Tuck and I work together a lot. I guess you heard he and Cassie split."

I finger-combed my hair back from my face. "Yeah, Sandra and I happened to be passing them in the hall when it happened."

"Oh, that must have been rough."

"It wasn't pretty. How's he doing?"

"Truthfully? He's fine. Really. A bit awkward since she's been very vocal about it all. But between you and me?" He paused, leaned toward me, then whispered, "He's extremely relieved. Ol' Tuck got hog-tied into that one from the start."

"Hog-tied?"

"Hog-tied. The Judge called up Tuck's dad, and the next thing you know the kids are dating. I think he was okay about it at first. Then Cass just started assuming things, making plans—basically just tugging Tuck along in the process. The visit to the jewelery store . . ." He shook his head and blew out a long sigh. "Cass had already picked out a two-carat flawless diamond. Shelby, the thing had a $125,000 price tag on it."

"Oh my gosh."

"Tucker just laughed. He was sure she was kidding. Like it was some kind of joke."

"She wasn't?"

"Noooooo," he said, shaking his head with conviction. "She'd already made a down-payment to hold it." He took another sip of his Coke. "When Tucker said no, that's when *she* laughed. She assured him she didn't expect him to pay for it. The only reason she'd asked him to come was to see if he liked it."

"Ouch?"

"Yeah. Trust me, even to a broke resident with massive college loans hanging over my head, that's a low blow to any guy's ego. Instant emasculation."

"I get that."

"Seriously. But it was only a matter of time. If it wasn't the ring, it would have been something else. Tuck's heart wasn't in it."

"So if he's okay, how come he's been missing in action? I haven't seen him around the hospital or church or anywhere."

"Ah, that's our Tuck. He's trying to give it time to blow over. He's around. Just flying under the radar until the melodrama subsides."

"I'm glad he's okay. I can't believe I'm saying this, but he's too nice a guy to get bullied."

Trevor's brow dipped. "What's wrong with saying that?"

"Remember, Tuck and I have history."

"Ohhhh, that's right. I forgot."

"Trevor! When did you get here?" Sandra asked, clapping him on the back.

"Just a little while ago. Didn't see you here, *Senorita Garcia.* How's it going?"

She plopped down on my lap and swung her legs. "Good! Especially now that you're here!" She let loose one of her signature laughs.

We chatted and made more S'mores even though everyone else was starting to leave. I would have stayed all night. Under the stars, the wonderful scent of the wood burning, the cool night air. Heaven.

Instead, I helped Rachel and Rich finish cleaning up while Sandra and Trevor talked. And talked and talked. They laughed and talked some more. Rachel elbowed me, nodded her head in their direction, and raised her eyebrows. "Well?"

Well, indeed.

14

"JIMMY! Over here!" I was standing at the fence just off the tarmac at NAS Millington watching my brother plow down the steps of the huge cargo plane with a bunch of sailors.

He looked so different. So grown up. I'd have to get used to that. Still the same handsome face, same prominent jaw line, with the same seriously masculine air about him. His brown hair, same shade as mine, was surprisingly shaggy. Last time I'd seen him, it was practically buzzed. He'd filled out a lot too. As if he'd been working out. I couldn't believe how much he'd changed. Suddenly he started running toward me, then dropped his duffel and scooped me up in his arms.

"Moonpie!" He planted a wet sloppy kiss on my cheek and hugged me hard. "You look great!"

"So do you! I can't believe you're finally home!"

"It's about time, huh?" He set me back down and gathered his gear. "Let's get out of here."

We wasted no time stashing his stuff in my trunk.

"I see the old man bought you a new Caddy. Nice wheels, Sis."

"Oh, I'm sure he's got one for you, no doubt a convertible all shined and polished. He'll probably hand you the keys before he or Mom even give you a hug."

"Here's hoping. He told me they've got a loaner for me here at Brentwood's so I can drive down to Birmingham."

"That's Dad. Always a step ahead."

I was so glad my brother was here. Safe in my car. All in one piece. No longer in the jungles of that faraway country where our defeat still defined the wounded soul of our nation. No longer on the other side of the earth. Home. Safe.

On the drive back to Memphis, we talked a mile a minute. It was a little strange, my annoying brother all morphed into this big soldier with a lot of mileage under his belt. I could tell he was happy to be back in the states, and especially glad to be back in the South. My heart ached when I looked into those gorgeous brown eyes of his. They looked tired. Like eyes that had seen too much.

As we approached the skyline of downtown, he said, "Hey, I would kill for some ribs. Are you hungry?"

"Funny you should ask."

A few minutes later we parked just off Beale Street and made our way to the back alley entrance of The Rendezvous. The famous restaurant had always been Jimmy's favorite, so he wasn't at all surprised when I suggested it.

If you've ever been to Memphis, you've heard of the famous basement rib joint. The son of Greek immigrants, Charlie Vergos first opened his restaurant as a sandwich shop. But his sandwiches were different from others in downtown Memphis. Charlie smoked his ham and chicken in, of all things, a pit which was fitted into a coal chute. His sandwiches sold by the hundreds. When a meat salesman one day left him a case of ribs, Charlie decided to spice them up a bit. His secret blend of Greek and American spices became the famous dry rib seasoning which would set his restaurant apart and delight customers for decades to come.

But it wasn't just the ribs and side dishes that made the Rendezvous so unique. Charlie took good care of his employees. Many have been with him since the '50s and '60s, and a few of them had kids of their own who now worked there. It was truly a family affair.

He stopped, closing his eyes as he inhaled the scent of barbecue that filled the air. "You have no idea how long I've dreamed of this moment—to taste these ribs again.

I laughed and patted him on the back as he rubbed his stomach in anticipation. "Which is precisely why I drove you straight here from the base!"

Of course, he had *no* idea we wouldn't be dining alone.

As we descended the staircase, I scoped the dining area for familiar faces, hoping I wouldn't see any. For a Sunday evening, the place was unusually busy. I gave our name to the head waiter with my back turned to my brother. "Colter. Party of two." I winked. A warm smile spread across his dark face as he acknowledged the name. "Yes, ma'am. Right this way."

He led us toward a private room in back, throwing open the doors as the crowd inside shouted, "WELCOME HOME!"

"What have you done, baby sister?" Jimmy shouted, planting his hands on his hips.

"I wanted you to know how happy I am to have you home, so we threw a little party!"

He wrapped me in his arms and kissed the top of my head. In a moment he was swept into the room filled with friends new and old. Tucker bear-hugged Jimmy before we'd barely entered. The greetings went on for several minutes, mostly by his old childhood friends. I took my time introducing him to some of the girls from work, and of course, Sandra.

"Hola, Jimmy! You're even more handsome in person!" she shouted, giving him a hug. "¡Bienvenido! Welcome to your party, hermano mayor!"

Rachel waddled over and gave him a hug. "You don't know me, but I'm Rachel, Shelby's roommate from Samford. I've prayed for you for as long as I've known her. It's so good to finally meet you!"

"Nice to meet you too, Rachel. I've heard a lot about you."

She swiped at a renegade tear. "And this is my husband, Rich."

Rich shook my brother's hand. "Welcome home!"

Jimmy took it all well, considering he's usually not one for all the fuss. He seemed impressed with the huge banner we'd made and all the red, white, and blue balloons bobbing around the room, but mostly he enjoyed getting reacquainted with old friends and making a few new ones.

Eventually we all took our seats as the waiters brought in family-style platters of the famous ribs, chicken, brisket, and all the sides. Jimmy didn't hold back, devouring the ribs on his plate along with the companion beans and slaw. I hoped he didn't make himself sick. Tucker teased him mercilessly. It was good to see them both laughing like that.

I was surprised how well the different factions of our little group blended. Everyone seemed to have a great time and lingered for several hours. Somewhere around 9:30, I realized it was just the four of us—Jimmy, Tucker, Sandra, and me. We settled in over last bites of dessert and coffee, enjoying the afterglow of the evening.

Jimmy nodded at Tucker and me. "Who would have thought, after all these years, that you two would actually be *friends*? Seriously, Tuck, after that stunt you pulled putting Ex-Lax in her chocolate malt, I didn't think she'd ever speak to you again."

I doubled over, remembering the awful experience and the

horrible after-effects. "Oh, Jimmy, please. Did you have to remind me?" I punched Tucker in the arm. "That was terrible!"

It took him a while to stop laughing. "Y'know, for the life of me I can't figure out why we were so mean to you."

"Well, that's a no-brainer," Jimmy said. "She was an easy target. Made our mischief all the more fun."

"Didn't you ever retaliate?" Sandra asked, before licking the last bite of chocolate from her fork.

"Believe me, I tried. I stole their beloved baseball cards. I hid my old Barbies in their lunchboxes—"

"Now, for the record, that was just wrong," Tucker interrupted, holding up his hands. "Do you have any idea how much flak I caught when I opened my lunchbox that day? The guys teased me about that for over a year, no thanks to you." He fake-punched my shoulder.

"I make no apologies. It was well-deserved and you know it."

"Atta girl, Shelby," Sandra cheered.

We chatted a while longer, then Jimmy asked, "Tuck, where's this fancy girlfriend of yours? How come she's not here tonight?"

An uncomfortable silence drifted across the table until Tucker finally answered. "Well, old buddy, I'm afraid you're a little late. We're no longer together, as of a couple weeks ago."

"Oh," Jimmy said, sitting back. "I'm sorry. I had no idea."

"No problem," Tucker answered quickly. "Really. It's all good. Just wasn't meant to be. Which puts me in the same boat with your sister here." He nodded at me, giving me one of those looks you give someone who's been where you've been. *Sort of . . .*

"That's right, Moonpie," Jimmy said, after draining the last of his coffee. "Mom and Dad said the reason you moved here was to get away from all the stress after dumping Will."

"Jimmy, I did not 'dump' Will."

"Sure you did. And it's a good thing. He's Navy. Need I say

more? You deserve a lot better." He winked at me, then added, "Someone like Tuck here."

"Oh, please," I groaned, hoping to cover my embarrassment. "With our history, that would be *most* unlikely."

"Yeah," Tucker added, refolding his napkin. "I'll always be Chubby Tucker to her. Not exactly the stuff of romance."

"And I'll always be Moonpie to him."

"I feel so left out with no nickname," Sandra said, faking a good pout. "What's a girl gotta do to get a nickname with you guys?"

"Jimmy, what do you think?" Tucker studied my roommate.

"I don't know, Tuck. Something Puerto Rican? Something a little spicy perhaps?"

Jimmy snapped his fingers. "I've got it! We'll call you Chiquita. Our favorite little banana."

Sandra laughed, clapping her hands. "I like that! Chiquita it is."

Our waiter stopped by to refill our coffee cups. "It's been a real pleasure to serve you this evening," he said, emptying his carafe into Jimmy's cup. "And especially to you, sir. Welcome home and thank you for your service for our country." He extended his hand, and my brother shook it.

"Thank you, I appreciate that."

"However," he said, setting down the carafe then reaching for our remaining dishes. "We got to move you all outta here. We got a private party coming in and that means it's time for you all to skedaddle."

"Whoa, that's a late party," Tucker said as we got up and gathered our things. "I didn't realize you all were open that late."

"We aren't," he said. "But sometimes ol' Charlie gets a call with a special request and we make allowances." His brows danced as he left the room.

"Well, I guess that means we're done here." I pulled down the banner to give to Jimmy. "So, big brother, did you enjoy your party?"

He wrapped his arm around my shoulder as we left the room. “I sure did. Thanks for going to all the trouble. And for including Chubby Tucker. That took guts.”

“I heard that,” Tuck chimed in as he escorted Sandra up the stairs behind us.

As we made our way down the alley, several cars suddenly pulled up on Beale Street as we rounded the corner. Doors flew open as a bunch of men and women emerged from the long white vehicles. *Limousines?* We tried not to stare, but curiosity kept turning our heads back.

Then, just before we rounded the corner to head to our cars, we saw him. Though to be honest, it was more of just a *glimpse* of him. Elvis Presley hustling out of a limo with a beautiful girl on his arm.

“Did you see that?!” Sandra squealed. “It’s Elvis!”

“Are you sure?” Jimmy asked. “All I saw were the sideburns. Could’ve been anyone.”

“No, it was him! I recognized Dr. Nichopoulos with him too. His doctor friend. I see him around Baptist all the time, don’t you?”

“So many celebrities, so little time,” Tucker quipped.

And so it was, that late Sunday night on a sidewalk mere steps from The Rendezvous, I had my first official, grown up Elvis sighting.

It would not be my last.

15

We dropped Jimmy off at Brentwood Cadillac on Monday morning on our way to work. Mom and Dad were anxious to see him, so he headed for Birmingham but promised to come back and visit soon. Sandra and I drove the rest of the way to the company of Rick Dees.

"Thirty-five after seven this *beauuuuutiful* spring morning. We've got 63 Dees-grees this morning, heading for a high of 84. Sound good to you, Mr. Mayor?"

"Yessuh, Mistah Dees," said a raspy old voice.

"Good, good. Gotta keep the politicians happy."

The sound of a door creaking open preceded a deep, velvet voice. "Good morning, Dees."

"Sammy Soul, what brings you here this fine morning?"

The voice, another of Dees' parodies, sounded like Barry White. "Wanna lay a little somethin' on ya this morning."

"You best watch what you lay on me, Sammy. How 'bout you stand over there. Waaaay over there. Daz' good. Now, whatchu gonna lay on me, bro?"

"I gots me a song t'sing, Dees."

"Well, ain't that just real nice, Sammy. But you've gotta hold on, my brother. We've gotta take a break for a Tidy Bowl commercial."

"I gots t'wait for a tow-let commercial? Whas' matter you?"

"Just calm your pipes there, Sammy. This is Rick Dees at WHBQ Memphis and 'we'll be *this* right after *back*!'"

"Sandra, they should make it mandatory to have two cups of coffee before listening to this guy. He's making my head spin this morning."

"Yes, but how dull to start a day without our Rick."

When we arrived at the hospital, we realized our day was about to take a very bad turn. Mrs. Baker was back. To say she was on the war path would be an extreme understatement. Apparently she'd drilled Sarah Beth when she got home over the weekend. Clearly, our senior hostess had ratted us out. A sign was posted on our notice board:

HOSTESS MEETING - 9:00 A.M.
CONFERENCE ROOM B
MANDATORY ATTENDANCE
NO EXCEPTIONS

Needless to say the atmosphere in the office was frigid at best. Those of us who tried to make small talk with Mrs. Baker, welcoming her back from her trip, were rewarded with short, polite answers and nothing more. I grabbed my clipboard and disappeared with some of the others to the cafeteria. We ate breakfast in near silence, none of us willing to talk about the lashing that surely awaited us.

And oh, what a lashing.

I'll spare you the blow-by-blow. It wasn't pretty. But I have to say, I think we all needed it. And oddly enough, we all left that conference room feeling renewed. Determined to restore her faith in us and in ourselves.

By the time I got to Nine, I was emotionally spent but eager to visit my patients. I started with Mr. Underwood who had already paged me.

"You made it! I'm so glad!" he said, greeting me with an unusual burst of enthusiasm.

"Good morning, Mr. Underwood. How are you this morning?"

"I'm fine, but I need your help. The SU-BA-RU people called and they need some more information." He held up what looked like a ream of paper. "Can you help me fill out these forms?"

A thousand excuses floated through my head before I remembered my new promise to work harder at the job I was blessed to have. "Sure thing. Where do we start?"

I spent about forty-five minutes sorting through the legalese forms before I left to make copies for him downstairs. As luck would have it, Mr. Wilcox was standing outside his door.

"Miss Colter! I was hoping to see you today. I wondered if you might check on some statements the insurance office sent up this morning. I don't know what they mean. Could you take a look at them for me?"

"How about I put in a call and have one of the insurance counselors come up to talk to you? They'll be a lot more help to you than I could ever be."

"Well, then, I suppose . . ." His countenance fell. "But I also had something else I wanted to show you. I had DeeDee bring my railroad scrapbook from home. I thought you might like to take a look."

"Oh," I said, envisioning hours on end getting a detailed tour of that scrapbook and another history of the entire railroad industry in general. "I'm afraid I'll have to come back later. I still haven't made all my rounds, and I've got several errands I need to run." I started backing away from him when I heard my name.

"Shelby?"

I turned just as a new patient was wheeled around the corner.

"Donnie? Donnie!" I couldn't believe it. One of my best friends from college. I caught up with him and leaned over to give him a hug.

"What are you doing here?" he asked as the orderly continued pushing his wheelchair down the hall.

"I work here. But the more important question is, what are *you* doing here and why are you in a wheelchair? Are you sick?"

He made a face. "Me? Sick? Do I look sick?" He pressed the back of his hand to his forehead then his cheek.

"Stop! I'm serious. Are you okay?"

"Good question. I guess we'll find out. That's what hospitals are for, right?"

Donnie was one of the funniest people I'd ever known. We had a long history going back to our freshman year at Samford when we both worked part-time at the infamous Taco Barn. I couldn't think of Donnie Rogers without smiling or literally laughing out loud. We were good, good friends, and I absolutely loved the guy.

Unfortunately he didn't look too good. His hazel eyes looked drawn and he'd lost a lot of weight since I'd last seen him. He was wearing his straight dark hair shorter than I'd ever seen it, but it was the fatigue in his face that concerned me most.

The orderly from Admissions backed Donnie's chair into 919. "How about we get Mr. Rogers settled then you all can catch up."

"It's a beautiful day in the hospital ward . . ." Donnie began, singing the familiar tune. He winked. "Come see me in a few?"

"Perfect. I've got to run an errand downstairs, then I'll be back up to see you."

"Oh goodie. You can help me with the catheter."

"Then again, maybe I *won't* be back to see you."

He fluttered a silly wave with his fingers as the door closed.

Oh, Donnie.

Just as I stepped off the elevator on the main floor, I heard my name paged. Apparently it was going to be one of those days. After I made copies for Mr. Underwood, I called the switchboard who connected me to my caller.

"Hey. Shelby. It's Tucker."

"Hey, how's it going?"

"Good. I was just wondering if you've got lunch plans. Want to meet in the Madison Restaurant?"

Well then. "Sure. Sounds good. What time?"

"I've got a consultation in a few minutes. Is 12:30 too late?"

"No, that actually works better for me."

"Good. See you then."

I wondered why he'd suggested the restaurant instead of the cafeteria. Then again, it was a lot quieter. And nicer. And out of the way. And for reasons not fully understood, I felt a smile warm my face as I headed back upstairs.

After getting Mr. Underwood settled with the copies he'd requested, I hurried down the hall to check back on Donnie.

"Come in, come in," he greeted, sitting up in bed. No hospital issue gowns were suitable for Donnie Rogers. He wore a pair of navy blue cotton pajamas piped in white with a matching white monogram over the left pocket.

"Well, aren't you just the dapper one?" I approached his bed. "You look great, Donnie. So what's going on? Why are you a guest on my floor?"

"*Your* floor? Sit! Sit. You first. Tell me what you're doing here. You're obviously not a nurse, dressed in that pricey ensemble. What are you—an administrator? Vice president?"

I took a seat beside him, pulling the chair closer. "Hardly. I'm a hostess. In fact—" I stood back up and launched into my standard hostess spiel using my best stewardess voice.

"Welcome to Baptist Memorial Hospital, Mr. Rogers. I'm Shelby Colter, your hostess, and it will be my privilege to serve you while you're a guest here with us." I handed him my card and brochure as I continued, using exaggerated hand gestures. "You'll find lots of helpful information in our brochure, with a list of extensions should you need to place calls within the hospital, as well as the number on my card there. Feel free to call me *any* time you need assistance, whether you need something from the gift shop like magazines or newspapers, help from the insurance office, or simply a friendly visit. And now if you'll fasten your seat belt and put your tray table in its upright position, we'll prepare for take-off."

"And if you put on a life vest and show me how to breathe through an oxygen mask, I'm outta here," he said, his expression deadpan.

I took my seat again, laughing at his tone. "Okay, sorry. But you get the gist of it. I love it. It's a great place to work."

"How long have you worked here? And why are you in Memphis? Why aren't you sailing the ocean blue with your sailor boy?"

I scratched my eyebrow. "Yeah, about Will. That's not gonna happen. I called it off."

He leaned his head back. "Well, thank God!"

"Huh?"

"When I didn't get an invitation to the wedding, I thought you didn't love me anymore."

"As if I'd forget you?" I pinched his shoulder.

"Ouch?" he whined, rubbing where I'd tweaked him. "A little compassion, please? Hospital patient here."

"Okay, so out with it. Why are you here?"

He busied himself, straightening his blanket and picking some non-existent lint off his sleeve. "Chest pains."

"Really?"

He finally looked up.

"Yes, but it's not the first time. Seems my ticker is rather temperamental."

"That sounds serious, Donnie."

He arched his eyebrows. "That's because it is. Anyway, I happened to be in town for a meeting and had to be rushed here by ambulance last night. I've been in your lovely emergency room most of the night as they tried to figure out what to do with me."

"Need I remind you that you're much too young for this?" I hoped I sounded a lot more lighthearted than I felt.

"I know. I have Donald Senior to thank for this. Coronary artery disease. If you'll recall, Dad died when he was 35. Back when I was just a little bugger."

"I forgot about that. Wesley was your step-dad. Speaking of Wesley, have you called home to let your mom know what's happened?"

He reached out, placing his hand over mine. "No, and I don't want them called. Mom's health isn't that great now either, and I don't want to stress her. I'll just handle this little scare on my own. She doesn't need to know."

I tilted my head, questioning his reasoning, but left it alone.

The door opened as my charge nurse walked in carrying a flip chart. "Mr. Rogers? I'm Helen, and I need to ask you a few questions."

I stood up. "That's my cue. Donnie, I'll check in on you later, okay?"

"Okay. Thanks for stopping by, Shelby. Good to see you again."

"Helen, use the *biggest* needles you have on this guy," I fake-whispered to her. "Preferably The Screamer, okay?"

"The Screamer?" Donnie mouthed as I left the room.

Donnie? Having heart problems? I couldn't believe it. He'd been through a lot—raised by his mom until she remarried while he and his twin sister were still in high school. He and Wesley had never really gotten along which made his relationship with his mom stressed to say the least. I hoped I'd have time to visit with him more, catch up on old times. I said a silent prayer for him, then noticed it was almost 12:30.

Time for lunch with my favorite anesthesiologist.

16

"Sorry I'm late," I said a few minutes later, taking a seat across from Tucker.

"No problem. I'm off duty so as soon as we finish here, I'm heading home to crash for a few hours.

The waitress took our order and I straightened my silverware, waiting for him to say something.

"You look nice today, Moonpie."

"I should have known I'd have to re-train you after having Jimmy in town last night."

He quirked a look at me, confused.

I leaned forward, whispering, "Remember? We were going to dispense with the whole nickname thing?"

"Oh!" He laughed. "My apologies. Old habits are hard to break."

"Yeah, well, try harder," I teased.

"It was great seeing Jimmy again. He seemed to really enjoy his party last night."

The waitress brought our beverages. Coffee for him. Iced tea for me.

"It was nice, wasn't it?" I said, emptying a packet of sweetener into my glass. "Thanks for getting all the guys to show up. I think that was his favorite part. Seeing all the old gang again."

We continued the small talk until the waitress returned with our meals. I was surprised when Tucker asked if he could pray before we ate.

"Sure," I said, bowing my head.

"For Your blessings, for Your mercy and Your love, we thank You, Lord. And thanks for new beginnings."

"Amen," I murmured wondering what in the world that meant. It didn't take long to find out.

"So, I was thinking about what Jimmy said last night."

"What's that?" I reached for my club sandwich.

"About you and me being in the same boat."

I'd just taken a bite but stopped chewing and stared at him. Was this a joke? Was he teasing me? I slowly resumed eating and waited to see what else he might say.

"Anyway, I thought . . . y'know, he's got a point. You're no longer in a relationship, and as the whole world seems to know, I'm no longer in one either. So I was thinking . . . well, I wondered if you might, uh . . ."

Oh no.

". . . like to go out sometime. Y'know, just something simple. Dinner. A movie. Something like that?"

I tried to swallow but it wasn't easy. When I finally managed the deed, I stalled by taking a sip of my tea. Then I wiped my mouth with the linen napkin. Then I'm pretty sure I gave him a really lame smile.

"I know, it's kind of weird," he jumped in.

"You could say that," I croaked.

"But it doesn't have to *be* weird. We're both grown now. I'm not that irritating punk anymore—"

"You sure about that?" I said, smiling.

"And you're not that irritating kid sister always begging to be pranked anymore—"

"*Begging* to be pranked? Oh, please."

"Anyway, it just seemed like something we could do. No pressure, no expectations, just a chance to go out and have some fun. What do you say?"

My heart thundered. There was something so wrong about this. It was awfully soon after his breakup with Cassie. As in only a few days? And I wasn't really interested in dating right now. Still, I couldn't help it. I wanted to say yes. The thought of dating him wasn't completely foreign to me, even if I didn't want to admit it. But would I ever be able to think of him as someone other than Chubby Tucker?

I wasn't sure. I just knew I wanted to try.

"I'd love to, Tuck."

"Really?"

"Sure. That sounds fun. Just promise you'll leave the Ex Lax at home."

He smiled broadly. "I promise."

"Well, well, what have we here?"

We both looked up as Dr. Love approached our table. "Two of my favorite people. Isn't this nice and cozy?"

Tucker stood, stretching his hand to our pastor. "Dr. Love. Nice to see you."

"Have a seat! I insist. How are you, Miss Colter?" he asked, taking hold of my hand.

"Fine, thank you. Would you like to join us?"

"Oh, thank you for the offer, but I'm meeting with the family of one of our members. He's not expected to make it much longer, and they wanted to discuss arrangements for his memorial service. So you two have a nice lunch. How's the clam chowder, Dr.

Thompson?"

"Excellent."

"Shelby? I'll see you Wednesday?"

"I'll be there."

He gave me a thumbs up and a wink, then made his way to a back table.

"Well, then."

"Well, then?"

"It's settled."

"What's settled?"

"Dinner and a movie. How does Friday night work for you?"

"Perfect," I said, "as long as I get to pick the movie."

"Uh oh. I was hoping we could go see the sneak preview for *Smokey and the Bandit.*"

"And I was hoping to see *Annie Hall.*"

"Hmm. Let me see. Action packed comedy with Burt Reynolds and Sally Field . . . or another goofy Woody Allen oddball movie. Tough call." He turned his head to the side as if in deep thought. "Oh, okay, fine. *Annie Hall* it is. Is it a date?"

"It's a date, Tucker."

"So, are you and Dr. Thompson an item now?" Dr. Love asked as he took his seat across from me in his office, his face beaming with expectation.

"What? Oh, no. No! We've known each other for years. He and my brother were best friends growing up." I blew out a raspberry to punctuate how silly I thought his misconception was.

"That's nice, but the fact he and your brother were friends growing up doesn't necessarily prevent you and Dr. Thompson from being an item. You sure looked nice together at lunch the other day." He took a sip of his coffee, his warm eyes crinkling along with his mischievous smile.

"No, Dr. Love. We are not 'an item'."

"And why not? He's a nice-looking young man, good family, good future . . ."

I pursed my lips trying to convey my insistence. "Just friends, thank you very much."

"Well, that's too bad."

"Why's that?"

"I think it's time you move on. You've made a lot of progress just in these past couple of weeks, Shelby. You're a lot stronger now. Much different from the young woman I found crying in our church library that morning."

I smiled at him. I'd already grown to love this dear man. I'd always had such a different impression of pastors, assuming most of them were a bit "holier than thou" up close and personal. Dr. Love wasn't that way at all. He was down to earth, humble, and he had such a genuine passion for people. You never felt like just another pew-sitter or name on the church roll in his presence. He made you feel like a long lost friend. Someone he cared deeply about. Never once had he made me feel like I was taking his time. Never once had he rushed me out the door for another appointment. I wasn't sure how he did it, with such a large congregation. I only knew it came very natural for him. I guess that's what it meant to be "called" to the ministry.

We talked through some other issues, including my still-shaky matter of trusting men. I talked a good talk, but apparently Dr. Love saw right through me.

"At some point you will be able to accept the fact that your sailor's deceit was an isolated case. Not every young man on the planet is a con artist or heart breaker. I understand that you may still need more time to believe that here," he said, thumping his heart. "But the day will come. Hopefully sooner than later."

"I'm scared, Dr. Love." I looked up into his eyes. "Actually, that's not completely truthful. I'm positively *terrified* to take a chance on falling in love again."

"Doesn't surprise me in the least," he said. "In fact, I'd be more surprised if you—" He paused, then coughed, whipping out a handkerchief to cover his mouth. I'd noticed he seemed short of breath, but then, he was a little on the heavy side. Everyone knew Dr. Love had a passion for good food. He was solid, built like a barrel with a broad waistline. And then there was that nasty cigar habit.

Still, I couldn't help be concerned. "Are you okay?"

He waved me off. "Oh, for heaven's sake. Just a little cough. Where was I?" He stuffed his handkerchief back in the pocket of his slacks. "Oh, yes. Trusting again. You know the good Lord had a lot to say about trust. Might be a good idea to dig into your Bible and let Him remind you just how trustworthy He is."

"It isn't God I have trouble trusting."

"No, but trust begins with Him."

I thought about that for a moment. I knew it was almost time to go. "Dr. Love, did you ever have your heart broken?"

He blinked at my question, then smiled. "Oh, of course I did."

"Really?"

"Yes, I most surely did." He paused again, as if debating what to say. Then quietly he said, "Her name was Magnolia Witherspoon."

"Wow," I said. "That's a name you don't forget."

"Oh, I'll never forget Maggie. She was the belle of the south. Prettiest little thing you ever saw. And I was so in love with her, I could hardly function."

I smiled, trying to envision a younger version of J. Thomas Love courting a young debutante. "What happened?"

His gaze was far off. "I proposed to her the night before I left for England. I was stationed there during the war. A chaplain with our boys in the Eighth Air Force. We made plans to marry when I was home on my next leave. The last letter I had from her, she was busy with wedding plans and dress fittings and what not."

I waited, anxious to hear more.

"Then the letters stopped coming. Not one more . . ." He stared somewhere over my shoulder, lost in his thoughts. "And I was preoccupied with the troops under my care. We'd sustained heavy losses. My heart was so heavy for the young men I served. So many of them not even twenty years old yet, either killed in action or missing. It was a terrible time.

"When I was finally able to come home on leave, I was desperate to see Maggie. That's when I found out why the letters had stopped." He looked at me, his eyes misting over.

"Why?" I whispered.

He clenched his jaw, looked down, then continued. "My brother. You see, in my absence, she'd fallen in love with my brother."

"But—"

"Oh, they didn't mean for it to happen. He was 4-F. Had a bad leg from an old football injury. So he stayed home during the war, helping in the family business. He'd promised to keep an eye on her for me while I was away." He looked straight at me with a sad smile. "Apparently he did a pretty good job of it."

"I'm so sorry," I said, not knowing what else to say. "How horrible."

"Yes, well, it's made for some awkward moments through the years. But they eventually moved to Alaska. I haven't seen them in twenty years, to be honest. Probably just as well."

"How did you get over it? Not just her, but your brother. How could you even be in the same room with them? How could you ever trust anyone again?"

"Shelby, that's what I'm trying to tell you. God's ways are not always our ways. I eventually learned that the good Lord allowed that whole mess to happen for a lot of reasons. Not the least of which was because He had someone else picked out for me."

"Elsie?"

He smiled again. "My Elsie has brought the greatest joy to my life. She's the best thing that ever happened to me, and I mean that with all my heart. She's a wonderful mother, she loves being a part of my ministry, and she makes me laugh. Oh, my goodness, how she makes me laugh! And there isn't a day goes by that I don't thank God for breaking my heart with Maggie and instead bringing Elsie into my life."

"How do you know you wouldn't have been just as happy with Maggie? If you don't mind my asking."

"Because in the end, that pretty little debutante struggled with all the attention her beauty brought to her. She's remained married to my brother, but she's broken his heart over and over, finding it all too tempting to ignore the attention men have always given her. She's had at least three affairs over the years. And those are only the ones he knows about."

I felt like crying. Why did life have to be so messy? Why did people have to be so unfaithful? So heartless to those who love them?

"I would never have wished such a life for my brother," he continued. "And yet he's never seen a need for God in his life—even in the midst of all the drama he's experienced in his marriage. He always thought of me as quite the fool for going into ministry. I'm not saying God's punished him through Maggie's infidelities, but he's clearly been out from under God's hedge of protection. Whereas I, on the other hand, have been blessed beyond measure with the sweetest, most faithful woman I've ever known. Like I said, God moves in mysterious ways."

Later, as I drove home, I kept thinking of Dr. Love's story.

How God saved him from what surely would have been a marriage from hell. For anyone, of course, but especially for a pastor. What a nightmare that would have been.

And then I wondered why I'd never thought to thank God for saving *me* from the same kind of nightmare. I wondered why I'd been so focused on never being able to trust again . . . instead of thanking God for interceding before I walked down the aisle.

17

"What is that SMELL?!"

I'd just walked into the apartment after work on Friday. I'd dropped Sandra off at the sidewalk in front of our townhouse, then drove around to pick up our mail near the clubhouse. When I returned and walked into our apartment, the stench nearly decked me. Something was dead. I just hoped it wasn't in the oven.

"Sandra! Where are you?"

She came flying into the living room. "I can't find it! Do you smell that? It STINKS! It smells AWFUL!"

I covered my nose and mouth with my hand. "It's horrible! What is it?"

She rattled off a long diatribe in extremely animated Spanish.

"English!" I demanded.

"Dead mice! It has to be dead mice. Our neighbor told me she'd been having problems for several weeks. Now they're here! This is DISGUSTING!"

"Where?" I said, cringing at the thought.

"In the walls. She said they get into the walls then can't get out and they just die in there. I think I'm going to puke!"

I held my nose and took the stairs up to my room. The odor wasn't quite as bad up there, but it was still pretty ripe. I dreaded the thought of inhaling this all weekend. We had to open the windows and get some fresh air coming in.

"AAAHHH!"

Sandra's scream reached all the way up the stairs, through my bedroom, and into my bathroom. I ran to the landing. "What is it? Why did you scream?"

"I SAW A MOUSE!"

"What? I thought you said they were in the walls?"

"NO! IT JUST RAN INTO THE KITCHEN!"

"It's alive?!" I ran down the stairs and found my roommate standing on one of the dining room chairs.

"SHELBY, GET IT OUT OF HERE!" She shrieked more in Spanish, but I had no doubt what she was saying. I dashed into the hall closet to grab the broom. I wasn't sure what I was going to do with it, but at least I was armed. Just as I turned to go back to the dining room, something scampered by my foot.

"AAHHH!" I jumped up into the chair beside Sandra. "It almost ran over my FOOT! But it came from the bathroom, not the kitchen!"

"THERE'S MORE THAN ONE?!" she screamed, clinging on to me for dear life.

Just then doorbell rang.

"COME IN!" we both yelled in unison.

The door opened and there stood Tucker. He looked at us then narrowed his eyes. "Have I come at a bad time?"

Sandra and I both screamed, talking at once, simultaneously telling our situation in two different languages.

He raised his hands. "Whoa! Wait a minute—one at a time. Shelby, what's the matter? And what is that *awful* smell?" he asked, covering his nose.

"MICE! Dead ones in walls and LIVE ONES IN THE HOUSE!"

"Are you sure?" he asked, stepping carefully as he came closer.

Our neighbor Bonita walked in the open door behind him. "Sandra, what's wrong? I heard the scream–" Her hand covered her nose. "Uh oh, you've got the mice in your walls. Oh, that's horrible. That's even worse than mine!"

By now Sandra had started whimpering. "I HATE this! Get them out of here, Tucker!"

He turned back toward us. "Me? What do you want *me* to do?"

I handed him the broom. "Chase them out the door or something. Just hurry! There are at least two that we know of. DO SOMETHING!"

"I'll get Harry. Be right back." Bonita rushed back out the door.

"Who's Harry?" Tucker poked the broom here and there.

"Her cat."

Tucker looked back at us. "You know, I've seen this in cartoons before, but I've never really experienced it. The whole screaming-women-standing-on-chairs thing. I wish I had a camera."

"SHUT UP!" Sandra yelled, though I could hear the break of frustrated laughter in her voice.

Bonita walked back in with a large tabby in tow. "Here, let Harry get to work. He's the best mouser I've ever owned." She put him down and he took off down the hall.

Tucker introduced himself to our middle-aged neighbor. She wore her usual housecoat with a red cardigan wrapped around her. There was a pink curler dangling in the back of her once-blonde hair.

"I spoke to the landlord last week," she said. "He promised to have someone come and see what the problem is with all these mice. I think we've got a major infestation, but he wouldn't admit to such. I'm just glad to have Harry. He's kept them out of my place for weeks. Course, he can't do anything about the ones in the walls. Isn't that the worst smell ever?"

I had to admit I felt kind of queasy myself. I wondered how long it would take that smell to dissipate since we couldn't get inside the walls to get rid of their wretched little corpses.

"OH MY GOSH, OH MY GOSH! HE GOT ONE!" Sandra shrieked again.

Sure enough, here came Harry, proud as he could be with the little critter dangling from his mouth. Mickey's tail whipped back and forth letting us know he was still very much alive.

"Tucker, kill it!" I yelled.

"I'm not gonna kill it! Let's just try to get it outside. Here Harry, here kitty kitty kitty." Harry sat down, holding his back ramrod straight as if he'd just found the crowned jewels.

"Get it out of his mouth, Tucker, or it'll take off again," I suggested.

"And just how do you expect me to do that?"

"I know!" Sandra yelled. "Get those pliers out of the kitchen drawer then try to grab it by the tail."

We both looked at her like she was crazy.

"That's not a bad idea," Bonita said, making her way into the kitchen. She yanked open the drawer and grabbed the pliers.

Tucker looked at us, then shook his head. "I can't believe I'm doing this." He cautiously approached the cat who pulled back. In a flash, Tucker clamped the pliers on Mickey's tail. Harry refused to relinquish his prize catch . . . until another one flew by him. We all screamed, startled by the blur of gray fur that dashed by Tucker's feet. But Tucker was too busy holding the little varmint by the tail as it swung back and forth trying to free itself.

"GET IT OUT OF HERE!" we shouted.

He hurried to the door and ran outside. Through the dining

room windows, we watched him run across the parking lot to the open field by the lake where he released it. He returned just in time to see Harry prance out of the kitchen with another one in his mouth.

Sandra ripped forth with another string of Spanish, clearly saying what I was thinking. This was bad.

Later, half an hour after Harry and Tucker had repeated their routine six more times—yes, SIX—we decided we were mouse-free. Except for the wall-encased corpses, that is. Sandra and I finally came down off our chairs. Bonita took Harry and returned to her apartment, promising to give our landlord a piece of her mind for us. But there was no way we could stay in our apartment. At least not tonight.

“Just grab some stuff and come stay at my place,” Tucker said, putting the broom away.

“Oh, we can’t do that,” I said, uncomfortable with the idea.

“Why not? I’ve got an extra bedroom. Besides, I’m on a 48-hour shift tomorrow starting at the crack of dawn. You’ll have the place to yourselves the rest of the weekend. Maybe by then your landlord will figure something out.”

Sandra looked back and forth between us as I pondered what to do. With a huff, she said, “You don’t have to ask *me* twice. I’m outta here.”

“Are you sure?” I asked. “I really hate to impose.”

“Get your stuff. Besides, we were supposed to go out tonight. Remember?”

I’d completely forgotten. I blew my hair out of my face. “You still want to go out after chasing the beasts out of our house?”

“Are you kidding? I’m starving! Hurry up!”

I had a feeling this would be a first date I’d never forget.

We'd invited Sandra to join us, but she insisted she'd rather just stay in and watch a movie on TV. I knew better. She knew I was nervous about going out with Tucker, and she didn't want to be a third wheel. Tucker showed us around his house, pointing out where everything was. Food in the refrigerator, television, stereo system, a guest bathroom . . . It was a beautiful older home in midtown, not far from Overton Square. I was shocked at how clean and tidy it was, wondering if he had maid service. He was a doctor, after all.

Half an hour later, Tucker and I sat down at a trendy Italian restaurant called Luigi's. The ambience was cozy and dark, with director-style chairs at sturdy wooden tables. We ordered our meals and made small talk.

"I don't know about you, but I'm not really in the mood for a movie tonight," he said, taking a bite of the crusty garlic bread the waiter had brought in a basket.

"No, I think I've had about all the excitement I can handle for one night."

"That was some nasty smell back there." Tucker shook his head. "I hope they can do something about it."

"Me, too. But thanks for your brave, chivalrous rescue," I said with a smirk.

"Darn right, it was brave!"

"You were kinda scary with those pliers. Remind me to keep those out of sight next time you stop by."

"So noted."

This was just too weird. I was actually relaxed with him. Not nervous in the least. We talked non-stop for the next hour, enjoying steaming plates of pasta. He told me all about med school and what it was like interning at Vanderbilt Hospital in Nashville. I was fascinated with the stories he told me about his classes, instructors, and labs. But I especially loved how his eyes lit up when he talked about his patients.

"What field are you specializing in?" I asked. "Or does that come later?"

He pushed his last piece of bread through the sauce still clinging to his plate. "I'm in anesthesiology. Can't believe I've never told you that. Basically I pass gas."

"Ah, yes. Now *that's* the Tucker Thompson I remember. Quick with the jokes. But why anesthesiology?"

"Why *not* anesthesiology?"

"Such a specialized field. But I would think it would be rewarding. And a little frightening at times?"

"Sure, when things go badly. But that doesn't happen often, thank goodness."

"What do you like about it?"

"Knowing what I do is vital to what my colleagues do. Without us controlling the level of pharmaceuticals to keep their patients under, they wouldn't be able to do what they do in surgery. That's very gratifying."

"I'm impressed, Tucker. I really am. I can't believe all that mischief you and Jimmy got into could have resulted in such a productive member of society. It's incredible. It's really—"

Suddenly my eyes were at table level. Literally. Tucker looked down at me in disbelief. I was too shocked to move.

"What happened?" He tried not to laugh as he made his way around the table toward me.

"I don't know . . ."

He helped me up and we looked at the chair. . . . that stupid director's chair with the cloth seat stretched between the wooden legs. Somehow the fabric had slipped off the bar, giving way. My backside had dropped down and plopped onto the cross-bars below, my legs folded beneath me. I'm surprised the table didn't rip my nose off on the way down.

"Oh, sorry about that" Our waiter laughed as he approached our table. "Sometimes that happens."

"You mean, it's happened before?" Tucker's smile disappeared.

"Yeah. Whenever we take them off to wash them. Sometimes they don't get put back on right. Y'know, like they don't get locked back in place. Slippage." He hiked his shoulders and smirked as if it was no big deal.

"Slippage?" I asked, still feeling the heat in my face.

"Yeah. You okay?" The kid was still smiling, obviously getting a kick out of the whole situation.

"Other than my bruised ego, I guess I'm okay."

"Do you realize that's a lawsuit just waiting to happen?" Tucker pressed.

"Uh, no. Hadn't thought about it," he said as he started gathering our empty plates. "You guys want dessert?"

Tucker just stared at him. "No, we don't want dessert. What we'd like is an apology."

He blinked a couple of times. "Oh. Yeah. Okay . . . sorry?"

Tucker stared at the kid. A muscle in his jaw twitched.

"That's okay, Tuck. Let's just go." I pulled his arm.

"Oh, okay," the waiter said. "Let me grab your check."

Tucker put his hand on the small of my back, moving me toward the door. "No, *you* can take care of that check tonight. And I suggest you tell your manager to get some new chairs."

The kid's mouth hung open as we walked away. It took a few minutes for Tucker to calm down.

"You sure you're okay?" he asked.

"I'm fine. But don't you think we should pay for our meal?"

"Absolutely not. Do you realize how badly you could have

been hurt? You could have snapped your ankle plopping down like that, or busted your nose—"

"But I'm fine."

"And I'm glad," he said, opening the passenger door for me. "But I don't appreciate his lack of concern. That was out of line. And just telling him of our concern wouldn't faze that kid. If he has to pay for that meal out of his own pocket, maybe he'll actually do something about those chairs. Or at least tell his boss about them."

He shut my door and walked around to his side of the car and got in.

"Hey, are you okay?" I asked. I'd never seen this side of Tucker. Annoyed. Agitated.

"Yeah. I just don't appreciate it when people are inconsiderate of others." He started the car. "Let's go home."

Let's go home.

As he put the car in drive and pulled out, I realized I liked the sound of that.

And the way he'd stood up for me back there.

And the way he'd put his hand against the small of my back . . .

What a strange weekend. After Tucker and I got home that night, we talked for a little while then said goodnight. He had to be up at 5:00 the next morning, with a long 48-hour shift ahead of him. It had been such a bizarre evening. Hardly what I would consider a legitimate first date. Who knew if there would be a second? Or third? Still, it was really nice of him to let us stay at his house while we got the townhouse aired out.

By the time we went back to the apartment Sunday night, the

smell had subsided considerably. I'm guessing they kept our windows open the entire weekend. An exterminator had been by and said he didn't find any more mice inside, though there was nothing he could do about the dead ones in the walls. Sandra and I had a long talk and decided to start looking for a house to rent. Nothing as nice as Tucker's, of course. But we both agreed it would be nice to live in a real house and not share the "joys" of neighborly problems like mice.

Or so we hoped.

18

Monday morning when I walked into the office, an enormous bouquet of red roses feathered with a mass of baby's breath sat on the corner of Mrs. Baker's desk. I guessed there were easily two dozen roses in the arrangement.

"Who's the lucky girl?" I asked as Mrs. B looked up.

"Why, you are, Shelby. Aren't they lovely?"

I stopped in my tracks. "For me? Oh, I'm sure there's been some mistake."

Sandra whipped around me, grabbing the card out of the arrangement. "Nope. No mistake. Says *Shelby Colter* clear as day. Ooohh, I wonder who could have sent them?" she teased, waggling her perfectly sculptured brows.

"And that's not all," Debra called from the back. "Your mystery admirer sent something for the rest of us too."

Now this was just too weird. Who would send me flowers and something else to my co-workers? I snatched the card from Sandra's hand and opened the envelope.

Shelby,

How about a do-over first date?

Saturday night at the Peabody.

I reserved us a booth . . .

(Chairs can be hazardous

to one's date, you know.)

Tucker

My face began to warm.

"Well? Who sent them?" Sandra stomped impatiently. "I bet I know," she sang like the tattletale she apparently was.

"Yeah, Shelby, who sent the Moonpies?" Rebecca shouted from the back office.

"Moonpies?" I said, the heat on my face now scorching.

"Two boxes of them!" Chelsea chimed in, already enjoying one of the chocolate confections. "Our card isn't signed. It was just addressed to *The Hostesses of BMH.*"

I made my way to the back office and grabbed the card from Chelsea's hand. Tucker would definitely hear about this.

Mrs. Baker stood in the doorway. "Well, Shelby?"

I straightened by back and headed to my cubicle to stash my purse. "They're from Tucker Thompson," I said quietly. "We're just–"

"I knew it!" Sandra clapped her hands. "Flowers after a first date? How sweet is that? He must really be stuck on you!"

"You had a date with Dr. Thompson?" Chelsea asked, wiping chocolate from her mouth. "Whoa, girlfriend, that didn't take long."

"No, it isn't like that! We're just–"

"Yeah, yeah, you're just friends." Debra taunted. "Of course you are. Which is why you went out on a date and he sent you roses. Riiiiiight."

"All right, girls, that's enough," Mrs. Baker said. "Get your things and get to work. Time's a wasting."

I couldn't get out of there fast enough. I gathered my supplies, reached for my new patient cards, and headed out the door while trying to ignore the seductive scent of those roses wafting through the entire office. Instead of breakfast in the cafeteria, I decided to go on up to my floor and get to work. I wasn't sure why I was so embarrassed that Tucker had sent me roses—and those blasted Moonpies to the girls—but I didn't want to think about it at the moment.

I made my rounds early then stopped in to see Donnie. I'd dropped by to see him after church on Sunday, but he was downstairs having more tests run. I'd left him a silly note and a bag of jelly beans. His favorite.

I could tell when I walked in, he wasn't feeling well. "Hey, buddy. How are you this morning?"

"Hey, Shelby. Thanks for the jelly beans. You forgot to take out the red ones, of course."

I put my hand over my mouth in fake-shock. "I forgot. Will you ever forgive me?"

"I doubt it." He took a deep breath and waved me over to sit down.

"Talk to me, Donnie. What's going on?"

"It's rather frightening, actually." Not a trace of humor on his face or in his voice.

Oh, please, Lord. No.

"I'm having a brain transplant. Mine is useless, you see, and they—"

"You are *not* funny." I swatted his arm.

He quirked a lazy smile at me. "Oh, come on, you have to admit that was pretty funny."

"Not in the least."

"But I had you going there for a minute, didn't I?"

"I don't like you any more. In fact, I'm going to put in a

request and have you moved to the psyche floor. They have lovely robes up there that tie in the back. You'll look dashing."

"Well, that's not gonna work."

"Yeah? And why's that?"

"Because I'm having bypass surgery today around noon. Which means I've had nothing to eat and I'll have to skip the yummy gruel at lunch."

I stared at him. Then I narrowed my eyes. "Is this another joke?"

"Oh, if only it was, my dear."

"Donnie, I'm so sorry."

"No, don't be sorry. It's all good. Better they unplug me now than plop me on a cold hard slab in your mortuary. I've got sixty-five percent blockage. Not good. Even at my age."

He told me all about the tests, the consultations, and the conflicting diagnoses he'd received. It was so rare to have that much blockage at his age. But in the end, they all agreed surgery was mandatory.

"Are you scared?" I asked, reaching for his hand.

"Me? Scared?" he scoffed. He creased a fold in the blue blanket over his legs. "Out-of-my-mind-and-*then*-some scared," he whispered.

I felt my eyes sting. "But you know you'll feel so much better afterward, right?"

He just nodded then turned to look out the window.

"Donnie, would you let me pray with you?"

He inhaled then let it out slowly. "Oh, that's really sweet, Shelby. But I don't think so."

"Really?" I said, before stopping myself. We'd both been active in Campus Crusade at Samford. Donnie sang and played the piano with our praise band. He'd even gone on a mission trip with us to the Dominican Republic. I remembered how great he was with all the kids. They loved him.

But then, we all loved him.

"I'm not into the whole God thing much anymore." He avoided eye contact with me.

I felt like I'd been sucker-punched. "Oh . . . I'm sorry. I just assumed—"

"Oh, I know. We were a bunch of Jesus freaks and all that. But it was just a phase. At least for me."

I couldn't figure out what to say. Or what *not* to say.

He squeezed my hand. "But that doesn't mean I don't respect you if you're still into all that stuff."

All that stuff? How could this be the same Donnie I used to sing duets with? How could this be the same Donnie who gave such a beautiful testimony to those kids in the Dominican about how God loved him in spite of his shortcomings and sins? Where was the joy that used to sparkle in his eyes when he shared his faith with others? I couldn't believe it.

"Donnie, I want so badly to ask—"

"And I promise, we'll talk about it. We will." He squeezed my hand again. "I just can't right now. Not right before my surgery. I hope you understand."

I nodded even though I didn't understand at all. Now it was my turn to take a deep breath and blow it out. I peeked at him sheepishly. "But I'm still gonna pray for you. Today. And tonight. And tomorrow while you're in surgery—"

"Pray away, Sister Rayce Catherine. Pray away."

I held up my hand, moving it in the sign of the cross like a priest giving a blessing, an attempt of a smile plastered on my face.

He mimicked my actions, adding a monkish Latin-chant-incantation as he moved his hand. *"My-father-plays-dominoes-better-than-yours-does . . . ah-ah-ah-mennn."*

"Love you, Donnie."

"Love you, Shelby."

I rode the elevator down to the main lobby. Just as I stepped out of it, I heard my name paged. I wasn't in the mood for any more teasing back in the office, so I picked up the nearest hall phone. "You paged Shelby Colter?"

"Yes, Miss Colter," the switchboard operator said. "I'll connect you."

"Shelby?"

Tucker? I couldn't believe he was calling. What would I say about the roses?

"Oh, hi, Tucker. I, uh—"

"Shelby, I wanted to let you know. They just brought Dr. Love into the emergency room."

"What?" My heart pounded.

"I only have a minute. I'm due in surgery with another patient, but I wanted to let you know. Just pray."

"Oh, Tucker, what—"

"I'll call you when I get out. Gotta run."

I hung up and just stood there. I couldn't think what to do. Should I go up to the prayer room on my floor and pray? Should I go down to the emergency room waiting area and look for Elsie?

Just then Mrs. Baker whipped by me. I reached out to catch her arm. "Oh, Mrs. Baker, did you hear—"

"I know. I'm on my way. Let's go."

The waiting room in the ER quickly filled with members of First Baptist. Mrs. Baker immediately engulfed Elsie Love in a hug and didn't leave her side. I recognized a lot of faces but didn't really know these people yet. Almost as soon as that thought drifted through my mind, Rachel arrived.

"Oh, Shelby! I came as soon as I heard." She looked across the room at Elsie and Mrs. Baker. "Is Dr. Love okay? What happened?"

"I don't know yet. Tucker just called and told me they'd brought Dr. Love in."

"He seemed fine at church yesterday. I can't imagine—"

"Wait," I said. "When I met with him last week he seemed really short of breath."

She tugged my arm toward the chairs and lowered herself into one. "He's had some health issues in the past. We've always worried about him, carrying so much weight. The man does love to eat." I sat down beside her. "Shelby, we should pray." She reached for my hand and bowed her head. Rachel had the most natural faith of anyone I'd ever known. Her soft-spoken prayer came right from her heart and brought tears to my eyes as she asked God to protect our pastor from whatever had brought him here. If only I could have prayed with Donnie like this.

As we chatted with some of the church members, we learned that Dr. Love had been at his weekly breakfast with a group of men he mentors. They said he kept losing his train of thought and had trouble using his fork. A couple of the men who were there said they were afraid he was having a stroke.

Just then, Elsie was called back to talk to the doctor. At her request, Mrs. Baker accompanied her. A short time later my boss returned and filled us in.

"Thomas is stable. They're monitoring him and have him scheduled for some tests. They'll definitely be admitting him, so we'll need to move to the first floor waiting area until we hear more. Elsie is going to stay with him for now and she said to thank you all for coming. Those of you who wish to stay, follow me."

Everyone gathered their belongings and went upstairs with Mrs. Baker. I followed Rachel to her office. "Are you okay? You look a little flushed, Rachel."

"I know. I'm not sure how much longer I can keep working." She lowered herself into her chair behind her desk as I took a seat across from her. “I’d hoped to work until my ninth month, but I think little Cooper has other ideas.” She picked up a file folder and started fanning herself.

“I hope you’ll give notice and start getting some rest. I can’t imagine how you’ve managed this long.”

“Once I got past the morning sickness, I was fine. But Cooper keeps parking on my sciatic nerve and the pain can be pretty unbearable at times. Dr. Forsythe says I need to get off my feet as much as I can. Rich wanted me to stop working a month ago. So we’ll see.”

“Listen to your husband. Let someone else count the BMH beans for a while.”

She laughed and leaned back in her chair. “Wait. Back up a sec. Earlier, when we were down in the ER waiting room, did you say Tucker called you about Dr. Love?”

“What? Oh. Yeah. He paged me. He was going into surgery but he’d heard they’d brought—”

“Am I missing something here?” She tilted her head slightly.

“What do you mean?”

“Tucker called you.”

Then it hit me. Rachel and I hadn’t had much time together lately. She had no idea.

“Oh. Well, we . . . uh . . .”

“You? And Tucker Thompson?” Her face lit up.

I shot her a silly smile.

“What?!” She spun her chair to face me directly. “Shelby! You didn’t tell me you were dating Tucker!”

“Rachel, we aren’t ‘dating’ per se. We just went out the other night. And the whole evening was actually kind of weird.”

“Weird how?”

I told her about our strange date, starting with the mice then the chair incident at the restaurant, ending with my weekend stay at his house with Sandra.

She grinned from one ear to the other. "And?"

I busied myself studying my cuticle. "And he sent me flowers this morning," I mumbled.

"He sent you flowers?" She was clearly enjoying our conversation. "What kind of flowers?"

"Roses. Lots and lots of roses," I said with a sheepish grin. "With a funny card asking for a 'do-over' first date."

Her smile grew wider.

"At the Peabody."

Her eyebrows lifted at least half an inch up her forehead. "The Peabody?" she whispered.

"Yes. The Peabody."

"Well, then. I suppose that tells me all I need to know."

The expression on her face was so goofy, I had to laugh. I cleared my throat and stood up. "And on that happy note, I need to get back to work."

"I'd get up but—"

"Don't you dare. And put in your notice, Rachel. Go home and go to bed. Dr. Colter's orders," I said as I walked out her door.

"Let me know if you hear anything about Dr. Love," she added.

"Will do. Oh! By the way. I forgot to tell you Donnie Rogers is up on my floor."

"Donnie? From Campus Crusade?"

"One and the same. He's having bypass surgery at noon today. Can you imagine? I'm really worried about him."

"He's too young to have bypass surgery!" She fanned herself even harder.

"Tell that to his doctors. Anyway, keep him in your prayers. I'd tell you to stop by and see him, but you need to stay off your feet."

"What room is he in?" She grabbed a notepad and pen then

looked up at me.

"You don't mind very well, do you?"

"Room 9—"

"He's in 919."

"Thanks, Shelby."

"Sure. Just don't blame me if you go into early labor."

"Bye, Shelby."

"Bye, Rachel."

19

As soon as I walked out of Rachel's door, I headed for Donnie's room. I jumped on the elevator, praying I'd make it upstairs before he was wheeled away to the OR. As I stepped onto the floor, I caught a glimpse of him on a gurney being wheeled to the back elevators.

"Donnie!"

The orderly stopped, and Donnie glanced in my direction.

"Hey sweetie," he said, clearly a little loopy from some pre-surgery meds.

I reached for his hand. "How are you, buddy?"

"Feeling no pain, my dear. Dancing on clouds with fairies and unicorns." He inhaled, closing his eyes. "Is that cotton candy I smell?"

I winked at the orderly. "Sure is. They always serve cotton candy before surgery."

"Mmmm," he moaned happily. "With Hershey's on top?"

"Anything for you, buddy."

I leaned over and kissed his forehead. "I'm praying for you, Donnie. Whether you like it or not."

"That's nice." A lazy smile graced his face.

"I'll see you later, okay?"

"Okay. Tell Big Bird hi for me."

"Will do. And Bert and Ernie too."

"You're the best, Shelby."

"Love you, Donnie. Sweet dreams."

After his gurney disappeared from sight, I decided to spend some time in my prayer room. I tapped on the door to make sure no one was using it. When no one responded, I walked into the dark, quiet room. It felt good to spend time talking to God about Donnie. I was still baffled by his easy dismissal of the Lord when we'd talked, but I didn't want to worry about that right now. So I prayed for Donnie's surgeons, for his protection during the procedure, and for a speedy recovery. I couldn't imagine having such serious health problems at our age. And to think it wasn't the first time he'd had problems.

I let my mind wander back to the days when we hung out together. I couldn't think of Donnie without smiling or laughing. He had the most contagious laughter of anyone I knew. Which got us into all kinds of trouble when we worked together. I have vivid memories of working the counter at Taco Barn, waiting on customers, while Donnie crawled on the floor beside me, out of the customers' view, and pulled my knee socks down. I shrieked, of course, and lost it when I looked down to see him rolling on the floor laughing at me. It was so silly, so ridiculous, but one of my favorite memories of Donnie. Him, sprawled out on that nasty floor, laughing so hard he had tears running into his ears.

And then there were the roach races. I still can't believe we did those. Late at night, after the restaurant had closed and we began our closing duties, Donnie came up with the idea of racing roaches in the deep fryer. I know, I know . . . we should have been arrested for such cruelty to those disgusting bugs, but at the time we were just young and stupid. Then again, it was a way to get rid of them. And we *only* raced them when it was time to change out the grease. Still, I have to admit, I've always been a little leery of eating at fast food restaurants ever since.

Donnie loved making people laugh, and he was *so* good at it. A natural. He should have been a stand-up comic. It suddenly dawned on me, I hadn't asked what kind of work he was doing these days. What kind of meeting had he been attending in town? Some friend I am. I'd have to remember to ask.

Oh Lord, he's such a teddy bear. Keep him safe. Help him heal. And show me how to help him find his way back to You.

I then turned my thoughts and prayers to my pastor.

I was just finishing my rounds when I looked up and saw Tucker approaching me.

"Hey," he said, nodding his head toward the back hall. I followed him around the corner.

"Have you heard anything?" I asked.

"Just came from Dr. Love's room. They've moved him to Seven. Still running tests but he seems to be doing better. Sounds like he just had a series of mini-strokes. He doesn't seem to be incapacitated and isn't showing signs of paralysis. Which is good."

"Thank goodness." I could literally feel the relief wash over me.

"He's joking around with the nurses, and that's a good sign."

I blew out a puff of air, not realizing I'd been holding my breath. "How's Elsie doing?"

"Good. Much better now that he's responsive. Of course, they had to post a *No Visitors* sign on his door or he'd have a steady stream of well wishers from the church."

"Though, hospital employee that you are, that doesn't apply to *you*, does it?" I teased.

He pinched my elbow. "Or *you*, for that matter." He leaned back against the wall, hiking a knee with his foot braced against the wall. "You look nice today, Moonpie."

I glared at him, unable to be completely mad. And then I remembered. Moonpies and roses. "Oh, Tucker—I forgot to thank you for the roses!"

He smiled. "Well, I didn't want to bring it up. Tacky to fish for a response, y'know?"

"They're so beautiful. But I was . . . well, I would never have expected something like that." I could feel my face heating and wondered if there was a medical cure for excessive blushing.

"Which is what makes it all the more special." He took hold of my hand. "I'm glad you liked them. So what's your answer?"

"My answer?"

"Didn't you read the card?"

"Oh. The Peabody. Saturday night." I looked into his eyes, surprised how tender his expression was. "I don't know, Tucker. That's awfully fancy, don't you think?"

"Oh," he said, obviously not expecting that response. "Well, we can go back to Luigi's, if you like. I hear they've just cleaned the director's chairs again."

"No, no. That's not necessary."

He squeezed my hand. "C'mon. It'll be fun. We can go early and watch the duck parade and have a nice quiet dinner. Say you'll go."

I looked at our hands, his thumb rubbing my palm, and wondered when all this would stop feeling strange. I glanced back up at him. "Sure, Tuck. I'd love to."

"Good. It's a date."

"So how did your surgery go this morning?"

"It was a gas!" His eyebrows did a two-step as he gave my hand a final squeeze and turned to go.

"You need some new material, Thompson."

"Duly noted, Colter. Gotta run."

20

By lunch time, I felt like I'd put in a full day. Donnie was in surgery. And I didn't want to intrude on Dr. Love just yet. I thought I might stop by later after I got off work. So I joined some of the girls in the cafeteria, glad for a break. I'd just taken my seat when Sarah Beth walked by carrying her tray.

"Hello, girls." She didn't stop to join us.

Close on her heels was a distinguished looking gentleman in a dark suit. "Ladies," he said, giving us a nod of the head as he passed our table. He and Sarah Beth took a table for two near the windows.

"Can I assume that is Raymond?" I asked, stirring sweetener into my iced tea.

"Raymond McCracken, crackerjack undertaker," Mindy quipped. "Try saying that three times in a row really fast."

I snickered, recalling some of the office chatter about Sarah Beth's husband of two years. He was actually very handsome, looking every bit the part of his family's prominent Memphis funeral company. The McCrackens had several locations throughout the greater Memphis area, though Raymond worked at the original home over on Poplar Avenue. As I watched him across the room with Sarah Beth I thought they were surely a match made in heaven. Sarah Beth was Type A all the way, and from what I'd heard, she'd met her match in Raymond. I could envision the two of them "taking over the world of undertaking" with great moxie.

"Get this," Sandra said, speaking quietly. "Today Sarah Beth was on another rant about her stellar housekeeping. She told me she routinely irons everything in the house. Their sheets. Their dishcloths—"

"Get out of here," Debra scoffed.

"Their hankies—both his and hers, of course."

"Oh, please," Leila groaned.

"And–" Sandra paused with flair, "she even irons dear Raymond's *boxers*."

We all hooted, then hushed ourselves, not wanting the McCrackens to overhear us.

"Sandra, you're making that up," I said, still laughing.

She crossed her heart and held up her hand. "As God is my witness, I'm telling you exactly what she told me."

"Who irons *underwear*?" Leila asked. "I mean, what's the point?"

"I asked her the same question," Sandra said, "and she said you just feel different knowing you're pressed from head to toe. 'Besides, what our mothers always said was true. You never know when you might be in a car accident and you certainly wouldn't want the paramedics to find you in wrinkled uns."

"Which is always my top priority when the paramedic is scraping me and my starched uns off the pavement," Rebecca added.

"Well, I don't know about you guys," I said, "but when I die, I'll rest so much easier knowing my undertaker has starched and ironed undies on."

We roared again. I tried really hard to get rid of the image of the tall undertaker wearing starched boxers under his expensive suit. Never in a million years would it ever cross my mind to iron my panties. Who comes up with this stuff? Then again, Sarah Beth and I were definitely not cut from the same fabric. I'm not even sure we were from the same planet.

"So Shelby, spill the beans," Debra said. "Let's hear all about the mysterious Dr. Thompson. How long has this been going on and why all the secrecy?"

I stabbed a fork in my salad and quickly took a bite. I wish I'd remembered to eat in my car or take a walk to the park. I didn't like dishing out private information like this. Especially since I had no clue what this whole thing with Tucker was all about. I swallowed hard and took a sip of tea.

"We went out to dinner, the chair I was sitting in broke, Tucker got kind of upset with the waiter, we left and that was that. Apparently he felt bad about how it turned out, so he sent me flowers. No big deal. End of story."

"Roses. Not just flowers. He sent you *roses*," Sandra added.

"No big deal?" Mindy garbled over a mouthful of French fries. "Look, I don't know how they do things in Alabama, but around here, when a guy sends flowers—"

"Roses."

"Thank you, Sandra. When a guy sends roses after the first date? It is a *big* deal. Especially since Tucker Thompson hasn't been back on the market all that long."

"I rest my case," Sandra said.

"Okay, fine. Whatever. I just wish you all would understand. We've known each other a long time. It's all very strange. So if I asked you to back off with all the questions, what are the chances?" I looked each of them in the eye, one after another. They looked at each other in silent consultation.

“Nahhhh,” Mindy droned.

“Not gonna happen.”

“Nice try, though.”

Sandra leaned over and gave me a side hug. “See? We’re all just like your sisters. Una gran familia feliz. One big happy family!”

“Nosy, but happy,” Debra added.

I nodded in resignation. “Thanks. Really.”

“Miss Colter. Miss Shelby Colter.”

At that moment, I wanted to find that woman behind the paging microphone and kiss her right on the lips. “Bye guys, I’m outta here.”

The call was from Samantha, one of the nurses on my floor. She said Mr. Underwood needed to see me right away. Bless his little heart. He rescued me from the inquiries of my fellow hostesses.

As I arrived on my floor, I noticed Mr. Underwood coming toward me.

“There you are!” he said, dressed in street clothes. “We’re about to leave, and I was hoping to see you before they take me downstairs.”

“You’re leaving today?”

“Yes, I’m afraid they won’t let me stay here any longer since I seem to have fully recovered.”

“But what about Mrs. Underwood?” I knew she was still in serious condition. She’d been released from ICU but every time I’d visited her on Eight, she’d been asleep. The pain medications still kept her heavily sedated.

“Margaret is being moved to a convalescent center. I believe it’s located not far from here. They’ve made arrangements for me to stay with her since I refused to go anywhere else. Our son Billy is coming to help us get settled. He’s awfully busy with his job, but he was able to take off a couple days to come.”

I'd met Billy several times. He seemed like a nice enough guy, though I kept wishing he would take charge and be more assertive about his parents' dire situation. If they'd been my parents, I would have insisted they be transferred to where I live so I could be more help. Then again, I'm not walking in Billy's shoes, so I've tried to give him the benefit of the doubt. I know he works hard to pay his bills and care for his family, so who was I to judge?

"I'm just so surprised you all are leaving so soon," I said. "But I know you'll have excellent care. We'll sure miss you, Mr. Underwood. I'll keep you and Margaret in my prayers. "

His eyes quickly misted and he slowly held open his arms for an embrace. I gave him a hearty hug, smiling as I inhaled his Aqua Velva.

"You've been just wonderful, Shelby. I never would have made it without you." He took a quick swipe at his eyes.

"Well, I don't know about that, but it was my pleasure to help. I wish you and Margaret the best and a speedy recovery."

An orderly showed up with a cart for his belongings and a wheelchair which was required for his departure.

"Well, there's my ride. I better go."

"Take care, Mr. Underwood."

"You too, Miss Colter."

I would always think of him fondly as Mr. SU-BA-RU Underwood, the sweet little man who helped me get my feet wet when I first started at Baptist.

As I made my way back to the nurses' station, I heard someone call out my name down the other hall. Mr. Wilcox was taking a walk down the hall with his wife. I felt bad, avoiding him like I had, so I asserted myself more than usual.

"Hi, Mr. Wilcox, Mrs. Wilcox. Nice to see you up and about this afternoon," I said, hoping to sound more chipper than I felt.

"Hello, Miss Colter," he said, slowly closing the gap between us. "You remember my wife, DeeDee?"

"Sure I do. How nice to see you again. How's our patient here doing?"

"The doctor said he can go home tomorrow if he has a nice bowel movement today," she said with all the pride of a mother whose baby just took its first step.

"Well then . . ." I couldn't think of an appropriate response. I looked at Wilbur, expecting to see him blushing or avoiding eye contact with me. But no. He was beaming. I reminded myself to steer clear of his room for the rest of the day, fearing he'd want to give me a detailed description of his . . . *production.*

"Wilbur's always been regular as rain, so it shouldn't be long now," DeeDee added, still glowing.

And that would be my cue to leave the floor. "Good to know!" I said, turning to leave. "If I don't see you before you leave, you take care and get well, okay? Bye now!" And off I dashed to the closest elevator.

The images flashing through my mind weren't too pleasant, so I opted for a break in Mindy's prayer room. As I leaned against the wall, waiting for the elevator, I noticed a gurney pushed by an orderly and wondered if it could be Donnie. I checked my watch and realized it was probably too soon. But as the patient was wheeled around the corner, I recognized that slap-happy smile coming my way. A knot lodged itself in my throat.

"Hey there, Donnie. How do you feel?" I asked, keeping pace as the orderly continued toward his destination in 919.

He licked his dry lips slowly. "Like I've been through a meat grinder. And you?" His voice was raspy, no doubt from intubation during surgery.

"I'm good, but thanks for asking. You don't look half bad after surviving a meat grinder."

"Looks can be deceiving, princess."

I waited as they got him settled in his room again. When they left, I slipped in for a quick visit. I knew he needed to rest.

"Hey, big guy. That was quick. I didn't expect you back until later in the day.

"Seems they cut me open and couldn't find a heart. Looked everywhere. Wasn't there. But then you always used to call me heartless, you know . . ."

"Very funny. I'm just thinking quick surgery and recovery room visit means good news."

"Who knows. They didn't tell me anything."

"Nor will they until later."

"Ah. My little fountain of medical knowledge."

"Can I get you anything? Some pork rinds? Maybe some deep fried roaches?"

He started to laugh then grimaced from the pain.

"Oh, Donnie! I'm so sorry. No more jokes. I swear."

He took a couple of long, shallow breaths. "What, no fork stabs in the eyeballs? You're really good at this whole Nurse Nancy gig." He closed his eyes as a lazy half-smile crept slowly across his face.

"More like Nurse Ratched, eh?"

"Fitting, as I feel rather cuckoo right now . . ."

I could tell he was drifting off to sleep.

"Well, you just get some rest, Mr. Rogers, and I'll go tell Bert and Ernie you came through surgery just fine." I leaned over and kissed his brow which he'd knotted, clearly not remembering our pre-surgery chat. "I'll stop by later, okay?"

"Mmmm."

Pleased to see my good friend resting comfortably after his ordeal, I finally made my way down to the prayer room on Five. Our little hideout was crowded today, but I squeezed onto the sofa between Chelsea and Rebecca. I told them how well Donnie had come through surgery, then decided to tell them all about my favorite train man who would be released as soon as Mother Nature did her magic with his bowels. The girls exploded in laughter, adding some rather gross puns on the subject.

Suddenly the door opened and there stood Mrs. Baker. A young couple in tears stood behind her. Our boss stared at us, her jaw dropping as she looked around the room. We quickly snapped out of our shock and ran like a bunch of rats fleeing the Titanic.

Literally.

I couldn't think where to go so I raced to Rachel's office. Thankfully she was gone. I closed the door and collapsed on her loveseat, dropping my head in my hands. I couldn't remember ever feeling like this. Ashamed. Embarrassed. Mad for such a stupid lapse of judgment. Mad at myself and my friends. We were dead meat, and we knew it.

About twenty minutes later, I heard myself paged along with every other hostess who'd been lounging in that prayer room. Even Mindy.

This would not be pretty.

She was huffing. Actually huffing. Pacing back and forth across the floor of our tiny office and huffing like a dragon ready to pounce its prey. I'd give anything not to be her prey.

"I've a mind to fire every single one of you right this minute. You deserve it. You know you do!" Her chest heaved with all that deep breathing, but I only know because I peeked when I saw her turn to go the other direction. Otherwise my eyes were glued to the floor.

"It's not enough that my day started with my friend and pastor brought in by ambulance, fighting for his life." Her voice cracked. And even though I knew it was an exaggeration (after all, Tucker had told me Dr. Love was upstairs laughing with his nurses), I felt bad for her. I knew how close she was to Dr. Love and Elsie.

"It's not enough that I took care of an entire waiting room of church members, all of them immersed in prayer on behalf of their beloved shepherd." She blew her nose into her handkerchief. "It's not enough that I'd barely come back to the office after making sure he was stable, when I heard about friends of mine who were here, awaiting the birth of the daughter they were adopting, only to find out the baby was stillborn . . . and then I lead that poor grieving young couple into one of our sacred prayer rooms only to find the whole lot of you in there, sacked out like a bunch of LAZY COWS!"

Her voice echoed in our office. I felt the first of my tears break free. If only the floor would open and swallow me whole. All of us.

"How DARE you?" she bellowed, her voice breaking again. "How dare you . . ." This time she lost her voice altogether.

We all broke down, the quiet sobs bouncing around the small room like one of those beach balls at a rock concert. This was worse than awful. This was wretched.

She continued pacing, wiping her nose, and obviously trying to compose herself. After five of the longest minutes of my life, she slowly took a seat, took a deep breath, then leveled her gaze at us. "I'm so profoundly disappointed, I'm in absolute shock here. What you don't know—what I haven't yet told you is that our program is in trouble. With the current economic situation, there will be a lot of employee cuts in the coming months. There are many programs a hospital simply can't survive without. Ours is not one of them."

We took turns looking at each other, startled by this unexpected news. *Did she mean what I thought she meant? Could the hostess program be axed? Would Dr. Grieve's pet program be on the chopping block?*

I hadn't thought things could get worse. I was so wrong.

"Right now, I can't even begin to think how to handle this . . . this absurd situation you've put me in. So for now, I want you to gather your things and go home. I need you to be out of my sight, because at this moment in time, you disgust me."

And with that, she stood up and left the office.

You might think we would've had a few things to say about what had just happened, but you'd be wrong. In utter silence, we gathered our purses and went home.

21

On our drive into work on Tuesday, Sandra and I quickly discovered we had no tolerance for Rick Dees and his craziness that morning. Sandra hadn't been part of the crowd lounging in Mindy's prayer room yesterday, but she'd been there many times before. She felt bad for me, but nowhere near as bad as I felt about myself. My eyes were still pink and puffy from crying half the night. No amount of Maybelline seemed to disguise the misery etched on my face.

Mrs. Baker wasn't in the office when we got there, though a half-empty cup of coffee was on her desk along with her reading glasses. We quietly made our way to the back office and put our things away. A lot of silent communication roamed the air as we went about our regular routine, getting ready to go to work. I was just thankful Mrs. B hadn't returned by the time we left the office. The others made their way to the cafeteria as always, but I had no appetite for breakfast. I quickly hopped on the elevator to go to my floor.

When the elevator stopped at Seven, I almost got off to go see Dr. Love until I realized that's most likely where Mrs. B was. I stepped back, thankful I hadn't made that blunder. I made a mental note to go see him later.

On Nine, I checked in at the nurses' station and went over the updated list of patients. Next, I stopped by to see Donnie but the respiratory therapist was there working with him. I told him I'd come back later. I made all my new patient visits and had just started my revisits when I heard myself paged.

And I knew.

Ten minutes later I entered one of the administrative conference rooms where Mrs. B, the other prayer room slackers, and the rest of the hostesses had gathered. I said a silent prayer, wondering if this might be my last day at BMH.

"Come in, Shelby. Have a seat." After I did so, she continued. "I'll address my opening comments to those of you I caught in the prayer room. But I'm well aware you seven aren't the only ones who've been lollygagging up there, so that's why you're all here. As well as some announcements I need to make.

"But first, we might as well clear the air. When you seven went home yesterday, I hope you had time to think long and hard about what happened in that prayer room. I spent a lot of time in prayer over it last night. It breaks my heart, girls, to think that you have so little respect for your jobs that you would even consider doing something like that. And after a few phone calls, I've learned it's hardly the first time."

Uh oh.

"Apparently it's become quite a routine for most of you to hide out in that prayer room. As I searched my soul last night, I tried to understand why any of you thought that would *ever* be an acceptable thing for you to do. Of course, there is no answer because it's completely unacceptable. When I think about the trust and responsibility you've been given by this hospital and by Dr. Grieve himself, it literally makes me sick."

She didn't sound mad, which surprised me. She sounded resolute. Which could be very, very bad. I closed my eyes as she continued.

"That said, I suppose part of this is my fault. I gave you girls complete and total freedom to do the job you were hired to do. I've never checked up on you, and I've never asked the staff on your floors how were you doing. Why? Because I thought I could trust you.

"Clearly I was wrong. So here's what I've decided to do. Starting today, I will begin a systematic routine of checking up on each and every one of you. Systematic, in that I'll cover every floor, but you will never know when I might show up on *your* floor. You will never know when I might stop in a patient's room to see if he or she has had a hostess visit. You will never know when I might have a little chat with your floor staff to see how you've been doing."

Oh my goodness. I swallowed hard.

She held up her hand. "I realize by these actions, I'll be treating you like irresponsible children instead of young adults. But let's be honest. You give me no choice."

"Mrs. Baker," Debra interrupted. "I can't begin to tell you how sorry we are. I don't think any of us got much sleep last night. We feel so badly about what's happened."

"I appreciate that, Debra."

"She's right," Chelsea added. "It's inexcusable. You have every reason to be ashamed of us. We're ashamed of ourselves."

We all murmured in agreement.

"Be that as it may," Mrs. B said, "I have no choice but to put you all on probation. For the next month, your behavior while on the job must exceed my expectations, or I'll be forced to let you go. As I mentioned yesterday, I'm fearful our program may soon be on the chopping block with all the upcoming budget cuts. At the very least, we may have to reduce our number of hostesses. I'm fighting as hard as I can to save your jobs—*our* jobs. But unless you all start stepping up and performing the job you were hired to do, then I'll be forced to let you go long before those cuts come through."

She looked around the room, making eye contact with each of us. Again.

I couldn't figure out why we'd let ourselves slide back into such lazy habits. I loved my job. So why did I take it for granted? Why did any of us?

"Now, I've said what I had to say. But I want you to understand something. I know part of this job involves simply waiting for pages from your patients. I also understand that you can only visit your patients so many times, and if you have patients who have family members with them, then your services aren't as needed. I really do understand that. Of course, that's why I've always allowed you to remain in the office once mid-afternoon rolls around. That's why I've not insisted you be present on your floors the entire time you're here.

"As I was thinking about all of this last night, I realized we may need to make some changes. Perhaps, by having nothing to do at times, you've grown complacent. Some of you rush through your visits and errands in order to zip down to the office to work on your knitting or needlepoint. Or whatever. Perhaps I'm to blame for allowing such complacency."

Why do I have the feeling things are about to change drastically in our little office?

"So I'm going to talk to Vice President Evans about the possibility of expanding our responsibilities in this hospital. I'm thinking we need to have a hostess working in the ER waiting room. In the ICU waiting room. In the surgical waiting rooms. We can add these to your responsibilities on a rotating basis."

"Mrs. Baker, that's a great idea," Leila said. We all stared at her, but I have to admit, I agreed. Rather than just running errands, we could offer more assistance to those in critical situations.

"Good. I'm glad you think so. I hope you *still* think so when it's your turn to work third shift or on the weekend."

"Whoa," Debra said below her breath. "Weekends?"

"Yes, weekends. After all, that's when there's the greatest need in the ER. Of course, some of you may prefer those shifts, giving you days off during the week. But we'll sort all that out later.

"Now, one more thing. I've talked to Chaplain Perkins, and he's agreed to begin meeting with us once a week. I've asked him to lead us in a Bible study specifically focused on our call to serve others. I think it's time we all started taking the ministry God has given us here at Baptist more seriously. Attendance will be mandatory, and there will be homework involved. But more than anything, I hope it will give us all a fresh new perspective about our jobs and the Lord's expectations for each and every one of us.

"Oh, and I will be meeting with each of you individually in the next few days. A little one-on-one time of sharing, if you will. I'd encourage you to do some serious thinking about your job, your service, your attitude . . . and be prepared to give me some darn good reasons why I should keep you on."

She whisked around the table and made her way to the door. "That's all."

After she left, we sat there and tried to take it all in.

"Ouch?" Debra whispered.

We all laughed quietly. Actually, it wasn't so much a "laugh" as a collective release of nerves.

"Well, at least she didn't give us the ax," Chelsea said. "Could've been a lot worse."

"I don't know about you guys, but I think it's a wake up call,"

Mindy said. "She's right. We've all gotten really lazy. I think this is going to make us better. And I'm actually kind of excited about the idea of working in the ER or the ICU, aren't you?"

A variety of different reactions skittered around the table. Some shrugged their shoulders, some nodded in agreement, and some weren't so excited.

"I didn't take this job to work weekends," Sandra piped in.

"Which is fine, Sandra, because it sounds like the ones who want to can opt for those shifts," Leila said.

"You know, all things considered, I'm relieved," I said. "It's like the air has been cleared. Now we just have to regain her trust and prove to her we're worthy of it again."

Sandra patted me on the back. "Well said, Shelby."

"Well, all I can say is, it's about time." And with that, Sarah Beth stood up and left the room.

After which, we all had a good hard laugh.

22

"So you basically got your butt chewed, is that what you're telling me?" Donnie rearranged the blanket covering his legs.

"Oh, yeahhh," I groaned. "But we deserved it. Honestly, I can't figure out why we all got so lax in our jobs. Why would we do that?"

"Oh, don't be so hard on yourself. It happens. I remember taking our own sweet time back at Taco Barn. Remember, when business was slow how we'd sit on the back counter, munching on nachos and talking for hours?"

"Yeah, but then we wouldn't finish closing til two or three in the morning. How stupid was that?"

"Exactly. We were young and stupid. And maybe you girls just fell back into young and stupid. It is what it is. Stop beating yourself up."

"That reminds me, Donnie, you've never told me what kind of job you have. You said you were in Memphis for a meeting when you had those chest pains. What kind of meeting?"

"I'm in hotel management. I work for Holiday Inn."

"Which explains why you were in Memphis. Their

headquarters is here."

"Smart girl. I just started in their PR department in January. I'm in the southeast division, primarily the Florida panhandle. I moved to Tallahassee right after Christmas."

"I can't believe I lost track of you so soon. Some friend I am."

"Well, it goes both ways. I haven't kept in touch with much of anyone."

There was a sadness in his eyes which I didn't quite understand. He caught me staring at him.

"What?"

"I'm worried about you."

"Well, I'd hope so. They just rooted around in my heart yesterday. I'd be worried if you *weren't* worried."

"No, not that. It's just that—you've changed. Something's missing. I can't quite put my finger on it."

He patted my hand like I was a school girl. "And I suggest you keep those fingers to yourself or I might have to report you to that mean devil boss of yours."

I laughed. "She's not mean, but I'll try to keep my fingers off you. Donnie, I'm serious. What's going on? Besides your heart condition. What have I missed that you're not telling me?"

He turned and looked out the window. I waited.

"Life just gets messy sometimes, Shelby. You know that."

"You're right. I do. But what's messed up your life?"

"Oh, it's just this heart thing. I wasn't completely honest with you about it."

"How so?"

"You remember my sister, Megan?"

"Sure. Your twin. Did you ever forgive her for choosing UT over Samford?"

He turned his gaze back to me. "She died, Shelby. Last Thanksgiving day."

"Donnie, no . . . what happened?"

"To no one's great surprise, Megan had the same heart defect I have, only it affected her much worse. Three days before Thanksgiving, she had a massive heart attack while at work. They did the same bypass surgery I just had yesterday." His face crumbled. "Only she didn't make it."

I grabbed his hand and held it tight as he wept. I couldn't believe it. Beautiful Megan. So young and full of life. She'd often visited her brother when we were at Samford, and we loved having her around. She was every bit the comedian he was, maybe even more so. The two of them together kept us entertained with a whole repertoire of outrageously funny routines they'd performed for years.

"I'm so sorry. I just can't believe it. She was so young . . ."

"Much too young," he whispered, his voice husky.

"No wonder you were so scared before your surgery. Why didn't you tell me?"

He wiped his tears. "I couldn't talk about it. I was quite sure I wouldn't survive the surgery either. I told you I was terrified, but that didn't come close to what I was feeling. Losing Megan was like losing part of myself. I can't seem to get beyond it, to let her go."

"But Donnie—"

"And I can't forgive God for taking her."

I stopped, clamping my mouth shut. Now it all made sense. *I'm not into the whole God thing much anymore,* he'd said. He blamed God for not saving Megan's life.

"All my life I'd been told how great and loving God was," he said quietly. "How He answered our prayers. All those years of believing everything I heard, believing it all to be true. All those mission trips, telling people how to trust Him and believe in Him. Leading worship songs proclaiming how awesome He was and how He hears the prayers of those who called Him Father. Yeah, well, where was He when *I* needed Him? When *I* begged Him to save my sister?"

"But surely you know—"

"No, Shelby!" Tears coursed down his face. "Surely I *don't* know. All I know is when I trusted Him to keep His promise, He wasn't there. He was silent. *Deadly* silent. When I needed Him most, He was nowhere to be found. And there's no way you can sit there with all those Christianese platitudes we all used to spew out to anyone who would listen and tell me He's real. He's *not* real. It's all a big joke, Shelby. One big, ridiculously pathetic joke."

I wiped my eyes, trying to think what to say. All those answers on the tip of my tongue were the exact ones he was talking about. Platitudes? Surely they were more than just words. I'd had my doubts along the way. Doesn't everyone? When I found out Will had deceived me, it shook my faith hard. But that was more about trusting in other people than my faith in God. Still, I hadn't walked in Donnie's shoes. There wasn't a single word I could say in this moment that wouldn't sound like a platitude, regardless of how sincerely I meant it.

I reached for his hand and wrapped it in mine. *God, help me here. Want can I say? What would* You *say?*

And before the thought had even passed through my mind, I knew.

"I love you, Donnie. I don't know anything else to say. But I love you."

He reached for a Kleenex and blew his nose hard, grabbed another one and wiped the tears from his face.

"You sure about that?" he sniffed, his eyes still leaky. "Even if I'm a *God-forsaken heathen*?" he mimicked, using his best TV evangelist voice.

I matched his mimic. "Even if you're a *God-forsaken, wretched, pond-scum of a worm heathen*—can I have an amen, brother?" I rasped. "Even then, I'll always love you."

He waved me toward him and I gave him a smothering hug ending with a wet, slobbery kiss on his cheek.

"I love you too, Shelby."

I stood back up and dashed away the tear tracks on my face. "How much longer will you be here? Have they told you yet?"

"No, not yet. The doctors want to run more tests. And there's some specialist from Vanderbilt that's coming in tomorrow to talk to me. Maybe they'll do exploratory surgery on my sad little thumper or put me on the heart transplant list."

"Isn't that still rather experimental?"

"Well, yeah, but what are my options? I can't lie in this bed forever."

I pursed my lips and glared at him. "I don't know, but maybe I'll do some research."

He rolled his eyes. "Oh, good. I'll rest so much easier knowing you're digging into your Junior Encyclopedia Britannica. Just remember, it's spelled h-e-a-r-t."

"Oh, gee, Donnie. Thanks. And all this time I thought you spelled it c-r-e-e-p."

"Go. Leave me. You're giving me heartburn in what's left of my aching heart."

I turned to go. "Yeah? And how do you spell that—g-a-s?"

I ducked as he threw his empty barf tray at me. It hit the door and clattered onto the floor. I peeked back in and blew him a kiss.

"I'm calling your boss, Colter. I have her number right here . . ."

I closed his door, ignoring his threat.

When the door tapped shut, I lost it. I ducked into the staff restroom and hid in a stall and cried so hard I thought I would throw up. After last night's weep-fest over the whole prayer room mishap, I didn't think I'd ever cry again. I was wrong. I kept seeing Megan's beautiful face and hearing her laughter bouncing around in my head. I watched as Donnie and Megan performed one of their routines at our Campus Crusade meeting, leaving us all gasping for air from laughing so hard . . .

Megan. Gone.

And Donnie, scared to . . . death.

Oh God, please help me. Show me how to restore Donnie's faith in You. Please break Your silence.

I couldn't stand the emotional tsunami I seemed to be fighting. Had I really only been on the job a few weeks? I felt like I'd been here years. I needed to learn how to handle all of this better. How to be there for my patients—my friends—without falling apart. I needed to be stronger. I needed to know how to respond in these desperate situations.

But right now, I mostly needed God to show me how to help Donnie.

23

The day had taken its toll. Sandra had a date that night, so I had the townhouse to myself. I put on some music and took a long hot bubble bath. I tried to read while I soaked, hoping to escape into someone else's drama for a while, but I couldn't concentrate. A deep sorrow coated my heart, and I couldn't shake it. I put on my pajamas and tried to lose myself in some mindless television, but tonight even *Laverne & Shirley* couldn't lift my spirits.

I gave up about 10:00 and went to bed only to toss and turn and drive myself crazy. I heard Sandra come in an hour or so later, but I didn't feel like talking so I didn't let her know I was still awake. I heard her go to bed and waited another half hour before I finally gave up and got dressed.

Forty minutes later I was on the elevator at Baptist. It was such a different place at night, the halls so empty and quiet. I got off on Seven, went to the nurses' station, introduced myself, showed them my BMH ID card, and asked if by chance they knew if Dr. Love was awake.

Before you think I've lost my mind, coming to visit at such an hour, I should tell you that Dr. Love once told me how he could never get to sleep before one or two in the morning. I wasn't sure if his normal routine might be off schedule, what with him being in the hospital and all, but my own restlessness had led me here at this late—make that, early—hour.

The nurse smiled. "I was just in there. He's been talking my ear off. Normally I wouldn't let you visit this late, but since you're an employee and a friend, I'll look the other way this time. Besides, you'll be doing me a favor. He's a sweet old guy, but glory, can that man talk! You go ahead and say hello. Just don't stay too long."

"I won't. And thanks."

His room was the last one on the right at the end of the long hall. I tapped gently on the door.

"Come in, come! Whoever you are, come in!"

I peeked around the door. "Hi, Dr. Love."

"Shelby! What in the world are you doing here at this hour? You're not working, are you?"

He pointed at the guest chair beside his bed, and I took a seat. He looked remarkably good, all things considered. The head of the bed was raised so he sat up comfortably, his Bible open on his lap. He wore a charcoal gray robe over his white pin-striped pajamas and somehow still looked . . . *pastorly*? Even his thick white hair was nicely combed and clean.

"No, I just couldn't sleep. A lot on my mind, I guess. Then I remembered I hadn't been up to see you yet. And *then* I remembered you said you could never sleep til the wee hours of the morning, so . . . I thought I'd try and sneak in for a visit."

He reached over and patted my arm. "I'm so glad you did. It's ghostly quiet around here at night. Except for those nurses. My heavens, they pop in here at least once an hour all night long. Even if I was to get to sleep, they'd come in poking and probing and asking me this or that. Makes a fellow anxious to get out of here just to go home and get some rest!"

"True. I hear that complaint all the time from my patients," I said. "But how are you? How's the recovery going?"

"Oh, it's awful hard to keep an old codger like me down. They said I had some mini-strokes or something. But I feel fine. I keep telling them I was just trying to get a little attention."

I smiled. "Right. As if you needed some attention. You don't get enough, standing in that pulpit several times a week?"

"Shhh! Don't you be giving away my secrets, now," he said, chuckling.

"You sure gave us all a scare. That ER waiting room was packed when you came in."

"Oh, I heard. And poor Elsie. She's been hovering over me like a mama bear ever since they brought me in. I sent her home an hour ago. She wanted to stay again, but I could tell she was needing a good night's sleep at home in a real bed."

"I hope she'll get some rest. How much longer will you be a guest of our lovely hospital?"

"Ah, that's the million dollar question. I'm ready to go now, but Dr. Weir wants to keep me in a while longer 'for observation.' I told Ben that Elsie would do all the observing necessary, but he didn't buy it. I reckon I'll be here at least another couple days or so."

"He's good, Dr. Weir. You should listen to him."

"Enough about me. What's got you up this time of night?"

I blew out a puff of air and tucked my hair behind my ear. "Guess I'm just a little overwhelmed right now."

"How so?"

"Oh, lots of stuff. But I didn't come here to bother you with my problems."

"Nonsense. Neither of us can sleep. Let's have a nice little chat. What's going on? Problems with that handsome Dr. Thompson? You just say the word and I'll—"

"No! No, there's nothing—I mean, that's not a problem. He's not a problem. Tucker's great." I stopped stuttering for a minute. "No, he's the least of my problems."

"Good. I like Tucker. He's a good man with a good head on his shoulders."

"Yes, he is."

"Then, out with it, Shelby. What's upsetting you tonight?"

And I told him. All about the miserable mess in the office and how badly I felt about all that, especially for disappointing Mrs. B. He talked me through it, assuring me that "Virginia" would be good to her word and give us all another chance. He applauded me for wanting to step up to the plate and prove I was worthy of her trust again.

Then I told him about Donnie. I wept as I shared Donnie's story. I couldn't help it. He patted my hand like an understanding grandfather and listened attentively as I expressed my concern for my friend's loss of faith in God.

He leaned his head back against his pillow. "Oh Shelby, I can't tell you how many times I've heard similar stories like your friend's. We Christians are an odd lot. We think our faith is so solid, and then something breaks our hearts and we find out that solid foundation wasn't so solid after all."

"But what do you say? How do you help them find their faith again?"

"You don't. You can't. That's the job of the Holy Spirit. If Donnie truly believed in God before all this happened, chances are he hasn't really turned his back on that belief. He's just lost his way. Lost his bearings. He's obviously still grieving. And losing someone so close and precious—well, that's hard. Mighty hard."

"So I do nothing? Just pray for him?"

"You say that as if prayer's not that important. Of course you pray! And what's more, you pray hard. You storm the gates of heaven on his behalf. You cry out to God to pour His presence over

Donnie in such a way that he'll have no question whatsoever that God Himself has touched his life again."

"But why does God go silent at times like this? Why would He desert Donnie when his heart was broken—and in his case, quite *literally* broken. I'll never understand why God does that."

"Of course you won't."

"I beg your pardon?"

"You won't understand because you *can't* understand. God is God. We try so hard to put Him in a box and think he'll behave the way *we* think He should behave. But remember, He's got the bigger picture. Sometimes He allows us to go through things—why, things we find absolutely unbearable—and we shake our fists in His face when He doesn't respond the way we think He should. But my dear, He sees far beyond what you or I can see ahead of us. He sees miles on down the road, years into our future. As much as we might want to, we simply can't know what He knows."

The gentle Southern drawl in his voice soothed my spirit even if I didn't completely understand all that he was saying. Well, I suppose I understood it. I just didn't quite know what to do with it. It was nothing new, just a reminder of what I'd grown up knowing. But knowing and living it are two different things.

We talked a while longer before a yawn took me by surprise.

"Could I pray for you, Shelby? Pray for your friend Donnie?"

"I'd like that."

And he did. The kindest, most heartfelt prayer for my troubled spirit and for Donnie's doubts. By the time he said amen, I felt a wave of peace beginning to seep into my soul.

"Thank you, Dr. Love. And thanks for letting me bother you tonight. I'll bet you're glad none of the rest of your flock can sneak in late at night like this. You'd never get any rest."

"That's for sure. Although . . ." A mischievous grin played on his lips.

"Although what?"

He wiggled his index finger, motioning for me to lean closer. "You're not the only after-hours guest I've had tonight."

"Really?"

"Elvis was by earlier," he whispered. "Slipped in the back door when no one was looking."

I laughed, confident he was pulling my leg. "Sure he did, Dr. Love."

He sat up, cocking his head to one side. "You don't believe me?"

"Well . . . no, I guess I don't. Why would Elvis—"

"Good heavens, Elvis and I go way back, my dear."

"You're kidding, right?"

"Not at all. We've been good friends for many years. Many's a night he'll call at two or three in the morning just wanting to chat. Sometimes he'll ask me to drive over to Graceland and we'll talk for several hours."

"I had no idea, Dr. Love."

"Well, I don't tell too many folks. A fellow like him, with all that craziness around him all the time . . . he likes his privacy. He needs to know he can talk to me and not worry about our conversations showing up in some newspaper. My, how he loves to talk about the Lord, ask questions about theology and what not. We've had some interesting discussions, I can tell you that much. But I sure worry about him. He's surrounded by so many bad influences and people taking advantage of his kindnesses. But he's got a good grasp on what the Bible teaches. Problem is, like the rest of us, he has trouble living the life he knows he should."

I stared at him, realizing I was sitting in the same chair the King had no doubt occupied.

"So what's he really like?"

He laughed. "Oh, he's just a normal guy like the rest of us, Shelby. Puts his pants on one leg at a time just like the next guy."

"No, what's he *really* like? Is he as charismatic as everyone says?"

"Well, he can definitely put on the charm when he wants to. And he knows how to use it, believe me. But underneath all that, he's just a nice guy. A nice guy who's carrying a heavy load most of the time."

"Would you believe I met him once when I was really young?"

"You did? My goodness, that must have been quite a thrill for you!"

"It might've been except that I have no memory of it. He came down to Dad's showroom in the middle of the night to let his buddies pick out Cadillacs—his Christmas gift to them."

"Oh, that's right! It had slipped my mind that ol' Cadillac Jack kept Elvis stocked in Caddies for himself and his friends."

"And complete strangers, from what I understand."

"Oh my yes, he loves shocking folks by handing them the keys to a new Cadillac."

I stood up. "Well, I need to go. Thanks again, Dr. Love. You take care of yourself, okay?"

"I'll do that, Shelby. And thanks for coming by."

"My pleasure. Goodnight."

A few minutes later I walked out of the hospital into the cool night air wondering how someone like Elvis could play the game so well, flying under the radar to avoid all the pandemonium. What a life.

And to think I'd just missed him.

Again!

24

Things were different the rest of the week. I don't know how the other girls felt, but even the air seemed different around us. Maybe I was just paranoid, but it felt like Mrs. Baker was surely hiding around the next corner, trailing me all over the hospital, ready to catch me on a potty break. I could just imagine her barging into my bathroom stall, tsk-tsk'ing me as she peered over her readers, warning, "Time's a wasting!" It made for a most uncomfortable work environment, but the only thing I knew to do was work hard and go lots and lots of extra miles.

I was careful to watch my time for lunch and coffee breaks, but I still took them. Tucker met me for coffee on Thursday at the end of another of his 48-hour shifts. How he and the other residents pulled those long hours, I had no idea. He looked tired but good.

"They just released Dr. Love," Tucker said before giving his face a hard rub. "I had a chance to stop by before he left. He seemed to be doing a lot better."

"I'm glad he finally got to go home. I hope he can get some rest."

"Oh, I guarantee Elsie will see to that."

I leaned forward. "Did you know he and Elvis are good friends?" I whispered.

He smiled. "Doesn't surprise me."

"So you knew?" I asked.

"No, but I'm sure their paths have crossed a few times. And probably right here at good ol' BMH. Elvis is a regular customer around here, you know."

I swatted his arm. "I know, I know. I just think it's funny. Elvis and Dr. Love. I'd never figure them for friends."

Tucker sipped his coffee. "Think about it, Shelby. Dr. Love doesn't know a stranger. Elvis has . . . *issues*, shall we say. Memphis isn't that big. And you've gotta figure someone like Elvis would seek out some kind of spiritual counseling from time to time. In between all the concerts. And all the girls. And—"

"Okay, okay. I get it."

"But enough about Elvis. Are we still on for Saturday night?"

"Saturday night? Well, I'd planned to do some laundry and paint my nails. And I was thinking about sorting out my sock drawer. You mean besides that?"

His eyes narrowed, a trace of disappointment in them. "Shelby."

"I'm just kidding. But I had you going for a moment there, didn't I? Of course I remember. We're having dinner at the Peabody. But are you sure you want to do something that fancy? I'd be perfectly happy with fried green tomatoes at Frankie's."

"Nah, let's do something fancy. We can do Frankie's any time."

"Do I need to wear something formal? An evening gown? Should I dust off my tiara?"

"Dust away, Moonpie. You wear whatever you like. I'll probably wear surgical scrubs, but whatever floats your pretty little boat."

"Scrubs? Well, then. I'll just iron my PJs and the two of us will make quite the fashion statement."

"If we want to see the duck parade, I should probably pick you up at 4:30. I know that's kind of early, but I still think it'd be fun. Is that okay?"

"Works for me."

He grabbed our empty coffee mugs and headed for the conveyer belt. As he turned back around, he yawned, his face contorted.

"That's lovely, Dr. Thompson. Really lovely."

"Isn't it though? I practice those in front of the mirror for optimal effect." He put his hand on my back and guided me toward the cafeteria exit. "And now if you'll excuse me, I'm going home to sleep. I'll try to get up in time for our date."

"That's in two days."

"It sure is. Two days of blissful slumber. See you, Shelby." He tossed me a wink over his shoulder and headed toward the Union exit.

I was just about to go back upstairs when I heard my name paged. When I called, the operator told me Mrs. Baker asked me to stop by the office.

Must be my turn.

I'd heard the other girls talking about their one-on-ones with Mrs. B. For the most part they'd gone well, though I'd been warned our boss wasn't letting up on her steely new demeanor in these private sessions. But I was glad to have my turn and looking forward to putting it behind me.

We walked together to the same small conference room where we'd all met earlier in the week. The silence was unnerving, so I tried to make small talk as we entered.

"I understand Dr. Love went home today."

"Have a seat, Shelby. Yes, he did. Elsie will have her work cut out for her trying to make him take it easy. But I expect he'll do fine. Dr. Weir has indicated his progress has been remarkable, all things considered."

"I'm glad to hear that. I think the world of him."

"I do, too. Now. Enough about Thomas."

I took a deep breath, bracing myself.

"Shelby, I'd be lying if I didn't tell you how disappointed I've been in you. You came with such a high recommendation from Rachel Bauer. I'd never have dreamed that you would fall into the bad habits some of the other girls have apparently lapsed into."

"I know, Mrs. Baker. I'm disappointed in myself too. And I hope you won't hold it against Rachel that I blew it. It's actually completely out of my character to do something like that, and I want to apologize—again. I give you my word that I'll never let that happen again. I love my job. I want to be the best I can be."

"Good. I'm glad to hear it."

For the next twenty minutes she reiterated much of what she'd said in our meeting on Tuesday, with an occasional direct question thrown in. I wasn't too sure why this one-on-one meeting was necessary, but I suppose she thought it would drive home her message by making it more personal to us.

"Shelby, I've accepted your apology and outlined what's expected of you. But do not forget that you are still on probation. The next time—well, just know that you won't be given another chance if there's ever a next time. Are we clear on that?"

I swallowed hard. "Yes, Mrs. Baker. Absolutely clear. And you have my word. There won't be a next time."

Later, as Sandra and I made our way to my car in the employee's parking lot, we compared notes about our one-on-ones. All the girls had them. Not just the Shameful Seven, as we'd come to call ourselves. To be honest, I was tired of the whole subject and asked Sandra if we could talk about something else on the way home.

Instead, she talked me into stopping for an early dinner at

Buntyns, a small restaurant right by the railroad tracks near the MSU campus. We had to wait in line for almost fifteen minutes, which I found odd since it was only 4:45 when we arrived. I soon found out why.

The restaurant was nondescript with booths covered in blue vinyl, tables covered in worn red Formica, and not a lot in the way of decor. But whatever was lacking in ambience was more than compensated by the most incredible home-cooked food I'd ever tasted. Sandra had recommended the chicken and dumplings, and after just one bite I thought I might just die and go to heaven then and there. I'd never tasted anything like it. Meals came with the most enormous yeast rolls I'd ever seen. To tell you they melted in your mouth would be a scandalous understatement. I could have made a meal of them.

"Sandra, you have to stop taking me to places like this. I'll be the size of the entire BMH complex if you don't. But first pass the jam, okay?"

She handed me the small dish of peach preserves then closed her eyes, savoring another bite of the creamy chicken. "This has to be sinful. There's no way it's not."

"So when are we going to start jogging? We keep talking about it but so far that's all we've done. Talk won't get these pounds off."

"Oh! That reminds me! I knew there was something I wanted to talk to you about. My charge nurse, Lori Ann, told me today one of her rentals is available. It's near the campus, so maybe we can drive by after we finish here."

"Yeah? What did she tell you about it?"

"It sounds perfect, Shelby. Two bedroom, two bath, hardwood floors, all new appliances, and she just had the kitchen and bathrooms updated. I think it's probably a little smaller than our townhouse, but she promised me she's never had trouble with mice."

"That's all I need to know. But can we afford it?"

"Two-fifty. I know it's a little more than what we're paying, but think how much we'll save on gas living so much closer to town."

"Sounds great. Let's go check it out. Can we get inside?"

"Not tonight, but Lori Ann said if we're interested she'll meet us there this weekend to give us a tour." Sandra waved her hand. "Waitress?" When the uniformed waitress stopped by, she ordered two cherry cobblers ala mode.

I wiped my mouth. "Sandra! I'm stuffed! Why would you order dessert?"

"Two reasons. One, Buntyns' cobbler is life changing. You've never tasted anything so delicious in your life."

"And two?"

"And two, we're going to be living near MSU. We can get up and run their track every morning before work. So the cobbler is our celebratory farewell to unwanted extra pounds."

"Your logic makes no sense."

The waitress returned with the biggest bowls of cobbler I'd ever seen, each with a huge scoop of vanilla ice cream drizzling over it.

It only took one bite. "Oh, yeah. Now I get it." I wanted to put my face in that concoction and just eat without restraint, but I refrained. It was *amazing.*

Later, we drove to the address Lori Ann had given Sandra for the rental. The house was adorable, with a wide front porch stretching the entire width of the house. Four concrete steps led up to it from a sidewalk lined with hostas and impatiens. Two rocking chairs and a swing graced the porch. The house was painted a pale sage green with white shutters on each of the front windows. A bright red door with a brass kick plate stood ready to welcome us to our new home.

Just as we got out to look around and take a peek in the windows, a car pulled up behind us. A woman in a white nurse's uniform stepped from the sedan.

"Sandra! I was hoping I'd catch you."

"Lori Ann, we love it! Can we see inside?"

"Of course you can. I was just stopping by to make sure they finished painting the bathrooms today."

Sandra stopped and turned back toward me. "Oh, I almost forgot. This is my roommate, Shelby Colter. Shelby, this is Lori Ann Trussell, the charge nurse on Eight."

I extended my hand to her. "Nice to meet you."

"Ah," she said, shaking it, "you're the one dating Dr. Thompson, right?"

Huh? How on earth did she know that? I shot a look at Sandra who shot me back a look of innocence.

"I've just seen you two in the cafeteria a lot, that's all. We love Dr. Thompson up on Eight."

"Oh, I see. Well, Tucker—I mean, Dr. Thompson and I are just friends. Really."

"Ah, well. Whatever you say," she said, chuckling. "Now come on in. Let me show you around."

I couldn't believe how perfect the house was. If I had the money, I would have bought it on the spot. If I'd built it myself, I would have designed it exactly the way it was. Sandra and I each claimed our bedrooms then started planning how to arrange our furniture in the living and dining rooms.

"When can we move in?" Sandra asked, doing her little dance.

"Any time."

"After the mouse problem we've had at the townhouse, our landlord does *not* want to cross us, so I'm guessing we can get out of our lease by the end of the month."

"Perfect," Lori Ann said. "I'll have the papers drawn up, and we'll make it official."

As we drove home, we talked non-stop about our new home

and all our ideas for fixing it up. But as we drove up to our complex and stopped by the drive-by mailboxes, I had to ask.

"Sandra, I don't get why everyone thinks Tucker and I are dating. It's not like we've been going out every night or paging each other all the time. Why is everyone at Baptist so into everyone else's business? I have to say, it's really annoying."

"Clearly you've never worked in a hospital before," she said, throwing in a sarcastic laugh as I handed her the wad of letters and junk mail.

"Obviously I haven't."

"It's just the nature of it. Actually, it goes on everywhere, but it's just amplified at hospitals. Like all those hospital soap operas on TV. Probably because we work with people who are sick and in critical situations. It's all very dramatic," she said, waving her hand for emphasis. "Makes for a melodramatic work environment. Don't let it bother you."

"But it does! I get that we're all caring for people who are sick and suffering. But that doesn't give everyone we work with the right to stick their noses into our private lives."

We got out of my car and walked toward our townhouse. "That may be, but why are you so embarrassed about people knowing you and Tucker are dating?"

I opened my mouth then slowly closed it.

I had no idea. Not a clue.

25

By Saturday afternoon, I was a mess. I couldn't believe how nervous I was about this "fancy" dinner date with Tucker, and it was making me a little crazy. I didn't want to be nervous, but the more I fought it, the more jittery I became. I had to reapply my mascara twice because my hands were shaking so badly. I growled out loud when I did it a third time.

"Again?" Sandra called from her bedroom.

"Don't even start with me"

She drifted into my bathroom, arms folded across her chest. "You're only making it worse. Let me help you."

"Help me how?"

"Sit." She shoved me to sit on the closed toilet and told me to tilt my head back. When she picked up the mascara wand, I held up my hands.

"Oh, no you don't! You'll have me looking like one of those Solid Gold Dancers."

"Hey! Give me a little credit here, will you?"

"Just promise me you won't bring in the ice blue eye shadow."

"You have my word. Now hold still and just relax."

I took a deep breath and tried my best to calm down. "This is so silly. It's not like I'm going out with Robert Redford. It's Tucker, for crying out loud. I've known him all my life. Why on earth should I be so jittery? I mean, what's the worst that could happen?"

Sandra continued brushing my lashes with mascara. "Hold still!"

"I am!"

"If you want my opinion, I think you're afraid you might just like Tucker Thompson more than you want to. You have this absurd notion that you all can't possibly connect on any other level than those kids you used to be who were always at each other's throats. You've got to get over that, Shelby. Tucker is a good guy. One in a million. And he obviously likes you—"

"But don't you think it's a little soon for that? It hasn't been that long since we witnessed his nasty little breakup with Cassie, remember?"

"Do I need to remind you that it hasn't been that long since you had a nasty little breakup with a certain sailor? Not that I knew you then, but how many long talks have we had about Will and everything that happened?" She nudged my face, focusing on the eyelashes on my left side.

"But that's different."

"How is that different? You were both recently engaged. You both recently broke off your engagements—"

"*He* didn't break off his engagement. He was dumped."

"I just don't see what difference any of it makes. Go out. Have a good time. It's not like he's going to propose or anything."

"Sandra!" I swatted her arm.

"Stop that! You almost got a streak of black up your cheek! Now hold still."

I took a deep breath and blew it out before tilting my head

back again. "The difference is, he's on the rebound. He has to be. And I don't want to . . . I just don't want to . . ."

She leveled her eyes at me. "You don't want to get hurt."

"I don't want to get hurt again," I whispered.

She moved my chin with her finger, finished applying the mascara, then recapped the wand. "And you won't. Shelby, just look at this as an elegant dinner at a beautiful restaurant with an old friend. Nothing more. You'll be fine. I promise."

I blew out another breath and nodded. "I'll try."

"Now then. What are you wearing?"

"Oh, I don't know. Pajamas?"

"What?!"

I had to admit I felt good in the little black dress Sandra dug out of my closet. She loaned me a beautiful matching shawl and helped drape it over my shoulders. She talked me into wearing the only pair of black heels I had, which were a little high for my personal taste, but they really did complete the outfit, especially paired with black hose. I was just putting on my lipstick when the doorbell rang. I capped the lipstick and headed downstairs to answer the door.

"Wow, Moonpie. You look . . . amazing." Tucker seemed surprised by my non-uniform ensemble. "I'm speechless here," he breathed.

"Oh, please. I put on a little extra lip gloss. No need to get tongue-tied."

He smiled and I felt my heart rate jump. He'd taken a pass on the scrubs, choosing a handsome black sport jacket, gray slacks, and a white button-down oxford shirt. I had to chuckle when I realized his tie had tiny golf balls and clubs on it.

“Why am I not surprised you golf? Do they teach that in med school?”

He looked down at his tie and laughed. “Absolutely. Second year. Mandatory. You can’t graduate unless you’re a scratch golfer.”

He closed the door behind me, and we walked out to his car. “You look really nice tonight, Shelby. I mean that.”

“Yeah? Well, you look pretty good yourself, Dr. Thompson.”

He helped me into his car, and we chatted all the way downtown. I couldn’t believe I’d fretted all afternoon, so nervous I almost made myself sick. Thankfully, the nerves had settled, and I was actually enjoying just being with him.

We turned onto the interstate. “Any more mice?”

“Oh, funny you should mention that. We found a house to rent. In fact, we’ll be living not far from you near the campus.”

“That’s great! Where’s the house?”

I told him about the house belonging to Lori Ann Trussell. He knew Lori, of course, and seemed genuinely pleased we’d be living closer to his neck of the woods. “That’ll be great. Think how handy it will be when the mice show up. Your knight in shining armor will be just around the corner now.”

“No more mice, thank you very much. Lori Ann assures us the house is varmint free.”

“Bummer. I’ll have to come up with some other reason to stop by. When are you all moving? Need some help?”

“Don’t offer if you don’t mean it. Of course we’ll need help. I’d rather not have to ask Mom and Dad to drive up again. They need to know I can handle these things on my own.”

“Just say when, and if I’m not working, I’ll be glad to help. Maybe I can rope in Trevor to lend a little muscle.”

“That’d be great. I haven’t seen much of Trevor lately. Where’s he been hiding?”

“He was out of town for a while doing some research with a

doctor up in Canada. Trevor's a gifted surgeon. He's already getting offers from all over the country. He can pretty much name where he wants to go when he's finished his residency."

"It's so hard for me to comprehend that he's a brain surgeon. Isn't that at the top of the pecking order when it comes to medicine?"

"I beg your pardon?" he scoffed in jest. "Anesthesiology is hardly chopped liver. Hey, those brain guys got nuthin' without us. How'd you like him digging around in that pretty little head of yours sans anesthesia? Huh?"

He had a point.

"Darn right. So let's just say neurosurgery is somewhere to the south of anesthesiology on that linear list of yours."

"Ok, then," I muttered. "Touchy subject?"

He threw his head back and laughed. "Nah, I'm just playing with you. Trevor's the best. And he's got a lot more muscle than me, so I'll make sure he shows up on moving day."

We pulled up at the main entrance of The Peabody Hotel. A doorman, dressed in top hat and tails, opened the car door for me.

"Welcome to the Peabody," he said with great flourish.

"Thank you." I had to admit, I enjoyed the pampering. Tuck handed the valet his keys and took my hand as we walked through the doors.

I remembered visiting the Peabody when I was a child. Jimmy and I loved to come and watch the duck parades. Each morning at 11:00, five mallard ducks, along with their duckmaster escort, ride the elevator down from the roof, then walk the red carpet to the hotel's Grand Lobby fountain. They spend the day there, floating and waddling along the fountain's edge, never leaving the area. Then at 5:00, the duckmaster shows up and leads them back to the elevator, and back to their rooftop home.

The lobby was already crowded with tourists, all waiting to see the parade. Tucker took my hand and pulled me to a spot along the roped-off area. In less than five minutes, a man dressed in a red jacket showed up to gather his brood. A recorded message filled the air, explaining the daily routine.

Tucker leaned toward me, his mouth close to my ear. "Do you know about the history of the duck parade?"

"I'm sure I did at one time, but I've forgotten."

"It all started back in 1932 when the general manager of the hotel and some of his hunting buddies came back from a hunting trip in Arkansas. As a prank, they put their live duck decoys in the fountain here. But the hotel guests loved it, and soon it became a popular attraction for guests and tourists. So they replaced the live decoys with five mallard ducks, and they've been doing it ever since."

"Whoa, those are some *really* old ducks," I teased.

He laughed. "Actually, they only work a three month gig, then they're retired. Sent back to the farm they came from."

Suddenly, John Philip Sousa's *King Cotton March* began to play and the five ducks jumped out of the fountain waters. All of them shook their tails for good measure, splashing water on several of the tourists to the delight of the many children in the audience. Then, the five lined up and headed back down the red carpet and onto the elevator, their escort right behind them.

As the crowd applauded and began to disburse, Tucker and I made our way to the restaurant. Evidently we weren't the only ones eating early. Apparently the duck parade brought in an early dinner crowd to the old hotel. The maitre'd seated us at a table in a quiet corner, close enough to see the tuxedoed piano player, but far enough that the music didn't interfere with our conversation. Tucker pulled out my chair for me then took the one directly next to it instead of across from me. I liked that. A succession of waiters immediately began looking to our every need. I couldn't help smiling at all the fuss.

"This is amazing," I whispered from behind my menu.

"Oh, I forgot to tell you. Feel free to order something other than fried green tomatoes. Though, now that I think of it, I don't even think it's on the menu." He searched the pages of the leather-bound menu then finally shrugged. "Nope, not here."

"Should we leave? Make a scene? What?"

"Nah, I bet we can find something suitable to your Southern palate."

"Is that so? Well then, what would you recommend instead?"

He leaned toward me, his brows dancing. "Well, I don't know about you, but I'd skip the roast duck. I mean, it's kind of tacky, don't you think? Parading them around the lobby then plucking their feathers and roasting their little carcasses?" He winced and produced a fake shiver. "That's just wrong."

"Good to know."

"However, their steaks are out of this world, if you're so inclined."

And so it went. Teasing conversation while lavishing in that extraordinary restaurant, waited on hand and foot by an exceptional staff. Our glasses never emptied and not a single crumb ever remained on the linen for more than a moment, quickly whisked away by the non-intrusive staff. The live piano music set a relaxing atmosphere, the talented musician playing a wide range of songs from Glenn Miller to Peter, Paul, and Mary, to Billy Joel's newest hit, "Just the Way You Are."

Tucker was right. The steak was the best I'd ever had. As was the Caesar salad which started our meal. The crisp-tender asparagus was cooked just the way I liked it as was the baked potato.

We shared an unforgettable slice of key lime cheesecake and sipped after-dinner coffee, our conversation never stopping even for a moment.

"Tucker, this is really lovely. I can't begin to thank you for bringing me here."

"Good. I was hoping to impress you," he said with a smile.

"Me? Why on earth would you feel the need to impress me?" I wasn't sure I really wanted to know.

He folded his napkin and laid it aside. "You really want to know?"

Goodness, is he into mind reading now?

"Sure."

"Because . . . because I hoped this might be a beginning for us."

Oh no.

Of course my face heated. Doesn't it always?

"A beginning?"

"Shelby, I—" He stopped, reaching for my hand. "I want to know if you'd consider seeing me. I mean, more than just as friends."

My heart pounded. *It's too fast. Too soon! I've barely gotten beyond thinking of him as Chubby Tucker. How can I possibly think of dating him?*

"I know it's fast."

There goes that mind reading thing again . . .

"I realize you must think I'm jumping the gun a bit. So let me explain something."

"Explain what?" I tried to keep my eyes on his and not on our entwined hands.

"Okay, I need to just say it. The thing with Cassie and me—"

I pulled my hand free. "Oh, Tucker, that's not necessary. Really. You don't have to—"

"But I do. You need to hear it. From me. Because if you just think I'm rushing into something after such a recent breakup, you'd be wrong."

"Wrong? How?"

He toyed with his dessert fork, pushing around the crumbs left on the plate. "I made a huge mistake with Cassie. And I didn't even realize it until . . ." He looked up at me. "Until you showed up."

I felt my mouth fall open.

"I know, I know. We have a pretty crazy history, you and I." He smiled, shaking his head. "Never saw this coming, that's for sure. But that day when I saw you by the elevators and realized it was really you . . . Shelby, everything changed."

I closed my mouth and swallowed hard. I'm pretty sure he must have heard it, even with *Misty* playing in the background.

"I can't even explain it, except that I knew immediately I wanted to get to know you again. To spend time with you. Which, of course, wasn't good, considering I was engaged at the time."

I arched my brows, nodding in agreement, but didn't even try to speak.

"And from then on, nothing was the same with Cassie. It's like it all came into focus—how we'd been pushed together. Her dad, my dad . . . I think I just went along for the ride at first, y'know? And then it just seemed to evolve on its own. She'd call me up, tell me what parties we'd be attending, what causes we'd support . . . and then last summer, while we were on vacation with her family in the Bahamas . . . I don't know. She kept wanting me to propose, to make it official there in that setting with her family all around."

I was imagining the two of them on a sandy beach, the sun setting behind them, the family looking on in expectation. "Let me guess. It would have been too awkward to disappoint them all?"

"Ohhhh yeah. Unbeknownst to me, the whole trip was a set up. Her mom, her dad and sisters—they were all in on it. And when push came to shove—quite literally, I might add," Tucker folded his arms across his chest and continued. "I guess what I'm trying to say is, rather than cause a scene, I just went along with it. I loved Cassie. I really did. And at the time, I thought I loved her enough to make a lifetime work with her."

"What changed your mind?"

"I already told you. You changed my mind."

I tried to keep my breathing calm. It wasn't easy. "But I would never have—"

"Of course, you wouldn't. And you didn't. This wasn't anything *you* did. It was me. That first day when I saw you, it's like my blinders fell off. I realized I was just allowing myself to be dragged along in the undertow of something that . . . something that was comfortable, but was anything but right. It wasn't fair to Cassie, for me to go along with the flow just to keep everyone happy. Not when my heart wasn't sold out to her.

"And you're probably not going to understand this, but I believe with all my heart that God used you to open my eyes to what had been happening."

I heard myself scoff. "You're absolutely right. I *don't* understand. And I'm not sure I want to be somehow responsible for causing you and Cassie to break up."

"No, that's not what I meant. You didn't cause it. It would have happened eventually. I just think God used the timing of your first day on the job as a means to plant a seed of doubt in my heart. To face up to what was going on. Please don't feel badly for my telling you this. I just wanted you to understand how it all fell in place."

I shook my head, trying to make sense of it. "But the fact remains, you didn't break up with her, Tucker. Cassie broke up with you. I was there that day. In the hall outside the cafeteria. I heard her tell you it was over."

"You did?"

I looked down to avoid his gaze. "Yes. Sandra and I both heard most of it."

He chuckled. "I'm not surprised. I had a feeling the patients on the entire Union wing heard most of it. Cassie is nothing if not vocal."

I smiled, wishing we could get off the subject. But I knew he had more to say.

Just then, the waiter returned with the folder. "I hope you enjoyed your meal. Please come again."

"We will," Tucker said, then quickly filled in the receipt and slid the folder aside. He picked up where he left off.

"Cassie called it off because I was lazy and hadn't done it myself. With every passing day I knew I needed to end it, but I was chicken. Cassie's a strong-willed woman. I knew it wouldn't go down well, no matter how I handled it. But I kept putting it off. And then the night she dragged me to Taylor's to pick out rings—"

"That had to be rough."

"You have no idea. But it was my own fault. I just couldn't make myself do it. And I have to say, it made me a little crazy. I'm not normally a pushover. So to keep putting it off, keep avoiding the confrontation to the point of actually shopping for rings? I mean, who does that?"

"But you didn't buy a ring, right?"

"Uh, no. No, I didn't. We got into a rather heated argument right there in front of that saleswoman. Which was also a set up. This woman had sold all of the McElroys their jewels for years. Cassie had obviously been there before and picked out exactly what she wanted. When I didn't respond and make a big fuss over it like she'd hoped, she got *really* upset. Then she informed me she would be purchasing the ring since I obviously couldn't. Which didn't set well with me. At all. And I have to admit, I did kinda gasp at the idea of buying a ring that cost more than my *house.*"

"Seriously?"

"Oh, yeah. Much more. But that wasn't it. I wouldn't have paid a penny by that point, but I didn't want to make a scene in the store in front of her family's friend. But Cass just stormed out and by the time I got out to my car, she was driving off in hers."

"Whoa, that had to be awful."

"Yes, but again, I had no one to blame but myself. So, like any good coward, I avoided her for a couple of days. I had a 48-hour shift which kept me out of sight, for the most part. And that day when she showed up at the cafeteria . . . well, you know the rest of my sad little story."

I took a final sip of my water and slowly set the crystal glass back down. "Tucker, I'm so sorry about all of this."

"No!" he said, reaching for my hand again. "Look, I didn't bring you here just to tell you all that. I really didn't. But you had to know. I really do believe God brought you back into my life when He did for two reasons. One, to finally get it through my thick skull that Cassie was not the one for me. And two, to give me a second chance."

He twisted the gold initial ring on my pinky for a few moments then said, "Please don't misunderstand. I'm fully aware it's awfully soon after my split with Cassie. I'm not suggesting we go ring shopping or pick out dishes."

"Well, that's a relief."

He laughed, then put his other hand on top of mine. "I guess I'm just asking for your permission to spend time with you. Go out together. Get to know each other again. But I'm done with being anything less than one-hundred percent honest. Which is why I'm telling you right up front that this is more than just Chubby Tucker asking Jimmy Colter's kid sister out for kicks."

"Oh, is that so?" I said, smiling.

"Oh, that is most definitely so."

He looked into my eyes for a moment more, then leaned over, slowly nearing me. I didn't even think about it. I leaned toward him, anxious for what I knew was coming. I closed my eyes, unable to breathe as he gently kissed me. He squeezed my hand once more then pulled away.

"You don't even want to know how long I've waited to do that," he whispered.

"I don't?" I asked coyly.

He smiled as he stood up. "Shall we go?"

Tucker held my hand the entire way home. We talked about all sorts of things—Baptist Hospital, the church, Dr. Love's recovery, and a lot more. I have to admit I was disappointed when I realized we were heading toward my townhouse. I'd hoped we might go somewhere else for awhile. I knew Sandra was home, and I didn't quite feel like sharing the rest of my evening with Tucker with her.

"I'm sorry to have to make it a short evening, but I've got to work at six in the morning."

"I'm convinced you're a mind reader. That's the third time this evening you've said something in response to a thought that just went through my mind."

"Is that so? And what thought was that?"

"Only that I was disappointed you were already taking me home."

"Yeah?" he asked, his face lighting up in the glow of the dashboard reflection. "I'll take that as a good sign."

"You should."

"Okay if I call you tomorrow sometime?" He pulled into my apartment complex parking lot.

"Sure. Preferably not at six, but I'll be up later."

"Good. I'll look forward to it."

He pulled to a stop in front of our townhouse, then a moment later, walked me to my door.

"I had such a nice time, Tucker." I stopped short of the welcome mat in front of our door. "Thank you so much for a wonderful evening."

Then, before I knew it, he wrapped me in his arms and pulled me close. I was sure he could feel my heart pounding through that little black dress. Then I realized I didn't care. He lowered his lips to mine and this time, there was nothing brief about it. I felt my knees go weak and he pulled back.

"Are you okay?" he said, his voice husky.

It took me a moment to catch my breath. "Sure. Why do you ask?"

"I felt you start to go limp there for a moment. Thought I was losing you."

I reached up and pushed a strand of hair from his eyes. "Not a chance, Tucker. Not a chance."

26

Much to my surprise, Tucker and I settled quickly into a comfortable routine. We didn't get to see each other every day because of his erratic work schedule, but we always talked by phone if we couldn't sneak in a moment or two together. On the nights he didn't work, he'd stop by and take me to dinner or pick up something so we could eat in. I loved how well he and Sandra got along, and how perceptive she was about giving us time alone now and then.

In only a couple of short weeks, I felt like Tucker and I had been together for a year or more. And I loved every single moment we spent together. I loved how he made me laugh. I loved the hint of mischief in his silly smile. I loved that his nose was just a tiny bit crooked—no doubt the trophy of a childhood prank or sports injury. I loved the way he hugged me when he was so tired he couldn't put a sentence together. I loved that he cried when a patient didn't make it through surgery. They weren't bodies. They were people with names and families and friends. I loved that he always put everyone at ease. I loved that he so easily made fun of himself.

And I love that he loved me.

On those long shifts when our paths didn't cross, he'd call me late at night and we'd talk until he got paged. We talked about anything and everything. I'd never known a guy so open and giving, so interested in who I was and what I thought about this subject or that. We both loved to read, and we'd discuss favorite books and characters and plot lines until there was nothing more to be said.

On the last weekend of May, Tucker and Trevor showed up bright and early on a Saturday morning to help us move. With their help, we had everything out by four that afternoon. When the guys took off with the last load, Sandra and I stayed behind to clean the townhouse.

We joined them at our house just after six. We were actually surprised to find them still there, but even more so when we walked in to find the dining room table set for four with a catered meal from Buntyns.

"Hey, can we rent you guys permanently?" Sandra asked, kicking off her tennis shoes. "I could really get used to this!"

"What—the meatloaf special from Buntyns," Trevor asked, "or the help of two manly-men?" He flexed his muscles like a bronzed body builder.

Sandra reached up and squeezed his upper arm. "Get a load of that beefcake, will you? So how exactly does a doctor like you have time to work out? I thought you brainiacs never got out much."

"Ah, mi amiga pequeña, those are secrets I'm not at liberty to share."

Tucker leaned toward Sandra in a fake whisper. "There's a gym over on the top floor of the Medical Center. Those aren't just doctors' offices, you know. He works out between shifts."

"Tucker, do you mind?" Trevor teased. "A man needs a little mystery. Thanks for spoiling my fun."

"You're welcome."

We all took a seat around the table and devoured the hot meal set before us. Meatloaf, buttery mashed potatoes, lima beans, a fresh fruit salad, and those life-changing yeast rolls.

"Please tell me there's no cobbler warming in the oven," I groaned.

"No cobbler," Trevor said.

"Thank goodness for that."

"Just a Mississippi Mud Cake. And we picked up some vanilla ice cream at the store to go on top."

"You did not!" Sandra scolded, jumping up to peek in the oven. Nothing there, but she quickly spotted a dark sheet cake sitting on the counter in a bakery carton. "Oh Dios mío! You'll have to roll me out of here come Monday."

"Hey, we can just let the guys have the cake. We don't have to eat it, you know."

"Are you out of your mind?" she scoffed. "Have you ever had Buntyns' Mud Cake?"

"Fine. Whatever. Just tell me which box my fat jeans are in."

The guys stuck around to help us move the last pieces of furniture where we wanted them. We would do the rest later. I was just moving another box into the kitchen when I looked out and saw Sandra and Trevor on the front porch swing. Trevor must have said something funny because my roommate threw her head back, laughing and holding her stomach. Trevor laughed too, so much that he could hardly breathe.

"What are you looking at?" Tucker said, coming up behind me. He wrapped his arms around my waist and looked over my shoulder. "Ah, the good Dr. Knight, weaving his magic on your delightful little roommate."

"They're good together, don't you think?" I mused aloud.

"Who, Trevor and Sandra?"

"Well, who else would I be talking about?"

"Ah, I don't know. They're pretty different, those two."

I turned around to face him, his hands still on my waist. "And different is bad because why?"

"Now, don't get all huffy. I just mean, it's okay for them just to be friends, isn't it? Do we have to pair them up just because he helped her move today?"

"Tucker, I didn't mean they should—"

He bear-hugged me, planting a kiss on my lips.

"What was that for?" I asked once he pulled back.

"Nothing. Just felt like doing it." So he did it again, this time slower and sweeter, gentler. I relaxed in his arms, ignoring the fact I was grimy from all the moving and cleaning we'd done. I was getting used to these sudden kisses. And I liked them. A lot.

He reached around me to grab his iced tea off the counter. "So did you decide about the singles camping trip?"

"When is it again?"

"July 4th weekend."

"That's a month away. Why do you have to know if I'm going?"

"Because I have to request the weekend off."

"Oh. I don't know, Tucker. You know I'm not much of a joiner for stuff like that."

"So? It'll be fun. C'mon, you know you wanna go."

"I do?"

"Sure you do. What's not to love? The fresh outdoors. A lake to swim in. Sleeping under the stars—"

"And about a hundred singles."

"Well, there's that. Though we've never had that many go. Usually only about thirty or forty. But they all know we're dating now, so I don't expect the Killer Bs to hit on you or anything. Besides, they're afraid of me."

"They are?"

"Yeah. Last week I told them you weren't available and to stop trying to get your number. I put on this whole tough guy thing. They were shaking in their boots by the time I was done."

"Why do I think you're lying?"

"Okay, well, maybe they weren't exactly shaking in their boots. It was more of a little wobble."

"Tucker?"

"Yeah?"

"Leave those poor guys alone, okay? They've got enough problems."

"So you should invite Sandra to come. They love Sandra. In spite of her Pedro stories."

"They know about Pedro?"

"You mean, do they know Pedro's a bird?"

"Tucker! You told them?"

"No! I didn't say a word! They just don't think this Pedro guy is anything to worry about. I heard them say something about seeing if the mice will play while the cat's away, or something like that."

"Please—we don't 'do' mice anymore. Remember?"

"Just say you'll go," he asked again, nuzzling my neck knowing full well how ticklish I was in that particular spot.

"Okay! Okay! I'll go. Now stop that!" I pushed him gently.

Just then, another raucous round of laughter spilled from the front porch. We watched as Trevor and Sandra giggled like a couple of school kids.

"I don't guess Trevor's planning to go on the campout, is he?"

"He's thinking about it. Why do you ask?"

"Nothing. I'm just thinking Sandra could use some fresh air, a lake to swim in, maybe a good night's sleep under the stars . . ."

27

The following Monday afternoon we had our first Bible study with Chaplain Perkins. Goodness, that man was boring. How anyone could make scripture that dull was beyond me. He was a nice enough guy, but teaching was definitely not one of his spiritual gifts. I fought to stay awake and noticed I wasn't the only one. But with Mrs. Baker sitting in our midst, we weren't about to risk nodding off. When it was finally over, I wanted nothing more than to get upstairs and visit my patients. Especially Donnie.

I was worried about my dear friend. He'd been a guest on Nine for four weeks. The flowers sent by colleagues and friends had all withered and died. Visits from co-workers at Holiday Inn's corporate offices had begun to taper off. Rachel stopped by as often as she could, but it was hard on her, especially since he refused her prayers as well as mine. I'd taped all his get well cards on the wall across from his bed. Quite a collection, but also a sad reminder he'd been here much too long.

His recent surgery hadn't helped as much as they'd hoped. Over the past couple of weeks, he'd undergone more tests and been examined by several more doctors, including the heart specialist from Vanderbilt. They were trying to decide if he would be able to withstand the extreme risks involved with a transplant. If he had any chance at all, he would have to be transferred to Columbia University Medical Center in New York—but only when and if a heart became available that was compatible to his blood type. Columbia was one of the only hospitals in the country performing organ transplants. And while heart transplants had improved greatly since the early days of Dr. Christaan Barnard in South Africa, they were still extremely rare and survival statistics were still not optimal.

But as Donnie said, what choice did he have?

I'd prayed constantly for him, but mostly I was worried sick.

"Hey buddy, how's it going today?"

Donnie looked up from a book he was reading. "Hey, Shelby."

He was so pale, almost ashen. And he looked more than a little frail. "How about a stroll down to the coffee shop? My treat."

"No, but thanks."

"C'mon, Donnie. You need to get out of here. Please?"

"Whining doth not become thee, fair maiden."

"And slothfulness doth not become thee, kind sir."

"I hate when you mock me."

"So humor me. I'll go get you some wheels. Make yourself decent and for heaven's sake, do *not* go commando this time."

"Never. I'm sporting my *Charlie's Angels* boxers. Wanna see?" He threw back his covers.

I covered my eyes. "No! You keep Farrah and the girls to yourself, thank you very much. Now get out of that bed. I'll be right back."

"Witch."

"Jerk."

"Cretin."

"Crybaby."

If he added another term of endearment, I didn't hear it. A couple minutes later I returned with a wheelchair. He'd wrapped his robe around himself and combed his hair. I helped him into the chair and off we went. I took him on a brief tour of the hospital first, using my best flight-attendant tone as I pointed out the various wings and points of interest.

"Here you see the world-renowned Baptist Memorial Hospital gift shop, featuring hymnals, Bibles, and communion wafers at special discounts for our Southern Baptist patients. Identification required, of course."

"What, I've gotta show my circumcision scars to get a wafer?"

"Shhh! Donnie!"

"Just asking."

"Well, stop asking and just observe."

He waved me closer. "Shelby, look."

"What?"

"Over there by the magazines. That's Ginger Alden, Elvis's girlfriend."

I peeked around a tall potted ficus tree and got a glimpse of the former beauty queen and the King's current girlfriend.

"Donnie, you know what that means!" I whispered urgently as I wheeled his chair around to go the opposite direction.

"Ginger likes communion wafers?"

"No, silly, Elvis is in the building!"

"Which explains why you're about to give me a whiplash, speeding down the hall."

I rounded the corner, hoping not to tip him over as I headed for the back elevators.

"Shelby! What on earth are you doing? Slow down!"

"I will, I promise." We rounded one more corner then I yanked Donnie's wheelchair to a stop, almost dumping him out of it. "Oh, sorry!"

He braced himself, palming his hand against the wall as I pressed the up button on the elevator. “Where are you taking me?”

“Shhhh! I'm not supposed to take you on these elevators, but it's the only way.”

The elevator chimed then opened. Thankfully, no one was inside. I whipped his chair around and pulled him inside then pounded number 16 on the panel list of floors.

“That's not my floor. What are you doing? And what about the coffee you promised me?”

I tried to catch my breath, leaning hard against the shiny silver elevator wall.

“Elvis is here! We're gonna ride up and see if we can sneak by for a peek!”

“Are you out of your mind? They're not going to let us just stroll by up there.”

“Sure they will. Aren't you forgetting? I work here. I'm in uniform. They'll think I'm just taking one of my patients back to his room.”

“Except that it's not my floor, and might I remind you, it's not *your* floor either. Won't the staff be a little suspicious?”

“I'll think of something. Just sit tight and keep your mouth shut.”

When the doors on Sixteen opened, I took a deep breath and slowly pushed Donnie's chair as if I had all the reason in the world to be on that floor. We took the first corner into the main corridor heading to the Union wing. I noticed no one was at the nurses' station except the medical records secretary whose focus was on a patient chart. I prayed she wouldn't look up as we passed. She didn't.

But just as we turned to go down the long hall toward the suite where I knew Elvis always stayed, Donnie reached back and grabbed my arm.

“Uh oh, looks like we're busted,” he said out the side of his mouth. "Call me crazy but those guys don't exactly look like your friendly Baptist orderlies."

I had to agree. Three guys decked out in black leather jackets stood guard about halfway down the hall. I noticed they all wore a lot of gold and carried a distinct air about them, leaving no doubt in my mind. These guys were part of the famous "Memphis Mafia," Elvis's entourage. They briefly glanced up at us then resumed their conversation. I thought if I casually pushed Donnie past them, acting as if he had a room down that hall, they might ignore us and just let us pass.

I was wrong.

"Ma'am?"

I kept moving, pushing Donnie's chair while nonchalantly looking up at them. "Yes?"

"You'll need to turn back around. This section of the hall is closed."

"Oh? I'm sorry. I guess I must have gotten off on the wrong floor. This isn't Fifteen?"

"No, ma'am. It's not. You're on Sixteen."

I faked a chuckle. "Silly me." I leaned down toward Donnie. "I'm so sorry, Mr. Rogers. I'll have you back on Fifteen in a jiffy." To the Mafia men, "Forgive me. Have a nice day."

I slowly began to turn around when Donnie started to cough. He was wheezing something terrible, and I suddenly felt foolish for my lame attempt for a glimpse of Elvis when Donnie wasn't up to it.

"You okay?" I asked, kneeling beside him.

He coughed again, sounding like he might just cough up a lung. I patted him on his back, thinking surely that would help. That's when he winked at me.

"Is he okay?" one of the guys in black asked, approaching us.

"I think so. Must have swallowed the wrong way or something. You okay, Mr. Rogers?"

He nodded but kept coughing, waving me off. I'd forgotten what a good actor he was.

"Can I get him something?" the guy asked. "Maybe some water?"

He stood right in front of us now, his Brut cologne overpowering us both. I wondered if Elvis bought the stuff by the case.

"No, I think we'll be fine. But thank you." I stood back and flipped my hair over my shoulder with as much flair as I dared. "Are you . . . are you visiting someone?" I hoped he didn't hear the quake in my voice. "I'm one of the hospital hostesses and we're here to help, so if you, uh . . . need some help or anything, I'd be happy to, uh . . . help."

"That won't be necessary. We know our way around, but thank you." He suddenly looked up and over my shoulder. "Hi, Marian. I was just getting acquainted with your hostess here." He looked back down at me. "I'm sorry, what was your name?"

Marian Cocke. Had to be. Elvis's nurse. The girls had told me about her. Something in the back of my mind uttered the term "mama bear." A shiver ran down my spine.

Time to go.

I quickly grabbed the handles of Donnie's chair and aimed him back down the hall in the direction we'd come. "Well, then. We'll just be on our way now."

She stood like a soldier in the middle of the hall, her arms folded across her chest. "And just where did you think you were going, Miss—" Her eyes lowered to my name tag. "Colter? This section of the floor is off limits."

"Shelby? What are you doing up here?"

As luck would have it, Sarah Beth arrived just in time to make matters worse. "Oh. Hey, Sarah Beth. I was just giving my patient here a tour of the hospital and we, uh, well, I wasn't paying attention and we got off on the wrong floor. Apparently. My mistake. We'll just be going now."

Sarah Beth folded her arms, making her a matched set with Nurse Cocke. "Does Mrs. Baker know you're up here?" She tilted her head just so and plastered a sarcastic smile on her lily white face.

"Of course not, Sarah Beth. I told you. I accidently got off on the wrong floor. Now if you'll excuse us?"

Donnie piped in with a pitiful cough, enough to convince Sarah Beth to move her sass out of the way for us to get by.

As we approached the elevator, I blew out a heavy sigh—along with a silent prayer apologizing for my little white lie.

"Seriously, Shelby, we should do this again sometime," Donnie said. "I'm told stress is really good for an ill-functioning heart."

"I'm *so* sorry, Donnie."

"Oh, don't I know it. I intend to hold it over your head but good."

"I'm your slave."

"Got that right. Now take me back to my room so I can write in my memoirs how I almost had coffee with my *former* best friend and almost met Elvis."

"As you wish."

"And Shelby?"

"Yes, your grace?"

"I'll be wanting a pedicure tomorrow so bring your supplies. Mr. Big Toe has a nasty green thing going on under his nail."

28

June came and went as summer got off to a warmer than usual start. We'd all settled in to our new responsibilities in the ER, ICU, and surgical waiting areas. It seemed strange, our schedules all different now, sometimes not seeing each other for days at a time. But Mrs. Baker seemed pleased with our added service to those areas of the hospital, and the feedback from the staff in those departments had been overwhelming.

I'd finally grown comfortable with the idea of being "Tucker's girl." In fact, I rather loved it. I was crazy about him. We spent every moment together we could, which wasn't always easy between his schedule and mine. Still, we found stolen moments together whenever we could.

As the first weekend of July approached, I even began looking forward to the singles camping trip. The Fourth actually fell on Monday, but tentative plans were to leave on Friday after work and return after lunch on Sunday.

I was disappointed Rachel wouldn't be going with us. She was much too close to her due date and couldn't take the chance of being out in the woods in case little Cooper decided to come early. Even though I'd looked forward to going, I hated to be out of town if she went into labor. I was having second thoughts.

"Tucker, I'll never forgive myself if I'm not here for Rachel when her baby is born."

"But Rich has my pager number," Tucker argued. "The minute we hear anything, off we go. Besides, didn't you just twist Sandra's arm to go with us?"

"Yes, but what does that have to do with it?"

"Because she'll bail if you do, and Trevor would be heartbroken."

"Really?" Suddenly, I found myself interested in going again.

"Okay, maybe heartbroken is a little strong."

"Tucker."

"But seriously, he did ask me if she was coming. I think he's kinda interested."

"Took him long enough. Hold on—are you making this up just to convince me to go? Because if you are, that's really lame."

"No! I'm not making it up. He asked me who all was going, I told him, then he said, and I quote, 'Is Sandra coming with Shelby?' See? He's interested. He wouldn't have asked if he wasn't."

Tucker finally persuaded me to go, promising he'd drive me back to Memphis if we got word that Rachel had gone into labor. Rich had lined up plenty of sponsors to help with the two-night trip so he could stay home with his bed-ridden wife.

Around 5:30 on Friday evening, thirty of us loaded our gear, got on the old church bus, and headed to Chickasaw State Park, about two hours east of Memphis. Trevor drove up later along with a few others who didn't get off work in time. Sandra and I were the only hostesses who made the trip, and I realized that was probably a good thing. A nice break. I still didn't know most of the girls and guys in the singles group very well, but they seemed like a lot of fun.

The day had been extremely warm, but out there in the wilderness the night was beautiful. We unloaded and started setting up camp. The guys built an enormous bonfire to help light our campsite. By the time the tents were up, we were all starving. Rachel had organized a team of girls beforehand to plan the meals, and they outdid themselves. I'm not sure why food always tastes better when you're out of doors, but everything they served was fantastic.

"Now, aren't you glad you came?" Tucker snatched a potato chip off my paper plate.

Trevor took a seat on the ground next to Sandra. "You weren't going to come?"

"I just hated to be away in case Rachel goes into labor."

"Nice cover," Tucker whispered in my ear.

Bobby snickered. "Now, none of that, you two love birds. You don't have to rub our noses in it."

Very funny. I wanted to deck one Killer B.

"Yeah, Bobby told me your boyfriend there told him to back off since you're 'TAKEN'."

Thank you, Killer B #2.

Tucker kept a straight face, pointing his plastic fork at the two goofballs. "And don't you forget it."

Sandra and Trevor snorted out loud at the exchange. He leaned against her shoulder almost knocking her over. I liked how those two were getting along. They made a nice couple.

"Not you too, Dr. Brainiac?" Bobby blurted, pointing at them. "Gosh, is there something in the water at that hospital? Gotta get me some of that!"

He and Burt lost it, laughing themselves silly over that one. Thankfully they turned their attention to some of the new girls in the group, carrying on about some big surprise they had planned.

After we ate, a couple of guys brought out guitars and we had the traditional Kumbaya sing-along. But I had to admit, with the roaring fire and the clear, star-covered sky, it was really fun. Dr. Krause talked for a while about how blessed we all were to live "at such a time as this" and how those blessings aren't to be taken for granted. He encouraged us to use the gifts God gave each one of us to share those blessings with a lost world. George always made God's word so up close and personal. He had a unique way of explaining scripture, making you feel like it was written just for you.

He closed with a time of prayer, we sang a little more, than we had some free time to enjoy the outdoors. The girls brought out the graham crackers, marshmallows, and chocolate bars for the traditional cooking of the S'mores, my personal favorite. Tucker made sure to burn my marshmallows, then smear the gooey mess over my face as much as possible. You can take the doctor out of the hospital, but you can never take the kid out of the doctor. Or something like that.

Later we said our good nights and headed into our tents. Earlier, Sandra and I had put our sleeping bags in an enormous luxury tent with eight other girls. After the mandatory final trek to the bathrooms, we all snuggled into our sleeping bags, ready to call it a night.

At least most of us did.

I realized Sandra was nowhere to be found. Normally, I would have been concerned, but the last time I saw her, she and Trevor were walking toward the lake. I smiled, envisioning them sitting on a log, enjoying each others' company as they gazed out upon the moonlit waters of Lake Placid. She still hadn't returned when I fell sound asleep.

When the sun began to rise, I awakened to the clatter of pots and pans and the distinct aroma of sizzling bacon. I noticed several of the girls in my tent had already rolled up their sleeping bags. I assumed they must be the ones out there cooking. I turned to find Sandra sacked out, snoring quietly with her mouth slightly opened. I nudged her with my foot.

"Hey, sleepyhead. What time did you get to bed?"

Her eyes flitted open, then she stretched into a vigorous yawn. "Huh? Oh . . ." Her lips curled into a smile as she closed her eyes again. "Mmmm, wouldn't you like to know?"

"Probably not, come to think of it."

She stretched again and rolled onto her side to face me. "I'm so glad you talked me into coming."

"Obviously," I smirked.

"Trevor . . . I've never met anyone quite like him. He's smart, he's funny . . . and oh my goodness, can that boy kiss!" she whispered.

"Shhh! Sandra? So that's what you guys were doing last night?"

"And if we were? We were just having some fun, that's all."

"I'm just saying, it's kind of fast, don't you think?"

"So?"

I stared at her for a moment and decided to let it go. It wasn't that I didn't like the idea of them together, it was just . . . well, I don't know. It just felt weird, out here, with all these singles around us. But Sandra was no fool. She could certainly take care of herself.

"Hey, forget I said anything. Let's get cleaned up so we don't miss breakfast."

I thought dinner was good, but breakfast was incredible. The girls had grilled up a mountain of eggs and bacon then cleared the camping stove to cook what looked like a hundred pancakes. They'd even warmed the syrup. I couldn't believe how hungry I was. Slowly, everyone wandered out of their tents and joined us. Tucker looked ridiculous when he popped out of his tent, his dark hair sticking up like a porcupine. He gave me a lopsided smile then sauntered off toward the showers, a towel slung over his shoulder. He was back in five minutes looking squeaky clean and wide awake, his wet hair still spikey.

"Whoa!" he said, pouring himself a cup of coffee. "Anybody else take a cold shower this morning?"

Bobby snickered, which of course made Burt crack up. I decided they were really just ten-year-olds masquerading as adults.

"No, I didn't mean *that*," Tucker groaned. "I meant there's no hot water. That'll wake ya' up and fast."

A few minutes later, he sat down beside me at the picnic table, his plate piled high with pancakes.

"Hungry, Dr. Thompson?" George asked.

"You betcha. I could eat a horse about now." He forked a huge bite of pancakes.

"Well, you'll be sorry to hear there's no horsemeat on the menu today. Just hot dogs for lunch and chili for dinner."

"Yes, but what's *in* the chili?" Tucker asked. "Therein lies the question."

An hour later, George led us in a morning devotional then encouraged us to go out into the woods and find a quiet place for some personal prayer time. Tucker took my hand and led me to a spot under some pine trees overlooking the lake. We sat quietly at first, then he just started to pray. It seemed like the most natural thing we'd ever done together. He talked to God as if the Almighty was sitting right there with us. Which, I guess, He was. He thanked Him for the beauty surrounding us, the fresh air, the scent of the pine needles beneath us . . . and then he thanked God for me.

It startled me at first. We'd never prayed together like this before, and I didn't really know what to expect. But I never thought he'd be so open, praying about me like this—especially with me sitting right there.

"Lord, I've already thanked You a thousand times for bringing Shelby back into my life. I still can't believe it, after all these years. Thank You for helping her see me as more than that snot-nosed kid who once put worms in her tennis shoes—"

"Hey!" I protested, elbowing him in the ribs. "That was you?"

"Shhh, Shelby," he whispered. "Can't you see I'm praying here? And Lord, please forgive her disrespect. She meant no harm."

I elbowed him again but said nothing.

"Thank You for saving me, Lord. Not just for saving my soul, but saving me from the mistake I almost made . . . for giving me a second chance. And for using Shelby to open my eyes."

I was glad his eyes were actually closed at the moment as I felt a tear slip down my cheek. We'd talked about it that night at the Peabody, but we hadn't mentioned it since. And certainly never in a prayer. I was speechless.

He pulled his hand free and wrapped his arm around my shoulder, pulling me closer. "Thank You, for this friendship You've given us. The sheer companionship of this relationship. It's such a blessing. Don't let us ever take it for granted, Lord."

He was silent for a moment, but I knew there was more.

"And Father, right here, right now, in this amazing expanse of your creation, I ask You to lead us. Whatever You may or may not have in store for us, show us the way. Help me be the friend Shelby needs me to be. Help her know how much she means to me . . . already. . . still."

I wasn't sure what he meant by that, but I liked the sound of it.

"And God, I want to commit our relationship to You in this quiet moment, and ask You to guide us each and every day to honor You with what You've given us. Thank You, even now, for what You're going to do. You are God, You are Abba Father, and we love You."

He took a deep breath and let it out, then squeezed my shoulder. I knew he probably wanted me to pray, but I couldn't. Even if I'd wanted to, I couldn't have uttered a word. After a few moments of silence, he said, "Amen."

We sat there, neither of us saying anything for at least ten minutes or so. Finally, he pulled me to my feet and we took a walk around the banks of Lake Placid. Occasionally we'd encounter some of the others in our group, but we tried not to disturb them.

I tried to figure out this man who'd dropped into my life and so radically changed it. I still had my reservations. I wanted to trust him completely. He'd given me no reason not to. Still, I had this check in my spirit, holding me back. Scared. I remembered my conversations about trust with Dr. Love. And as we walked around that lake, I prayed silently that God would show me how to let go and love this man the way he deserved to be loved.

29

The rest of the day we were at war.

The group was divided into four teams and we competed in all kinds of crazy games and skills. Tug of war, silly relay races, a scavenger hunt, and even a shaving cream fight followed by exploding sacks of flour. It was all so ridiculous, but we had the *best* time. I couldn't remember the last time I'd played so hard and laughed so much.

Thankfully the showers weren't completely cold when we all cleaned up, though I craved the steaming hot water of my shower at home. But by dinnertime, the last remnants of the pasty goo were gone, and we enjoyed chili and cornbread by the campfire. The Killer Bs were preoccupied with their "big surprise" and kept running off into the woods. I was convinced more than ever those two should have gone on a middle school outing instead of our singles adventure. One of the other guys had seen a stash of fireworks in their tent, so we all braced ourselves for whatever they had up their sleeves.

We sang again, then Dr. Krause talked to us about the

importance of staying sexually pure in a society that ridiculed such behavior. Thankfully, Burt and Bobby had scampered off so we could avoid their childish reactions to the topic. But George talked so sensibly about the subject, I don't think any of us were uncomfortable. He reminded us how the world had confiscated the beautiful gift God intended us to have, substituing it with a cheap knock-off. He gave examples of Hollywood's lies on the subject in the movies we'd all seen. And yet, he never talked down to us, never lectured us in that sense. I wasn't sure how he did it, but he was sure good at it.

I couldn't tell if it was the breeze against the night air or just a long day of lots of physical activity, but I was having a hard time staying awake toward the end of Dr. Krause's talk. When he finished, Tucker and I chatted a while then I begged off, wanting to call it a night and go crawl in my sleeping bag.

"What, and miss more-S'mores?"

"But I'm tired, Tucker."

"Too tired for Tucker? I'm offended."

"No, that's not what I said. I'm just beat."

"Okay, I promise I'll let you get some sleep if you go down by the lake with me for a few minutes first."

"Tucker . . ." I whined.

"A few minutes, that's all. I promise."

I tilted my head, already imagining the soft cool liner of my sleeping bag. I huffed for his benefit. "Okay-fine-whatever."

"Gee, don't sound so thrilled, Moonpie." He took my hand and led me down the path.

"Anyone ever tell you how stubborn you are, Tucker?"

"Yeah. You. About twenty years ago. Over and over and—"

"Well, that's because you take stubborn to a new art form."

"Stop whining. It's beautiful out here, see?"

We took a seat on an old tree log at the edge of the beach. He put his arm around me and drew me close.

"You're right. It is. I'm sorry. I don't mean to be so crabby. I'm just tired."

"Not used to shaving cream fights, eh?" He leaned his head on mine.

"Evidently not," I said, then changed subjects. "So, no pages from Rich?"

"Nope, not yet."

"I wonder how Rachel's doing. I can't imagine what she must be thinking right now. Wondering if any minute her baby will be born."

"Ever witness childbirth?"

I pulled back to look at him. "Me? Not hardly."

"It's a beautiful thing. Whether it's natural or c-section or something in between, it's beautiful. To see those little buggers twist their little red faces up," he said, acting out the part, "then belt out that first good cry—there's nothing like it."

"I'm looking forward to it someday."

"Yeah? You want a lot of kids?"

"I don't know. I haven't really thought about a number. I just know I want children. Don't you?"

"Absolutely. At least a dozen or so."

"A *dozen*?! Well, then. I guess—"

Suddenly, shots rang out. They came in rapid-fire succession, sounding like we were in a war zone.

"What the heck?" Tucker cried out.

"Stay down, everyone!" we heard George shout.

We could hear everyone shouting and rushing around, the voices wild with panic.

Tucker leaned close to me. "Stay here, Shelby! I need to go see what's going on."

"Tucker, no!"

"I'll be fine. Just stay low until I get back." With that he was gone.

The commotion continued as more shots rang out. Then I heard Tucker yell, "Is anybody hurt?"

I couldn't just sit there, so I crawled back toward the campsite. Everyone had hit the deck and seemed to be as bewildered as I was. As far as I could tell, no one had been hurt. More shots rang and everyone lowered themselves to the ground again. That's when the screaming commenced.

"OUCH! OUCH! OUCH! I'M HIT! I'M HIT!"

"PUT IT OUT! PUT IT OUT!"

Across the way to my far right, a spectacle of lights bounced erratically around the inside of a tent. Some of the lights shot right through the tent walls arcing into the night sky. Others seemed to just keep bouncing around inside. Against the backlight of all that commotion, we saw two silhouettes dancing wildly inside the tent.

Just then, another round of explosions went off. Bobby came flying out of the tent.

"I'M HIT! I'M HIT! HELP ME! I'M HIT!"

Burt followed close behind, backing out of the tent as more of the apparent bottle rockets chased him. He stumbled, falling back on the ground, then quickly back-crawled away from the fireworks which continued going off inside the tent.

"MY BUTT! MY BUTT! IT'S ON FIRE!" Bobby ran around the campsite, his hands on his backside, occasionally stopping to jump up and down and wail like a banshee.

"Trevor! Where are you? Go get the First Aid kit!" Tucker shouted, jumping up to help Bobby. "Calm down, Bobby! Just calm down!" he said, trying to grab hold of his arm.

"DON'T TOUCH ME! IT HURTS! I'M DYYYING! IT HURTS SO BAD!"

"Stop it! Listen to me!" Tucker said, yanking him to a stop. "You're not dying. Come over here on the table and let me take a look at it."

"SOMEBODY CALL AN AMBULANCE! I'M DYING! I TELL YOU, I'M DYING!"

"You're not dying, Bobby, so shut up!" Burt scolded, approaching his friend.

I rushed to Burt's side. "You don't look so good," I said. "There's blood all over your face. Come sit down."

"What? Oh my GOSH! I've been HIT! I'M HIT TOO!"

"You're fine, just calm down. We'll get Trevor and Tucker to take a look in a minute. Come here and sit down." I led him over to another table and helped him sit. Some of the others grabbed dishtowels and poured water on them so we could gently start cleaning Burt's face and try to find the source of the bleeding.

"NO!" Bobby screamed again, behind me. "You're not going to pull my pants down in front of all the girls! NO! Stay away from me!"

Tucker turned toward the crowd. "Ladies? If you'll move away from the campsite and give our friend here some privacy? George, you want to escort the ladies down to the water for a minute?"

Trevor returned with the First Aid kit. Once they convinced Bobby his female audience was gone, he let them attend to his wounds. I had my back toward him as I continued cleaning Burt's face, finally realizing the blood was coming from cuts on his forearms. Apparently he'd suffered some lacerations, then, while shielding his face, inadvertently smeared blood all over his face.

"You're going to be fine," I said quietly. "As soon as Tucker checks out your buddy over there, he can take care of those cuts. Okay?"

"I guess," he said, his voice shaky. "Is Bobby gonna be okay?"

I refrained from looking over my shoulder, not wanting to invade the other B's privacy and risk getting him riled up again. I could hear Trevor and Tucker discussing the situation as they worked.

"Is he going to be okay?" Burt called to them.

"Oh, I think he'll survive," Trevor said calmly. "But we

probably need to get him to the ER."

"YOU'RE TAKING ME TO THE HOSPITAL?!" Bobby screamed, just before breaking into a full-scale sob.

"Bobby! Knock it off! We'll get you cleaned up as best we can, but you need more medical attention than we can provide here. Wouldn't you rather be in a nice, sterile environment than out here in the woods?"

"Yeah-huh," he cried, sounding like a five year old.

"Good. Let us finish cleaning these wounds, then we'll make you comfortable and get you back to town."

"Okay," he whimpered.

"Take me, too!" Burt cried. "Look! See my arms? They're all shot to pieces!"

"We'll take you, Burt. Just calm down," Tucker said, obviously weary of the behavior. "Shelby, how's it look? Have you been able to stop the bleeding?"

"Not really. Can you take a look?"

He stepped over and checked out the multiple cuts on Burt's forearms. "Yeah, looks like you're going to need some stitches too. Burt, what were you guys thinking? Don't you know not to play with firecrackers?"

Burt turned his head. "I don't want to talk about it."

Tucker looked at me, rolling his eyes. He handed me a roll of gauze and some antibiotic ointment. "See what you can do."

Gradually, the others returned, helping where they could. Several of the guys secured the now-destroyed tent making sure there were no more surprises about to go off. Half an hour later, we watched as Tucker and Trevor drove off with the two Killer Bs in Trevor's Jeep, with Bobby stretched out in the back on his stomach, his legs awkwardly resting on Burt's lap. Bobby wouldn't be sitting for a long, long time.

The rest of us tried to get some sleep but the episode pretty much ruined the campout. We'd all been stung by the Killer B's tomfoolery. We decided to break camp after breakfast and just go home.

I decided it would be a long, long time until I ever embarked on another camping trip.

30

After we got home, I'd barely stepped out of the shower when the phone rang. I knew Sandra was taking a nap, so I quickly wrapped a towel around me and tiptoed over to the phone on my bedside table. I was relieved to hear Tucker's voice on the other end.

"So, how are the boys? Did they survive the trip to the ER?"

"What? Oh, yeah. They're fine. But I think you need to get down here. Rich just called and said he's bringing Rachel in."

"Oh, Tucker! That's wonderful! I'll get dressed and be there as soon as I can!"

"Shelby . . ."

"What? What's wrong, Tucker?" Something snagged my heart.

"Rich said Rachel hasn't felt the baby move in a couple of days."

No. NO! Absolutely not.

This isn't happening.

God wouldn't let this happen.

"Are you still there, Shelby?"

"Yes. I'm here. Is he taking her to the ER?"

"Yes. I'll meet you there. Just hurry."

I hung up then sat down hard on my bed. A flurry of horrible images floated through my mind. I had to stop them. I got dressed as fast as I could and jumped in my car. All the way to Baptist, I kept begging God to save little Cooper. I prayed for Rich and Rachel and their doctors, but I quickly realized I was snapping at God in those prayers, demanding He come through for us. I thought of Donnie and how he'd lost his faith when God didn't save his sister. I wondered if I would lose mine if—

No, God. Please, no. Make a way. Make a miracle. Just please don't let anything happen to this sweet baby. Or Rachel . . .

Fifteen minutes later I rushed into the ER waiting area. Several of Rachel and Rich's friends from church were already there along with a few of the singles who'd been on the camping trip with us.

"What have you heard?" I asked, joining them.

"Nothing yet," a guy named John answered. "Rachel and Rich got here about ten minutes ago. They're pretty upset."

"Have you seen Tucker?" I asked.

"He was down here a few minutes ago. He wants you to page him."

"Okay, thanks."

I picked up the wall phone, called the operator, and waited impatiently to hear his name called over the PA system. A couple minutes later he showed up. I was surprised to see him wearing scrubs.

"Come here." He took my hand and led me out to the hall away from the others.

I started to ask, but the lump in my throat got in the way for a moment. "How's Rachel? Is she okay?" I whispered.

"She's stable. They're monitoring her now. The baby's heartbeat is very weak, so they're going to do a c-section. He's got to come out now or he won't make it."

A sob escaped before I could stop it. He gathered me into his arms. "Shelby, I need you to be strong, okay? I've got to run. I'm putting her to sleep so I need to scrub up."

I stepped back, wiping my face. "I'm glad you'll be there for her. Will you tell her I'm here and I'm praying for her?"

He kissed my forehead and turned to go. "I'll do it. Just keep those prayers coming. They need every one they can get right now."

I dug a Kleenex out of my purse and tried to dry my eyes as best I could before going back to the waiting room. Just as I walked through the door, Dr. Love strode in from the ER bay entrance.

"Shelby, how is Rachel? I came as soon as I heard."

He still looked a little pale to me, but I was so glad to see him. "She's going into surgery as we speak. Tucker said they're doing a c-section. The baby's heartbeat is too weak to wait."

"Well, then. I think we should round up the troops and have us a time of prayer. What do you think?" He patted me on the back as we joined the others. Had it really only been a few short weeks since we'd done the same thing for him in this same room?

Forty-five minutes later, Rich appeared looking visibly relieved. "He made it! He's okay!" Crocodile tears gathered in his eyes before breaking free.

We all exploded in overwhelming relief, smothering him with hugs.

"How's Rachel?" I asked when I got my turn to hug him.

"She's still sedated. She'll be in recovery for at least a couple of hours, then moved to a private room if everything goes well. I'm so glad Tucker was in there with her. They wouldn't let me in, so I'm glad he could be there for her."

"And how's that son of yours, Rich?" Dr. Love asked, shaking his hand.

"He's going to be in Newborn Intensive Care for a day or two, but as far as we know, he's fine. Gave us quite a scare, but he's fine. Just fine."

"That's just great," Dr. Love said, pounding him on his back. "And what did you name the lad?"

"Cooper Christopher Bauer."

"Well, now! That's a fine name. Good and strong, just like his father's. Congratulations, Rich. Will you give Rachel my best when she wakes up?"

Rich wrapped him in a hug. "Will do, Dr. Love. Thank you so much for coming."

The crowd began to thin out after everyone had a chance to talk to Rich. Tucker showed up a little while later and promptly dropped into the seat next to mine.

"I don't know about you, but I'm exhausted."

I looped my arm through his. "Yes, but you helped make sure Cooper had a birthday today, so what's a bit of fatigue compared to that?"

He squeezed my hand. "Hadn't thought of it that way."

"And Rachel's really okay? I want to see her so badly, I can hardly stand it."

"No problem. Come along, my little Moonpie."

He stood and led me upstairs to the recovery room. I knew she'd still be sleeping, but I just wanted to see her with my own eyes. We approached her bed. I pressed my lips together, determined not to cry. She looked so peaceful sleeping there despite all the monitors hooked up to her.

"You must have done a really good job. The Rachel I know would never be sleeping if she knew her little one had arrived."

He draped his arm over my shoulder. "That's why they call me The Gasser, my love."

I leaned into him, surprised to hear the term of endearment, but content to watch my friend resting so peacefully.

Tucker yawned. "So, you wanna go check up on the boys now?"

I looked at him, trying to decide if he was serious.

"Because I'm sure they'd be happy to see you."

"Thanks, but I think I'll take a pass. I've had about all the drama I can stand this weekend."

I stepped over to Rachel's bedside and kissed her forehead before we left. On the way back downstairs, Tucker asked if I wanted to take a peek at Cooper.

"Are you serious? You can let me do that?"

"Hey, I've got clout around here, remember? Just follow me."

A few minutes later we stood outside the window of the neonatal ICU. Tucker knocked on the glass and waved at one of the nurses then pointed to one of the special newborn beds. She nodded, then gently rolled the bed close enough to the window for us to take a look at Rich and Rachel's precious bundle of joy.

I'd thought I was done with the tears, but I was wrong. He slept peacefully, just like his mother downstairs, his face a healthy pink beneath a small blue stocking cap. Even with that cap on, we could see the curly blonde hair sticking out every which way.

"Will you look at that . . . he looks just like a little Rich with a head full of Rachel's hair."

"Cute little fella, isn't he?"

Just then, Cooper's face pinched up and he stretched, his tiny fists poking up into the air.

"I'm so glad he made it. I can't tell you how scared I was," I whispered.

"We all were. You're looking at an absolute miracle, Shelby."

A miracle . . . an absolute miracle.

Then, the strangest thought crossed my mind. Why would God grant one miracle and not another? I wish I understood why He did what He did. Because this hospital was filled with people needing miracles.

"Tucker, I need to do something. Okay if I catch up with you later?"

"Sure. I'm going to check on Rich, then head on home. I'm beat." He walked me to the elevators then gave me a weary hug. "I'll talk to you later, okay?"

"Get some rest, Tucker."

A few minutes later I stepped off the elevator on Nine. Sunday afternoons were a lot like evenings around a hospital. Quiet. Deserted. Strange.

I tapped on Donnie's door. "Anyone home?"

He glanced at me and used his remote to mute the television mounted on the wall. "Hey girl. What are you doing here? It's Sunday. Oh, wait. Let me guess. You're here to see Elvis and thought you'd stop by since you were in the neighborhood?"

"Very funny." I reached over and mussed up his hair before taking a seat.

"Ah, I know . . ." He poked his foot out from under the cover. "You came to say hello to Mr. Big Toe and give him the pedicure, right?"

"Not hardly. But you're right about one thing. He's green. That's really disgusting, Donnie."

"Yeah?" he mused, sticking his toe up for a better look. "Well, bring some nail polish. Something in the burgundy family. We'll just give him a makeover and no one will ever know he's green to the gills."

"Will do."

"So?"

"So I'm here because Rachel had her baby."

"Congratulations! Girl or boy?"

"Boy. Cooper Christopher Bauer. Cutest little thing you ever saw."

"Well, I'd ask you to wheel me down for a look at the little gipper, but I don't trust you to wheel me *anywhere*."

"Very funny. But even if I wanted to, I couldn't. He's in neonatal ICU. He almost didn't make it."

"Oh, Shelby. I'm sorry. I shouldn't have teased about it. Is he okay? Is Rachel okay?"

"Yes on both. He's going to be fine, I think. Rachel's good too. They did a c-section, so her recovery will take a bit longer, but she'll be fine."

"Good. I'm glad to hear that."

I leaned back in my chair and folded my legs beneath me, Indian style. "Tucker said it was a miracle that he made it."

"That bad, huh?"

"Yeah. That bad."

He looked at me, as if waiting for me to say something. I couldn't find the words. Donnie waited, the silence a little strange between us.

"Something on your mind, Shelby?"

I studied his face. He'd lost so much weight. His color was worse. Even his voice had weakened. I hated what all that meant.

"Have you heard anything?"

"About what?"

"About a possible transplant."

"Oh. That."

"Yes, *that.*"

"They put me on the list last night."

"They did? Donnie that's great! I'm so relieved!"

"Why?"

"Because you're going to feel so much better when you have a new heart!"

He narrowed his eyes. "Do you hear yourself? You used those exact same words when I was about to have my surgery when they brought me in here a thousand weeks ago. 'Oh Donnie! You'll feel so much better once you have your surgery!'"

I didn't particularly care for his mimicry, but I certainly hoped I didn't sound anything like it. "Be nice. I was trying to encourage you. How could I have known the surgery wouldn't take care of your problem?"

"That's just it. Don't you see? There are no promises here. So what if I get some poor sucker's heart who gets his head shot off."

"Donnie!"

"Well, you don't exactly get to pick the circumstances for the donor's ability to 'donate,' if you catch my drift."

"Still. Don't be crass."

"Oh, I'll be crass if I want to. I'm just saying, someone's got to die in order for me to live. That's not much of a game plan. And even then, there are no guarantees. My body might reject it. And even if it doesn't, the survival rate after a heart transplant is fourteen to eighteen months tops. What's the point?"

"The point is, Mr. Glass Half Empty, your body will probably accept your new heart and you'll go on to live a long and productive life."

"Or not."

When I scowled at him, he just shrugged. "Well, as long as you're on that list, you can bellyache all you want about it, but when the time comes, you'll be glad you were."

"Is that so?"

"Yes, that's so. And for the record, someone's already died so that you could live, Donnie."

His face registered confusion but only for a moment. "Ah yes, and here comes the sermon. Shall I pass the offering plate first or do we want to sing a couple of hymns first?" He did a ridiculous imitation of Jim Nabors singing "Just a Closer Walk with Thee."

"Very funny."

"Oh, better yet—how about a little Elvis? *Then sings my soul . . .*" Donnie sat up, striking the famous Elvis pose complete with an imaginary microphone. *"How great Thou art . . ."*

"Enough! Enough. I get it."

He leaned back against his pillow. "Sweetie, we've been all through that topic and you know how I feel about it."

"I know," I said quietly, looking down at my hands. "I just witnessed a miracle this afternoon. And I'm thinking another one's due. That's all."

He took a deep breath and blew it out with great gusto. "Oh, my little friend, if only it was that easy."

"Who says it isn't?"

"Don't, Shelby. Please? I don't want to fight with you."

"Yeah? Well, I'm not giving up. Whether you like it or not."

"Pray on, sister. Just make it quick. If some schmuck doesn't cash it in pretty soon, it won't matter anyway."

"Stop talking like that!" I yelled. I jumped up and leaned over his bed, grabbing him in a fierce hug, suddenly losing all my composure. "I can't stand it! I don't want you to die, Donnie!" I buried my face in his shoulder, crying. "I don't want you to die . . ."

He didn't say a word, but I felt him shaking. Pretty soon, he was sobbing in my arms. We sat like that for a long time, neither of us saying a word. When he finally grew quiet, I leaned over, reaching for the box of Kleenex, snatching several for him and another wad for me.

He wouldn't look at me for the longest time. I didn't want to say anything that might upset him, so I remained silent. After what seemed like an eternity, he patted my hand and whispered, "Thank you."

I squeezed his hand, leaned over to kiss his brow, then quietly left the room.

It might not have been the miracle I'd hoped for, but it was a start. A crack in the armor.

And for now it would have to do.

31

No question about it, I was head over heels, hopelessly in love, and none too shy about the fact. I rushed through my patient visits every morning then bee-lined to see him. I didn't even care if Mrs. Baker walked by and saw him in my arms.

The first time Rachel placed Cooper Christopher Bauer in my arms, I couldn't stop staring at him, touching him, cooing over him. Without question, this little guy was a heartbreaker, and I was first in line.

Rachel looked on, her weary smile warming her face.

"You really should go home and get some rest," I whispered.

"Shelby, if I hear that one more time I'll scream. I'll go home when Cooper goes home and not before. End of discussion."

I walked slowly around the room, the sleeping bundle of love cradled in my arms. "I'm not sure, but I think your claws just came out. Remind me to keep my distance."

She'd been released this morning, but refused to go home. They wanted to keep Cooper a couple of more days just to make sure his stats all leveled out. He was a little jaundiced on top of everything else, but overall he was doing much better. Once he was moved to the regular nursery on Five, she stayed with him every moment they'd let her, rocking him in her arms as often as possible.

She rocked, closing her eyes. "Comes with the territory. I had no idea I possessed that kind of protective streak in me. Must come as a package deal with the raging post-partum hormones."

I lowered myself into the rocker beside hers and matched her rhythm, laughing as Cooper nestled in my arms. "Oh, Rachel, he is the most beautiful thing I've ever laid my eyes on. I'm so happy for you."

She reached over, pushing a tiny curl from his forehead. "I know. I can't take my eyes off him. And I can't stop thanking God for saving him."

"Me, too," I whispered. "Rich said your mother arrived last night."

"Her flight got in at seven and by ten, I think she'd already stocked the refrigerator with half a dozen meals. Rich is loving it. But enough about us. Tell me about you. How's it going with Tucker?"

"Good, I guess. He's been working so much, I haven't seen a lot of him this week. But we had a good time on the campout. Well, until the fireworks went off."

She laughed, resting her head back on the rocker. "I heard about it. I hate that I missed all the excitement. Burt and Bobby stopped by to see me Sunday night after they were discharged. I'd just been taken to my room and was still pretty out of it, but that didn't stop them from giving me a blow-by-blow account of the whole thing. Those guys . . ."

"Rachel, are they really that immature or are they certifiable? You're much more patient with them than I am. I just hope we can keep Bobby from showing off his shrapnel, if you know what I mean."

Rachel covered her face with her hands. "Eww?!"

I leaned over and kissed Cooper then gently handed him back to his mother. "Well, I'd love to stay, but I need to get back to work. I'll stop by when I get off later, okay?"

"Sounds good. Love you, Shelby."

"You too, Rachel. Bye, Cooper. Love you!"

I was still basking in a borrowed maternal glow when I stepped onto the elevator. A doctor leaned against the back wall studying a notepad. I knew he looked familiar but couldn't quite remember why. Just as the doors started to close, Mindy stuck her hand in, making the doors slide back open in time to catch a ride.

"Shelby, there you are." Mindy joined me standing against the side wall. "I just ran into Tucker downstairs. He's looking for you."

"Yeah?" I felt the elevator start to rise. "Well, shoot. This is going up. I meant to go down."

"I get on the wrong ones all the time. Goes with the territory." She turned toward the doctor behind us, still engrossed in his notes.

"Hi, Dr. Nichopoulos. Nice to see you."

He looked up and smiled. "You too, Mindy. How's baby land this morning?"

"Busy as usual. Must have been a full moon this weekend."

He chuckled and went back to his notes.

I felt my eyes go wide as I caught Mindy's attention. *That's him? Elvis's doctor?* I asked, asking by way of facial expression.

She smiled wide and nodded nonchalantly.

I stole another peek at the distinguished looking doctor of one of the world's most famous patients. Sure enough, embroidered in blue there on his white lab coat, it said *George C. Nichopoulos, M.D.* His thick head of white hair betrayed his age, but overall his Greek heritage had blessed him with a handsome face which was remarkably well-tanned even for July.

I shook off my distraction. "So, where'd you see Tucker?"

"He stopped by the office hoping to catch you. He was having a chat with Mrs. Baker when I left."

"I wonder why he didn't just page me?"

"No idea. I'll see you later." The elevator stopped at Sixteen, and Mindy and Dr. Nichopoulos both stepped off. I pushed the button for the lobby, but just before the door closed, another hand stuck in to stop it. The doors opened again.

"We'll talk to you later, Dr. Nick," one of the men said. "We're gonna head out to the house for a while."

"Sounds good," I heard the doctor reply.

The doors closed after the three—two men and a woman—joined me in the elevator. I must have been invisible to them because they continued talking as if I wasn't there.

"If you'd just stop aggravating him, he might get well. Every time you go in there telling him you won't go on tour, you just upset him again. His blood pressure skyrockets. You've got to stop that. And I mean now."

I didn't recognize the man talking, but I knew immediately who the other two people were—Ginger Alden and Vernon Presley, Elvis's dad. I smiled casually and looked back up at the numbers above them.

"Stop badgering me. I'm sick to death of you all running my life," Ginger growled under her breath.

Does she really think I can't hear her?

"Bud's right," Vernon said quietly. "Whatever's going on between you two, put it aside for now. He's got to get better. He can't do that with you aggravating him every time you walk in the room."

She turned her back to me, but I could hear every word as she stood only inches from Vernon's face. "Fine. I'll just stop coming. That'll make it easier for everyone, right?"

"Now, don't go and do that, honey," Vernon answered. "It's even worse when you don't show up. He starts gettin' all hot n' bothered that you're gonna leave him. You know how paranoid he is. Can't you just calm down and put it all aside until he's better?"

The elevator chimed and the doors opened. They stepped off into the lobby and went the other direction. I couldn't help smiling, wondering if that might be the closest I'd ever get to Elvis. First, Dr. Nick, then the girlfriend and his dad. Never a dull day at BMH.

As I approached the office, I could hear Tucker's voice.

"But the back nine is rough. Especially eleven. I almost always end up three-putting, no matter how close I get to the hole."

"Oh, don't I know it! Last week I had one of my best rounds ever going, then I took a four-putt on eleven. About threw my putter into the lake."

"Well, trust me. It would find lots of company in that lake. I know there's at least a couple of my Titleists in there."

They shared a laugh before Mrs. Baker waved me in. "Tucker and I were just discussing the conditions out at the club."

"Hey, Shelby," Tucker said, turning to see me. "Mrs. Baker gave me permission to borrow you for a little while. Is now a good time?"

I looked at her, then him, then back at her. "Oh. Okay. If you're sure that's all right, Mrs. Baker?"

Mrs. B smiled. Clearly Tucker knew a little golf chat would grease the wheels. "Go. Just listen for your pages, dear."

"I will."

As we left, Tucker guided me out the door with his hand on my back.

"What's going on? Why did you need permission to meet with me?"

"I need to talk to you. Let's take a walk."

"Okay." I felt the strangest sense of apprehension come over me. "Is everything okay?"

He nodded, directing me toward the Union exit. The warm summer air felt good against my skin as we walked out into the sunshine. Tucker put on a pair of sunglasses and took my hand as we walked.

"I had a surprise visitor last night."

"Oh? Anyone I know?"

"Jimmy."

"Jimmy?" I slowed our pace. "I had no idea he was in town. Why'd he come to *your* place?"

He didn't say anything.

"Tucker?"

"Shelby, I think something's going on with him."

"What do you mean?"

"He wasn't himself. Not even close."

I stopped. "You're starting to scare me. He wasn't himself? What exactly do you mean by that?"

"Have you ever known Jimmy to drink?"

"What are you saying? He was drunk?"

"Just humor me and answer the question. Does Jimmy drink?"

"I don't know. I've never seen him drink anything alcoholic, but I guess it's possible. I mean, he was in Vietnam, for heaven's sake. Who *wouldn't* drink after something like that?"

He started walking again, tugging me along. "I know. I had the same thought. And don't get me wrong—I've had a few drinks in my time, mostly back in college. I just couldn't remember Jimmy ever talking about it or ordering alcohol whenever we've been together. Granted, I haven't seen him much since you all moved to Alabama. Just now and then, I'd hear from him, or he'd call me up if he was in town. That sort of thing."

"Was he actually drunk last night? Or did you just smell it on him?" I wasn't sure I wanted to hear more.

"Oh, he was definitely drunk. Smelled like a brewery, and he walked in carrying two six-packs. I didn't think that much of it at first, though it caught me a little off guard."

"Tuck, I don't understand. Why didn't you call me?"

"Because . . . I think it might have been more than just alcohol."

I stopped again. Something in the area near my heart began to hurt. "Meaning?"

He wouldn't look me in the eye, instead focusing on something off in the distance. "I'm pretty sure he was also high on something."

I just stared at him.

"Look, Shelby, it's simple enough to understand. The guy's been through a lot. I don't know about you, but he never talked to me much about what happened in Nam, but I'm sure it kind of messed with him. And it's no secret a lot of stuff went on over there. It was a popular topic of discussion in med school, all the addictions that were coming back with those guys."

"Did you ask him? Did you ask if he'd taken something?"

"No, I didn't. I wasn't sure what I might be dealing with, so I just acted like it wasn't that big a deal. He drank more than half the brews he brought in. Kept slipping off to the bathroom, blaming his 'peanut bladder.' He got a little miffed that I wouldn't drink with him."

I kept staring at him, not wanting to believe a word he was saying. I even wondered if he might be exaggerating. Though, for the life of me, I couldn't figure out why on earth he'd want to do that.

"After a couple of hours, he started getting really loud. All worked up about something, but I couldn't follow his train of thought. He wasn't making any sense so I just let him talk. At one point he kicked over my coffee table and—"

"Oh, please," I scoffed, dropping his hand. "You expect me to believe that my brother got upset and started kicking over furniture?" I heard my voice getting louder, but I didn't care. "Give me a break, Tucker."

"Listen to me! I'm trying to tell you! He wasn't himself. I've never seen him act like that. And there was a lot more to it than just drinking too much. I . . . I noticed his pupils were like pinpoints. It's called miosis. That's not something caused by mere alcohol."

"Tucker, will you stop? Listen to me. You know Jimmy as well as I do. He's not violent. He's the kid who's always the life of the party. Always working on a prank or, or—getting into mischief. Of all people, *you* should know that! But he's not stupid. Sure, maybe he had a few drinks. Maybe he's trying to forget everything that went on over there. But he's *not* a druggie. And in my entire life, I've never seen him do anything even remotely violent."

He grabbed my arm, but I wrenched it away. We stared at each other.

"Shelby, do you mean to stand there and tell me you think I'm making all this up?"

"Just tell me one thing," I said, glaring at him. "Why didn't you call me? He's *my* brother. If there was something wrong with him, you should have called me."

"I didn't want you to see him like that."

"What do you think I am, a child? So he was drunk. I've been around a few in my time. I could've handled it." I started to walk away from him. "Where is he now?"

"He was sacked out when I left this morning. I assume he's still home sleeping it off."

"Stop saying it like that! Like he's some hopeless drunk! Good grief, Tucker. I can't believe this. I wish you just would've called me."

"Then I'm sorry. Forgive me for trying to protect you." His tone grated on my last nerve.

"I don't *need* protection!"

"Fine." He turned around, heading back to the hospital. "Then, assuming he's still at my house, stop by and see him when you get off work. I'm sure he'd be delighted to see you."

"Why are you acting like this?" I yelled, rushing to catch up to him. "Jimmy's your friend. Why are you treating him like some freak who just came home from the war?"

"I'm not treating him like a freak! I'm worried to death about him, Shelby! You're not the only one who loves the guy, okay? I think I might have a few more insights—"

I rolled my eyes. "Give me a break."

He stopped, snapped the sunglasses off his face, then folded his arms tightly across his chest. Something along his jaw line pulsed. "What exactly do you want from me, Shelby? I care about Jimmy. I think he's got a problem. After all, I am a doctor, and I've treated junkies before. I just want to help. Why does that make me the bad guy here?"

I stared at him, so angry I was shaking. "That's just it, *Doctor* Thompson. I don't want *anything* from you. I never have and I never will. And for your information, my brother is not a junkie!"

I stormed off, rushing into the hospital while trying to bite back the fury that was consuming me. Of all the ridiculous, absurd things I'd ever heard . . . To think I had fallen for someone so . . . so self-righteous and pompous. Give a guy a stethoscope and he thinks he's some kind of god with all the answers.

By the time I rounded the corner near our office, I could hardly breathe. I took a sharp right and dove into the nearest public restroom. I slammed the stall door and kicked the toilet lid down so I could sit on it. It took a good five minutes before I caught my breath enough to think straight. And when I did, all I could think of was what a fool I'd been to think a grown-up Tucker Thompson was any different from that fat little kid that used to hang around our house and drive me out of my mind.

With my jaw clenched tight and my heart pounding, I thanked God for helping me see Tucker for what he really was before it was too late . . .

Before I fell in love with him.

32

Before I left the hospital that afternoon, I called Tucker's house hoping to reach my brother. He answered on the fourth ring.

"Hi, baby sister! I was figuring I'd hear from you. Tucker tell you I popped in on him last night?"

He sounded fine. Perfectly fine.

"He did. But I'm jealous you didn't come stay with me. What's he got that I don't?" It wasn't easy to keep the conversation light, but I knew I had to.

"Well, for starters, I know where he lives. Imagine my surprise when I knocked on the door of your townhouse and some dude answered your door."

"Oh, Jimmy! I'm so sorry! Didn't Mom and Dad tell you I'd moved?"

"Huh? Oh. Well, no. I haven't been home in weeks. It was great and all when I first got back, but then I got really restless. They wanted me to enroll for classes at Samford or apply somewhere else, but I needed some time. And some space, I guess. Decided to get on the road and chill out for a while."

"Well, that makes sense. You've probably got a little culture shock going on," I added, trying to test the waters. "I think a road trip or two is just what you need."

"Yeah, it's been good. I don't really have a plan or anything. I just get in the car and drive."

"Well, I'm glad you're here. But come stay at my place."

"You got an extra bedroom?"

"No, but you can sleep on the couch. It's nice and big and really comfortable."

"Why would I want to sleep on your couch when Tucker has a guest room? I've got my own room, my own bed, my own bathroom . . . Besides, he'll be gone a lot. Guy works like a horse. I'll just stay here. But you're welcome to come see me."

Not gonna happen. I'm not about to step foot in Tucker Thompson's house ever again.

"No, I'd rather cook for you tonight. I'll give you my address and you can meet me at my place."

"What's for dinner?"

Men and their stomachs. Apparently it's true what they say. But for now, at least I had a chance to see what was going on with my brother—IF anything was going on—without having Tucker's hyper-suspicious presence.

An hour later, I welcomed Jimmy into my house.

"Hey, big guy! Come on in."

He wrapped me in a hug and I inhaled, trying to discern the trace of any alcohol. I didn't catch the slightest hint. Nothing. I smiled.

"Whoa, this is nice, Moonpie."

"Jimmy, please don't call me that."

"What?" He took a seat on the sofa. "Oh, that. I forgot. You're the big grown up now. Can't tolerate the silly nicknames anymore. Right?"

"Something like that." He had it partially right. He didn't need to know I was also avoiding all reminders of Tucker Thompson I could possibly manage. "I'd just rather not hear it any more. What can I get you? The lasagna will be ready in a couple of minutes. Would you like some tea? A Coke?" I held my breath.

"Coke sounds great. Lots of ice. I'll never understand why other countries never give you ice. It's barbaric. So where's Chiquita, your feisty little roommate? Or do you live here alone?"

"Sandra's working the late shift tonight." I stepped into the kitchen to get his drink. "They've just started having us work the ICU, ER, and surgical waiting rooms, so we have to have someone there around the clock. She's thrilled about it. Loves all the action that happens in the ER after hours." I handed him the iced glass of Coke and took a seat across from him. "Me? I'd prefer to keep my day shift, but we'll see."

"You like working at the hospital?"

"I love it. We've had a lot of stuff going on, some conflicts—that sort of thing. But overall, I love it. I enjoy helping my patients and meeting new people all the time. Which reminds me, Elvis is staying with us again."

"Again?"

"Well, he's a bit of a regular, I guess you'd say. He's apparently got a lot of health issues and checks in now and then to get checked out."

"Or cleaned out, from what I hear."

I just looked at him while trying to choose my words carefully. "There's a lot of rumors about him, that's for sure. But I've never heard anything to substantiate it."

"Don't be naive, Sis. Everybody knows he's doing all kinds of stuff."

I looked him in the eye. "Define 'stuff'."

He laughed. "I have no clue. I just see the headlines, hear things. Is he really as fat as those pictures show?"

"How would I know?"

"You said he's at Baptist right now. Can't you go up and see him if you want to?"

Now it was my turn to laugh. I told him about the whole botched attempt to sneak up on Sixteen with Donnie. He got a big kick out of my misadventure. Jimmy didn't know Donnie, but he'd heard me talk about him before.

Over dinner we talked a mile a minute. I kept checking his eyes, looking for those pinpoints Tucker alleged he'd seen, but saw only my brother's beautiful brown eyes. I could still see the fatigue in them, for sure, but nothing out of the ordinary. He shared some of his experiences over in Vietnam and in the Philippines, but only when I asked. I could tell he really didn't want to talk about it, so I didn't push.

Later, we watched some television and made fun of the actors like we always used to do, adding snide dialogue to the script. I was careful to observe Jimmy without him knowing it. No shaking hands. No twitching. No munchies.

He was clean.

"What are you smiling at?" Jimmy asked, tapping my foot with his. "You've got a really weird grin on your face."

I debated whether or not I should say anything, then decided I had no reason not to.

"I wasn't going to tell you, but Tucker and I had a big fight this morning."

"About what?"

"You."

"Me? Why on earth would you all fight about me?"

I couldn't help analyzing the way he responded, which was complete innocence, of course. Then I chided myself for doing so. "He told me you were plastered at his house last night."

"What?"

"Can you believe it? I mean, c'mon, Jimmy. I realize you may have a drink now and then. And that's your business. You're an adult. You can do whatever you like. But he said you walked in carrying two six-packs, and you were already smashed before you stepped foot in his house."

Jimmy leaned his head back and rubbed his face. "What a pal. You think you know someone but you never really do. I can't believe he'd lie to you like that."

"And that's not all. He said you were obviously 'on' something. He thinks you're on some kind of drug. Jimmy, I wanted to smack him upside that handsome face of his. I was so mad! And I still am!"

He stared hard at me, shaking his head. "That's out of line. I can't believe he . . . that takes some nerve, dishing up a bunch of lies to you like that. I ought'a go over there and—"

"No, don't. I don't want you to say a word about it."

"Why not? He can't get away with it, Sis. I don't know why he'd say something like that to you, but I'm not about to just sit back and let him—"

I sat up and grabbed his hands. "Do not say a word to him. Let's just let it play out. See what he's up to. You've done nothing wrong, so for now just let it go. Let's see what other kind of lies he may come up with. Then we can confront him together. Rub his nose in it."

"I don't know."

"Yes, you do. Promise me, Jimmy. This is so out of character for Tucker—or so I thought. There's got to be some reason he's done this. Let's just give it a little time and see what happens."

Around 9:30, Jimmy took off. He assured me he'd be in town for a while, so I just gave him a quick hug and sent him on his way.

As I closed the door behind him, I let out a long and noisy sigh of relief.

Yes, I was relieved. If Jimmy was some slobbering alcoholic, I would have known it. If he was doing drugs, I would have been able to tell. And after confronting him with Tucker's lies, he would have told me. We may not have always gotten along, especially when we were kids, but I never knew him to lie to me. He would have come clean if there was something going on. I just knew it.

Still, something kept nagging at my soul.

For the life of me I couldn't figure out why Tucker would have made up such a thing about his life-long friend. What was the point? What possible motive could he have for doing something so vile?

I had a feeling we would find out. One way or another.

33

Rachel and little Cooper checked out on Friday morning. I would miss seeing them every day, but I knew Rachel was anxious to get home and settled again.

Sarah Beth announced that Elvis had also been released. To hear her, you would have thought he'd sought out her permission before leaving the hospital, but I'm sure that's not quite how it happened. I was disappointed I hadn't been able to cross paths with the King, but there was always next time. And from what I'd been told, there was always a "next time" with Elvis.

Tucker called a few times at first, leaving messages asking me to call him. But I never returned his calls. Fortunately, I hadn't run into him at the hospital, but I knew it was just a matter of time. Mrs. Baker had put me down to work the ER waiting room both Saturday and Sunday. It would be my first time doing so. I'd worked the ICU and surgical waiting rooms, but not the ER. I hated the idea of working the weekend, but at least it was first shift. In by seven, out by three. Better than all night long. Still, I knew Tucker often worked weekends, so that had me a bit on edge.

Before I left on Friday, Sandra showed me the ropes about our responsibilities in the ER. She told me we helped inform visitors of their patient's progress, primarily just letting them know where their friends and loved ones were. The medical information would come from the nurses and doctors, of course.

"Sometimes it's crazy busy and sometimes you don't have anything to do. I always bring a book just in case. You just have to stay at the desk here and be available. There's a little sign here in the drawer that you put on the desk when you take a break or go to lunch. Same as in ICU."

"That's it?"

"Oh, I almost forgot. We're also responsible for keeping the coffee bar stocked and fresh."

"I think I can handle that. Same as ICU and surgery waiting rooms?"

"Exactly the same." She unlocked a cabinet beneath the bar and showed me where all the supplies were kept, then showed me where to get the water.

"You wouldn't believe how nasty all this was before we started helping out down here. I was on duty the first night and those urns were disgusting. Took me a couple of hours to clean them adequately and make this place shine again."

"All this from the girl who once—"

"Shelby, don't make me hurt you," she warned with a smile.

"I'm kidding. You've obviously worked a miracle on the whole room. I've never seen it look so clean and cheery."

"It's nice, isn't it? Just needed a little TLC, that's all. The rest of the staff never has the time to keep it up. You'll like it here. The time goes fast when it's busy. Plus, you get lots of opportunity to help people when they're really scared and anxious."

"Oh, so I can finally use all that magnificent training we've had from Chaplain Perkins?"

"Most definitely. Just don't kill them with boredom. They've got enough to worry about."

"Okay, is that it?"

"That's it. Let's go. It's quitting time, girlfriend!"

It had been a rough week, so I decided to stay in Friday night. Sandra was going to see *Star Wars* with a bunch of the girls, but I wasn't in the mood. I was hoping Jimmy might come over. I didn't have any way to reach him without calling Tucker's house and wasn't about to take that risk. Jimmy had stopped by the hospital that morning, and we'd had coffee together during my break. He told me he'd played it cool with Tucker, basically avoiding him when he could.

I finally gave up waiting to hear from him and took a hot bath. I decided to just go to bed early and read. I'd just started a new book called *The Thorn Birds* and couldn't put it down. It was after midnight when I turned out the light.

Saturday, my first morning working in the ER, went well though I stayed busy. An early morning accident on I-40 brought in a handful of worried family members. An altercation between parents at a Little League practice game sent half a dozen wounded adults in around eleven. And a string of other patients appeared from time to time, just enough to keep things hopping. I still didn't like the idea of working on a weekend, but I'd survived. Around 2:30, I started a fresh pot of coffee and gave the area a quick clean up. Rebecca would be in soon for the evening shift.

I'd finished my chores and sat down to wait for Rebecca when Trevor showed up.

"Will wonders never cease? A hostess? Working weekends?"

"Very funny, Dr. Knight."

"How are you, Shelby? Haven't seen much of you lately," he said, pulling up a chair.

"I could say the same for you, but thanks for asking. I'm good.

How about you? Saved any brains lately?"

"Every day, m'lady. Every day. I'm glad you all are helping out down here. That's a nice touch."

"What can I say? We're here to help."

"Any word on those two knuckleheads who tried to blow up the campsite last weekend?"

"Haven't heard," I said, realizing I hadn't bothered to find out.

"Ol' Tuck and I had a good time driving those boys in. We started discussing their injuries—using lots of medical jargon just to scare them. By the time we got them here, I think they were convinced they'd never come out alive." He laughed hard. "Oh, I wish you could have been there. It was a beautiful thing to behold, weaving those two geniuses into our wicked spell. Didn't Tucker tell you about it?"

I blinked a couple of times and tried on a fake smile. "No, but we really haven't had a chance to talk much lately. He's been working a lot. You know how that goes."

"Please. Since we got back from that sad excuse for a camping trip, I haven't had a minute to myself." He sat forward in his chair, resting his elbows on his knees. "Shelby, I wanted to ask you something. Is our Sandra seeing anybody?"

"Sandra? Well, let's see. What day is it?"

His eyebrows took a northern hike. "Seriously? She dates that much?"

"I'm kidding, Trevor. She goes out a lot, but she's not seeing anyone steadily, if that's what you mean."

"So who's this guy Pedro? Bobby was telling me something that first night at the bonfire. He said Pedro was her 'beloved' and he was really mean. Someone I should be worried about?"

I laughed so hard, imagining all the bull Bobby must have shoved Trevor's way. "Oh Trevor, I don't think you need to worry about Pedro. But I'd rather let her tell you about him."

“So you think she’d go out with me?”

“I think she’d love to go out with you. Give her a call.”

He smiled like a school boy. “I think I will.” He stood up, putting his chair back where he got it. “Thanks, Shelby. And who knows, maybe we can double with you and Tucker sometime.” He winked and disappeared down the hall.

Yeahhh. Like that’s *gonna happen . . .*

34

After I finished my shift in the ER on Sunday, I went home and kicked my feet up for a while. Sandra had made her famous red beans and rice, as only Puerto Ricans can make it. The aroma wafting from the kitchen almost made me drool. We were just about ready to eat when Jimmy showed up.

"Where in the world have you been?"

"What are you, my mother?" he quipped, giving me a hug as he walked in.

"No, but you said you were going to be in town for a while, so I was hoping to see you occasionally."

"Well, take a look and see me now. I'm here! And just in time for dinner, by the looks of it. What's that I'm smelling?"

"Arroz blanco con habichuelas. My mama's recipe for red beans and rice. Come join us," Sandra said. "You'll love it. Shelby, pour him a glass of tea."

"Hey, Chiquita. Nice to see you again." Jimmy made himself at home, taking a seat at the table as Sandra put a plate and silverware in front of him. I was really disappointed he'd been so out of touch the last few days, but decided not to bug him after his comment. "So where've you been keeping yourself?" I asked, placing a napkin in my lap.

"I drove down to Tunica. Some guys in my unit live down there. We checked out the casinos. You ever been down there?"

"You'll lose your shirt at those places, Jimmy," Sandra said, serving him a plate filled with the spicy red beans and rice.

"Oh, man, this looks amazing." He forked a bite.

"Slow down there, hermano! Those are hot off the stove."

He took a bite anyway then reached for his tea before he barely started to eat. "Whoa! Those are some kind of *hot*!"

Sandra shot me a look. "He's *your* brother." She served the two of us then took a seat. "So how much did you lose?"

He was still gulping down his tea, then set down his glass and let out a long sigh. "So what makes you think I lost? I'll have you know I won a thousand."

"You won a *thousand* dollars?" I gasped.

He just nodded, proud as a peacock.

"Okay, hot shot," Sandra began, "but how much did you invest *before* winning the thousand?"

"Invest?"

"Surely you didn't win on your very first try. How much had you lost before you won?"

"Oh." Jimmy got up to fill himself another glass of tea. "I dunno, around that much. Maybe a little more."

"Jimmy!" I gasped, for the second time.

Sandra shook her head. "See, no one ever includes that little bit of information. It's all about how much you win, win, win. Never mind that you lost, lost, lost before you won, won, won."

"In other words, you pretty much broke even?" I asked.

Jimmy sat down again. "Well, not really. I made more than I lost."

"Like what—a hundred?"

"Well, no, not that much. What is this, an inquisition?"

We changed the subject and chatted over the rest of dinner. Sandra served her famous flan for dessert. It was amazing. So creamy, with just the right amount of caramel. She was such a good cook. Though how she ate like she did and stayed so tiny, I had no idea.

"Chiquita, thanks for dinner." Jimmy placed his napkin over his empty plate. "Make your roommate chip in and help occasionally."

"Hey, I do my share." I picked up our empty plates and put them in the sink.

"Well, I'm outta here," he said, heading into the living room. "I need to get some sleep over at Tuck's. Haven't seen him in a few days, but just as well. I guess you know he's been over in Nashville."

Nashville? Why was Tucker in Nashville? It explained why I hadn't seen him around the hospital, but—but it really didn't matter, did it? He certainly didn't owe me any explanations.

Before I could say anything, my brother continued. "And by the way, I'm leaving in the morning."

"Again?"

He opened the front door. "Yeah, I'm driving down to New Orleans for a few days. Not sure when I'll be back, but I'll let you know."

"Great. I'll hold my breath to hear from you."

"Jimmy, stay away from those casinos down there!" Sandra yelled from the kitchen.

"Wonderful. Now I've got three mothers." He smacked a kiss on my cheek and stepped outside.

"Bye, Jimmy. Be good."

"Oh, I will."

And oh, how I hoped he would.

Since I'd worked Saturday and Sunday, I got to take Monday and Tuesday off. It was strange being home on a weekday, but I have to admit I enjoyed it. I slept late, putzed around the house cleaning up a little, then drove over to spend some time with Rachel and sweet baby Cooper. Actually, I spent time with Cooper. He'd been up most of the night and Rachel was exhausted, so I sent her to bed for a long nap.

Have I mentioned how much I love the little guy? I'm fairly sure he already knew that Auntie Shelby was permanently wrapped around his tiny little finger. All he had to do was flash those baby blues, and I was a goner. We had a nice long chat, but as is often the case with the men in my life, I quickly put him to sleep. I gently placed him in the cradle they'd set up in the family room, then stretched out to read one of Rachel's magazines.

Rachel woke up a couple of hours later and wouldn't stop thanking me for letting her sleep. "Any chance I could hire you to do this full time?"

"Very funny. I'm sure Baptist would collapse without my presence."

"Oh, that reminds me. Have you heard the news?"

"What news?"

Just then, Cooper let out a fussy wail. "Dr. Grieve announced his retirement this morning."

"What? How did you find out?"

"One of the girls in my office called this morning. I can't believe I forgot to tell you. Then again, I'm surprised you hadn't already heard."

"So what does that mean for the hospital?"

"I'm not sure." She picked up Cooper then took a seat in her rocking chair and nursed her baby. It was such a sweet sight, the two of them. "But there will definitely be some changes," she continued. "And not the good kind."

"I don't like the sound of that."

"Neither do I. Being on maternity leave puts me in a vulnerable position, to say the least."

"Oh, they'd never let you go, Rachel. You're the one who keeps them running."

"Ha ha."

"Now, as a fairly new employee myself, that's a whole different situation."

"I know. I feel bad, helping you get a job right before this unfolds. Course, I had no idea this was coming. The thing is, we could all be out of jobs. Who knows."

"Stop. You're depressing me."

"So, how's it going with Tucker?"

I didn't really want to talk about it, so I made my answer brief. "Came and went. End of story."

"What?!"

"Rachel, it was such a long shot anyway. Especially with our history. I'm just glad I found out early on that it wasn't meant to be. He's a jerk. Can we just leave it at that?"

"No, we can *not* just leave it at that. I can't believe this! Tucker is one of the nicest guys I know. Why would you call him a jerk? What happened?"

I told her the short version, ending with Jimmy's lucid visit last night. "What I can't figure out is why he would do such a thing, Rachel. But I have to tell you, I'm relieved. Good riddance."

She stared at me, still gently rocking her son as he nursed. "Why is it I'm having a difficult time believing you really mean that?"

I shrugged and looked away.

"Has he called you?"

"A couple of times. I let the answering machine take the call. I'm not really interested in hearing any more of his analyses of my brother. Did I mention he's a jerk?"

"Tucker Thompson is not a jerk. You all just need to talk it out. I'm sure there's just been some sort of misunderstanding. Why won't you at least give him a chance to explain?"

"Explain what? That he's such a brilliant doctor he can diagnosis someone from across the room? Seriously, Rachel, it's over. Just let it go."

She shook her head. "Well, you should at least come to some kind of truce on the subject. You attend the same church, you work in the same building with him—you'll run into him constantly. Why not make the effort to smooth things over?"

"We'll manage."

Rich arrived home, thankfully providing an end to the subject. He brought home a bucket of Kentucky Fried Chicken and all the trimmings and insisted I stay for dinner. But when I finally made my way home later, I couldn't shake the dark cloud hovering over me. Everything seemed so out of sorts. *Everything.* And I wasn't quite sure what to do about any of it.

By the time I got back to work on Wednesday, I found an office filled with gloom and doom. Mrs. Baker hadn't said anything, but all the girls seemed to think it was just a matter of time before we all got pink slips. I got so sick hearing all of them talk incessantly about who was hiring, what kind of transfers might be available, and a whole boat load of other options. I grabbed my things and headed upstairs, needing to be away from it all.

I made my rounds then stopped by to visit with Donnie. He looked terrible. I couldn't believe he'd been here so long. After two-and-a-half months, he'd become good friends with the entire staff on my floor, and I was so proud of them for taking such good care of him. I'd prayed and prayed for him to get that phone call, the one telling him a new heart was available. But so far, nothing.

We were into another round of verbal sparring when I heard my name paged.

"Be right back, Donnie. Not that you'll miss me, of course. You seem to keep yourself well entertained without me."

"You got that right. Besides, it's time for my soaps. Don't hurry back."

I answered my page, and the operator connected me to the hostess office.

"Shelby, it's Sarah Beth. Mrs. Baker asked me to page you. They just brought Dr. Love into the ER again. She wanted you to know."

I took a deep breath and thanked her, then hung up. I raced back down the hall to Donnie's room.

"Donnie, it's my pastor. He's in the ER again. I need to go."

"Sorry, Shelby. Go. You know where to find me."

This time the ER was fairly vacant. Apparently the church members hadn't heard the news yet. I found Mrs. Baker sitting with Elsie who was sobbing.

This can't be good.

Debra was at the hostess desk so I checked in with her. "Have you heard anything?"

"No, but it must be bad. No one's making eye contact. And you know what that means."

I certainly did. Working with patients day in and day out takes a toll. It's hard to be openly compassionate around the clock. And when a situation is more serious than the staff may want to portray to the family, they avoid eye contact. At least some do.

"Do you know if he was conscious when they brought him in?" I asked her.

"He wasn't, which probably explains why Mrs. Love is so upset. I feel so badly for her."

We looked at my boss who was trying to comfort her dearest friend. Mrs. B looked up and waved me over. I quietly approached them. “Shelby, go see if the prayer room is available,” she whispered.

If ever an area of a hospital needed a prayer room, it was the emergency room. Just around the corner from the main waiting area, this particular prayer room was larger than those on the other floors. It had more rows of chairs and a larger kneeling area at the front. Finding the room empty, I returned and waved to Mrs. B, who quickly escorted Elsie there.

The day passed agonizingly slow. Eventually, I went back upstairs and tried to work, but I’m sure my patients thought a zombie had replaced their hostess. I ran several errands, helped three patients check out, and even played cards with a dear lady who asked me to help her pass the time. We don’t usually do that sort of thing, but I was glad for the distraction.

Before leaving for the day, I checked back with Mrs. Baker and learned that Dr. Love was in critical condition. I just couldn’t believe it. And I definitely couldn’t bear to give anchor to the thoughts that kept waving through my mind.

I wish Tucker was here.

I blinked, wishing that particular thought hadn’t buzzed through my mind either. Still, he would be able to tell me more and keep me updated on any changes in Dr. Love’s condition. If we were talking, that is.

How did life get so messy? Why did bad things always have to pile up this way? There wasn’t a single area of my life that wasn’t in turmoil right now. My job. Donnie. Dr. Love. Tucker . . . And even though I knew Jimmy wasn’t into all the things Tucker had suspected, I still wasn’t pleased that he seemed to be a little lost, wandering here and there. And gambling?

I shook my head as I walked back to the office to get my purse and finally call it a day. Sandra grabbed my arm, dragging me alongside her out of the building. “Hurry! I’ve got to get home and change!”

“Why? Another date tonight?”

“Not just any date. I’m going out with Trevor Knight!” She let out a little squeal and did her signature dance right there on the sidewalk.

I had to laugh. “Have I ever told you how much I love you?” I asked, drawing her into a side-hug.

“Huh? I love you too, but why’d you say that now?”

“Oh, nothing. It’s been such a sad day, but you always know how to bring a little sunshine when the clouds roll in.”

She hugged me back. “Ah, I’m so sorry about Dr. Love. He’s such a nice man.”

“That he is. But tell me about your evening. Where’s Trevor taking you?”

“He has tickets to see the Commodores! I can’t wait! How did he know I *love* them?!”

“The Commodores? Oh, I’m feeling some major envy coming on here.”

“Hurry!” She looped her arm in mine and propelled me toward the employee parking lot. “I want to take a shower and have time to do my nails!”

“All right, all right. I’m hurrying! Besides. I need to get home too.”

“Yeah? You have a date?”

We climbed into Sandra’s car. “No, but I have to write a letter.”

She cocked her head and pinned me with a glare as only Sandra could do. “You have to write a letter. Pray tell who you’re writing?” She roared the engine to life.

“Pedro, who else? I think your ‘boyfriend’ back home should know about your big date tonight. . .”

35

I was clearly experiencing déjà vu. I'd been in bed a couple of hours, unable to sleep. Sandra had returned home earlier and already gone to bed after her "dream date" with Trevor. But once again, I couldn't stop thinking about Dr. Love. I kept picturing him in ICU, lying there with all those tubes and monitors hooked up to him. I'd prayed and prayed but couldn't seem to find any peace in it. I kept feeling the strongest pull on my soul to be there. At the hospital. Ridiculous, right? He was no doubt still unconscious. And even if he wasn't, they'd never let me in ICU the way I'd snuck in to see him last time. Still, I knew I had to go.

About 1:00, I quietly got dressed, slipped out the door, and made the six mile drive to BMH. The streets seemed unusually eerie this night. I literally felt my skin crawl. *Twice.* But I knew I was doing the right thing. I didn't know why. I just knew.

I showed my ID at the ICU desk and told the receptionist I was also a friend of Dr. Love's. Of course, she couldn't give me any information—patient privacy rules—but she did tell me he was still unconscious. I thanked her and took a seat in the waiting area, unsure what to do. At that point, I felt so silly for being there. I noticed a sign over at the hostess desk: *Back in 20 minutes.* I couldn't remember who was working tonight, but I wasn't really in the mood to talk to anyone. Then I remembered the prayer room down the hall, and once again, feeling that earlier tug on my soul, I went in.

It was quiet in there. So quiet. Soft lighting, extremely low. And nothing but the occasional, rhythmic clicking from a ceiling fan to disturb this peaceful haven. I made my way to the front, put my purse on one of the front pews, then knelt on the padded kneeling bench. At first I just repeated some of my earlier prayers, the ones that hadn't seemed to help at all when I was home in bed.

Then I just started thinking about Dr. Love. About that first time we met in the church library. I remembered the faint scent of cigar that I later learned was so characteristic of him. His hidden little secret . . . though I'm fairly sure everyone in the church probably knew. I smiled at the memory. I remembered how quickly he put me at ease, how genuine he was, and how surprisingly "normal" he seemed for one who pastored such a large metropolitan church.

I remembered my many visits to his office and all of our chats. How he always made it seem like he had all the time in the world for me.

All the time in the world . . .

Oh God, please give him more time.

The tears came slowly at first and then something inside me seemed to break free. Like a dam that finally gave way, I couldn't stop crying, my heart in so much pain for this good and godly man.

"Why him? Of all the people You allow to get sick—why him, God? I just . . . I just don't understand. This kind and gentle man, so beloved and so cherished by so many people. Why him?" A sob caught in my throat. I reached for the box of tissues on the edge of the platform then tried to dry my face. A useless attempt.

"Oh God, please . . . please spare him. Don't let him die. Not now. Not like this. Surely there's more You have for him to do on this earth." I hiccupped a couple of times and continued. "He did so much for me, Lord. He helped me learn to trust again. To find my way again. And I know I'm just one of thousands he's helped guide back to You. So why, God? Why?"

I cried silently, shaking my head, wishing I could find answers to my questions.

"Excuse me."

I jumped up, startled at the sound of a man's voice. He was sitting on the back row, the light all but non-existent in that corner of the room. And for the third time that night, my skin crawled. "I'm sorry," I said. "I didn't know anyone was—"

"No, I'm the one who's sorry. I didn't mean to intrude on your privacy."

My heart was pounding so hard in my ears, I had trouble hearing him. I tried to take a breath but it kept catching.

"I couldn't help but overhear and wondered if there's anything I could do to help?"

Something in his voice sounded familiar. Still, this was awkward.

"No, but thank you. I'm sorry I was speaking out loud. I didn't know anyone else was in here."

I noticed he was fairly large as he stood up and started toward me, but oddly enough, I wasn't frightened. Something in that voice was very reassuring. As he neared, he took off his glasses, and I felt my jaw drop. He made his way past the four short rows of pews until he was standing only a few feet away from me . . .

Elvis Presley.

"May I?" he asked, indicating he'd like to take a seat on the front row.

"Uh . . . uh . . ." Nothing else would come out of my mouth.

"Please," he said, this time indicating I should sit down just across the aisle from him.

I nodded, unable to get anything else to come even close to my lips as I slowly took a seat.

"I truly didn't mean to eavesdrop, ma'am. But if you don't mind my asking, any chance this good man you've been praying for is Dr. J. Thomas Love?"

"Yes," I said in something like a gasp. "Yes, but how—"

"Oh, that's easy," he said with that world-famous crooked smile. "Because that's why I'm here."

I grabbed another tissue, trying to restore some dignity to my hopeless appearance. "Mr. Presley, how do you know Dr. Love?"

"Please—call me Elvis. Oh, Tommy Love and I go way back. We first bumped into each other a long, long time ago at the Cadillac dealership in town."

Had to be Daddy's. Had to be. "You bought your Cadillacs from my dad."

"You're related to Franco Brentwood?"

"No, my father is Jack Colter."

"Cadillac Jack is your daddy? Well, what d'ya know. How's that for a small world? Wait a minute. Are you the one I—"

"Met on Christmas eve a long time ago? You were there letting your friends pick out cars for Christmas. Yes, that was me."

"That shy little girl I had to coax to sit on my knee? That was you?" His smile grew bigger.

"Yes, it was. Although, I have no memory of it. I've just heard the story told over and over my entire life."

"Well, ain't that somethin'? I hope you'll forgive me for not remembering your name."

"I'm Shelby. Although, at that time I went by my real name, Rayce."

"That's it—Rayce. And you were the prettiest little thing. Why, I can't believe that little girl was you."

I toyed with the rumpled mess of tissues in my hand. I realized there wasn't a trace of mascara on them. Which made sense since I hadn't put on any make-up before leaving the house. *Oh great. I finally meet Elvis Presley—again—and I look like a train wreck.*

I looked back up and found him staring at me. The hair was still jet black and thick, and he still had those beautiful blue bedroom eyes. His face seemed a bit puffy but I figured it was due to some of the medical issues he faced. I'd heard there were many. Still, the charisma was there. I could finally understand why hearts broke all over the world for this man. There was an aura about him, impossible to put into words.

"How's ol' Jack doing? Sure miss him."

"He's good. Still down in Birmingham. Still selling Cadillacs."

"Well, who knows. Maybe next time I get a hankerin' to buy some new ones, I'll just run down there and buy 'em from Jack. Good man, that daddy of yours."

"Yes, he is."

He scratched the back of his neck and let out a big sigh. "It's a real shame about Tommy. He's been a good friend to me over the years. I hate that he's in such bad shape. Tore me up seeing him lying there like that."

"You saw him? Tonight?"

"Oh, sure. I made a call. His doctor's a friend of mine."

Well, of course he got in to see him. He's Elvis.

I felt my eyes well up again. "Still unconscious?"

"I'm afraid so. I'm used to seeing his face all crinkled up in smiles, used to hearing that laugh of his. Sure not used to seeing him . . . so lifeless." He shook his head and looked down.

"He told me you snuck in to see him last time he was here."

He lifted his eyes. "Oh, I do a lot of sneaking around, little lady." He winked with that smile this time. "I even drop in for church now and then. Sneak in late. Sneak out early. Incognito, of course. Story of my life."

I smiled at the thought of Elvis in some strange disguise. "He told me you all are good friends."

"We are. I don't get to see him that much, but sometimes when I'm in town, I'll call him up. Ask him out to the house. We always talk for hours. He's got this gentle way of telling you what the Bible says, what God says, without hitting you over the head with it, y'know?"

"I know. He's been counseling me for several months. I just hope I get the chance to thank him for all the ways he helped me get my life—" I choked up before finishing the sentence.

He reached over and touched my hand. I looked at that famous hand on top of mine and just could not get it to compute in my head. *Elvis Presley. Comforting me.*

"I hope you do too, Shelby. But if you don't, then don't you worry about it. He knows. Tommy Love knows."

I wept quietly, so frustrated at my inability to turn off the waterworks. He handed me a fresh white handkerchief. I thanked him.

"Shelby Colter, may I ask you a favor?"

I wiped my eyes again, then looked up into his. "Me? You want to ask me a favor?"

"Would you mind if I sang a hymn for Tommy?"

A baseball lodged itself in my throat and the floodgates opened again. I nodded, my face crumbling again at the sweetness of what he wanted to do.

"This is an old Mosie Lister song called "His Hand in Mine." Tommy was always asking me to sing it to him. Somehow it just seems like the right thing to do right now."

I tried to smile, couldn't, so just nodded again.

And then he started to sing. That famous old hymn in a voice so quiet, I couldn't hear him at first. The lyrics, so beautiful, so reassuring, sung in that deeply reverent way Elvis always sings his hymns. I couldn't tell which affected me more—those lyrics or that voice. It was one of the most touching moments of my life.

When he was through, he bowed his head. I assumed he was praying.

After the longest time, he looked up, his face streaked with tears.

"I'm real glad I had a chance to meet you, Shelby—again. You tell your daddy hello for me, okay?"

"I will."

He took my hands in his, and I felt every one of those big rings on his fingers as the distinct scent of Brut cologne wafted over me. "You make me a promise."

"Me?"

"Yes, you. You promise me you'll keep praying for our friend in there. You and me. Let's keep Dr. Love lifted up before the very gates of heaven. Agree?"

"I promise. It was nice to meet you, Mr. Presley. Again."

"Now, none of that Mr. Presley stuff. We go way back, you and me, remember? You just call me Elvis, darlin'."

"Nice to meet you again, Elvis."

He squeezed my hand and then he was gone.

My knees gave out and I dropped back into the pew.

Oh, my goodness. *Oh, my goodness.* I found it hard to breathe as the reality of what just happened sunk in.

I met Elvis Presley.

I had a private concert by Elvis Presley.

No one is ever going to believe this.

I sat there for almost half an hour, going over and over every word, every glimpse at those beautiful eyes, every tone of his voice, every touch of his hand . . .

And I realized something. Even *I* didn't believe it. How would anyone else?

And then I realized something else. I had a white handkerchief wadded up in my hand. A handkerchief monogrammed with the initials *EP*.

36

The entire next day felt out of body to me. From the moment I woke up after only two hours of sleep, I was quite sure it had all just been a long and vivid dream. I chuckled at the absurdity of it. *Impossible.* I showered, dressed for work, and was about to head out the door, when I saw it. There in my purse.

The handkerchief.

It really happened? It really happened!?

"What's wrong? You look like you've seen a ghost," Sandra teased, passing by me as she walked out our front door.

I locked the door behind me and followed her to her car. "You're not going to believe it."

"Believe what?"

I told her as we climbed into her car.

"You're right. I don't believe you."

"Sandra! I'm telling you the truth! Why would I lie?"

She backed out and we were on our way. "I have no idea. It's not like you, but it's still unbelievable. When I got home last night, you were in bed asleep."

I pulled the handkerchief out of my purse.

"What's that?" she asked, keeping her eyes on the road.

I shook it at her. She glanced at it then did a double-take. That's when she slammed on the brakes.

"SANDRA! Look out!"

A car sped past us, its horn blaring as the driver flashed a universal hand gesture. She quickly pulled off the road into a convenience store parking lot and stopped the car.

"That's . . . you mean, that's . . ."

"Yes. It's his. He gave it to me because I couldn't stop crying."

She grabbed it from my hand. She pressed it flat on her leg, smoothing her hand over those initials. "Oh Shelby! ¿Tu conociste a Elvis Presley? You really *met* him?" Then she held it up to her nose and took a whiff. "Brut! You really met him! I can't believe it!"

We were almost late for work by the time we arrived at the BMH employee parking lot. I told her everything. Everything he said, everything I said, and the way he sang the hymn, so soft and intimate as if singing it in the very presence of the Lord. She cried hearing that part, little softy that she was. Then came the squealing and the mile-a-minute chatter, much of it in Spanish.

The chatter continued through the rest of the day as Sandra told anyone and everyone about my encounter with the King. The girls were all thrilled for me, with the exception of Sarah Beth. Apparently I'd inadvertently encroached upon her sacred Elvis territory. She waved it off, quite unimpressed. I couldn't have cared less.

It was hard to concentrate on my work, but I did my best. I was surprised to find "a return customer," of sorts. When I checked my patient list, there was Mr. Wilbur Wilcox, my favorite train engineer. I couldn't remember how long it had been since he was here—a month or so? The fact he was back so soon couldn't be a good thing.

I tapped on his door and walked in. "Mr. Wilcox! How nice to see you a—" I stopped the minute I laid eyes on him. He looked pale and withered, a shell of the man I'd seen only weeks ago. I was absolutely shocked. "Mr. Wilcox, I . . . I'm Shelby Colter, your hostess. Do you remember me?"

He slowly tracked his eyes toward me and gave only the slightest hint of a smile as he nodded. "Yes. I remember." I could tell it took a lot for him to get those three words out.

I approached his bed. "I would like to say it's nice to see you again, but that's not usually the case when you work in a hospital. How are you?"

He shrugged, looked away, then back at me. "I've been better," he said, his voice raspy and quiet.

I didn't want to tire him out, so I tried to make it brief. "I'm so sorry you're not feeling well. I'm sure the doctors and the staff will do everything they can to help you get better. I'll place my card here on your table in case you need anything. Don't hesitate to call me. For anything at all, okay?"

A slight nod of the head and a weak smile was the best he could do.

I reached down and touched his hand. "You take care, Mr. Wilcox. I'll be praying for you."

As soon as I left the room, I bee-lined to the nurses' station. "Helen, what's going on with Mr. Wilcox on 903? I can't believe he's already back. He looks so much worse than before."

"I couldn't believe it either. Apparently the procedure didn't work as well as they'd hoped. And to make matters worse, his wife didn't give him the right dosage on his meds. She told Dr. Wells she thought she could save money by only giving him one pill a day instead of the six prescribed. Poor thing. She was so devastated when she heard the doctor's response about that, she broke down and went home. That was about 4:30 yesterday afternoon. She hasn't been back."

"Helen, that's so sad! When they were here before, she never left his side."

"I know. Slept on that awful couch beside his bed every single night."

"I hope she's okay. Has anyone heard from her?"

"Come to think of it, no. Not that I know of."

I just shook my head looking down the hall toward his room. "Can they do anything for him?"

"I hope so. They're trying to figure out which approach to take at this point. He should have come back weeks ago instead of letting himself get so weak."

"Life gets so complicated, doesn't it?"

"You've got that right. We'll do what we can, Shelby. Thanks for asking about him."

I made the rest of my visits then headed to Donnie's room looking forward to a nice long visit. Just as I was about to tap on his door, I heard the Harvey team paged to ICU. We heard those pages all the time, but I always tried to whisper a silent prayer for the patient needing the assistance of that expert team. And this time, I prayed it wasn't Dr. Love.

I also prayed that my friend on the other side of this door would never need them. I knocked gently then entered Donnie's room.

"Well, look what the cat dragged in," he snarked. "You look awful."

"Gee, thanks, Donnie."

"Come. Sit. Tell Mr. Rogers what's going on. Shall I call for some cookies and warm milk?"

I took the seat next to his bed. "No, thanks. But where's your sweater that zips up the front, Mr. Rogers?"

He snapped his fingers. "I knew I forgot something. I'll call Goldsmiths and have them send over a couple. Any particular color preference?"

"Oh, one of every color, I'd think." I smiled.

He tilted his head and narrowed his eyes. "I bet you *think* that's a smile, but it's actually a rather pitiful *attempt* of a smile.

What's got you so blue today?"

I told him about Mr. Wilcox and quickly noticed his countenance began to fall. *Nice one, Shelby. Cheer up your severely cardiac-challenged friend with the tale of another serious cardiac patient's woes.* I waved him off. "You don't need to hear all this. I'm sorry for bringing it up."

"No, it's okay. I'm not the only sad heart on this floor. I'm sorry to hear about his situation. But I'm sure you brightened his day with your Susie hostess schlep."

"Cute. Very cute. Unfortunately, Mr. Wilcox was so weak, he couldn't respond much at all. But enough about all that. How are you?"

"Oh, just a laugh a minute. Having the time of my life." He pursed his lips and lifted a brow. It was one of my favorite Donnie-isms.

"You know all the nurses up here love you. They all have Donnie stories they love to share. You're quite the rock star up here."

He rolled his eyes. "I get that everywhere I go. Never a moment's peace. The autographs, the constant flash of the cameras, blah blah blah. Such is the life of a celebrity. But someone's got to do it, right?"

I grabbed his arm. "Celebrities! Donnie, I forgot to tell you! Guess who I met last night?"

"Well, let's see. I watched Johnny Carson on the Tonight Show, so it couldn't have been him. And I know Bob Hope is on tour again in some faraway war zone—" He stopped abruptly and sucked a lungful of air so fast, I thought he'd pass out. "You met ELVIS?!" he screeched in a half-whisper, half-squeal.

"I did! I finally did!" I clapped my hands like a shameless adolescent.

He threw his head back on his pillow, practically wheezing with laughter. "Tell me EVERYTHING. Don't leave out a single syllable. Sit! Start. Now!"

"Well, I couldn't sleep so I—"

"No!" He grabbed my arm. "No, I can't wait. Tell me now. Did he kiss you?"

"Donnie! Eww? No, he didn't *kiss* me! He's twice my age and besides—"

"Besides what? You don't like world famous celebrities who are filthy rich and have the world on a string?"

Now it was my turn to purse my lips. "No, I do not, thank you very much. And for the record, the thought never even crossed my mind. Now. Do you mind if I tell you what happened?"

He straightened his blanket over his legs, folded his hands on his lap, and shot me a look. "Do tell. I'm all ears."

And I told him. He asked a million questions, just like Sandra had. He made more wild jokes and we laughed so hard—something we both needed.

"Did he have on all that gold jewelry? Was he wearing the famous TCB lightning bolt necklace?"

"No, I don't remember seeing it, so I guess not. But he did have rings on every finger of both hands. Oh, and a gorgeous watch. When he put his hand over mine, I noticed how unique it was. A huge silver thing. Like antique silver, you know? And a wristband studded with a bunch of stunning turquoise stones and diamonds. It looked like something you'd buy in New Mexico."

"Or Vegas?"

I smiled. "Good point.

"No cape?"

"No cape. He was actually dressed fairly normal. I noticed he put a hat on as he left. Looked like a fedora. Maybe that was his low-key disguise to get through the hospital at that hour of the night."

"Bummer. I was hoping he wore the cape."

"You would."

"And he really sang to you?"

"Well, no, he didn't sing to *me.* It was more like he was singing for Dr. Love. Almost like a prayer on his behalf. It was really beautiful. I wish you could have heard it."

"You and me both. In fact, I'm not sure I'll ever forgive you for not inviting me down to join your private party."

"Donnie! It was hardly a 'party'! I was in that prayer room bawling my eyes out when he came in. What was I supposed to do? Say, 'Excuse me, Mr. Presley, while I go fetch my friend Donnie. You just wait right here until I get back.' Oh, that would have been class. Pure class."

He stuck his chin up in the air. "So you say."

"Don't be silly. And get this. He told me he sometimes sneaks into our church to hear Dr. Love preach. He comes incognito. The whole nine yards. Can you imagine?"

"What's his disguise? An Elvis impersonator?"

I laughed again at that one. "I don't know but it's not a bad idea, if you think of it. You better believe I'm going to be on the lookout next time I go to church. So tell me, what's the latest? Have you heard anything?"

"Yes. In fact, just today they told me they're renaming the whole wing for me now that I've officially become their longest-staying prisoner—er, guest. There's to be a ceremony, the posting of a plaque—you must come."

"I sent in my RSVP. Didn't you get it?"

"Good one."

"So, what are the chances of you telling me what really happened and not trying to pull my leg?"

"Okay, fine. Nothing new. There's never anything new. They run tests. They 'consult'. They run more tests. My levels are up. My levels are down. Meanwhile, I sit here on my butt, day after day after day. Case closed."

"I just can't believe it's been so long. It absolutely boggles the mind. But then, I'm not a doctor."

"And we're all grateful for that."

I whacked him playfully then stood up. "I need to go. I'll pop in before I leave this afternoon, okay?"

"Pop away, my dearest. Pop away."

As soon as I stepped into the office, I knew.

Mrs. Baker wasn't seated behind her desk. I found her crying in the back office. Several of the girls sat around her, consoling her, many of them crying as well. Mindy's arm was wrapped over her shoulder. I caught Sandra's eye and let my face ask the question. She nodded, confirming what I suspected.

Dr. J. Thomas Love was gone.

He had slipped from this world into the presence of His beloved Lord.

I turned around and left.

37

By the time Sunday rolled around, I really wasn't in the mood to go to church. I had such an ache in my soul, still desperately wishing I'd had just one last chance to thank Dr. Love. To tell him how much he meant to me, how much he helped me, and how much I loved him. I kept remembering that night in the prayer room with Elvis.

"I just hope I get the chance to thank him for all the ways he helped me . . ."

"Don't you worry about it. He knows. Tommy Love knows."

In the greater scheme of things, I suppose it didn't really matter. But it mattered to me. It seemed so strange to feel such deep sorrow for the loss of someone I'd only known a few months. But that's just the kind of man he was. He always made you feel like the dearest of friends. The world would be a sadder place without "Tommy Love." I knew mine would be.

Still, I hadn't been to church in a while, so I thought I should go. Sandra was working the ER that weekend, so I went alone. Even at 10:30 in the morning, the mid-July heat was miserable. Just walking from my car to the sanctuary, I could feel the perspiration beneath my dress. Everyone had told me Tennessee summers were hot, but this was brutal.

I stepped inside the foyer, thankful for the blast of air conditioning that greeted me along with the famous Candy Man. Everyone at First Baptist knew the Candy Man. Charlie Driscoll served as an usher, manning his post faithfully every Sunday, greeting worshipers with a bag full of candy. The kids loved him. The children's' teachers? Well, that was a different story. After stoking up on sweets, the kids would roar into Sunday school on a sugar high, leaving their teachers and workers at wits end.

I selected a wrapped peppermint, thanked Charlie, then made my way into the sanctuary and took a seat. As I unwrapped the candy, I felt someone brush against my back, passing through the row behind me. I turned just in time to see Tucker sit down. Our eyes locked for a split second. It was the first time I'd seen him this close since our fight. Sure, it had crossed my mind that he might be at church today, but I figured I'd just avoid him. Unfortunately, I didn't have a plan B.

"Hi, Shelby."

"Hi, Tucker."

"How are you?"

"Good, thanks. You?"

"Good."

So. It's come to this. Polite conversation and nothing more.

The organ saved the day, blaring into a majestic version of "A Mighty Fortress is Our God." I smiled at Tucker then turned back around, more than grateful for the interruption. Of course, my mind was focused on the individual sitting behind me, so little else during the service filtered in. Mrs. Baker's husband, the reverend, opened his message with a kind tribute to Dr. Love. Our programs included a picture of our pastor along with a brief note and a time for this afternoon's memorial service. As the sermon began, I looked down at Dr. Love's photograph, felt a sting in my eyes, and quickly tucked it inside my Bible.

When the service was over, I knew there was no way to leave without talking to Tucker. I decided to take the high road and act like nothing in the world was wrong.

"I hear you went to Nashville," I said as we each emerged from our rows into the aisle.

"I was. Spent about a week there for a conference. It's good to be home. Although I was sure sorry to hear of Dr. Love's passing. Trevor called and told me. Will you be at the memorial service this afternoon?"

"Of course. I want to pay my respects." I really wanted to get off the subject and keep the tears at bay.

"Well, then. I'll see you later."

With that, he turned and left. I hated this. Hated the awkwardness of it all. I'd had so little time to think about what had happened—no, I take that back. I'd *avoided* thinking about Tucker as much as I could. It all seemed so stupid. And yet, I could still feel the resentment, a slow burn deep within me. No matter how hard I tried, I couldn't convince myself Tucker was right about my brother. I knew better. I'd seen Jimmy with my own eyes. He was fine. Footloose, perhaps, but fine.

And yet . . . and yet, I missed Tucker terribly. Seeing him was even harder than I'd imagined. I'd missed his sweet smile, that goofy look in his eyes when he teased me, the compassion on his countenance for others. Regardless what I'd told Rachel, Tucker Thompson was a good, good man. He'd just stepped over a line. One I was not yet ready to forgive.

Not that he'd asked.

I grabbed a quick bite to eat at Danver's, then ran a couple of errands in town before heading back to the church for the memorial service. I knew the church would be packed, so I made sure I got there in plenty of time. Or so I thought. I had to park in the farthest parking lot, then as I got closer, I found myself blocked behind a large group of senior citizens, some with canes. I didn't know it was humanly possible to walk that slow. By the time I finally stepped inside the sanctuary, there were only a few seats left on the first floor. I ducked off to the right and took the stairs to the balcony, hoping for a better seat. It was nearly full as well. I found a seat on the back row and made the best of it.

When I finally looked below, I saw the casket. A stunning mass of red roses blanketed the coffin. I swallowed hard and reached into my purse for a tissue. There, beside my billfold and keys was the handkerchief. I felt a slight smile as I folded it into my hand. It felt right somehow, holding this reminder of the man who also loved my pastor. In a strange sort of way, I felt comforted just holding it in my hand.

The family entered as the organ quietly played "Jesus, the Very Thought of Thee." I spotted Mrs. Baker, not far behind Elsie in the procession. Not family, but certainly the best of friends. Reverend Baker was already on the platform. He would be giving the eulogy. Once everyone was seated, the service began. From start to finish, it was wonderfully befitting the man whose life we celebrated. Reverend Baker's message was touching, filled with humorous anecdotes of his life-long friend who loved to laugh. He told one example after another of the many lives forever changed because they'd crossed paths with Dr. Love. His voice cracked as he bid a final farewell on behalf of the family, friends, and church family.

"Shall we pray," he said, and we all bowed our heads.

But just as I started to bow my head, something caught my eye. I turned around after noticing a man in sunglasses standing just a few feet from me near the exit. His blond curly hair and beard struck out in stark contrast to his black pin-stripe suit. As I glimpsed his way, he scratched his head. I noticed his whole head of hair moved ever so slightly. As he nudged what appeared to be a strange toupee, I saw it—there on his wrist, a turquoise and diamond watch. I blinked twice to make sure my eyes weren't playing tricks. Just as he turned to leave, he looked my way. He paused briefly, lowered his sunglasses, and tossed me a wink. Just as quickly, he pushed his shades back in place, that wide crooked smile creeping up the side of his face.

I smiled back.

In fact, in spite of my sorrow, I don't think I stopped smiling the rest of the day.

38

The following weeks rambled on. I was in such a funk, I found no interest in much of anything. Sandra and Trevor were seeing more and more of each other whenever they could. They were so cute together—Trevor, over 6'4", and tiny Sandra, not even 5'2" in heels. I was really happy for them, but I missed having Sandra around at home. Of course, a resident's schedule doesn't leave much free time for extensive dating, but somehow they worked it out. I loved seeing her so happy.

But "happy" had long since disappeared from my horizon.

In fact, as happy as I was for them, their relationship seemed to mirror a sharp contrast to how much I missed Tucker. We'd run into each other from time to time at work or at church. It was always awkward, always strained. Once, during the worship service, I glanced over and caught him staring at me. But when I attempted to smile, he just looked away. It surprised me how much that hurt. I began avoiding church whenever possible.

Donnie was getting worse every day. I never missed a day's visit, but it was getting so difficult to be cheerful as I entered his room. Even harder to hide how scared I was for him.

As July melted into August, I still hadn't heard from Jimmy. It had been more than a month now. By this point, I was more angry than disappointed. The least he could do was call. I checked in regularly with Mom and Dad. They hadn't heard from him either, but seemed much more understanding than I was.

"He just needs a little more time to readjust," Mom had said.

I just hoped he hadn't lost his shirt down in New Orleans. I was half-tempted to drive down there some weekend and try to find him, but I nixed the idea. What would I do? Just walk through the Quarter and hope to bump into him?

The office atmosphere continued on a downhill slide as well. Chelsea and Rebecca had already handed in their two-week notice to Mrs. B, having found jobs elsewhere. The rest of the girls were busy scouting the paper for job opportunities. I knew I should be doing the same, but I couldn't make myself do it. Not yet.

As for Mrs. Baker, we'd all noticed how much she had changed. The loss of her friend and pastor had visibly affected her. I realized she wasn't scheduling afternoons off to play golf anymore. She kept mostly to herself, rarely coming into the back office to visit with us in the afternoons like she'd always done. And her smile was manufactured when needed. As if a great black cloud had descended over her and wouldn't go away.

I have to admit, I felt like it was hanging over me, too. It wasn't like me to stay down and blue like this. But I just couldn't shake it. I threw myself into my patients' needs, visiting them more than I ever had. Most of them seemed to love the extra attention—but not all.

I'd just knocked on 910 and said hello to Daphne Lee Crockett. She'd been here for a week now and was still waiting on results from all the tests they'd been running. I'd already stopped by several times and run a couple of errands for her.

"You again?" She let her newspaper fall onto her lap.

She sounded so terse I assumed she was teasing. I was wrong.

"Young lady, if I need something, I'll call you. I don't like to be constantly bothered, and I certainly don't need babysitting. So just scoot your little self right back out that door and leave me be."

"Uh . . . oh, okay. I'm sorry. My apologies." I ducked back out the door, wondering if she'd hurl a pillow at me if I didn't. I also wondered why everyone on the planet seemed to be in the pits. I took a deep breath, straightened my uniform, then tapped on 912 to check back in on Mr. Slidell.

"Oh, good. I was just about to call. Could you hand me the bedpan, miss?"

Not my job!

Some days you wonder why you even bother to get out of bed.

By mid August, I was actually relieved whenever my turn rolled around to work in the ICU or ER. On Saturday, August 13th, I was scheduled to work the 3:00 ER shift, which was good. It meant I still had a big chunk of the day to myself before I went to work. And since Saturday nights were always the busiest night of the week in the ER, I knew the time would fly by.

Before I went to work, I cleaned the house then decided to work on my pitiful tan. I stretched out on a lounge chair in our backyard and felt the heat against my skin while I listened to Stevie Wonder, the Eagles, Jimmy Buffet, and Fleetwood Mac on my radio. But the music didn't help. My mind kept traipsing off in directions I didn't want to follow, so I eventually gave up, showered, and went to work.

But when I arrived at the ER just before 3:00, I caught a brief glimpse of Tucker down the hall. *Just my luck. He must be working the same shift.* Thankfully, he wasn't in the ER for long and exited without seeing me. I hated this game we seemed to be playing. Or was it just me? Maybe he'd long forgotten what we had . . . or what we *almost* had.

I did my best to avoid him, which was fairly easy since anesthesiologists don't normally hang out in the ER unless they're called in for a particular problem. I'd managed to evade any face-to-face interaction right up until 10:30 that evening. That's when the ER receptionist asked if I would help an elderly woman back to see her husband in Trauma 2. I helped her to his room and made sure she was okay. Then, as I was making my way back to the waiting area, I spotted Tucker. I'm not sure why he was back in the ER again, but there he was—leaning against the wall, his right knee hiked up with his foot anchored against the wall behind him. It's how he always stood whenever we talked in the hall. Just a silly nuance, something I'd always found endearing. But this time, a very attractive nurse stood close to him, obviously sharing a joke. I didn't recognize her, but I could tell this wasn't a doctor/nurse consultation. This was much more personal.

I know it's absurd, but I felt like someone punched me in the stomach. I had no logical reason to react that way. We weren't in a relationship. He could talk to whomever he pleased.

Before another thought crossed my mind, the bay doors just beyond where Tucker and his friend were standing slammed open. Paramedics rushed in with a bloodied patient on a stretcher, shouting as they rounded the corner toward Trauma Room 1.

"Pedestrian hit by a truck. Multiple injuries. Contusions, abrasions, BP's falling, 72/40. Pulse 120. He's had two morphine and two liters saline."

The doctors and nurses went to work, guiding them into the examination room, Tucker and his friend joining them.

As I started to return to my post, I heard someone shout my name.

"Shelby!"

I turned, surprised to see Tucker rushing toward me, his face etched with concern. "It's Jimmy."

"What?" The air whooshed from my lungs. "That's not possible. He's—"

He gently grabbed my arm and nudged me toward a row of chairs lining the wall. "It's him, Shelby. It's Jimmy. Let me go back and see what's going on. I'll let you know. Just don't leave."

I nodded, unable to speak.

I lowered myself into a chair, my mind swirling with questions. *How could that be Jimmy? He's supposed to be in New Orleans, right? If he'd come back to Memphis, he would have called. I don't understand . . .*

Twenty minutes later I would understand—much more than I wanted to. Tucker came back down the hall toward me.

"Shelby, come with me. We need to talk."

Oh God.

Of all places, he led me into the prayer room.. He placed his hand on my back, moving me toward the back row where we both sat down.

"Tucker, you're scaring me. What's happened? Is Jimmy okay?"

"He's in bad shape, but I think he'll make it—"

"You *think*? What's that supposed to mean?"

"They said he was walking down the middle of Union Avenue—"

"What?"

"A delivery truck had just turned the corner and didn't see him. Plowed him down. It looks like he's got some broken ribs, a ruptured spleen, and a serious head injury from hitting the pavement so hard."

My shoulders began to shake as I completely lost it. I heard myself crying as if from across the room. "Oh, Jimmy . . . oh God!"

Tucker wrapped his arm over my shoulder, his head resting atop mine. "Shelby, listen to me."

I kept sobbing. I felt like I might get sick.

He lifted my chin, making me face him. "Listen to me. They need to operate on his spleen STAT. I need you to get a hold of yourself and sign some papers for me. Can you do that?"

I seemed to have no control over my extremities. Everything was trembling. "But Tucker—"

"We can talk more later. I promise. I've got to get upstairs to give him his anesthetics, so we need to do this now. Right now."

He stood up, helping me to my feet. I wasn't sure I could stand on my own. "But Tucker—"

And then he wrapped me in his arms. He rested his head on mine again, saying my name softly, over and over. I gripped the front of his shirt so hard and buried my face against his shoulder, my tears soaking his white lab coat.

"Shelby, I have to go. Here—" He handed me his handkerchief. I would have laughed at the irony of it if I hadn't been crying so hard. "We've got to get those papers signed, sweetheart. Come on." He grabbed my hand leading me back out into the ER hallway as I wiped my tears.

In less than a minute he was gone. I signed the papers and turned just as he ran out the door toward the OR.

In something I can only describe as a dense, thick fog, I made my way back to the prayer room, stumbled toward the front of the room . . . and collapsed.

Over the next hour I talked to Mom and Dad twice, called Sandra and asked her to come, paced the ER, prayed in the prayer room, and cried enough tears to fill the Atlantic. Mom and Dad promised to be on the road to Memphis as soon as they could get dressed. Sandra showed up and quickly came to my rescue, helping calm me down and stop pacing. She was such a rock. I couldn't have made it without her. Trevor showed up a few minutes later and offered the kind of reassuring presence only a doctor can. He had the access we didn't to find out what was happening up in the OR. He quickly escorted us upstairs to the surgical waiting room then disappeared to find out what he could.

Through it all I prayed constantly. Aloud. Under my breath. Silently. I prayed. Begging God to spare Jimmy. To give him another chance. And I took a U-turn whenever my thoughts tracked too close to the reason he was in that OR. I couldn't handle that right now.

After the longest three hours of my life, the surgeon and Tucker pushed through the doors and into the waiting room.

"He made it," Dr. Lewis said, his mask hanging from his neck. "Your brother did just fine, all things considered. He's not out of the woods yet and has a long road ahead of him, but he's stable. And that says a lot."

I thanked him profusely, wanting more details, but knowing those would come later from Tucker.

"He'll be in recovery for a good while yet. I won't release him to a private room until I'm sure he's a little more stabilized. But you can let go of that breath you've been holding now, Miss Colter."

I did just that and shook his hand, thanking him again.

Tucker gave me a side hug. "You doing okay?"

"Yeah, I think so. Was it bad up there?"

Sandra and Trevor closed ranks in our little circle as Tucker told us about the surgery. I didn't understand most of it, particularly in my emotionally drained state of mind. He continued, and while I couldn't comprehend what he was saying, his tone told me what I needed to know. Jimmy would be okay.

"That's a good sign," Trevor added. "Basically means he won't suffer any long-term memory loss. Though he might not remember the accident. Which might not be a bad thing."

"Tucker, do you have any idea what happened?" I asked. "Did the paramedics explain how he was hit?"

He looked exhausted, raking his hand through his hair. When he looked up, I couldn't read the expression on his face. "Maybe you should wait and discuss this with the police who worked the scene."

"Why? Why can't *you* tell me?"

"Shelby . . . I just don't think I should be the one to—"

"What aren't you telling me, Tucker?" I pushed. "Please—this is Jimmy we're talking about!"

"Precisely," he said, in a much-lowered voice, "And as you'll recall the last time we talked about Jimmy was the end of us."

"We're gonna take off," Trevor said, giving me a hug. "You take care and we'll talk soon."

Sandra hugged me, too. "We'll be in the building. If you need me, just have me paged, okay?"

"I will. Thanks, Sandra."

As they left, Tucker suggested we take our conversation somewhere more private. We decided on the hostess office since no one would be there. After we entered and turned on the lights, we each took a sofa in the back office and resumed where we'd left off.

"Look, Shelby. I'm not trying to be mean or obstinate here. I'm trying to do what's best. For both of us. And I just think the police will be able to tell you the facts much better than I can."

I folded my legs under me and tried to get a grip. "I appreciate that. I do. I realize I came down on you awfully hard when we—when I . . . And no offense, but right now I have to think about Jimmy. If it causes another rift between us, so be it. I *have* to know."

He studied me for a moment then gave in. "If that's your preference—"

"It is."

"Shelby, he was drunk. His blood alcohol level was at 0.15. More than twice the legal limit. I doubt he had any idea he was walking down the middle of Union. I doubt he had a clue *where* he was."

I stared at him, trying to keep my mind open.

"And . . ." He paused.

"Go on."

"They found marijuana on him. A pretty big stash of it. Along with some pills which we suspect are amphetamines. I'd guess speed. Who knows what the toxicology report may show when it comes back."

I dropped my head in my hands.

"I wish I didn't have to tell you this, especially after everything we've been through."

I nodded, my head still in my hands. "Oh, Jimmy."

I felt the warmth of his hand on my back as he took a seat next to me. "I'm so sorry, Shelby."

"No. No, I'm the one who should be apologizing." I looked up at him as a tear spilled down my cheek. "You tried to tell me, and I wouldn't listen. Oh Tucker, if only I hadn't been so stubborn! If only I had listened instead of snapping your head off. Maybe I could have helped Jimmy instead of . . . of . . ."

"We can talk about all that later. Right now you just need to be there for Jimmy. Neither of us really know what's been going on with him. God knows he's been through hell during the war. They all have. But at least he's alive. He's going to recover. And then we can get him some help."

I wiped my tears away, *so* sick of them. I tried to think of what to say, but I couldn't stand it another minute. I wrapped my arms around him, burrowing my head on his shoulder. "I'm so, so sorry."

He held me for the longest time in the silence of that small room. "There's a lot we need to talk through, but I've got to get back to work. I've got another 24 hours on my shift. But when I get off, I'd like to go somewhere we can talk. Are you open to that?"

"Yes, of course. I'm not leaving. My parents are due anytime, so I'll be with them until then. At least until Jimmy is moved to his own room."

As we stood to go, he pulled me into his arms and held me tight. "I'm here for you, Shelby. Please let me."

I nodded against his shoulder. He kissed the top of my head then was gone.

39

The next 24 hours seemed like a blur to me now. Mom and Dad finally arrived. They were frantic by the time they finally walked into the hospital. We had a good cry together as I filled them in on everything—including Jimmy's troubled road. They were shocked then deeply grieved that they'd missed any of the warning signs. As was I. Jimmy was moved to a private room on Twelve around midnight on Sunday. We immediately moved in with him, not willing to leave his side.

I couldn't help thinking of all my patients whose family members stayed with their loved ones around the clock. And I thought of those with no visitors at all. Hospitals could be a place of comfort in the worst of circumstances, but they could also be one the loneliest places on earth.

When Jimmy finally came around he wept openly, seeing us all there, and didn't stop crying for a long, long time. The accident had opened a wound that was much deeper than any of those on his body. He poured out a story filled with unimaginable, horrific scenes played out in the jungles of Vietnam, over and over throughout his tour of duty. He shared the nightmares that consumed him, most filled with endless visions of floating body parts and the empty stares of buddies who never made it home. He wept as he told of the gut-wrenching fear he faced every second he was there . . . and the blessed, numbing effects of the alcohol and drugs he willingly turned to.

But we were probably more shocked when he admitted lying to us about his extended tour of duty. He stayed in that part of the world because he was too afraid to come home. Too afraid to let his family know the ugly truth. The grip of his addictions held allurement; going home scared him to death. Even though his tour of duty was over, he'd basically wandered around Thailand, Malaysia, and the Philippines for most of those two years after the fall of Saigon. Occasionally he'd find a job to make a little money, but mostly he just roamed those foreign soils and got high.

For more than two hours, he aired out the haunting memories and anxieties that still chased him. He told us of waking up on a street in a small village as little children poked sticks at him and dogs sniffed him. He had no clue how he got there or what he'd done for the previous ten days. That's when he decided he had to clean himself up, get his act together, and go home. And that's just what he did. He slowly weaned himself off the worst of the drugs, started running to get back in shape, and finally put a plan in place to get himself back home.

"Wait a minute," I said. "If you were no longer in the Army, how did you get a hop back stateside on a military plane?"

"I'm a veteran now, Moonpie. I knew I could get a lift if I talked to the right people. I just made a few phone calls and called in a few favors."

I thought back to the day I'd picked him up at the base in Millington. He'd been wearing his Army fatigues. Carrying an Army duffel. He looked so healthy and tan and had obviously been working out. But that had all been nothing more than a grand performance, staged to make us think he was finally released from his military deployment and perfectly fine.

How easily we'd been duped.

Except Tucker, that is. He'd been able to see what none of the rest of us could—a crack in the armor of Jimmy's well-orchestrated façade.

When Jimmy finished, we smothered him with love and assurances, our own tears mingling with his.

The healing had begun.

Tucker called Monday morning and asked if I would have dinner with him Tuesday night. My parents had booked a room at a hotel near the hospital; Mom and Dad taking turns staying nights with Jimmy. By then, the thought of being away from Baptist sounded good to me. Really good.

He took me to Frank Grisanti's over on Main, a quaint and cozy Italian place where Dean Martin tunes played quietly in the background. We dined on steaming plates of pasta and crusty garlic breadsticks. And I was overwhelmed with relief as we quickly fell back into rhythm with each other.

"This is nice. Thanks for inviting me, Tucker."

"You're welcome. I'm glad you and your parents had a breakthrough with Jimmy."

"Well, it's a start. He knows he needs serious counseling to deal with all the demons he brought home with him, but it seems like he's genuinely ready to start."

"That's half the battle. Admitting you need help. Good for him."

We talked a while longer, then I pushed my near-empty plate aside and folded my napkin. "Are we okay, Tucker?"

He took a sip of water and set his napkin aside. "I think so. But we need to clear the air. You up for that conversation?

"I am if you are." My heart rate spiked, but I knew we needed this to happen.

"Then let me just put it out there. I have to be completely honest with you, Shelby. It *killed* me how quickly you threw us away. We had an argument. That happens. All relationships hit road bumps now and then. But the minute it happened, you were done with me. You wouldn't take my calls. You avoided me at the hospital, until I finally got the message. And I just couldn't believe it. I couldn't believe you'd give up on us that way. And what I need to know is why? Why were you so ready to bolt the first time we had a fight?"

I lowered my eyes, avoiding his penetrating stare. "That's a fair question, and one I've asked myself many times over the past few weeks. I wish I knew. I really do, Tucker. Initially, I think I was so shocked by what you'd told me about Jimmy—and it made me crazy, wanting to defend my brother."

"Which I understand. Blood is thicker than water, isn't that what they say?"

I looked back up at him. "Yes, but I'm no idiot. It's no secret that a lot of our guys came home with problems, and not just war fatigue. But I could not, in my heart of hearts, believe Jimmy would ever do something so stupid."

"In all fairness," he interrupted, "under the circumstances, I wouldn't call it 'stupid'—he just needed help to deal with what had happened to him but he didn't know how to get it."

"Maybe you're right. I don't know. But after we argued that day, I should have searched my soul and at the very least, considered the possibility. *Regardless* of the fact he's my brother. We're all frail at different times in our lives. How could I not even allow myself to consider the possibility that Jimmy could have succumbed to the pressures around him? How could I be that naive?

"But instead of coming to terms with that, I spent the last few weeks stewing over what I considered a cruel, unfounded attack on my brother. I was more willing to shoot the messenger than even consider that the message could be valid. It was a childish reaction and I'm sorry. I'm so sorry."

He reached for my hand.

"As for bolting so quickly, I don't know. I was so sure I'd finally learned to trust again. I have Dr. Love to thank for that. But apparently I wasn't as secure as I thought I was. I think I just freaked at this first rip in our relationship. I was scared, Tucker. Scared you weren't the man I thought you were. Scared that if I didn't turn and run, I'd stand by and watch my heart get trampled all over again."

He sighed heavily. "But surely you knew me better than that? You have to know I'd never trample your heart."

I laced my fingers through his, swallowing back a lump in my throat. "No, Tucker, I didn't know. But that's because I felt a crack in my new resolve. It felt like the ground beneath me was starting to give way again. And I was simply scared out of my wits."

He rubbed the top of my hand with his thumb. "So what are we going to do? How can we go forward if every time we have an argument or hit a snag along the way, I have to worry about you taking off again? How can I earn your trust, Shelby?"

I didn't answer right away. Was it really possible for me to trust him so completely that I'd never turn tail and run again? I wanted to believe I could. Oh, how I wanted to believe it.

I had trouble finding my voice when I finally spoke. "Let me try. Give me another chance. Will you?"

He looked into my eyes, but I was sure he could see right through to my soul. "Shelby, I love you. And I might as well tell you—I have *always* had a special place in my heart for you."

My head jerked. "What?"

"All those years Jimmy and I used to torment you when we were kids? At least on my part, it was all an attempt to get your attention and try to make you like me."

I chuckled. “And somehow you thought putting a frog in my underwear drawer was the way to do that?”

He laughed. “Hey, I was only twelve at the time. What would you expect?”

“You’re serious? I had no idea. I thought you were just playing the part of Jimmy’s partner-in-crime, always coming up with schemes to make my life miserable.”

“And I can’t imagine how you might have thought that . . .” He fashioned a face of innocence. “Nothing but a schoolboy’s clumsy crush.”

I sat back in my chair. “You have no idea how this confession of yours has set my world off its axis. I don’t know what to say.”

“Say you love me, Shelby.”

My heart began playing a tympani solo, the driving beat nearly taking my breath away. But I wasn’t about to blow it this time. “I do love you, Tucker. I have for a long time now. I only wish I’d told you sooner.”

A huge smile beamed back at me. “Now’s as good a time as any. I’m just happy to finally hear you say it.” He leaned over and placed the most gentle kiss on my lips . . . the most gentle, perfect kiss. As he leaned back, he added, “There’s just one more thing I’d like to hear you say.”

“Yeah? And what’s that?”

“Say you’ll marry me.”

I’d held them in as long as I could—those wretched, pesky tears. But hearing those words kicked the floodgates wide open. I felt the tears flow freely down my face as I answered. “Yes. Yes, I’ll marry you! Nothing could make me happier. I love you, Tucker Thompson.”

He was on his feet and before I could blink, he took my hand, helped me up and into his arms. He kissed me and kissed me and kissed me again, completely oblivious to the other patrons in the small restaurant. And I knew if I died that very moment, I would die the happiest woman on earth. He hugged me so tight, I think I wheezed through most of our kisses. Suddenly he broke away, reached for a spoon, and tapped his water glass repeatedly.

"Ladies and gentlemen, if I could have your attention?" He paused just long enough for them to turn our way, then lifted our hands in the air. "SHE SAID YES!"

The room broke into applause and we laughed so hard, we couldn't speak. When the applause died down, Tucker paid the bill and we were out of there.

"C'mon, Moonpie. I think it's about time we spread some good news for a change, don't you?"

40

After leaving the restaurant, we went straight to the hospital and were pleased to find both Mom and Dad in Jimmy's room. They were thrilled with our announcement and gladly welcomed some good news after all that had happened. Jimmy seemed happy for us too, though his was a more sarcastic response.

"After all we did to you, Moonpie, you're gonna *marry* him?"

We all laughed and started reminiscing over some of the more memorably epic pranks the boys had played on me.

"Just don't tie the knot before I get outta here," Jimmy said. "I need time to plan the traditional decorating of the get-away vehicle so you can leave in style."

"I don't even want to know," I groaned.

"No problem, Jimmy," Tucker added. "We can't tie the knot until they let you go seeing as how you're my best man. If that's okay with you."

Jimmy's eyes misted and he struggled to find his voice before answering. "It'd be my honor, Tuck."

Mom kept hugging me and hugging Tucker amid a steady flow

of tears. Thankfully, these were tears of joy.

When I got home, Sandra and I had our own squeal-fest when I told her my news. She kept sliding into Spanish out of sheer excitement which only served to ramp up the celebration. I decided then and there I must enroll in a Spanish course at MSU so I could keep up with whatever in the world she was always saying at times like this. Once we settled down, she made us each a cup of tea and wanted every detail.

"Don't leave out anything!" she insisted.

Tuesday morning arrived much too early after such an unforgettable evening. As we drove in to work, Sandra and I gabbed incessantly. Of course, we had to stop and turn up the radio when Rick Dees started an Elvis segment. It seems the King reportedly had a midnight visit to the dentist office for some kind of tooth ailment. Later in the day he was leaving on tour to Portland, Maine and didn't want to leave with a sore tooth. Or something like that. It was always hard to tell what was real and what was "The D'Man's" antics when he got on a roll.

"If the King says he gots a toothache, then he gots a toothache," Dees said in his Sammy Soul voice, his faux-Barry-White character.

"Nah, he just likes the happy gas they give him before drilling," Dee's sidekick countered.

"Now, don't you be talkin' 'bout the King like 'at. Me 'n Elvis, we're tight. Know what I mean? And you know the Big E packs heat."

"What's that supposed to mean?"

"It means, you be nice when you be talkin' bout my man, Elvis. And dat's alls I got to say about dat."

"Well, sure thing, Mr. Soul. I'm shaking in my boots here. See?"

"No, you be's shakin' in dem' blue suede shoes!"

Suddenly the voice of Rick Dees resurfaced. "Twenty-five after eight 'Dees morning' on WHBQ Memphis, with you on your way to work. And what's a Tuesday without a little Elvis?"

The introduction to "I'm All Right, Baby" filled the car as we made our final turn into the BMH employee parking lot.

Sandra immediately started rambling about shopping for wedding gowns and bridesmaid dresses.

"Sandra, promise me you'll take it down a notch or two when we get to the office in light of all that's been going on," I begged. "I just don't want to waltz in there and be obnoxious about Tucker's proposal."

She shot me a look. "Are you out of your mind? This should be the happiest day of your life! Why not spread a little joy? C'mon, don't be such a kill-joy."

I rolled my eyes. "Fine, then. Just don't get carried away. Promise?"

"I'll make no such promise." She pulled into a parking spot, turned off the engine, and smacked the steering wheel as if playing a set of bongos. "It's just SO EXCITING!"

Needless to say, she didn't hold back anything once we got to the office. Then again, the girls all knew how animated and noisy Sandra could be. I'm not going to lie and tell you I didn't love it, because I did. At breakfast I was bombarded with wedding suggestions, tips on training husbands, and a random list of suggestions for honeymoon destinations. I hadn't had a split second to think about any of that, but they seemed content to keep it coming.

As soon as I got my gear together, I stopped by to see Jimmy. He was still sleeping, thanks to the pain meds he was on, so Dad and I stepped out in the hall to talk. Mom had stayed with him all night and was back at the hotel sleeping. Dad seemed upbeat and encouraged about Jimmy's progress. He said they'd had a long talk, and he believed Jimmy was truly ready to get well. As we talked, Dad kept bear-hugging me, saying over and over, "I can't believe my little girl is getting married!" I loved it. I told him I'd check back later then headed up to Nine.

I grew impatient waiting for the elevator door to open on my floor. I couldn't wait to tell Donnie my news! I had called Tucker to see if he could come with me, but he was down in the ER. There'd been an early morning pile-up on I-40, and he couldn't get away. Tucker had visited Donnie as often as he could and the two had struck up a quirky friendship. I should have known they'd hit it off. They clearly came from the same DNA, what with Donnie's roach races back in the Taco Barn days and young Tucker's endless critter pranks of his own.

Still, I couldn't wait on Tucker. I had to share the good news with Donnie. I didn't even check in at the desk. I raced straight to his room.

"DONNIE, I'M GETTING MARRIED!" I yelled as I banged open his door.

I froze.

The room was empty. Two members of our housekeeping staff were sanitizing the room.

"What—"

No. Oh please no . . .

I tried again. "Wh-where's Donnie?" The words fell out in whisper-croak.

The two women looked at each other and shrugged. "We don't know. You'll have to ask at the desk.

I pushed my fears down hard as I ran to the nurses' station. "Shirley, where's Donnie?!" My voice broke and I covered my mouth with my hand, so afraid what I might hear.

She came around the counter and grabbed my hand. "Shelby, he's okay. He got the call!"

"What call?"

"They have a heart for him! They air-lifted him out this

morning at 7:45 to catch a private jet. It all happened really fast, honey."

"But he's okay? He can handle the surgery? He was so weak, Shirley. I've been so worried about him."

She put her arm around my waist. "I know, but he's going to be fine. We just need to pray his body accepts that heart."

"I just can't believe it. After all this time. Wait—where did they take him? To Columbia?"

"Yes, to Columbia University Medical Center in New York. Oh! I almost forgot—he left you a note." She reached over the desk for an envelope and handed it to me. "He kept saying over and over, 'Don't forget to tell Shelby!' As if we would?" She shook her head. "Oh, we're going to miss that young man *so* much. He's been here so long, he's like family. And we all loved spending time in there with him. Such a cut up, that one."

"Major understatement. So there's no way I can call and talk to him until after his surgery?"

"Oh, goodness no. They're in a race against time to get that heart in him."

I hugged and thanked her, then headed to the prayer room around the corner so I could read his note. I took a seat and gently opened the envelope. I smiled, imagining the expression on his face as he'd written his note on BMH stationary. I carefully opened the folded note and began to read.

> *Dear Shelby,*
> *I can't believe I'm leaving without saying good-bye to you. (Let's just hope that's in the temporary sense as opposed to the permanent. Ha ha.) I wonder if my donor was in a wreck? They probably scooped up some poor man's heart off the pavement and shoved it in an Igloo cooler for me. Sweet, huh? I*

just hope he liked Mexican food and Krispy Kremes.
If not, I may demand a replacement.
I'm not afraid. Really. So don't worry about me. I'm ready to go home. Whether that's Tallahassee or the great beyond.
You've been the best friend in the world to me. You lifted my spirits every time you walked in my door, Shelby. I'm so glad we've had these months together. Lousy excuse to do it, but there it is.
So, off I go. Promise you'll come see me soon.

Love you,

Donnie

p.s. And if you wanted to say a prayer or two, that'd probably be okay . . . just this once. ♥D

I fought the tears—again. It was all such of mix of happy/sad, I didn't have a clue what to do. I slid down on my knees and begged God to get Donnie to the hospital in New York in time and for the surgery to be a success.

The alternative? Unthinkable.

After my mind and heart came to terms with it all, I ducked in the restroom to freshen myself after this latest tear-fest, then kept myself busy the rest of the morning with patient visits. I purposefully left Mr. Wilcox for last, not sure I was up to anymore angst this morning. He seemed slightly better after receiving the treatment and medications he needed. His color was much better and he seemed more like himself, though still weak.

I noticed an oversized book over on the wall-to-wall window sill. "What's this?" I asked, making my way around his bed. The title read *My Life on the Line.* I had to bite back the irony of those words, but it was obviously a scrapbook of his career as a railroad engineer. And I knew immediately how to cheer Mr. Wilcox up.

I pulled up a chair close to his bed and took a seat. "I'm all done with my visits this morning, Mr. Wilcox. Any chance I could twist your arm into telling me all about your book here?"

Cheapest, fastest-working meds on the planet if that smile is any indication. An hour and a half later, he was the happiest camper on the floor, and I'd never felt so gratified.

When I went back downstairs for lunch, I stopped by the office first and noticed Mrs. B had put a sign on our note board:

HOSTESS MEETING AT 2:00 P.M.

CONFERENCE ROOM B

ATTENDANCE MANDATORY

Our boss had been subdued for weeks and hadn't interacted more than necessary with any of us for some time. Curiosity took away my appetite, but I forced down a few bites. In the cafeteria, the girls and I had a horrible feeling this meeting wasn't about an office picnic.

We were right.

"Thank you for coming, ladies," she began, after we all arrived. "I have some rather unfortunate news to tell you, but it's not really going to be much of a surprise, I'm afraid."

The tuna in the salad I had just eaten did a triple spin off the high dive.

"Today is your official two week notice of dismissal."

A collective groan filled the room.

"Our program will cease to exist in two weeks. You will each receive a severance check in your final paycheck. And I would be most happy to write a letter of recommendation for you as you pursue other employment."

She took off her glasses and gently wiped the outer edges of her eyes with a handkerchief. "I suppose it was inevitable, as the economy has continued on a downslide. Even a grand hospital such as ours must cut corners in times like these."

The side door opened and in walked Dr. Grieve, our president. We all sat a little straighter as he entered, all of us trying to maintain our composure.

"Ladies, Dr. Grieve would like to say a few words to you." Mrs. Baker motioned for him to go ahead as she stepped back against the wall.

"Ladies, no one is more disappointed than I am at the news Virginia has just shared with you. As you are all aware, the hostess program was one of my proudest achievements during my tenure here at Baptist. You have been the welcoming face to all our patients, offering them an extra portion of kindness and service during their stay. I was never so proud as the first time your predecessors made their rounds making our hospital 'more hospitable,' if you will, by offering a smiling face, a cheerful message of service, and a willingness to do those little things that told our patients we wanted to make their stay as pleasant as possible.

"I was proud then, and I'm proud today. I'm proud of each and every one of you and all your accomplishments. And that's why it's especially hard for me to have to close down something I feel so strongly about. But these are difficult days in our hospital, our city, and our country. We've had to make some painful decisions, not the least of which—at least for me—is the one that concerns each of you.

"As you know, I'm stepping down soon to begin my retirement. I've had a wonderful life, especially while here at the helm of this great institution. But it's time for me to move on and spend as much time as God sees fit to give me with my wife, my children, and my grandchildren. Most of you, on the other hand, are at the beginning of your careers. And this is not the way I'd hoped to see you leave us. That said, I trust God will help each and every one of you find the job He has for you. A job that will take you closer to your dreams, whatever they may be. Who knows but what a future nurse or doctor or chaplain or hospital administrator is sitting in this room. Perhaps your time here at Baptist has sparked an interest in such a career. I'd like nothing more.

"And so I bid you farewell, with my utmost thanks. Thank you for your service here at Baptist, thank you for the way you made me so proud, and thank you for the blessing you've been to each and every patient you visited." He paused, held his fist to his mouth, then seemed to clear his throat. He blinked away tears, held up his hand, and with a graveled voice said, "God bless you."

As the door closed behind him, we all broke out the tissues. Mrs. B wiped her eyes again, folding and refolding her handkerchief. When she was able, she continued. "Girls, tomorrow morning when you come in, we'll meet briefly to discuss how to wind down our work here, how to inform your floor staff, that sort of thing. In the meantime, I would like to invite you all to be my guests a week from Thursday, at *Top of the 100,* the revolving restaurant atop the Union Planters building downtown for a final dinner together and a chance to celebrate the times we've shared."

I couldn't help but think . . . our office picnic had become the last supper.

41

As we left the conference room, I think we all felt numb. I know I did. You'd think we'd be moaning and groaning about the situation, or at the very least, ranting to some degree about what the heck we'd all do. Instead, an unusual eerie silence surrounded us. Mrs. Baker stayed out of the office. I can only assume she was avoiding us—not because she didn't care, but because she hated what she just told us, hated the predicament, and maybe even hated the thought of saying goodbye in the very near future. I couldn't blame her for disappearing for a while. It was all so surreal.

I looked at my watch—2:30. I tried to reach Tucker, still on his shift, but I was told he was with a patient in the ER, so I decided to go back up to Jimmy's room. I just needed someone to talk to. I needed my daddy.

Dad was working a crossword puzzle and my brother was still lights out. Dad came back out in the hall with me and we found a couple of chairs. I unloaded about my crazy day. He was such an amazing father, always knowing when I just needed to talk things out.

When I finished, he pulled me into a side hug and said,

"Sweetheart, I'm so sorry, though I have no doubt in my mind that you can do anything you set your mind on. But my goodness, when it rains it pours, doesn't it? What a week it's been. Your brother's accident, you got engaged, your friend's about to undergo a heart transplant—and now this."

"I know. Weird, isn't it? The highs and lows are about to give me whiplash. Makes you wonder, what's next?"

What's next . . .

No sooner had those words left my mouth, than I heard myself paged. When I called the operator, she connected me to Sandra in the hostess office.

"Shelby! OH MY GOSH, Shelby, have you heard?" She sounded out of breath and more than a little hyper.

"No, what's going on?"

"Elvis! It's all over the news. They're saying he's dead!"

"WHAT?" I didn't mean to shout, and immediately looked around, hoping it wasn't as loud as I thought. Clearly it was. Dad rushed over to my side, his expression asking what was wrong. "*Who's* saying he's dead?" I asked more quietly.

"Supposedly they're bringing him here to Baptist by ambulance right now. Some reports on the radio are saying he's dead. Others say they're still trying to resuscitate him. I can't believe it! I just can't believe it! Oh Shelby, meet me in the Union lobby so we can see what's going on. Hurry!"

I told Dad what Sandra had said, gave him a hug, then ran down the hall and impatiently pressed the down button by the elevators. It was taking forever so I opted for the stairs, taking them as fast as I could in my wedged heels.

When I pushed open the door on One, it hit me hard.

I could *physically* feel it. Something was in the air . . .

Ask anyone who was there that day and they'll tell you. The air literally crackled with electricity. As if a nearby transformer had blown and all of us could feel the hairs lift off our arms, our necks. The Union Avenue lobby quickly filled as employees rushed to see for themselves. Their questions, hushed but urgent.

Is it true? Please tell me it's not true!

Surely it's just a rumor?

Elvis Presley . . . our Elvis . . . dead?!

Word had spread like a Tennessee wildfire throughout the hospital . . . an ambulance carrying the King of Rock 'n Roll was racing through the streets of Memphis from Graceland to "his" hospital, flanked by police cars and motorcycle cops.

Elvis? Dead? How can that be?

I spotted Sandra immediately and rushed to her side. She grabbed my hand in a death-lock grip with both of hers. We held our ground there by that expansive wall of windows overlooking the Emergency Room bay. I couldn't breathe, and except for an occasional whisper or whimper, no one else seemed to be breathing either. Doctors, nurses, bookkeepers, administrators, gift shop clerks, cafeteria workers, visitors, even a patient or two—some in wheelchairs pushed by family members—and most of my own coworkers . . . we all stood there. Waiting, hoping, praying.

Shrouded in silent grief, we waited for him to arrive, fearing the worst.

Don't ask me why, but just then I looked up at the clock on the wall—2:56. Then flashing lights suddenly rounded the corner as a long line of emergency vehicles made the final stretch of the ER entry. As the ambulance rolled into sight, I felt a tear slip down my cheek, then another. I felt Sandra's arm slip around my waist, pulling me closer. I felt someone else's arm drape over my shoulder. In moments, the girls were all around us, drawing even closer as the crowd behind us pushed for a better view. I could hear Sandra's whispered prayers in her native tongue. And then I caught a waft of Mrs. Baker's familiar cologne and heard her utter,

"Oh, dear Lord . . ."

I knew it wasn't possible, but at that precise moment, the whole scene seemed to slip into slow motion. The incessant flash of cameras created a surreal landscape of strange strobe-like movements as people rushed across the lawn below us toward the ER. The barrage of flashing red lights bounced off glass-covered medical buildings as the wailing sirens echoed in that valley of concrete and glass.

And then the sirens went silent . . . all of them, leaving an eerie, foreboding hush in their wake.

Oh God, please don't let Elvis die . . .

We waited and waited. The halls and lobbies of BMH filled to near-capacity. Rumors ran wild. I thought I would lose my mind. After an hour with no validation as to what was going on in that ER, I looked up and saw Tucker threading his way through the crowd toward me. When our eyes met, he waved me toward him. I grabbed Sandra's hand and we slipped through the pack of onlookers.

As we neared him, he held out his arms, beckoning me to that safe place I'd come to cherish most. I quickly melted into his embrace, desperately needing some sort of stability in the madness of this moment.

"Tucker, what have you heard?"

"I was there when they brought him in."

"You were *there*?" Sandra shrieked, her hands grasping his arm.

"Shhh, c'mon. Let's go somewhere we can talk." He pulled us to a corner as far away as we could get from everyone else. He looked around to make sure we were out of earshot.

"Is it true?" I asked, clutching onto him.

"Is he dead?" Sandra whimpered.

He dropped his head, then looked back up. "I'm afraid so."

Sandra let out an unexpected cry, and Tucker quickly brought her under his other arm. "Shhh, we need to keep this under wraps until an official announcement is released. Dr. Nichopoulos is on his way to Graceland to tell Elvis's dad. After that takes place, they'll go public."

"What happened?" I asked as quietly as I could.

"Well, that remains to be seen. Apparently he was discovered in his bathroom unconscious. Or so they said. From what we could tell, he'd been gone for quite a while by the time they got him to the emergency room. Livor mortis had clearly set in—"

"Rigor mortis?" Sandra asked.

"No, *livor* mortis. It's a purple skin coloration. If it doesn't blanch out when you press your finger against it—meaning, it remains purple—that's a sign that the patient has been dead for two or more hours. Plus, when you factor in that the body was also stiff—indicating an onset of rigor mortis, which you're obviously familiar with—he was obviously dead long before he arrived here."

"How horrible," I said.

"In fact, one of the nurses on the Harvey team verbalized what we all were thinking when she asked why in the world we were working on a corpse. He was visibly blue and unresponsive. Someone told her, 'Because it's Elvis.' Like most of us, she hadn't recognized him. Honestly, I had no idea it was him. He was extremely bloated and like I said, very, very blue."

Can this really be happening? This kind-hearted man I met only a few weeks ago—now dead? First Dr. Love, now Elvis? No matter what Tucker said, I just didn't want to believe it.

We all lingered at the hospital, hoping against hope there had been some bizarre mistake. People reminisced, others couldn't stop crying, but none of us wanted to believe it. We kept hearing reports that the entire section of town near Graceland had come to a standstill because of all the traffic. Masses of people were gathering there as they had here, all of them hoping it was just a sick, elaborate hoax.

I had lots of questions too. I peppered Tucker with them over and over until he asked me to stop. His long shift was finally over and he just wanted to go home and get some sleep. Sandra and Trevor left, as did the rest of the girls in my office. But I didn't want to go home yet. I wanted to spend some time with my family up in Jimmy's room.

Mom and Dad were both there, Mom looking much more rested, but terribly sad. She'd always loved Elvis, having met him several times at Dad's dealership. She had every one of his albums and played them constantly, especially when we were kids. It finally dawned on me—maybe that's why I wasn't a big Elvis fan growing up. I'd heard one too many tunes by the King when I was younger.

But that all changed that day in the prayer room. I'd met the man, not the image. And he couldn't have been kinder. His heartfelt despair over Dr. Love's imminent passing had drawn out that beautiful, unforgettable hymn, quietly sung in the softly lit prayer room.

They'd called his time of death at 3:30. According to the Shelby County medical examiner, the cause of death was listed as heart failure—which he announced *before* the autopsy. Others speculated that Elvis had died from a drug overdose. Those reports broke my heart. We all knew he'd had problems for years, which explained so many of those weeks he'd stay with us at Baptist, trying to overcome those afflictions. But it seemed grotesquely wrong for reporters to jump to conclusions when no autopsy had yet been performed.

Maybe we were just naive, but we were surprised at the

vastness of the television coverage. When local news finally gave way to the networks, we found ourselves glued to the set in Jimmy's room, watching Chet Huntley and David Brinkley detail the news coming out of Memphis. As Mom helped Jimmy try to eat a few bites of red Jell-O and applesauce, we listened to the animated conversation of a young reporter named Geraldo Rivera. He seemed overly agitated about the whole situation, making all sorts of wild speculations about what went on in that bathroom at Graceland, and even more so, in Trauma Room 2 in Baptist's ER. So much misinformation seemed to be flying all over Memphis, and across the world, for that matter. After a while, we grew weary of it all and turned off the set. I said my goodbyes, promising to see them again in the morning.

In the days that followed, the entire spectacle surrounding the death of Elvis Presley warped out of control. Everyone was stunned to hear that his body was already lying in state at Graceland the next day. *The next day.* How could they have possibly pulled that together so fast? Thousands lined Elvis Presley Boulevard hoping to pay their respects. It was estimated that more than 80,000 people filed by that open casket.

I found it all very distasteful. Why an open coffin for complete strangers to stare and gawk over? It seemed like more of a staged event for curiosity seekers than an opportunity for genuine fans to pay tribute to a beloved entertainer. The most devoted of fans took it the hardest, many collapsing and fainting after hysterical outbursts. I couldn't imagine being over there in all that chaos, especially in the sweltering 94-degree heat. Yet one of the nurses on my floor later told me she'd gone with her husband, waiting in line more than nine hours for one last look at her beloved Elvis.

"I'm so sorry I went, Shelby. The body in that casket didn't look a thing like Elvis. It looked like one of those figures at Madame Tussaud's Wax Museum. Nothing looked right. And now I'll forever have that image locked in my brain instead of the Elvis I loved."

I found it equally baffling that the funeral took place the very next day on August 18th. How on earth had they been able to arrange a funeral of that magnitude in less than 36 hours? A small funeral with only 200 invited guests was held in the living room at Graceland. Floral arrangements blanketed the entire front lawn of the mansion. Local florists had been inundated with orders from friends and fans around the world.

Later, television coverage showed the seventeen white limousines following the hearse with Elvis's casket on the drive over to the cemetery. Daddy jumped up, pointing to a silver Cadillac leading the procession ahead of the hearse shown on television. My dad choked up and couldn't speak. Even Cadillac Jack was grieving.

Elvis was laid to rest next to his mother at Forest Hill Cemetery. Eleven days later three men broke into the cemetery and tried to steal his casket. Charges were later dropped when they admitted they were just trying to prove it was an empty casket, convinced Elvis was still alive. Elvis's dad, Vernon, would later have both Elvis and his mother moved to Meditation Garden at Graceland.

I have to admit, I'm one of those who was always intrigued by the supposed misspelling of Elvis's middle name on his grave plaque. Over the years, all kinds of explanations have been offered for what *could* be the world's worst typo. To this day the plaque reads *Elvis Aaron Presley*, though every Elvis fan knows his middle name was spelled *Aron* on his birth certificate—a name significant if you look just across the garden at the memorial plaque for Elvis's stillborn twin, Jesse G<u>aron</u> Presley. Then, again, maybe

Vernon just misspelled it the day Elvis was born. That same original document lists his first name as "Evis." Which should tell us that spelling wasn't a high priority in the Presley household.

I'm not sure why, but it took me a long time to get over the death of Elvis. Tucker was strangely silent when I tried to ask him about what all happened in that ER Trauma Room and all the other strange facts surrounding his death. I assumed it had more to do with professional ethics than anything else.

But time heals all wounds, and eventually it healed mine. Life got back to normal—well, the "new" normal, I suppose. Our office finally closed at Baptist, though I still found myself mourning over that loss too. True to her word, Mrs. Baker treated all of us to an unforgettable dinner at *Top of the 100.* It gave us some sense of closure and a chance to say goodbye. The girls and I had pitched in to buy a crystal vase for Mrs. B with all our names etched on it. She seemed genuinely touched by our gift.

Jimmy began his recovery, getting a little stronger every day. When his injuries were well enough, he began going through rehabilitation at a highly respected local retreat center for those needing help to overcome addiction. I was so proud of him the day he graduated, clean and restored.

As for me? I had a wedding to plan!

In four short months, Tucker and I were married in a small service in the chapel at First Baptist on New Year's Eve. Tucker surprised me during the ceremony (a dangerous thing to attempt where brides are involved) by including an acoustic rendition of Elvis's *Hawaiian Wedding Song,* sung by none other than Trevor Knight. It was such a sweet and unexpected gesture of love—and a not-so-subtle hint about the secret honeymoon he'd planned for us. We left the next day for two weeks in Hawaii and had the time of our lives. All too soon it was time to come back home to Memphis where we began our lives together as Dr. and Mrs.

Tucker Thompson.

That's Mrs. Moonpie Thompson to you.

EPILOGUE

Present Day

I leaned back, suddenly weary from sharing my long story. Darkness shone through the windows. How was that possible? We'd chatted all through lunch earlier in the day—a nice chicken salad and fresh fruit plate which I served out on my back porch. When dinner rolled around, my guest seemed delighted when I made Belgian waffles served with heated maple syrup chocked full of pecans. I lost count on how many cups of coffee we'd both enjoyed.

I looked over and noticed my new friend Chip was comfortably molded into my easy chair, a serene smile on his face. He'd started out with a Q&A about my memories as a hostess at Baptist hoping to mine some helpful ideas for a similar program at the hospital where he worked in California. But after our long day's visit, I felt like we'd taken a trip back in time together.

He sat up in his chair, dropping his notebook and pen on the coffee table. "Do you have any idea how compelling your story is? And beautifully told, I might add. I feel as though I've been watching a movie of your life. I feel like I actually *know* these people you've been talking about. You tell a great story, Mrs.

Thompson. I can't begin to thank you enough."

"You're most welcome, Chip. And I hope somewhere in all of this, you can find some ideas for your own hospital."

He paused then raised a finger. "If it's not too much to ask, would you mind telling me the rest of the story? What's happened in the years since you left Baptist?"

"I'd be happy to tell you. Let me think a moment. Oh—you might be interested to know that Donnie survived his transplant. In fact, he was even able to come to our wedding. When we found out he would be able to come, Tucker graciously invited him to be one of our groomsmen. It was such a delight to see him looking healthy again. I just prayed he wouldn't pull any of his crazy pranks while we were standing there at the altar. And thankfully, he didn't. Cried like a baby through the whole ceremony." I chuckled at the memory of it.

"Unfortunately, as with most of the heart transplant patients in those days, Donnie's recovery was short lived. He lived for two more years before passing away. But those were two of the happiest years of his life. Before his health began to deteriorate, he fell in love and married a wonderful girl who just adored him. Bethany and I remain good friends to this day. But I still miss him so much.

"Jimmy was there at our wedding too, serving as Tuck's best man. He truly cleaned up his act and has lived a wonderful life. He's married with four kids, if you can believe it. Serves as a deacon in his church down in Birmingham. When Dad retired about twenty years ago, Jimmy took over the dealership. Folks call him 'Cadillac Jim' and it still cracks me up. But the real hoot is that when Dad retired, he bought himself a red Ferrari!"

My guest laughed out loud with me. If only he knew my dad.

"Tucker enjoyed many good years as an anesthesiologist here in the Memphis area. In fact, he set up a practice and brought in five others. They were all quite successful, and I'm happy to say, all five were very involved in their churches and local charities and a good many mission projects. Every year they hosted an event called 'The Gas Blast,' a big '40s-style swing dance to raise money for medical projects in third world countries. We always had such a good time working on those together.

"But Tucker was diagnosed with cancer a few years back, and I lost him just eighteen months ago. I miss him terribly. Not a day goes by that I don't catch myself asking him a question or telling him about something clever I heard on TV. Can you imagine? After all these months? I suppose I'll eventually stop doing it, but I hope not. It helps me feel his presence here with me."

"Did you and Dr. Thompson have children?" Chip asked.

"Yes, we have two kids. Dana is married to a recording engineer in Nashville. They have two little angels, Lizzie and Missy. I get to see them a lot since we're not that far apart. Then our son Josh just started his internship in Dallas. He plans to specialize in sports medicine."

"Ah, another doctor in the family."

"Tucker would've been so proud. Oh, and you might like to know Sandra and Trevor married six months after our wedding. When our program closed down at the hospital, Sandra went to med school. They're now medical missionaries in Africa—with six children, if you can imagine! But they have a precious family, and they're doing some amazing things over there."

"That's incredible."

I smiled. "I think the hostess program opened our eyes to all kinds of possible career paths. After my kids were in school, I enrolled at MSU for my master's degree in counseling. After my experience with Donnie and so many other of my patients, I realized how important it was for people with serious health problems to be able to talk through their concerns and fears and questions with someone. Doctors and nurses don't have that kind of time. Or training, for that matter. I was able to go back on staff at Baptist, counseling full time. I did that for more than twenty years and loved every minute of it."

"So you went full circle, returning to Baptist," he said.

"Well, yes and no. I worked for Baptist Memorial Hospital, but at its new location out east of town. As we discussed earlier, the original building, located in the midtown medical area, was closed down and leveled many years ago."

"That's such a shame. I would love to have taken a tour of it with you."

"I would have loved to have *given* you that tour," I said, meaning it.

He capped his pen, closed his notebook, and put away his mini-recorder. "Mrs. Thompson, this has been such a treat for me. I must admit, I came here on an assignment to learn some facts. But I'm leaving with much, much more. You've given me so much to think about."

"Chip . . ." I hesitated.

"Yes?"

I mulled it over in my mind, wondering if I should tell him. But something deep inside kept nudging me to do it. I looked him straight in the eye, motioning him to sit back down. "There is one more thing."

He slowly sat down. "Please, go on."

I smiled at him, still not sure if I should. Tucker wouldn't be pleased. But as I reminded myself daily, Tucker's no longer here. At least not in the physical sense.

"I'd like to tell you about our anniversary."

I'm not sure what he expected me to say, but this certainly wasn't it. His eyebrows shot up. "Your anniversary?"

"Yes."

He waited, those brows locked in place about halfway up his forehead.

"I fell in love with the islands of Hawaii when Tucker and I spent our honeymoon there. So I was thrilled when he suggested we return there for our tenth anniversary. Though, this time around, we stayed in a quaint village on Maui. Very secluded and off the beaten path, but with all the spectacular ocean vistas and lush majestic mountains. We stayed in a condo right on the beach, and I told Tuck I could stay there with him the rest of my life and die a happy woman.

"We'd been there about a week when . . ." I paused again, still hesitant.

"When what?" I noticed he was sitting on the edge of his seat.

"When we happened on a small beachside restaurant right up the road. It was open air, with live entertainment, and some of the best island food we'd ever eaten. We'd paid no attention to the sign by the door which listed the entertainer for the evening, so we were surprised when a performer who called himself 'Elvis' came on stage. Tucker and I laughed ourselves silly over it. Considering our own particular 'history' with the King? Then to come here ten years later, in this completely out of the way hole in the wall in Hawaii—to find 'Elvis' doing a whole set of his famous songs? What are the chances?

"He definitely had the look—the white studded jumpsuit with pleated bell bottoms, the oversized uniquely-shaped glasses, the jet black hair and long sideburns, and enough gold jewelry to supply an armada. He wasn't slim, but much thinner than the Elvis we'd seen in all the pictures just days before he died. But the face wasn't quite right and while he tried to mimic that famous voice, he missed it. At one point I leaned over and whispered to Tuck, 'Elvis would roll over in his grave to see this guy. Doesn't look anything like him! Besides, he does a lousy Elvis voice. How embarrassing!'

"We actually got quite tickled, biting our lips to stop the laughter, and not succeeding most of the time. Whenever a snicker or snort would slip, the singer would look our way, smile a corny Elvis-style smile and keep going. Apparently our response was merely egging him on. It was such a small audience, he started looking our way more and more, winking at me—the whole shtick. Which, of course, only made us laugh harder.

"Toward the end of his set he said, 'I'd like to dedicate my last song to this pretty little lady right over here.' I thought, oh no, no, noooo! But sure enough, he came off the stage, walked right up to me, and took my hand in his. 'What's your name, lil' darlin'?' he said.

"I shot a look at Tucker who was all but rolling on the floor by then. I looked back at 'Elvis' and said, 'Shelby. My name is Shelby.'

"'And what are you doing here on our lovely island, Miss Shelby?'

"'I'm here celebrating my tenth anniversary with my husband.'

"'Well, now! Ain't that a thrill? And who's this lucky man?' he said, facing Tucker.

"'This is my husband, Tucker,' I said, wishing this would all be over.

"He took hold of Tucker's hand, shook it, then asked, 'Mind if I sing a love song to your lil' missus?'

"Tuck held up both hands and said, 'She's all yours, Elvis.' The crowd loved it.

"Then he dropped to one knee and started singing those famous lyrics to "I Can't Help Falling in Love With You." He had all the right moves, but his version was nowhere close to the original Elvis rendition of the song. But it was so corny and absurd, I finally just decided to give in and play along. When the song ended, he kissed my hand and draped his white scarf around my neck, then said, 'Aloha, Shelby.'

"The audience—all twenty or thirty of them—went wild. He made his way back up on stage as the background music ramped up. 'Thank you, ladies and gentlemen! Thank you for coming out tonight. I'll be here all week! Aloha!'

"When it was finally over, we eventually stopped laughing long enough to order dessert and coffee, hoping to stay a few more minutes just to enjoy the ocean breeze and chat a little. The waitress brought us our pie—along with a note from 'Elvis' asking us to stop by his dressing room before we left. I mean, he even signed it *EP.* Which only sent us into another round of uncontrollable giggles."

Chip laughed, clearly enjoying my story. "Tell me you're making this up! Oh, what I would give to have been there and see this all play out. Oh my goodness, how on earth did you keep a straight face?"

"Well, it took us a while to regain our composure, but we finally did and decided to accept his invitation. The waitress showed us back to this tiny, cluttered closet of a dressing room where Mr. Elvis greeted us warmly.

"'Come in! Come in! I'm so glad you decided to stop by.' He stuck out his hand, shaking Tucker's hand then mine. 'Elvis Presley. It's nice to see you again!'

"Chip, he had this ridiculous smile on his face and a part of me began to wonder if the guy was perhaps delusional, thinking he really *was* Elvis. I moved closer to Tucker, grabbing his hand.

"'Okay, then," Tucker said, 'Elvis it is. *Mr. Presley,* we really enjoyed your show tonight. We, uh, . . . we enjoyed hearing all those old songs again.'

"He struck the infamous Elvis pose, continuing the façade. 'Why, thank you. Thank you very much.'

"Naturally he'd use the famous 'thank you' lines, same as he'd used after every smattering of applause during the show. He obviously thought he was genuinely funny.

"For a moment we just stood there, the three of us staring at each other with plastered smiles on our faces, though his seemed more real . . . well, more *Elvis* real.

"'Oh, I beg your pardon. Please, have a seat' he said. He moved a bunch of costumes and scarves and makeup totes off a couple of rickety chairs and offered them to us. We sat down wondering what in the world we'd gotten ourselves into. He kept staring at me to the point I was growing extremely uncomfortable.

"'Shelby, it's been a long time.' By the way he said it, I had the impression he wasn't talking about our little scene that just took place during the show. I was totally confused. I looked at him. He smiled at me. I looked at Tucker, whose face reflected the worry in mine. Was this some kind of joke?

"'I'm sorry,' I said. 'What did you say?'

"'Oh, come now, Shelby, it hasn't been *that* long. Don't you remember our visit that night in the prayer room when ol' Tommy Love was on his deathbed?'

"'Wha . . . wha . . .' I wheezed, only this time there wasn't a trace of laughter in it. Or oxygen, for that matter. By that point, I should tell you, the room began to spin and I was quite sure I would be sick. He looked over his glasses and gave me a wink. Just like he'd done at Dr. Love's funeral.

And just like then, as he reached for those glasses, the turquoise and silver watch peeked out from beneath his cuff.

"I stared at him a split-second more then promptly threw up all over those white bell bottoms . . . and his blue suede shoes.

I kept telling myself to take a deep breath, get a hold of myself and calm down. Tucker tried to help me, taking the scarf off my neck to help me clean myself up. 'Elvis' took off and came back with a damp cloth.

"'Here you go, let me help you—'

"I slapped his hand away. 'Don't touch me! Who ARE you? And why are you doing this? How do you know—'

"'Okay, now, let's just get you back in that chair,' he said, motioning for Tucker to help me sit back down.

"Tucker said, 'Look, buddy, I don't know who you are, but you need to cut the act. It was fun while it lasted, but can you just drop the façade and explain how you know what you just said?'

"'Sure, sure,' he said, busying himself as he wiped the remains of my mahi-mahi off his bell bottoms. I wanted to apologize for it but couldn't find a breath in me. Finally he took a seat in his director's chair.

"He said, 'Well, I could've spent half an hour trying to convince you who I was, but you wouldn't have believed me. So I figured I'd just cut to the chase.' He looked down at Tucker. 'See, one night I snuck into the hospital to visit my good friend Tommy Love. And after they let me see him, I just wanted to be alone and pray. So I went to the prayer room on that floor and slipped onto the back row.'

"Chip, I have to tell you—as he talked, I kept thinking over and over to myself—*this isn't happening, this isn't happening! What did they put in our drinks out there? Who could have told him about that night? Who's playing this elaborate joke on us and why?*

"But it just got worse. He went on and on, spilling out every detail of that night, including the name of the hymn he sang, and the fact he gave me his handkerchief to dry my tears. By then, I was no longer sick, but pretty sure I would pass out.

"That's when Tucker jumped in again. 'Nice try, buddy. But what you *don't* know—I was in the ER the day Elvis died. I'm a doctor. And I saw his dead blue body. So why don't you give it up and tell us who put you up to this? Was it Trevor? Or Shelby's brother, Jimmy?'

"'All staged,' he shot back, 'As for the funeral? Those folks at Madame Tussaud's did a good job, don't you think? The papers all said I looked waxy, but what corpse doesn't? My makeup guys did an amazing job. Fooled you, didn't he?' Then he just sat there and smiled. I noticed he had that same lopsided smile Elvis always had, but of course that was likely just another of his affectations for the gig.

"Then he said, 'If you really want to know, I'll tell you. And I'd make you promise not to tell anyone, but I figure you won't believe me anyway. Which is part of the fun—no one ever does! And I'm not really worried about you telling anyone else because even if you did, they wouldn't believe it either.' He threw his head back and laughed. 'Genius. Pure genius. I never dreamed it would work out so well.'

"'Anyway, I'm sure you probably heard all the conspiracy stories about me faking my own death. Well, I'm here to tell you they're true. We *did* fake my death. We worked on it for more than two years to put the plan in motion. Only a handful of my closest associates were in on it. And trust me, they're all living off the high price tag of keeping the secret. Not that anyone would believe them if they spilled the beans. Course, Dr. Nick had to jump a few hurdles and lost his license for a while, but he didn't need it anyway. He'll never want for anything for the rest of his life. He's got a house not far from mine here. We play racquetball several times a week.'

"Tucker and I sat there spellbound. Neither of us said a word. He continued telling his the story.

"'C'mon, my life was a mess. I *had* no life. Couldn't go anywhere. Never had a normal relationship— aside from Priscilla, of course.'

"'Does she know?' I heard myself asking.

"'Oh sure,' he said. 'She and Lisa Marie fly over to see me a couple times a year. They've even stopped by to see my show. The tourists and locals love it. They're clueless, of course, but they love it. Lisa Marie and I always do a few duets together. That really wows them, and I love singin' with my baby girl.'

"Tucker and I looked at each other, each trying to figure out how it was possible, but slowly beginning to wonder . . . Then, even as those thoughts rolled through my mind, I noticed he pushed up his sleeve and there it was again. That turquoise watch."

Chip's jaw hung somewhere in the vicinity of his chest, and he looked a little glassy-eyed, but I continued.

"Finally, Tucker couldn't hold it in anymore and said, 'But why? Why here? Why like this?'

"'Oh, that part's easy,' he answered. 'First of all, I've always loved these islands. Ever since I made *Blue Hawaii,* I knew some day I'd live here. Then it all got so crazy, and I couldn't do it anymore. I needed to get my health back, needed to get my *life* back. And one day it just hit me—what better place to hide than playing an Elvis impersonator? Heck, I even do some of the competitions in Vegas. Haven't come close to winning!' With that he roared with laughter, throwing his head back."

I looked over, watching Chip Carouther's expression morph into disbelief. I couldn't help but smile. Sandra and Trevor had the same reaction when we told them upon our return from Hawaii.

Finally, he rubbed his hand roughly over his face. "With all due respect, Mrs. Thompson—"

"Oh, I know. Trust me. I know. It's quite unbelievable."

He blew out a lungful of air. "Exactly. I mean, it makes for a *great* story. One of the best I've ever heard."

"Doesn't it?" I said.

"But let's be honest. With no viable proof, that's *all* it is—a great story."

"Oh, yes, I totally agree." I leaned forward and opened a small leather box sitting on my coffee table. "Of course, *seeing* is believing." I handed him the photograph taken that night at the little restaurant in Maui. Elvis had asked one of the waitresses to snap a picture of us with him there at the club. He found it hilarious to provide us proof we'd been together, knowing full well no one would ever believe it was really him.

"I'll say this much," I finished, "he has a great laugh. Elvis has a *great* laugh."

Chip stared at the photograph, studying it for a moment or two. I could tell he was holding his breath. Then suddenly, he blew it out. "Nah. That could be one of a million impersonators. Sorry."

I reached back in the box and tossed a stack of Christmas cards on the table, all tied up in a blue ribbon. "Then I guess you probably think these are fake as well."

He pulled them out, one by one, each signed *EP*, postmarked from Hawaii, year after year after year. Each with a personal note.

I chuckled quietly as I watched Chip frantically shuffling faster and faster through the cards. He held the last one in his hand, carefully studying the personal message written and signed by *Elvis*.

Suddenly, he stopped and slowly looked up at me. A momentary hint of possibility flashed across his eyes as a slight smile took form.

I knew what he was thinking . . . *"Everyone knows Elvis left the building."*

Or did he?

ABOUT THE AUTHOR

Born in Texas and raised in Oklahoma, Diane Hale Moody is a graduate of Oklahoma State University. She lives with her husband Ken in the rolling hills just outside of Nashville. They are the proud parents of two grown and extraordinary children, Hannah and Ben.

Just after moving to Tennessee in 1999, Diane felt the tug of a long-neglected passion to write again. Since then, she's written a column for her local newspaper, feature articles for various magazines and curriculum, and several novels with a dozen more stories eagerly vying for her attention.

When she's not reading or writing, Diane enjoys an eclectic taste in music and movies, great coffee, the company of good friends, and the adoration of a peculiar little pooch named Darby.

Visit Diane's website at **dianemoody.net** and her blog, "just sayin'" at **dianemoody.blogspot.com**

ACKNOWLEDGMENTS

Without the help of my friends and family, my stories would lack their sparkle. I'm so grateful to be surrounded by such willing hearts who always help make my literary babies shine.

To Glenn Hale, my faithful "Eagle Eye" who always spots my typos and then some. The fact that you actually enjoyed this story makes it even better. What would I do without you? Love you, Dad.

To Sally Wilson, my fellow author and forever friend who helps put the final spit and polish on my stories. Thanks for blazing the trail on this unique path to publication. I never would've dipped my big toe into these waters had it not been for you. Love you, missy.

To John "Sockmonkey" Robinson and Joy DeKok, two of my favorite sounding boards. Thanks for all your feedback and advice, but most of all your friendship. One of these days we must get together—preferably in the same city! Wouldn't that be a switch?

To Jessi Hill, CRNA, my go-to source for all things anesthesiology. I'm so grateful for the time you spent answering my questions and educating me about your special world. I take full credit for any mis-statements coming out of Tucker's mouth.

To Dr. Kelly Carden and Martha Smith at Sleep Medicine of Middle Tennessee for giving me back my life. Sleep is a beautiful thing! I never dreamed it was possible to write a full-length novel in just two months. WOW. And don't worry, Dr. Carden. The secret about your Elvis Presley bikini is safe with me. Mum's the word.

To my good friend Veronica Beard who I met at First Baptist Church of Indian Rocks, Florida back in the '90s. Veronica was born in Chili and has the most beautiful accent, especially when she refers to her husband's "Yaguar" (that would be Jaguar to the rest of us.) Veronica, thanks so much for all your help with Sandra's Spanish. I just hope I got it right. Oh, and keep an eye out for that case of popsicles I've sent you. Your favorite kind, of course!

To Don Riddle, my inspiration for Donnie Rogers. I've known Don since Tulsa Memorial High School days when we discovered how difficult it was to mark time while giggling. Oh, the trouble we got into . . . And yes, we did indeed work together at a taco establishment which shall remain nameless. I'm not sure anyone on the planet has made me laugh as hard as Don. Like Donnie, Don has heart problems, but he's currently doing fine, still terrorizing the greater Houston area from what I understand. Don, I loved spending time with you via Donnie's character. Thank you for giving me so much material to work with. Love you, buddy!

To Sandra Perez Graham, my favorite Puerto Rican who still holds such a special place in my heart. We met on my first day at Baptist Memorial Hospital, became the best of friends and eventually roommates. Sandra, I couldn't possibly write your character using a different name, so I hope you'll forgive any potential embarrassment I may cause you. Thanks for all the precious memories of our time in Memphis! ¡Te quiero, Sandra!

To all my fellow hostesses who shared that tiny office on the first floor of the Madison wing and ministered to every floor of our beloved hospital. My characters may be fictional, but each of you played an important role in the memories I tried to put on paper. Wherever you are, may God richly bless you!

Other Books by Diane Moody

Confessions of a Prayer Slacker

Don't Ever Look Down:
Surviving Cancer Together
co-authored with Dick and Debbie Church

The Runaway Pastor's Wife
available in paperback and Kindle

Tea with Emma
Book One of the Teacup Novellas
available on Kindle

Strike the Match
Books Two of the Teacup Novellas
Available on Kindle

Blue Christmas
Book One of the Moody Blue Trilogy
Available in paperback and Kindle

Also available from OBT Bookz

Ordained Irreverence
by McMillian Moody
available on Kindle

Made in the USA
Lexington, KY
15 May 2012